KT-379-866

Kate Ellis was born and brought up in Liverpool and studied drama in Manchester. She has worked in teaching, marketing and accountancy and first enjoyed literary success as a winner of the North West Playwrights competition. Keenly interested in medieval history and 'armchair' archaeology, Kate lives in north Cheshire with her husband and their two sons. *The Funeral Boat* is her fourth Wesley Peterson novel. *The Merchant's House*, *The Armada Boy* and *An Unhallowed Grave* are also published by Piatkus.

Praise for *The Funeral Boat*:

'sense of the abiding presence of history
adds another dimension to an already intriguing tale'
Northern Echo

'moody mystery . . . a splendid piece of whodunnit, and when?'
Newcastle Evening Chronicle

Praise for *The Merchant's House*:

'A very attractive first novel . . .
good, straightforward story-telling with lots of
interesting characters'
Birmingham Post

'A highly readable novel . . .
a good start to what promises to be an entertaining series'
Historical Review

Fascinating first novel . . . has the feel of a Wycliffe novel . . .'
The Bookseller

Praise for *An Unhallowed Grave*:

'Kate Ellis is a fine story-teller . . . and this one
gripped me to the end'
Shots

Also by Kate Ellis

The Merchant's House
The Armada Boy
An Unhallowed Grave

The Funeral Boat

Kate Ellis

PIATKUS

In memory of Andrew Arden who loved South Devon and who first introduced me to 'Tradmouth'.

For more information on other books published by Piatkus, visit our website at www.piatkus.co.uk

Copyright © 2000 by Kate Ellis

First published in Great Britain in 2000 by
Judy Piatkus (Publishers) Ltd of
5 Windmill Street, London W1T 2JA
email: info@piatkus.co.uk

This edition published 2000

The moral right of the author has been asserted

A catalogue record for this book is available from the British Library

ISBN 0 7499 3216 3

Set in Times by
Phoenix Photosetting, Chatham, Kent
Printed and bound in Great Britain by
Mackays of Chatham plc, Chatham, Kent

Prologue

The boy's heart pounded rapidly as he searched for a place to hide. He ran on through the field, the tall grass cool against his legs, caught between terror and thrill.

He knew they were coming after him; he could hear their teasing calls, their excited laughter mingled with the sound of the rising lark. He pressed himself against the hedgerow but jumped away swiftly as the nettles stung his bare legs. He looked down, fascinated, as the raised red weals formed on the pale skin above his socks. But there was no time to register the prickly pain of the nettle stings. He had to hide.

He saw the wooden outbuilding ahead, the planks flaky grey and weathered. The place looked sheltering, inviting. He stared for a moment, summoning the courage to go in. Then he heard a yell, like a fox-hunter's cry. With trembling fingers he pulled the great door open a little, just enough to slip through.

But he wasn't alone. The stench of fumes from the throbbing engine made him put his hand to his nose and cough. They kept a tractor in here sometimes. But this didn't sound like a tractor. He saw the car through the fug of exhaust smoke . . . and the figure in the driving seat.

The boy made his way round to the driver's door, choking, sobbing. She sat quite still, her familiar, beloved face flushed red; her sightless eyes wide open in a parody of life. He opened his mouth to scream but no sound emerged. He tried to cry but no tears came.

When the other children found him he was sitting on the

1

path, rocking to and fro, staring ahead with empty, terrified eyes.

It was six months before the boy uttered another word.

Twenty years later

Ingeborg Larsen drove cautiously down the single-track road towards Tradmouth, hoping she wouldn't meet an oncoming vehicle and be forced to back her car up into a distant passing place. It was with some relief that she looked in the rearview mirror and glimpsed a car following close behind: any car she met now would have to back up for both of them. The other vehicle followed, almost on her bumper, seemingly impatient to pass. But passing wasn't an option on this road. The driver would have to be patient.

The first impact came as a shock, jolting Ingeborg forward so that her seat belt locked, only just preventing her chest from hitting the steering wheel. Her heart began to beat faster. An accident. She should stop . . . exchange insurance details: she knew that was the way things were done here.

Taking a deep breath, she put her foot gently on the brake pedal, only to be thrust forward again by a second push from the car behind. What was the idiot doing? People like that shouldn't be on the roads. Perhaps they thought that a foreign car was fair game. She sat for a few seconds collecting her thoughts as she slowly unfastened her seat belt.

She didn't have time to look round as the car door flew open and the evil-smelling pad was pressed firmly to her face. Then her wide, blue eyes flickered shut as she drifted into oblivion.

Chapter One

AD 997
The Danes ravaged in Cornwall, Wales and Devon and did
much evil by burning and slaying many. Word has come to
our house that they went up the Tamar, slaughtering and
burning. Then they burned Ordulf's monastery at Tavistock
and took much plunder. We pray the Lord to defend us
against this evil.
  From the chronicle of Brother Edwin, monk of Neston Minster

Daniel Wexer looked across the flowery pillow at his young wife,
reached out his hand and gently touched her thick, fair hair. He
was a lucky man. Little had he imagined when she had come to the
farm to help with the accounts that he would now be lying beside
her in the huge iron bed that had belonged to his parents and their
parents before that. The thought made him smile; a small, sly
smile of satisfaction.

He could still smell Jen's perfume – the stuff he had bought
her for her birthday, the stuff he liked – and he felt the stirrings
of desire. He reached over, slid his hand beneath the duvet and
began to caress her firm, youthful body. 'Jen' he whispered in
her ear, his voice low and thick with yearning. 'Do you fancy . . .
er . . .'

'Not now, Dan. I'm tired.' She turned over, as if to make the
point, and closed her eyes tightly.

Daniel Wexer lay still for a while, coming to terms with his
disappointment. Then something made him hold his breath and
listen. He was used to the noises of the countryside but this was
different . . . man-made. There it was again – a vehicle engine

outside, gently throbbing. Daniel left the bed; careful not to disturb Jen, and slowly, carefully, made his way to the window.

But his consideration was in vain. When the crash came Jen sat up with a start. 'What the hell was that?' she asked, panic in her sleepy voice. 'Dan . . .'

The sounds from downstairs were now distinct. The door had been forced open and the intruders were moving from room to room, smashing, opening drawers.

'I'm ringing the police.' Daniel reached for the phone on the bedside table as his wife sat, her eyes wide and fearful, clutching the duvet to her chest in defence. Daniel stabbed at the buttons with his index finger. Again and again he tried. Then he turned to his wife. 'They've cut the bloody wires, Jen. They've cut us off.'

'The mobile . . .'

'It's in my coat downstairs.' He reached for the towelling dressing gown on the back of the door. 'I'm going down.'

'No, Dan. It said on the telly that they're armed. They threatened that farmer over at Dukesbridge.'

'It might not be the same ones.'

'Don't be stupid, Dan. They could kill you.'

'Not if I've got this they won't.' He picked up the shotgun propped against the wall by the bed, placed there each night since the farm robberies began. Over the past couple of weeks alarming tales had been reported on the local TV news: isolated farmhouses had been stripped of valuables by the audacious robbers, desirable vehicles taken, and the hapless farmers and their families threatened with a sawn-off shotgun to ensure their acquiescence.

Jen leaned over and grabbed her husband's arm. 'No, Dan. Please . . .'

'I've had enough, Jen.' He pushed her restraining hand away. 'It's about time they learned their lesson.'

He marched from the bedroom, his eyes blazing with righteous fury. His farm was threatened, all that he had inherited from his father and built up. His only livelihood, for so long jeopardised by economics and regulations, was now under siege by mindless, grasping thugs. He flicked the safety catch off. This was war . . . and Daniel Wexer wouldn't surrender without a fight.

He kicked at the parlour door and it flew open.

They had switched the main light on, making no pretence of

4

stealth. His opponent stood there, black-clad, his face hidden by a knitted ski mask.

Daniel felt no fear as he pointed the shotgun. 'Get out,' he shouted, his voice cracking with fury. 'Get out of my house and off my land.' The robber didn't move. 'Now!' he screeched, increasing the pressure of his finger on the trigger.

Daniel Wexer felt a tearing pain in his left leg which sent him hurtling backwards. The shotgun seemed to leap from his hand and he heard a second shot which sent a shower of plaster fluttering down from the ceiling onto his balding head.

Still conscious, he reached down to his leg, gasping with pain. His hand was wet with blood. His head swam as he listened to the retreating footsteps and the noise of the car engine – something big, a Land Rover . . . his new Land Rover. The sound faded as the vehicle drove away.

A nervous scampering in the doorway announced Jen's terrified arrival. She looked down at her husband's prone body and screamed, the scream echoing in Daniel's ears as he fell into unconsciousness.

The two men pushed open the swing-doors to Tradmouth Hospital's C Ward, trying their best to look purposeful.

'I still don't know why we had to come down here, Wes,' said the larger of the pair, a big man in his late forties with tousled hair, a badly ironed shirt and a noticeable Liverpool accent. 'I thought Stan Jenkins's sergeant was going to deal with this one. Stan did offer his services when we were pushed.'

'He's away at a conference . . . Policing for the New Millennium. Apparently he was very keen to go.'

The big man emitted a sound of disgust. 'I'll start going to ruddy conferences when the villains start holding 'em. Couldn't Rachel or Steve have done this?'

'Rachel offered to come but I wanted to have a word with Mr Wexer myself while the events are fresh in his mind.'

'That's very noble of you, Wes, but don't forget Heffernan's fifth rule of life.'

'What's that, sir?'

'Never volunteer.' Detective Sergeant Wesley Peterson suppressed a smile as they reached the ward's desk. 'Morning, love. Police,' said Heffernan cheerfully.

The plump, navy-blue-clad sister at the desk looked up at the newcomers: the large, scruffy one and the well-dressed young black man, rather good-looking with an air of confident intelligence. She might have taken the latter for a new doctor assigned to the ward . . . if it weren't for the company he kept.

Heffernan flashed his warrant card. 'We're here to see Daniel Wexer, love. Have we come to the right place?'

The sister pushed her paperwork aside and managed a weak smile. 'Yes. He's over there on the right.'

'How is he?' Wesley enquired politely.

'He's comfortable,' said the sister in an official tone. 'And the doctor thinks he'll make a good recovery.'

The inspector turned to his colleague. 'Right, Wes. You lead the way. Do you think we should have brought some grapes?'

'He might not like grapes.'

'I didn't mean for him, I meant for me. I didn't have any breakfast this morning. Remind me to get a bacon butty on the way back to the station, will you.'

Daniel Wexer wasn't hard to find as his position was marked by a young uniformed constable who had made himself comfortable on a bedside chair. The constable looked relieved to see them, a welcome distraction from his tedious vigil.

Heffernan looked down at the sleeping patient. 'Has he said anything yet, Wallace?'

'He hasn't made a proper statement yet, sir. He was in an awful lot of pain before he went down to the theatre so he couldn't say much . . . just that he'd disturbed an intruder who fired a shot at him and made off in his new Land Rover. That's about all.'

'Nothing else?'

'Not really. Do you think it's the same lot, sir?' He looked at Heffernan anxiously.

Heffernan turned to his sergeant. 'Well, Wes. What do you think?'

'Same modus operandi,' said Wesley thoughtfully. 'But it's the first time they've actually fired at someone. Perhaps they panicked.'

'It's possible. Let's just hope they're caught before their aim improves,' Heffernan said with sincerity.

A small groan from the bed made the three policemen look round. Daniel Wexer's eyes had opened and he was attempting to sit up. Wesley, the son of two doctors, rushed to the patient's aid. 'Take it easy now. Take your time,' he said gently.

'I'm okay,' Wexer gasped. 'I'll be all right.' With Wesley's help he managed to sit, propped up by a trio of plump hospital pillows. PC Wallace handed him a glass of water and drew the curtains around the bed.

'Is Jen okay?'

'Your wife's fine,' Wallace assured him confidently. Wesley and Heffernan exchanged looks. This young lad would go far.

'I want to make a statement,' said Wexer, his voice gaining in strength. 'I don't want to see the bastards get away with it.'

Gerry Heffernan and Wesley Peterson listened carefully as the farmer made his statement while Wallace dutifully wrote it down. It was a familiar story. Isolated farmhouses in the area were being systematically raided for valuables and vehicles ... and the robbers were armed and unpredictable. With the summer tourist season and its associated problems rapidly gaining momentum, this was the local force's worst nightmare.

Exhausted by his efforts, Wexer lay back and closed his eyes. He had thinning hair and the rugged complexion of one who had spent much of his life out of doors. Wesley found it hard to guess at his age, which could have been anything between forty and sixty.

Gerry Heffernan nudged his sergeant. It was time to go. They mumbled a few words of encouragement to PC Wallace and were about to leave when the curtain drawn round the bed parted.

A girl, dark-haired, skeletal and aged about sixteen, rushed to the man in the bed. His eyes followed her with loving anxiety. 'Dad ... are you all right?' she asked before looking up at Heffernan. 'Are you the police? Do you know who did this? Have you got them?'

'We'll do our best to find 'em, love,' Heffernan assured her. 'Did you see anything last night?'

The girl shook her head. 'I wasn't there. I live in Neston with my mum.'

Heffernan nodded. There was nothing more to be learned from the newcomer.

'We'll be off now, love, and leave you to talk to your dad.'

The girl sat on the bed, peering anxiously into her father's face. 'Mum sends her ... well, she asked how you were.'

Before the farmer could reply the curtain parted again, this time to admit a fair-haired woman. She was in her late twenties, tall with a turned-up nose and freckles. There were dark shadows beneath her green eyes. She looked as though she hadn't slept.

'This is Mrs Wexer, sir,' said Wallace helpfully.

Wexer's daughter's facial expression changed dramatically. Concern for her injured father was replaced by a glowering of deep hatred directed at the newcomer. 'I'll be off,' she announced curtly, standing up. She pushed past Jen Wexer and left, her father's eyes watching her helplessly, pleading with her to stay.

'What was all that about?' asked Gerry Heffernan bluntly. Wesley looked at the inspector, uncomfortable: sometimes tact wasn't his boss's greatest asset.

Jen Wexer sighed. 'We, er . . . don't get on. My husband split up with her mother, his first wife, and Penny and her brother seem to blame me.'

'Oh, Jen, come on, it was hardly your fault. The kids'll come round,' said the optimist in the bed weakly.

'Let's not talk about it, Dan. How are you feeling? How's the leg?'

Wesley and Heffernan looked at each other. It was time to leave. They had done their bit.

'Not much love lost there,' Heffernan commented as they left the hospital.

'You can say that again. It can't be easy for these kids when their parents . . .'

The electronic buzzing of the mobile phone in Wesley's pocket announced that he was needed. When he had finished his brief conversation, he turned to the inspector, not quite knowing how to break the news.

He decided on the direct approach. 'A body's been found at a smallholding just outside Stoke Beeching, place called Longhouse Cottage. Call came in from a lad who turned up a skeleton while he was digging a drain. I said we'd be straight over.'

'Longhouse Cottage?' Gerry Heffernan pursed his lips and let out a long low whistle. 'It's my bet the chickens have come home to roost.'

'Chickens? Well, it is a smallholding,' said Wesley with a

smile. It wasn't often that Heffernan's pronouncements were so cryptic.

'If a body's been found there, I reckon I know who it belongs to.'

'Really?'

Heffernan took a deep breath before embarking on his story. 'Jock Palister was a farm labourer who came into money about twenty years ago and bought Waters House, a big place on the hill above Longhouse Cottage . . . origin of windfall unknown. I was a young constable at the time and I remember there was talk . . . and a couple of bank robberies in Plymouth that went unsolved,' he added meaningfully.

'So?'

'Jock led what seemed like a blameless life for a good few years – in other words he didn't get caught – then he disappeared suddenly leaving his loving wife, Maggie, and sixteen-year-old son, Carl, in the lurch with a load of debts. They had to sell Waters House and most of their land and move into an old farm worker's cottage down the hill . . . tatty old place called Longhouse Cottage. Now they just about scrape a living from three or four acres with some hens and a few scraggy sheep . . . if you can call it a living.' He took a deep breath. 'I think old Jock's turned up again.'

'Buried on his own land?'

'It wouldn't surprise me. His disappearance was always a bit of a mystery.' He sighed. 'Why did old Jock have to choose now to pop back up, eh?' He rolled his eyes to heaven in an uncharacteristically theatrical manner. 'Oh, Wesley. What have we been doing to deserve all this?'

As Wesley drove out of Tradmouth past the low glass and concrete comprehensive school and the architecturally uninspiring swimming baths, he tried to organise his thoughts.

Just under a year ago, Wesley and his wife Pam had needed little persuasion to leave the cosmopolitan bustle of London and settle in the ancient Devon port of Tradmouth with its quaint quaysides and steep, narrow streets tumbling down to the river. But Wesley had been kept busy since his arrival and something told him that things were going to get worse. Criminals, unlike the invading army of tourists, did not come to Devon to take a holiday.

It was a glorious day: the temperature was in the seventies and the sky was a spectacular shade of unbroken sapphire blue. To Wesley's right the ground rose to hilly, hedged fields. To his left the pasture sloped down to meet the sparkling sea. This was hardly the landscape he'd known in London. And it wasn't the sort of day to contemplate violence and murder . . . but he feared that was what waited for them at Longhouse Cottage.

Gerry Heffernan slumped back in the passenger seat with his eyes closed, seemingly asleep, while Wesley slowed the car down, peering out of the window, searching for the gateway to the smallholding. He noticed two driveways a few yards apart; the first bearing a rustic wooden plaque with the name 'Waters House' in bold letters, the second a home-made sign with the barely legible words 'Longhouse Cottage'. A pair of gateposts, covered in flaking blue paint, loomed up on his right. He flicked the indicator and executed a right turn onto a track that would make any self-respecting car owner fear for his suspension.

He wasn't sure whether the low stone building he eventually reached was Longhouse Cottage or some sort of outbuilding, such was its dilapidated state. There was an ancient and disreputable-looking Land Rover parked in the stony rectangle that passed for a yard. An array of half-dismantled vehicles at the side of the house, perched on bricks, made the pair of gleaming police cars parked beside them look positively Space Age in comparison.

Wesley studied the building with its protruding central porch. Longhouse Cottage – the name should have told him. He judged that it had enjoyed a few additions in its long lifetime, but the central section had remained relatively untouched. A fine example of a classic Devon medieval longhouse – with accommodation for the farmer at one end of the building and the animals at the other – dating back to . . . he hardly liked to hazard a guess. It had probably been abandoned at some stage in its history by the farmer of the land, who had built himself something more fashionable and allowed his workers to live in the old building. It wouldn't have survived in this form otherwise – unmodernised and apparently unloved. He looked up to the top of the gently rolling hill where a large white house stood, half hidden by trees. presumably this was Waters House; home to Jock Palister and his family in wealthier days.

Heffernan had woken up with a jolt when the engine stopped

and now both men climbed out of the car, amazed to see Detective Inspector Stan Jenkins walking slowly towards them, a look of relief on his face.

'Hello, Stan. Wasn't expecting to see you around this morning,' said Gerry Heffernan. 'I thought you had a hospital appointment.'

'Yes, I did, Gerry. I went first thing and I was in and out in half an hour. Saw the consultant private,' he added in a whisper.

'Everything okay?'

Stan looked down and shuffled his feet. 'Well as can be expected, Gerry.'

'What's wrong exactly?' Gerry Heffernan always believed that beating around the bush had never advanced the sum of human knowledge.

Stan's face reddened. 'Oh, er . . . the old trouble,' he muttered mysteriously. 'I'm due to go in on Friday so I'm afraid I'll have to leave you to deal with this one. Don't want to start a case then have to drop it after a couple of days, and with my sergeant away . . .' He shrugged his shoulders apologetically. 'Did you see that farmer who was shot last night?'

'Yeah. He didn't tell us much we didn't know already. Looks like the same lot, all right. His leg's in a bit of a mess . . . but so would yours be if it was blasted with a sawn-off shotgun.'

Stan Jenkins shook his head in disbelief. 'Terrible,' he mumbled. Stan always seemed amazed at the extent of human wickedness . . . an odd reaction, Wesley always thought, for a policeman of so many years' experience.

'So what have we got here, then?' Heffernan asked bluntly. 'This body, is it Jock Palister's?'

Stan pushed back his thinning grey hair, a worried expression on his face. Wesley had heard rumours of Stan's imminent retirement ever since he had arrived in Tradmouth – and there were those who said it was long overdue. But something – perhaps the fear of long days spent in the company of Mrs Jenkins, if station gossip was anything to go by – kept Stan at his post. 'I really don't know, Gerry. It was Carl Palister who called us: that's him over there in the field with his mum. He was digging a drain near the edge of the field when he turned up a human skeleton. I reckon Carl and his mum look worried about something . . . especially her,' he said significantly. 'But if they'd known the bones were there, surely they wouldn't have called us out.'

'Yeah, Stan. You could be right.'

'And Jock only disappeared three years ago,' continued Stan. 'This body looks as if it's been in the ground a lot longer than that.'

'Has Dr Bowman been called?' asked Wesley.

'He's on his way ... should be here any time.' Stan turned to Heffernan, a look of relief on his face. 'Well, Gerry, I suppose this one's yours. I'll leave you to it. Good luck.'

'Thanks, Stan.' Heffernan tried to sound as if this fresh addition to his considerable workload didn't bother him in the least.

'The body's over in the field,' said Stan, climbing wearily into one of the police cars. 'Go and have a look for yourselves.'

Gerry Heffernan led the way. Wesley, following behind, hoped he wasn't about to witness anything too gruesome. He came from a medical family – his parents had both come to England from Trinidad to train as doctors and his sister had read medicine at Oxford – but his stomach for such things was weak.

They made their way across the field, carefully avoiding the molehills and sheep droppings that littered the uneven ground. A gang of dirty-looking sheep watched them, chewing grass insolently. They reminded Wesley of the bored adolescents who hung around outside the amusement arcades of Morbay.

A pair of uniformed constables stood in the far corner of the field, peering down into a hole in the ground. A well-muscled young man, with dark curly hair and minus his shirt, stood nervously to one side, talking to a middle-aged woman who wore a shabby, flowered frock. She watched Wesley intently as he approached and whispered something in the young man's ear.

Heffernan nodded to the woman. 'Morning, Maggie. Still keeping us in work, then?' The woman said nothing but glowered at the inspector.

The two constables stood aside and watched as Wesley reached the hole, a gash in the earth; ten foot long and five foot deep.

The young man spoke, glancing nervously at Gerry Heffernan. 'There were a load of stones down there . . . put there deliberate, I reckon.' He regarded Wesley with anxious eyes, as though desperate to prove that this gruesome find had nothing to do with him.

'Carl,' said Heffernan, in a friendly tone. 'How are you keeping?'

'Okay, thanks, Mr Heffernan,' Carl replied with a tentative smile. He leaned on his spade, the sweat glistening on his muscular torso. There were many who forked out good money in Tradmouth's flashy new gym to achieve a body like Carl's. But the demands of the smallholding saw to it that his fitness regime came free of charge.

The niceties over, Carl's mind returned to the matter in hand. 'I found this in the soil.' He handed a small coin to Heffernan, who in turn handed it to Wesley. 'It's dead old, ain't it? That wasn't put there a couple of years ago,' he concluded smugly. He gave Gerry Heffernan another swift glance, ensuring that he'd made his point.

Wesley studied the coin. It was in good condition, the inscription quite clear. 'A silver penny . . . Saxon,' he announced. 'Ethelred the Unready.'

'How old is it, then?' Carl asked.

'Late tenth . . . early eleventh century. About a thousand years.'

Carl Palister raised his eyebrows and leaned over to take a fresh look at the treasure he'd discovered. 'Is it worth much?' he enquired greedily.

'They're not uncommon. Actually more are found in Denmark than in England – Ethelred paid the Vikings off with them to stop them raiding. It was protection money . . . called Danegeld. But it didn't make much difference – like most self-respecting gangsters they kept coming back for more.'

'Nothing much has changed,' mumbled Gerry Heffernan philosophically.

Wesley turned his attention to deeper matters. 'Let's have a look at this body, then.'

'Dr Bowman's on his way,' said the smaller of the two constables helpfully.

Wesley looked down. The brown-stained skeleton lay at the bottom of the pit, on its back in an orderly fashion, its arms by its side. Somebody had taken the trouble to lay it out.

Carl looked Wesley up and down. 'Are you police, then? You don't look like police.'

'I'm a detective sergeant.'

Carl shrugged. The well-spoken young black man with a detailed knowledge of ancient artefacts wasn't like any policeman he'd ever come across before . . . and he'd come across a fair few in his time.

13

Wesley climbed down into the pit to examine the bones more closely, careful not to disturb anything. The skull grinned up at him, greeting him like an old friend as he studied the soil around the body. He was hardly equipped to begin a detailed excavation, but he brushed some soil away gently with his fingers, recognising two small rust-encrusted objects that he found during his cursory search.

'He's got a degree in archaeology, you know,' he heard Gerry Heffernan announce proudly to anyone who cared to listen. Heffernan leaned over the edge of the pit. 'Well, Wes, what have you found? Don't keep us in suspense.'

'When Dr Bowman's examined the bones, I'd like Neil to have a look at the grave.' He turned to Carl Palister, who was watching, open-mouthed. 'A friend of mine works for the County Archaeological Unit, and there's something here I'd like his opinion on. You weren't thinking of filling this hole in just yet, were you?' Carl shook his head, speechless.

'So what is it, Wes? Come on.' Gerry Heffernan's voice was impatient.

Wesley looked up at the expectant faces. Even the flowery-frocked woman, whom the inspector had addressed as Maggie, had deigned to join the group and was staring down at him with barely disguised hostility.

Wesley looked down at the bones again, then at the tiny objects he held in his hand. 'I can't really say anything for certain at the moment but I'll tell you one thing.'

'What?' said Gerry Heffernan, curious.

'There's a nasty hole in the top of this skull. I reckon he was murdered.'

In the CID office on the first floor of Tradmouth police station, Detective Constable Rachel Tracey was feeling hot. She said as much to her colleague, DC Steve Carstairs, but regretted the words as soon as they had left her mouth.

'Take something off, then,' he leered. 'I won't look.'

'Steve.'

'What?'

'Get lost.'

'Only making a suggestion.'

Rachel picked up a witness statement and began to read,

sending the message that the conversation was over. But Steve didn't take the hint.

'Where's our Wesley, then? Bet you'd have taken something off if he was here.'

Rachel looked up, her blue eyes ablaze with indignation. 'I've told you once, Steve. Get lost.'

'No need to be like that,' said Steve, all injured innocence. 'I just wondered where him and the boss had got to.'

'Last I heard they were off to the hospital to interview that farmer who was shot last night. Then they went straight over to Stoke Beeching, apparently. A body's been found there but I don't know any details yet.'

Steve rolled his eyes. 'Let's hope it's not more bloody work. Mind you, it might not all be bad news . . . we might get teamed up for some night-time surveillance, eh?' he added suggestively.

Rachel ignored him. She stared at the statement, not registering the words. If only Steve could be transferred back into uniform, resign, be posted to another division, be abducted by aliens – anything – it would make her life a lot easier.

'How's the boyfriend?' Steve began again, still leering. 'Still the Aussie, is it? Know what they say about Aussies?' He had made enough racist quips about Wesley in his time; now it seemed he was about to add Australians to his unpleasant repertoire.

'Steve,' Rachel said, exasperated, 'haven't you any work to do? Last I heard all the criminals around here hadn't gone on strike.'

Steve looked affronted. 'I've got all these statements to sort out. Then I'm going over to Morbay for a meet with my snout this afternoon,' he swaggered self-importantly. 'Someone must know something about these farm robberies. I can't believe these villains have no local knowledge.'

Rachel looked across at him, pleasantly surprised. Steve Carstairs had made an intelligent observation – that made a change. The telephone on her desk rang, summoning her down to the station's front desk. When Steve asked where she was off to, she said nothing but shot him a look that she hoped was mysterious. He could mind his own business.

Sergeant Bob Naseby, the large and avuncular guardian of Tradmouth police station's front desk, greeted Rachel with a wink and told her that a lady was waiting to talk to someone from CID.

He pointed to a woman who stood with her back to them, studying the array of colourful posters on the station notice-board.

Rachel walked over to her. 'Excuse me,' she said quietly, not wishing to startle her.

The woman turned, and Rachel could see that she wasn't the type to startle easily. A tall, capable-looking creature, probably in her late forties; well-built bordering on plump. Her hair was a brassy shade of auburn that owed more to the chemical industry than to nature. Rachel, a natural blonde, held a low opinion of those who resorted to the bottle.

'I'm Detective Constable Tracey. Was there something you wanted to report?'

The woman looked around, as if afraid she might be overheard.

'We can go into one of the interview rooms if you like,' Rachel suggested helpfully.

'Oh no. It's nothing really.' The woman looked uneasy, as if anticipating imminent arrest. 'My husband said that it was early days . . . that I shouldn't be bothering the police about it yet.' Her accent wasn't local. Rachel, who considered herself to be good on accents, put her somewhere up near Birmingham.

'So what exactly do you want to report, madam?' she asked. It was always best to know what you were dealing with right from the beginning.

'A missing person,' the woman stated dramatically. 'A Danish lady. She's just vanished off the face of the earth.'

Chapter Two

AD 997
*It is said that those they did not slaughter were taken, men,
women and children, and put aboard their ships to be sold as
slaves, treated as common plunder. The people of our town
gathered within the Minster this day to pray that as these
heathens from the north come around our coast, they pass by
our river and do us no harm. Oh Lord defend us.*
From the chronicle of Brother Edwin, monk of Neston Minster

Rachel knew from long experience that a good cup of tea oiled
many wheels and even more tongues. She sat opposite the woman
in the interview room, sipping the hot, reviving liquid, and
listened patiently.

'I was worried, you see,' the woman said. 'She's left everything
in her room. Her clothes, shoes . . . everything. She went out in her
car two days ago and she hasn't come back.'

Rachel had discovered by gentle questioning that the woman's
name was Barbara Questid. And that she ran a small but select bed
and breakfast establishment – with *en suite* facilities and
magnificent views over Tradmouth harbour – up on Newpen
Road.

'I mean, it's the height of the season and I can't let the room
again, can I?' Barbara continued anxiously. 'Not if I don't know
whether she's coming back.'

'So you last saw her on Monday?'

'Yes. At breakfast it was. She had toast and marmalade. I do the
full English, of course, but that's all she wanted . . . toast and
marmalade.'

17

'Did she say what her plans were for the day? She was over here on holiday, I presume?'

'That's what she said. She told my husband she was going to Neston. She'd read about the town walls there. Apparently they date back to Saxon times . . . or that's what my husband told her. He said she was very interested . . . but I told him she was just being polite. He can be a bit of a bore at times. But she said she was going to spend the day there and set off at about ten in the morning. That's the last I saw of her.'

'How long was she planning to stay in Devon?'

'Just for the week. She arrived last Friday and said she'd probably leave next Saturday. I told her it was a shame because she'd miss this big festival they're having in Neston at the weekend. The Viking Festival . . . they were from round her way, weren't they, the Vikings? I had a little joke with her about it but she didn't seem to understand. Do you think I can relet her room? Will you have to search it or . . .'

'I think we should take things slowly, Mrs Questid. After all, most missing persons turn up safe after a few days. She might have met someone . . . gone off with them and not thought to tell you. I don't think we should be worrying too much yet.' Rachel smiled reassuringly, suspecting that Barbara Questid was more worried about the loss of revenue from her unoccupied luxury *en suite* room than about her errant Scandinavian guest. 'If you'll just give me some more details about this lady . . .'

'She was about my age . . . thirty-five.'

Rachel tried hard not to smile at Barbara Questid's economy with the truth. She was forty-five if she was a day.

'Slim, shortish fair hair . . . about your colour. About five foot eight. Nicely dressed. Attractive, my husband thought,' she added disapprovingly.

'And what was her name?'

'Larsen. Ingeborg Larsen.' Mrs Questid's plastic chair creaked dangerously as she sat back and drained her cup of tea.

Neil Watson, crouching in a trench beside the south wall of Neston's magnificent medieval parish church, cursed as he pulled his mobile phone out of his pocket and stabbed, with soil-covered fingers, at the button that would stop its importunate whining.

'Feel like helping the police with their enquiries?' asked a familiar voice on the other end of the line.

'Wesley. I'm a bit pushed at the moment.'

'Still in Neston?'

'Yeah, we've just opened up another trench inside the church,' Neil replied cautiously. 'Why?'

'Could you do me a favour?'

'What?' Neil asked suspiciously. 'Not looking for a baby-sitter for your Michael, are you? I'm no good with babies.'

Wesley smiled. It was hard to imagine Neil in the Mary Poppins role. 'Nothing like that. A skeleton has just been unearthed at a place called Longhouse Cottage; it's a smallholding near Stoke Beeching. The doc's having a look at it now and there are a couple of things in the grave that I'd like you to see.'

'Interesting?'

'If my suspicions are correct it could be very interesting indeed . . . interesting bordering on exciting.'

'What is it?'

'I'd rather you had a look for yourself.'

Neil, suitably intrigued, said he'd be over right away. He put his mobile phone, his one personal concession to high technology, back into his pocket, straightened himself up, and persuaded himself that a quick visit to Stoke Beeching would do no harm.

The sheep in the field beside Longhouse Cottage had never witnessed so much activity. They stood in a group, a safe distance away from where Dr Colin Bowman was examining the unidentified occupant of the grave, and chewed insolently, unworried by the police presence in their domain.

'Well, Gerry,' Colin Bowman said cheerily, 'I think our friend here might have been dead a very long time. Not that I can tell you how long now, of course – we'll need tests to tell us that.'

Wesley held out a hand to help the pathologist out of the trench. 'I've asked Neil Watson to come over,' he said. 'I'd like the bones lifted carefully if that's okay. And I've seen something in the trench that I'd like his opinion on.'

Colin Bowman stripped off his rubber gloves. 'Something I should know about?'

'I can't tell yet. I'll let you know.'

Gerry Heffernan, who was watching the proceedings with

19

interest, looked round. The Palisters had returned to the house: there was nobody apart from the two attendant constables to hear his next question. 'Is there any chance it could be Jock Palister, Colin? Any chance at all? He disappeared three years ago.'

Colin Bowman looked down into the trench. 'Did he have a dentist?'

Heffernan looked puzzled. 'No idea.'

'It's just that our friend here didn't seem to have one . . . couple of missing teeth but absolutely no dental work that I can see. And I reckon he was over six foot. How tall was this Jock Palister?'

Gerry Heffernan looked crestfallen. He had to admit defeat. 'About five foot eight . . . five foot nine.'

'Sorry, Gerry. It's not him'. He turned to Wesley. 'When you've got him out of the ground, I'll have a proper look at him down at the mortuary. Come down for a cup of tea . . . I've found this rather good Darjeeling.' Colin Bowman always managed to make his place of work sound positively cosy, more like a tea room than a place of death.

'Thanks, Colin. I'll be in touch.'

The pathologist waved a genial hand and marched off towards the gleaming Range Rover that awaited him in the yard.

As he drove off, a battered yellow Mini appeared, chugging slowly up the pitted track. The thing looked fearful for its exhaust as it rode over the potholes and furrows that Colin Bowman's Range Rover had negotiated with ease. The Mini came to a halt, and Wesley watched as Neil Watson emerged from his disreputable vehicle and extracted a box containing the tools of his trade from the boot. He strode towards them with determination. He wasn't going to waste time.

'Well,' he shouted to Wesley, 'what is it and where is it? Come on, I haven't got all day.' He grinned impudently. He and Wesley went back a long way, having met in their first year at Exeter University, where they had both wrestled with the intricacies of archaeology. Then their paths had diverged. Wesley – influenced by a grandfather who was a senior detective in Trinidad and an adolescent taste for the mysteries of Sherlock Holmes – had joined the police force, while Neil had embarked upon an archaeological career in Devon.

'Come over here and take a look at this,' Wesley shouted back. Neil marched over to the grave and bent down, noting the stones that were heaped around the hole. 'Where did these come from?'

'They were in there . . . piled on top of the grave. There was a silver penny of Ethelred the Unready in the soil near by.'

Neil stood above the body and took a long hard look, assessing what he was dealing with.

Wesley produced a plastic evidence bag from his pocket and passed it to Neil. 'There are loads of them down there. Where the ground hasn't been disturbed they seem to be in some sort of line. What do they look like to you?'

Neil studied the three rust-encrusted objects and nodded. He recognised them. 'Rivets. Any wood preserved?'

'Haven't seen any yet. These aren't coffin nails, are they?'

'No way.'

'Are you thinking what I'm thinking?'

Gerry Heffernan was becoming impatient. 'Oh, come on, Wes. Don't be so ruddy mysterious.'

'I'd just like Neil's opinion.'

'It's impossible, Wes. There's no record of anything like that being found around here. Now if we were in Scandinavia, or Orkney, or even Yorkshire . . . I'll take a look.'

Neil picked a trowel and small-finds tray out of his box and let himself down carefully into the trench. He was silent as he scraped away at the earth surrounding the bones. A dozen or so loose rivets found their way onto the plastic tray and he noted the position of those nearer the body. They formed a distinctive pattern that he recognised.

Wesley watched, breath held, for the verdict, while Gerry Heffernan made a superhuman effort to control his impatience.

'Well?' said Wesley. 'What do you think? Am I right?'

'You could be. We'll have to get the bones examined and dated but I think someone's gone to a great deal of trouble to bury this chap in some sort of small boat. The question is why?'

'I can't see a boat. Where is it?' Heffernan mumbled, shifting from foot to foot impatiently.

'The wood rots away,' said Wesley. 'Only the rivets are left.' He called down to Neil. 'There seem to be some flakes of something dark fused to the right arm bones. Could it be rust?'

'It's possible. He could have been buried with a sword or something like that. But if the rivets are still there it's unlikely something as big as a sword would have rotted away. Strange.' Neil took his mobile phone from his pocket. 'I'll get Matt and Jane over here to help me lift these bones properly and get all this lot recorded. I'd ask you to help, Wes, but I can see you're not dressed for it. This is very interesting. I'm glad you called me over.'

'So what's all the fuss about? What is it you've found?' Gerry Heffernan's patience had finally snapped.

'Ever heard of the Vikings?' asked Wesley.

' 'Course I have. They were big and hairy, wore horned helmets and went in for a lot of rape and pillaging. Well . . . what about them?' The truth slowly dawned. 'We've not got one here, have we? No, you're wrong, Wes. They were cremated in boats . . . blazing boats sailing off into the sunset . . . I've seen it in the films,' he said smugly.

Wesley and Neil looked at each other and grinned.

'Well, Hollywood isn't exactly renowned for its historical accuracy,' said Neil patiently. 'Your average Viking warrior was just buried in a boat or, failing that, a boat-shaped grave made out of stones. I'm pretty certain that what we have here is a Viking burial.'

Heffernan shook his head in disbelief and turned to go. 'I'd better get back to the station. I'll leave you to arrange for the bones to get to Colin Bowman, seeing as how you like digging things up. Don't be too long here, Wes . . . and try and have another word with Ma Palister, see how she reacts when you mention Jock. I'm still not convinced it isn't him we've got down there, you know,' he said, leaning over to look at the skull. 'I recognise that shifty grin of his.'

Gerry Heffernan didn't see Neil and Wesley exchange a conspiratorial smile as he marched away, the two attendant constables following a little behind like burly bridesmaids.

Wesley's stomach told him it was lunch-time. He had indulged himself for half an hour, watching Neil and his colleagues carefully lift the skeleton and search the rest of the grave. They had found more rivets – hundreds of them. The theory that the body had been buried in some sort of smallish boat which had since rotted away, leaving only its rivets behind, seemed to be gaining in credibility. When the mortuary van had left, bearing the remains into Colin Bowman's care, Wesley's conscience had dictated that he return to the station in Tradmouth.

But the brain doesn't function well on an empty stomach, and as Wesley drove back he anticipated a crisp, well-filled, warm pasty from the pasty shop in the High Street. He could almost smell it, taste it, as he approached the town.

He parked the car and marched swiftly past the Memorial Park. The pavements were packed with meandering holidaymakers, cruising slowly past the shop windows, Devon ice creams clutched in their hands. He strolled back to the police station, pasty in hand. The ecstasy of the first bite came when he was sitting back at his desk on the first floor, thinking how quiet the office was for a change.

The thought didn't last for long as Gerry Heffernan burst in carrying a pile of tattered files. 'I'm going to go through these, Wes. Jock Palister used to be a busy lad in his younger days. Clever and all . . . made sure we never had any evidence against him that'd stand up in court. We knew he was behind whatever it was, of course, but it was the Devil's own job to prove it. I reckon we've got him now, though. I know what Colin said, but it's got to be Jock in that grave. I mean, Colin only had a quick look, didn't he? How can he tell properly till he gets him back to the mortuary? Buried so close to the house . . . it's just got to be him. His disappearance was always one of the Great Unsolved Mysteries of Tradmouth CID.'

'Did his wife report him missing?'

''Course she did. She would, wouldn't she. I reckon we were only called today because Carl didn't know she'd bumped his dad off. It was Carl who reported the skeleton, and Maggie couldn't really have told him not to call us without giving the game away, could she?'

'What makes you think it was her? If he had criminal associates . . .'

'Oh, Wesley, didn't they teach you anything in the Met? Most murders are domestics. And a complete stranger wouldn't bury him in his own field in full view of his wife and son, would they?'

'Neil thinks the body was buried in a boat which rotted away,' said Wesley patiently.

'Stoke Beeching is near the coast, you know. Someone might have happened to store an old boat there years ago . . . nothing to do with the body. No, Wes, I'm convinced it's Jock. Here.' He drew a photograph out of the top file and handed it to Wesley. It showed a thickset man in his thirties with cropped dark hair – not the sort to encounter on a dark night.

'What about Mrs Palister? What do you know about her?'

'She comes from a well-off family who disowned her when she took up with Jock. And she's a sharp one is Maggie Palister . . . always ready with an alibi for her nearest and dearest. Give her her due, though, she has kept that smallholding going. And Carl's not a bad lad. He's only known to us for very minor offences – spot of vandalism, possession of cannabis – which means she's managed to keep him out of his father's league . . . so far.'

Heffernan sighed and picked up the files again, ready to carry them off into his office. Then, as an afterthought, he turned back to Wesley and handed him a sheet of paper. 'Here's a list of the things that were nicked from Wexer's Farm last night. Put it in the file, will you. It seems they just took some jewellery. There's a description of a Victorian locket there, quite distinctive . . . used to belong to Wexer's grandma. Details have been circulated to all the jewellers in the area. Forensic haven't come up with much. No fingerprints; no footprints; and no sign of the Land Rover that was nicked. It seems an old armchair took most of the blast from the shotgun; Dan Wexer's leg only got the tail-end, which at least shows they weren't necessarily shooting to kill . . . this time. And there was that second shot, possibly aimed at Mrs Wexer in the hall outside the room.'

As the inspector disappeared into his den, Wesley prepared to read the file on Wexer's Farm. Whether its contents would help them catch the robbers was debatable, but there might, just might, be something Gerry Heffernan had missed. He had hardly begun to read when he heard a voice at his shoulder.

'I've just been talking to the landlady of one of those bed and breakfast places up on Newpen Road.' He turned to see Rachel standing behind him.

'Thinking of moving out of the farm, are you?' asked Wesley with a grin. Rachel had often expressed her dissatisfaction about living on her family's farm with her parents and three brothers.

'Not at the moment, but there are times when I'm tempted,' she answered meaningfully, perching herself on the edge of his desk and showing a good deal of leg. 'This landlady came to report that one of her guests has gone missing.'

'Any cause for concern?'

'I don't know, Wesley.' She shoved a statement form in front of his nose. 'What do you think?'

'Ingeborg Larsen, eh? Ingeborg is the loveliest of the girls . . .'

'I beg your pardon,' she said, sounding mildly affronted. It wasn't like Wesley to utter such sexist sentiments . . . unlike others she could think of.

'"Ingeborg is the loveliest of the girls." It's a piece of Viking graffiti found in a place called Maes Howe in the Orkneys . . . written in runes.'

Rachel's eyes started to glaze over at the mention of archaeology. 'Fascinating,' she said insincerely. 'What do you think we should do?'

'She's a grown woman. Unless we have some evidence that she's come to harm there's nothing much we can do.' He shrugged his shoulders.

'That's exactly what I told the landlady.'

'Then let's hope our Ms Larsen turns up safe and sound.' He looked at his watch. 'I'd better crack on. I promised Pam I'd be home at a reasonable time tonight . . . wedding anniversary.'

Rachel nodded, passing no comment, and returned to her desk. She had a bad feeling about Ingeborg Larsen.

Pamela Peterson had decided on a takeaway Chinese banquet to celebrate her fifth wedding anniversary. Tonight she and Wesley would enjoy an oriental feast, followed by a walk to the old part of the town for a quiet drink. Wesley had promised to be home at a reasonable time . . . but his wife wasn't banking on it.

But Wesley was as good as his word. Having come to a natural break in his paperwork, he had left the station at half past five and had walked back up the steep, narrow streets to his modern detached house, perched at the top of the town. The smell that greeted him at the front door made him realise that he was hungry again, and his spirits lifted as he walked into the kitchen and saw the parade of foil dishes lined up on the table. Chinese was his favourite.

They were halfway through the meal when the phone rang. Pam was busy trying to spoon baby rice into little Michael's reluctant mouth, so Wesley abandoned his lemon chicken to answer it. It was Neil, asking if he could meet him in the Tradmouth Arms. Wesley hesitated and told Neil to wait. This would need careful handling: abandoning his wife on the evening of their anniversary might not be the wisest of moves.

But he was amazed to find Pam agreeable to the idea. She had planned for them to go out for a drink and she had already arranged a baby-sitter. Lost for words at this unexpected twist in events, he muttered to Neil that he'd see him later and returned to his lemon chicken.

At eight o'clock, with the meal cleared and the baby-sitter installed, they strolled arm in arm down the steep hill towards the heart of the town. Tradmouth was a medieval town, once made prosperous by trading wine, wool and Newfoundland fish. Although the fringes had undergone the inevitable development of the twentieth century, the centre, built around the harbour, had kept its picturesque character: this was what caused the tourists and yachtsmen to flock there each year in the summer months. They made their way down the restaurant-lined street that ran parallel with the river until they reached the Tradmouth Arms, a hostelry unspoiled by juke-box or fruit machine, which stood at the end of an expanse of cobbled quayside.

The pub was fuller than normal. But most of the summer visitors had taken their drinks outside onto Baynard's Quay, where they sat on the benches watching the boats moving on the river while their children caught fat crabs on thin nylon lines which dangled off the quayside. Wesley and Pam didn't bother looking for Neil outside. Alfresco drinking wasn't Neil's style.

It was Pam who spotted Neil first. She made straight for him, Wesley trailing behind. Neil's face lit up with a grin.

'Hi, Pam . . . Wes. I understand commiserations are in order . . . wedding anniversary, isn't it?'

'You're turning into a crusty old cynic, Neil. You could do with a bit of romance in your life. Did you ever get round to ringing my friend Anne?' Pam asked with a teasing grin as she sat herself down beside him. She knew Neil of old. Although he had expressed interest in her widowed friend, Anne, he had been too lazy – or too busy digging up the past – to take any action. Now Anne was away for a few weeks, but Pam would persevere when she returned: she rather fancied herself in the role of matchmaker, and Neil was a challenge.

'So what's the latest on Longhouse Cottage?' asked Wesley before Pam could get another word in. Since Neil's phone call Wesley's mind had been on matters archaeological: he hadn't come to sit around, burdened with unanswered questions, while his wife tried to sort out their friend's love life.

Neil sat back and held out his empty glass. 'Get us a pint and I'll tell you.'

Wesley fought his way through the members of the yachting fraternity drinking at the bar, who were exchanging tales of ports, moorings and uncooperative harbour authorities. Some of them looked at him curiously, a stranger in their nautical world. Laden with drinks, he returned to the cosy scene in the corner, where Neil, who had now started reminiscing with Pam about their shared student days, seemed to be enjoying himself.

Wesley asked his question again. This time Neil was ready to co-operate.

'I got Matt and Jane over and we did a bit of digging. We found loads more rivets. It's certainly a boat, but not a big one ... probably a rowing boat. You could see the shape quite clearly when the skeleton was removed, and I found a couple of pieces of wood too, although most of it had rotted away. But the most exciting find was a beautiful axe-head we found underneath the boat. I'm going to get it X-rayed and examined but I'd lay money on it being Viking. Those dark flakes fused to the skeleton were interesting too. They certainly looked like rust ... we'll run some tests. And there were some more, similar small flakes on the side of the skull too. I wonder ...'

'What?'

'Whether someone's dug the grave up before and removed whatever it was. Some farmer probably kept what he'd found as a curio. It happened all the time – skeleton discovered with grave goods, grave goods nicked, skeleton either left there or the bones dug up and scattered. Even so-called experts in days gone by perpetrated all sorts of destruction that'd give any self-respecting modern archaeologist the vapours.'

Wesley nodded. He had heard all this before. He glanced at Pam, who was listening with what seemed like genuine interest.

That was good. He had more questions to ask. 'So what are you going to do about it, then?'

'Oh, we've recorded everything, photographed it and covered the site with plastic. I told Carl not to fill it in for now. I know it's not official or anything, but I'd still like to have a dig around . . . for my own curiosity.'

'What about the Palisters?'

'The mother's not keen on us being there. She doesn't say much but I can feel the vibes, if you know what I mean. But the son seems interested . . . positively enthusiastic.'

Wesley smiled to himself, more certain than ever that the skeleton didn't belong to Jock Palister.

'How's the dig in Neston going? What is it exactly?'

'They're replacing a section of floor in Neston parish church and we've been asked to see if we can find any trace of the first church built on the site. Most local historians seem to believe that it could have been an Anglo-Saxon minster, as Neston was such an important place . . . a burgh . . .'

'What's a burgh?' asked Pam.

A big voice, reminiscent of the banks of the Mersey, boomed in reply. 'It's a big furry animal that lives in a cave. Hi, Wes. Didn't think you'd be in here tonight. You never mentioned it.' Gerry Heffernan stood grinning reproachfully, glass in hand.

The only trouble with the Tradmouth Arms, Wesley thought, was that it was virtually next door to his boss's whitewashed cottage at the end of Baynard's Quay. He felt guilty for resenting Heffernan's presence – after all, the inspector was a widower, alone in the world and longing for a bit of off-duty company, and he did like the man. But the prospect of being joined by his superior each time he wanted a quiet drink with his old university friends didn't fill Wesley Peterson with feelings of unmixed delight. However, he forced himself to smile as he made room for his boss to sit down.

'I had to get out, Wes. Those holidaymakers don't half make a racket outside my house . . . it's like Piccadilly ruddy station in the summer.' He looked across at Pam. 'Hello, love. How's things? I understand you're to be congratulated for putting up with our Wes for five long years.'

'That's right.' Pam smiled. 'Not that I see much of him these days,' she added ruefully, glancing over at her husband.

'Not my fault, love. Blame our villains. When they work overtime so do we.' Gerry Heffernan took a long drink.

'Anyway, how are you, Gerry?' asked Pam tactfully. 'I've not seen you since Michael's christening.'

'I'm bearing up under the tidal wave of crime.' He winked at Wesley. 'And my lad's coming home for the holidays tomorrow. He's at Liverpool University . . . training to be a vet,' Heffernan said proudly.

'That's nice,' said Pam with sincerity. 'What about your daughter?'

'She's gone off to Salzburg with a group from the music college . . . some sort of course,' he said, sounding disappointed. 'Anyway . . .' He changed the subject. 'How come the taxpayer spends a ruddy fortune on your education and you lot don't know what a bear is?'

'A burgh,' said Neil, smiling smugly, 'is a fortified town. Alfred the Great set up a load of them so that people would have some defence against Viking attack. Neston had become a burgh by the tenth century, as well as a market town. It even had its own mint . . . made its own money.'

'So what about this minster?' asked Pam, interested.

'Well, there's a theory that as Neston was such an important place a thousand years ago it must have had a minster church . . . a sort of monastery and principal church of the district. So if we can find traces of the Anglo-Saxon minster on the site of the parish church . . .' His face suddenly clouded. 'Unless they built it out of wood, of course, then it's the Devil's own job to find anything . . . all you get is a few post holes and a bit of stained soil, and under a building that's been developed over the years, you'd be lucky to find them.'

'And did the big hairy Vikings manage to attack Neston then?' asked Pam teasingly. She was beginning to enjoy herself, and found the conversation a refreshing change from endless days of baby care.

Neil leaned towards her. 'Well, we don't know for certain. There are stories, of course . . . I mean this Viking Festival next weekend is cashing in on local legends. It was started by some local history society in 1997 to commemorate the thousandth anniversary of the supposed Viking raids.'

'I saw some leaflets about that. They're looking for volunteers to take part,' said Pam thoughtfully.

29

But Neil wasn't listening. 'Although there were some very bad raids on Devon in 997,' he continued. 'The town isn't actually mentioned by name in the Anglo-Saxon Chronicle. But I intend to discover the truth . . . whatever it is.'

Pam glanced over at Gerry Heffernan with a secretive smile on her face, while Neil drained his glass dramatically and flicked his long hair out of his face with soil-stained fingers. Wesley said nothing but sat back, thinking about the bones buried deep in the field at Longhouse Cottage.

At dusk Josiah Beaumont climbed into his tractor, more than ready for home and maybe a quick last pint at the Crown before bed. He chugged slowly out of the field onto the narrow lane, getting down wearily to close the gate behind him.

He progressed up the single-track lane at a stately pace, knowing that behind the high hedgerows lay acre upon acre of rolling countryside; the loveliest in England. But that evening his mind wasn't on the appreciation of nature or the contemplation of beauty. He had lived with this landscape all his life and took it for granted . . . couldn't see what all the fuss was about.

As he drove along past crossroads and isolated cottages, his thoughts flew to lower matters: whether his wife would go on at him again about the broken washer in the tap; whether he would miss that programme on ITV with all those sex scenes; and whether that car with the foreign number plates would still be there on that grass verge when he passed.

He slowed down as he reached the verge, next to a sudden widening of the road, broad enough to accommodate three smallish vehicles. It was still there. A white car, an Opel – quite new, quite nice. But foreign, left-hand drive, with strange foreign number plates. He saw lots of foreign cars about in the holiday season – Dutch, French or German mostly. From his elevated position he could watch the drivers' expressions of deep concentration as they negotiated the blind-bended lanes from an unfamiliar side of the road while he, Josiah, sat smug in the familiar security of his slow-moving tractor.

This white car was foreign all right. But where was its driver? There were no houses near by . . . there was nothing near by except fields. And it had been there since Monday. If it had broken down surely it would have been recovered by now. Josiah drew up alongside, left his engine running and climbed down to have a quick look.

He peered into the white car's windows, but the light was fading and he couldn't see clearly. But he could make out a coat on the back seat, a woman's coat, and some sort of bag. He put a nervous hand on the door handle. To his astonishment it was unlocked and the door opened with a slight creak. Josiah shut it again quickly, the bang seeming to echo in the evening air. He would leave well alone.

He squinted at his watch in the half-light. Quarter to ten. That programme would be starting any minute. He might ring the police in the morning if the car hadn't gone by then.

But that night it wasn't only the thought of the naked writhings he had witnessed on the television screen that occupied Josiah's mind, depriving him of sleep while his wife snored gently beside him. He kept asking himself the same question. Who would leave a car abandoned and unlocked for days in an isolated place? As he lay awake his unease turned to fear – a gnawing feeling that something dreadful had happened.

First thing the next morning, before he dressed and sat down to breakfast, Josiah Beaumont telephoned the police.

Chapter Three

AD *997*

Many arrived in our town today from villages round about. They too had heard of the horrors that the men from the north had wrought upon Lydford and Tavistock. Some stay with kin but many have sought the shelter of the Minster. The brothers pray the danger does not last long as our house must provide sustenance for all.

There are some nuns of the district who take refuge with us. I pray the Lord to keep His people in safety.

From the chronicle of Brother Edwin, monk of Neston Minster

The last thing Wesley Peterson wanted to face first thing in the morning was a visit to the mortuary. But at least today Colin Bowman had only called him over to discuss the bones that had been found at Longhouse Cottage . . . hardly as gruesome as a full post-mortem.

Wesley told himself as he walked to the hospital that there was nothing to be squeamish about; that he would see only dry bones, nothing worse than he had seen during many an archaeological dig in his student days. But there was something about the mortuary itself – the smell of death; the clinical surroundings which masked the true purpose of the place – that filled his heart with dread each time he stepped through the plastic swing-doors.

He found Colin Bowman in his cosy office and was immediately offered some excellent coffee and a superior chocolate biscuit. Colin Bowman had a taste for the best things in life. As Gerry Heffernan had commented more than once, they certainly knew how to live down at the mortuary.

Wesley liked Colin and found him a genial host, but he was anxious to get the business over with . . . to leave this place of death and get back into the sun. But Colin Bowman couldn't be hurried. After a long discussion about Michael's sleeping habits, Wesley's sister Maritia's medical career, Mrs Bowman's new part-time job in a local antique shop, Gerry Heffernan's son's home-coming and a few other subjects besides, Wesley at last managed to steer the conversation around to death.

Reluctantly, Colin put the packet of biscuits away and led Wesley to a spartan white room. On a trolley in the centre of the room lay a skeleton.

'There he is. Our six-foot-two-inch male of unknown origin.'

'Can you tell me anything else about him?' Wesley asked tentatively.

'I can tell you that he was probably in his thirties when he met his end and that he most likely died from a severe blow to the head.' Bowman indicated the back of the skull.

'What was he hit with? Can you tell?'

Bowman shook his balding head and smiled. 'Actually, it looks rather like an axe wound, but I can't tell you any more than that. There's one interesting thing, though.' He turned his attention to the skeleton's shoulder bone. 'See that nick there on the clavicle . . . the collar bone?'

Wesley bent down to look. The bone looked as though it had been nicked by something sharp. 'Yes. What is it?'

'Well, I did some experiments to see what could have caused it and I think I've come up with the answer. I have a friend who collects old swords . . . he's got quite an impressive array of the things. I borrowed one of his older swords and matched it with the cut to the bone. I'm certain it's a sword cut. I can't prove it, of course, but . . .'

'Could that have killed him?'

'Not there, no. It would only have wounded him. Of course, I can't say he wasn't wounded then dispatched with a blow to the head as he lay writhing in agony. After all this time it's impossible to tell.'

'So he's old?'

'I think so, yes. Look at his teeth. He's not had the pleasures of a modern refined diet . . . and no dental work. I'd say he's very old. Certainly over seventy years, so you won't have to start an investigation into how he died. I've let the coroner know. But as to exactly how old he is, we'll have to wait for the result of Neil's radiocarbon dating of the bit of bone he took . . . he said it could take months.'

'Yes. Unfortunately it does. So can we be sure this isn't Jock Palister?'

'Absolutely sure, I'd say. Once we get the results of Neil's test even Gerry won't be able to argue with science.'

'I wouldn't bank on it,' said Wesley with a grin. 'Well, thanks very much, Colin. I'd better get back to Gerry now . . . break the bad news.'

'Oh, there's one more thing, Wesley. I found this fused to the inside of one of the ribs. It's possible he was wearing it around his neck on a leather thong: the leather rotted and it fell through. That's my guess anyway.' He passed Wesley a stainless-steel dish. In it was a small amulet with a hole at the top from which it could be suspended on a chain or leather strip. It was in the shape of a stylised hammer. Wesley had seen something like it before.

'I think I know what this is. It's Thor's Hammer. Pagan Vikings used to wear them around their necks for luck. May I take it to show Neil?'

'Of course.' Colin Bowman raised a hand in farewell. 'I hope Gerry doesn't take the news too badly.'

Wesley put his new-found treasure in a plastic exhibit bag and walked out through the swing-doors into the bright light of day, wondering how he was going to break it to his boss that Jock Palister wasn't lying, silent and dead, on a mortuary trolley.

Gerry Heffernan sat at his cluttered desk, head in hands, contemplating the wickedness of the world. He raised his head and shouted through to the main office. 'Get us a coffee will you, Rach. I'm spitting feathers 'ere.'

Rachel looked up from her paperwork, seething. Why did he always expect her to provide the refreshments? Why not Steve? Gerry Heffernan was a good boss but there were times when she suspected that the concept of feminism had never entered his benighted world.

Then she had an idea. She looked across at WPC Trish Walton, who was on secondment to CID. Trish was earnestly typing information into a computer. She looked awkward and self-conscious in her everyday clothes, having been used to wearing a uniform to work. 'Trish,' said Rachel smoothly, 'the inspector wants a coffee. Could you, er . . .'

Trish jumped up without a word and went to the coffee machine outside the office while Rachel sat back, feeling triumphant. Delegation was a wonderful thing . . . and it was something she would have to get used to if she was going to make Chief Constable.

She saw that Steve was watching her. 'I don't know what you're looking so smug about, Rach. I've had a call from a farm worker: a Josiah Beaumont. Josiah . . . what kind of a name is that?' He smirked.

Rachel gave him a withering look. 'What did he want?'

Steve sat back, teasing. Dark-haired and in his mid-twenties, he was good-looking and he knew it. If he hadn't tried so hard to emulate the tough cops he'd seen on television Rachel might have considered him attractive. But as it was he had absorbed all the undesirable features of his fictitious heroes – their insensitivity; their dim view of racial minorities; their predatory attitude to women. Steve Carstairs longed for the mean streets of some grimy metropolis, but stayed in Tradmouth because his mother did his washing.

'Well, come on, Steve. What did he say?' Rachel asked impatiently.

'He's found a car abandoned.'

'The one that was stolen from Wexer's Farm? The Land Rover?'

'No. A white car . . . foreign number plates.'

'Have you told Traffic?' As soon as the words were out of her mouth she made the connection. Her mind had been so occupied with the farm raids that she had almost forgotten Barbara Questid's visit and the missing Danish woman. Hadn't Ingeborg Larsen driven a white car? She stood up, went over to the cabinet and drew out a wafer-thin file.

'What was the make of the car?' she asked, scanning Barbara's statement.

'I thought you said we should tell Traffic . . . get it moved.'

'No. Hang on, Steve. I've got an idea. What was the make?'

'Don't know. He didn't say. Why?'

'What about the nationality?'

35

Steve shrugged. 'He just said foreign.'

'I'd like to have a look at this car. Where is it?'

Steve reluctantly parted with the information, wondering why Rachel was so interested in an abandoned car. Before he could enquire further, Rachel was marching towards Gerry Heffernan's office with a determined expression on her face.

Trish Walton had been pleased to get out of the office. She hadn't realised that she would encounter so much paper working with CID: somehow she had seen it as more glamorous than being in uniform, and form-filling was hardly Trish's idea of glamour.

Rachel had had the choice of taking Steve or Trish to look at the car. She had chosen the latter, as she found that Steve's macho posturings got in the way of his judgement. Besides, she thought it was about time Trish saw some action other than that provided by a flickering computer screen.

They found the white car easily enough. It was unlocked, and it was a tribute to the honesty of the local citizens – or the isolation of that particular lane – that the bag and coat Josiah Beaumont had described were still there on the back seat.

Rachel walked around the car, deep in thought. 'Well, Trish, have you noticed anything out of the ordinary?' she asked, testing the novice.

'There are no skid marks. But there's a bit of a bump at the back. Look.'

Rachel walked round to the back of the car. 'Well spotted. The rear light's broken. It looks as though something's bumped into it from behind. But the damage isn't enough to stop anyone driving the car, is it?'

Trish shook her head. 'And if the driver had to abandon the car, why did they leave the things on the back seat?'

Rachel stood looking at the vehicle for a few moments. The nationality sticker on the back bore the letters DK . . . Denmark presumably. She thought of Ingeborg Larsen as she pulled on a pair of disposable plastic gloves. Things were not right here . . . not right at all.

She opened the car door slowly and put her head inside. 'Trish,' she called, 'come here. Can you smell something?' Rachel stood to one side as Trish poked her head into the car.

'Yes. A sort of hospital smell . . . I don't know what it is. Any ideas?'

Rachel opened the back door of the car and took the bag out carefully. She carried it round to the bonnet of the car and opened it, her heart beating quickly as she examined the contents. Trish hovered just behind, straining to look.

'There's everything in there,' Trish exclaimed. 'Her purse, her passport . . . look, there's her make-up. Is there a name?'

Rachel flicked open the passport . . . a Danish passport. She knew what the name would be. 'See if you can find anything in the front, will you, Trish. Any note or . . .'

'Do you think it could be suicide, then?'

Rachel didn't answer but continued to examine the contents of the bag. A minute later Trish emerged from the car waving a plastic exhibit bag containing something white.

'I've found this. It's a pad of gauze or something . . . doesn't half stink.'

Rachel looked at the object and reached for her mobile phone. Things weren't looking too good for Ingeborg Larsen.

Pam Peterson stood in the hall and listened. Silence. Michael was still asleep. She went into the living room, opened the sideboard drawer and stared at the yellow leaflet inside. Why not? She had six more weeks before she returned to work after her maternity leave. This was the perfect opportunity to get out and try something new – meet new people, broaden her horizons.

A wail from upstairs told her that Michael was awake. She fetched the baby down and placed him in his car seat. She would drive over to Neston now and arrange things.

Parking proved difficult owing to the determined invasion of tourists eager to sample the delights of the picturesque town of Neston, eight miles downriver from Tradmouth, with its Elizabethan houses, castle and assorted New Age emporia. But she found a space and headed for the community centre, Michael's push-chair whizzing before her like a tank to clear the way.

The community centre prided itself on being wheelchair-and push-chair-friendly. As Pam pushed Michael's conveyance up the wooden ramp into the half-timbered building on the High Street, she saw more people milling around with yellow leaflets in their hands – young people with ears and noses burdened by dangling metalwork; the earnest middle-aged dressed in a vaguely ethnic manner, the prosperous retired; a fair cross-section of Neston residents. She felt a fresh wave of determination.

The girl manning the rickety reception desk looked up. Her nose was decorated by a jangling ring, while her mousey hair, arranged in tiny plaits, matched her long, dull garments. Pam, dressed simply in a checked summer dress, felt at a sartorial disadvantage. She explained what she was there for.

The girl looked her up and down. 'Are you sure you want to take part in the re-enactment?' she said, sounding genuinely concerned. 'We need people to help with stalls and refreshments as well. Perhaps you'd rather . . .'

'Oh, no. I fancied the re-enactment. I'm a teacher, you see . . . and it's on the national curriculum. I'll be doing that period of history with my class next term,' she added. This explanation probably sounded a little feeble, but Pam felt she had to justify her decision somehow. 'Er . . . can you tell me exactly what's involved?'

'Right, then,' said the girl, clearly dubious about Pam's suitability. 'How much do you know about the Vikings?'

Gerry Heffernan stood next to Wesley, watching the scenes of crime officers go about their painstaking business examining the area around the white Opel. The car itself had been taken away on a low-loader for more detailed examination.

Rachel stood beside Wesley, Trish having been dispatched back to the office to continue her paperwork as soon as things hotted up.

'So what do you think, Wes?' asked Heffernan bluntly. 'Have we got an abduction or what?'

'Looks that way, sir. I mean, you don't use a chloroform pad on someone to ask directions, do you? I've arranged for everyone who lives round about to be interviewed. Someone might have seen something.'

'Roads don't come much quieter than this. Wonder what she was doing here.'

'Her landlady said she was going into Neston on Monday. These lanes are used as a short cut by locals,' said Rachel. She had been born and brought up in the district and knew the place better

38

than most: 'But she could have got lost ... taken the wrong turning. It's easily done.'

'I think it's time we went to see her landlady ... found out more about this mysterious Danish woman. I think we'd be justified in searching her room, don't you, Wes? You go with Rach.'

Wesley gave Rachel a smile. There was nobody he would rather take with him to search the room of a missing woman. Rachel's powers of observation and common sense had often proved invaluable. And she was good with people, too: she would soon have the landlady giving her secret opinions about Ingeborg Larsen, and probably recounting her own life story too if they weren't careful.

The SOCOs continued their search as Wesley and Rachel climbed into Wesley's dark blue Ford and drove off towards Tradmouth, leaving Gerry Heffernan engaged in what he claimed to be his second-favourite occupation – watching other people working.

The sound of an inexperienced organist practising for some future wedding provided a dubious musical accompaniment for Neil Watson and his colleagues as they dug deeper into the foundations of Neston parish church. They were fenced off in the south-western corner of the impressive medieval building, trying to cause as little disruption as possible to visitors and worshippers as the life of the church carried on around them.

But by the time they had suffered Mendelssohn's wedding march for the sixth time, Neil had had enough. Even his colleague Matt, who had fleetingly considered putting his relationship with Jane, the classy blonde squatting next to him in the trench, on a more permanent footing, had been quite put off the idea of marriage by the musical aversion therapy.

A shout from Neil made Matt look up from the fragment of old tiled floor he was starting to uncover. 'Matt, Jane, come and have a look at this.'

Without a word they crossed over to the deeper trench where Neil was working. They could see that Neil's eyes were shining with excitement as he pointed downwards with his trowel. 'Look. Can you see the blackened section? And look there just below it where I've started to uncover the wall. That's Saxon stonework. I'm sure of it.'

Matt looked at Jane in a purely professional manner. 'Are you thinking what I'm thinking?'

'This ties in with all the stories that are flying around this place,' Jane answered, matter-of-fact. 'At some point in its Saxon days Neston was attacked and the church burned to the ground. And we can all take a guess at who was responsible, can't we?'

Neil nodded. 'I'll say one thing for the Vikings – nobody could have accused them of being idle.'

Barbara Questid was nervous. Rachel could tell. When they had first entered the house – a large, three-storey villa reputedly built for a sea captain in the early nineteenth century – she had offered tea. But the offer was forgotten as soon as they announced the reason for their visit. Barbara stood in the hallway wringing her hands, muttering the words 'that's awful' like a mantra. An elderly couple appeared at the top of the stairs – Ingeborg's fellow guests. As soon as Barbara spotted them her manner changed and an ingratiating smile appeared on her face which disappeared as soon as the newcomers were greeted and dispatched out of the house in the direction of the town centre.

'Of course you must search her room. I mean, if she's been kidnapped or something . . .' She didn't finish the sentence, just shook her head at the horror of it all.

'Did she tell you anything about herself, Mrs Questid?' asked Wesley.

'Oh, I can't remember. She taught English and she came from Copenhagen . . . I think that's all she told me. I'm always welcoming to the guests – I chat to them and all that – but to be honest half of it goes in one ear and out the other, if you know what I mean.'

Wesley nodded. He knew what she meant all right.

'My husband might remember something. He's just in the back mending a lamp from one of the guests' rooms at the moment. Do you want to see him?' There was a slight hint of disapproval in her voice.

'Perhaps later, Mrs Questid. If we could just see Ms Larsen's room . . .'

'Of course,' she said, slipping easily into the role of hostess. 'This way. You did say you wanted tea, didn't you?' She seemed to have recovered from the initial shock of their news, Wesley noticed. It would take more than a missing guest to put Barbara Questid off her stride for very long.

She showed them into a spacious first-floor room. The decor was pink, flowery and spotlessly clean.

'Have you cleaned in here since Ms Larsen left, Mrs Questid?' asked Wesley. The desire for cleanliness often destroyed evidence.

'I've dusted and hoovered . . . just gave the *en suite* a wipe round like I always do. The bed was already made so I didn't have to do much. She was a very tidy woman . . . not like some.'

With this grudging eulogy ringing in their ears, Wesley and Rachel began to search the room of the very tidy woman. Barbara Questid sniffed, took the hint and left them to it.

The room was indeed preternaturally tidy, and Wesley observed with disbelief the clinical precision with which Ingeborg Larsen's possessions were arranged. In the drawers sweaters and T-shirts, even underwear – sporty rather than lacy – were folded, shop-style, in colour-coded rows. The neat, tailored clothes in the wardrobe hung in order of length. A white jacket hanging at the end of the row was still swathed in the thin, clinging polythene used by dry-cleaning firms, a pink ticket pinned to the label.

'Obsessive,' was Rachel's only comment on the matter. 'I always thought I was fairly tidy but . . .'

'Not really natural, is it?' said Wesley, grinning. 'At least it'll make our job easier,' he added with sincerity. There was nothing worse than having to search through a jumbled mess of belongings.

It didn't take long to search the room. Although Ingeborg hadn't necessarily travelled light, she had certainly travelled in an orderly fashion. There was a bottle of pills in the drawer of the bedside table, and beside them was a bulky paperback book. Beneath the book Wesley found a photograph. A blonde woman, slender and lovely, standing framed in the porch of a white-painted wooden house. Next to her stood a tall, fair-haired man. Wesley picked the photograph up and studied it. The woman was Ingeborg Larsen – he recognised her from her passport photograph. But this image, unlike the official one, showed her true beauty.

He turned his attention to the book. Although he couldn't understand the Danish title, the cover told him that it was a steamy historical saga set in the age when bodices were ripped with monotonous regularity. Ingeborg's reading taste didn't appear to match the cool order of the rest of her life: perhaps a desire for romantic, uncontrolled chaos simmered somewhere beneath the smooth surface.

But was Ingeborg Larsen really so cool, so precise? He went over what they knew about her: she was thirty-eight, had a taste for neatness, lived in Copenhagen and taught English. But why was she holidaying in Devon alone? Her passport had listed her next of kin as a Sven Larsen. Was he her husband? Brother? Father? Was he the man in the photograph with her? Had she come to Devon to meet somebody? The unanswered questions irritated Wesley.

There was a shy knock on the door and a large man stepped into the room. 'I'm Ralph Questid. My wife sent me up with some tea. Is that all right?' The man looked at Wesley and Rachel appraisingly. He had a mane of steel-grey hair which he wore tied back in a neat ponytail. Well built rather than fat, he wore a colourful waistcoat and exuded the laid-back air of a semi-retired hippie. Wesley and Rachel exchanged a glance. They had imagined Barbara's partner to be a small, balding, henpecked man. This apparition was quite unexpected.

After Wesley had introduced himself and Rachel, he thought a plea for co-operation might be in order. 'Mr Questid, we're sorry if we're inconveniencing you but we are rather worried about Ms Larsen and . . .'

'Actually . . .' Ralph put the teacups down and looked round conspiratorially. 'I did want a word with you. Ingeborg . . . er, Ms Larsen . . . asked me to do her a favour. She was, er, a very attractive woman, you understand.' He winked at Wesley, man to man. 'And I didn't tell my wife at the time so I'd be grateful if you wouldn't mention it . . . avoid misunderstanding and all that.'

Rachel was growing impatient. 'What exactly did you want to tell us, sir?' she demanded with disapproval in her voice.

'Well, I offered to help Ingeborg out. She was a foreigner . . .'

'Was?' Rachel seized on the word like a terrier.

'Sorry . . . is a foreigner, alone in a strange country. She had a little prang in her car. No damage to hers luckily, but she was backing out of a parking space in Tradmouth on Saturday – the day after she arrived – and she just touched someone's nearside wing. Just a little bit of damage apparently but she was rather confused about the procedure with the insurance companies and the man in the car had been rather unpleasant. I made a few phone calls for her . . . sorted things out. There was no problem, but with the other driver's aggressive attitude and . . .'

'Are you certain there was no damage to her car, sir?'

'Quite sure. I had a good look. It was fine.'

'What was Ms Larsen like?' asked Wesley. Mr Questid had clearly known her better than his wife had.

'A lovely woman . . . very, er, cool, very beautiful, but with a sense of humour. Always a twinkle in her eye, if you know what I mean.' There was certainly a twinkle in Questid's eye as he described her. She had made quite an impression.

'Sexy?' suggested Wesley, sensing Rachel's disapproval of this cool, beautiful creature who flirted with other women's husbands.

A wide smile appeared on Questid's face. 'Oh, very, Sergeant. That's exactly the word I'd use.'

'And did she talk about what she was doing in Devon . . . about her life in Denmark . . . anything that might help us?'

'She taught English in some kind of college. She'd been to Devon before, when she was young, and she'd always wanted to come back.'

'What did she do while she was over here?'

Questid shrugged. 'Sightseeing mostly. She said she'd been to the castle and been on one of the river cruises. The usual tourist stuff.'

'Did she say that she'd met anyone here she knew?'

'She never mentioned it to me if she had,' he said regretfully. 'And before you ask, she never said when she was here before or where she'd stayed.'

'And was she married?' asked Rachel.

'She was divorced. But she'd just moved into a flat with her brother. I had the impression the divorce was fairly recent. In fact she said that was why she decided to come back to Devon now. She needed a break and she remembered that this part of Devon was very beautiful. She came on impulse, she said . . . a spur-of-the-moment decision.'

'Did the divorce cause much ill feeling, do you know?'

'Oh, no. Ingeborg said they'd been separated for a while and it was all very civilised. You know what the Scandinavians are like . . . very modern,' Questid said regretfully.

Wesley pictured Questid's own marital circumstances. The brassy Barbara would probably not have approved of 'modern' arrangements. In fact he wondered how Ralph had managed to become so well acquainted with the ins and outs of Ingeborg Larsen's life in such a short time under his wife's roof.

'So you were getting to know Ingeborg quite well before she disappeared?'

'I wouldn't say well. We passed the time of day.'

'You seem to know her better than your wife does,' Rachel said, watching for a reaction.

'Well, I think Ingeborg's more of a man's woman, if you know what I mean. Nothing wrong in that. Some women just seem to get on better with men than with other women.'

'Quite,' said Wesley. He was building up an interesting picture of Ingeborg Larsen – the beautiful, neat, sexy woman with a twinkle in her eye who enjoyed her power over men. She had probably been more than capable of sorting out her own insurance, but she knew how to play the helpless foreigner when it suited her. But last Monday Ingeborg, for once, might have encountered a situation that she couldn't control.

'You said the driver she backed into was aggressive. Did she tell you his name, by any chance?'

'Yes. It was Proudy . . . Laurence Proudy. Youngish, address in London. He said he was here on holiday, but I don't know where he was staying.'

Rachel frowned for a moment, deep in thought. 'I'm sure I've heard that name before . . . but I can't remember where.'

The journey back to the station was a silent one as Rachel dredged her mind for the elusive information. Where had she heard the name Laurence Proudy before?

Chapter Four

AD 997
A traveller came to the Minster this day seeking shelter on the
way to Exeter. He said that the Danes had sailed around the
coast, attacking many dwellings and churches. They had come
ashore at Stoke Beeching and had burned the church there to
the ground. Some men of the village had defied them and had
fought bravely but to no avail. All that the people possessed
was plundered and many were taken as slaves. Then Mass
was said and prayers offered for those dead and enslaved by
these enemies of God.

[Note in margin of the text] *I pray that my father and*
mother came safe through the outrage at Stoke Beeching. Oh
Lord hear this my prayer.
From the chronicle of Brother Edwin, monk of Neston Minster

Neil Watson felt pleased with himself. He had found Saxon
foundations underneath Neston parish church – he was certain of
it. And they had not been simply demolished to make way for a
bigger and more up-to-the-minute structure in Norman times: they
had been destroyed by fire. Neston's Saxon minster had met a
violent and fiery end only to rise, phoenix-like, from the ashes at
a later, more peaceful, date. They had found other things too. Late
Saxon pottery and a number of styli, Anglo-Saxon writing
implements, all of which fitted in with Neil's minster theory – a
house of learned monks in the heart of the walled town,
ministering to the people of the area.

Neil sat back on his heels and looked at his handiwork. It was
coming on nicely – which was more than could be said for the

playing of the amateur organist, who was still murdering Mendelssohn up at the church's east end.

'Coming to the pub for lunch, Neil?' asked a well-bred female voice from the next trench.

'Er . . . no thanks, Jane. I think I'll pop along to Longhouse Cottage.'

'I thought you'd finished there. Any word from the museum about those rivets?'

'They say they're early . . . won't give an exact date, though.' He paused for a minute, thinking. 'I wanted to speak to the people at Longhouse Cottage . . . see if they know anything about the history of the place. It's probably a long shot but . . .'

'Well, you know where we are if you change your mind,' said Matt, wiping his hands on his black T-shirt. He and Jane walked out of the cool, dark church in amicable silence. Those two, Neil thought, are becoming more like an old married couple every day. Resolutely single, he watched them leave without envy.

The heat came as a shock to Neil when he stepped outside the church. He had spent the morning shaded from the warmth – the happy result of a ridge of high pressure hovering over the south-west of England – and, like most of his fellow countrymen, had been totally unprepared for an outside temperature which was greater than that indoors. He walked down Neston High Street past men with pallid legs displayed beneath ill-fitting shorts and women in diaphanous dresses, resolutely staying out of doors to make the most of the rare heat wave. When he reached his car, he found it hot enough inside to bake bread in. He wound the windows down and drove the ten miles out to Stoke Beeching, where a pleasant breeze blew in off the sea, making the temperature more bearable.

Maggie Palister must have spotted him as he drove up the bumpy track to Longhouse Cottage. She waited for him outside the front door, arms folded. Her expression was hardly welcoming.

'I thought you'd finished. What do you want?'

'Is Carl about?' Carl, at least, had been interested in their discoveries.

'He's seeing to the hens. He's busy. And he's filled in that hole. He had to lay the drainage and he thought you'd finished,' she said accusingly.

Neil sensed that she regarded him as a nuisance, interfering with the running of their precarious livelihood. He'd have to tread carefully.

'That's okay. I just wanted to ask you if you knew anything about the history of this place.'

Maggie regarded him suspiciously. 'You're a friend of that policeman, aren't you . . . the black one?'

Neil wondered why she had mentioned Wesley. Did concern about his friend's occupation indicate a guilty conscience? 'Yeah. We were at university together. Why?'

'Did he say anything . . . about my husband?'

'Not to me he didn't,' said Neil, casually. He did remember Gerry Heffernan saying something about a Jock Palister – presumably Maggie's husband – but he hadn't been taking much notice, his mind being filled with thoughts of Viking raiders. He changed the subject to one he considered more appealing. 'I think the burial in your field might date back to the late tenth century. I can't be certain yet, of course, but . . .'

'I don't know what that's got to do with me.' Maggie looked at Neil with contempt. She had once been pretty; Neil could tell that. She wore a shabby frock which needed a whirl round a washing machine, and disintegrating slippers which appeared to be held together by dirt. Her face was lined with the hopelessness that resulted from years of struggle against financial ruin. But her voice was accentless, educated. Neil suspected that at some point she had made a social descent and, by her resentful expression, had lived to regret it.

He carried on regardless, hoping his enthusiasm for his subject would be at least mildly infectious. 'We're on the brink of a big discovery in Neston. We think the first Saxon church there – a minster – was burned down in a Viking raid. Your skeleton was buried inside a boat, which is a Viking custom. I know Neston's ten miles away, but if we could establish a link . . .' He didn't bother finishing his sentence but he detected a flicker of interest in Maggie's eyes. 'I just wondered if I could have a look inside your house, see if there are any clues to how old it is. If it's not convenient . . .'

'No, it's not convenient,' she said with some hostility, as if she suspected Neil of planning to nick the family silver. He decided that persistence wouldn't succeed and changed the subject. 'Have you ever heard any stories about the place?' Sometimes local legends held a kernel of truth.

Maggie shrugged her shoulders and the neckline of her dress fell back to reveal a washed-out bra strap. 'There's only that story about the stones. Someone in the village told me about it. Probably a load of rubbish,' she added dismissively.

'What stones?'

Sensing that she wouldn't get rid of Neil until she had made a token effort to satisfy his curiosity, she led him round to the back of the building without a word, glancing back nervously at the house, and began to march up a scrubby sloping field, Neil following a few feet behind. They reached a stream, just a trickle in the summer heat. She pointed downwards. 'Those stones there . . . the red ones. See?'

'What about them?'

'Well, an old woman in the village told me this field was known as Blood Field: she said those stones in the stream were stained with blood.'

'Yes,' said Neil, growing impatient. 'But when? What happened here?'

'How should I know? You'd better ask her. It was that old biddy who used to run the post office. She lives in that little pink house by the church. I don't remember what she said except . . .'

'What?'

'Except I think she said something about Danes.'

Maggie led the way back to the farm and stood, arms folded, seeing Neil off the premises with obvious relief. As he climbed into the Mini, he glanced back quickly at the house and saw a dark shape flit across one of the upstairs windows.

Neil wasn't the only one who took it into his head to slip away from his duties that sunny lunch-time. Gerry Heffernan rolled up his shirtsleeves to reveal a couple of large, nautical tattoos, left his office on the first floor of Tradmouth police station, and lumbered through the crowded narrow streets of the town towards cobbled Baynard's Quay.

The holidaymakers were out in force, swarming around the quay, strolling up and down between the small defensive castle at one end and the Tradmouth Arms at the other. Children perched on the edge of the quayside with crabbing lines, squealing with delight as their clawed prisoners made their bid for freedom, scrabbling sideways towards the water. Parents sat on benches enjoying the view across the river and a drink from the Tradmouth Arms until their offspring tired of their captive crustaceans and threw them back into the river, no worse for their ordeal.

Some holidaymakers turned and stared as Gerry Heffernan let himself into his whitewashed cottage at the end of the quay. He resisted the temptation to make some witty comment in retaliation and closed the front door behind him.

Since the death of Kathy, his wife, three years before, Heffernan had become used to returning to a silent, empty home. But the raucous rock music blaring from the living room told him that his son had returned to the fold. For a few weeks, at least, Gerry Heffernan's quiet and lonely domestic routine would be completely disrupted . . . which didn't upset him overmuch.

Sam Heffernan looked up guiltily as his father entered the room. 'Dad. I wasn't expecting you back till tonight.'

'Thought I'd call in and see if you'd arrived. How are you, son.'

Sam stood up and gave his father a tentative hug. He was taller than his dad. And dark, having inherited Kathy's good looks. 'Good to see you, Dad. How are you keeping? Sorry I've not been in touch much this term, but you know how it is.' He shrugged.

Gerry Heffernan knew how it was all right. He had been young himself once, as he kept reminding everyone at the police station. He knew the pull of booze and members of the opposite sex as well as any. But alas, unlike Sam and Wesley, Gerry Heffernan hadn't had the advantages of a university education. At the age of sixteen he had joined the merchant navy and gone to sea. He had worked his way up to first officer when disaster had struck and he had developed appendicitis as his ship passed by the Devon coast. He had been winched off by helicopter and taken to Tradmouth Hospital, where he had fallen heavily for Kathy, his nurse. He had then forsaken his native Liverpool, stayed ashore, joined the police force, and the rest was history.

'I see you've had something to eat,' Heffernan said, noticing the fall-out of a ham sandwich on a discarded plate. 'Made any plans for this holiday yet?' he asked, trying not to sound like the heavy-handed father.

'I'm a bit short of readies, Dad. I was thinking of getting a job.'

'Well, there's lots of seasonal work about.'

Sam made no comment. He didn't tell his father he'd been thinking along completely different lines. A job in a café or hotel would hardly make a dent in his student loan. There were more lucrative options.

He thought it wise to change the subject. He stood up, walked over to the fireplace and lifted a picture postcard of a white wooden colonial church. 'Nice card, Dad. New England, is it? Have you been keeping something from me? Who's Susan?'

Gerry Heffernan reddened. 'Er . . . she's, er, a lady I know. I met her not long ago when her next-door neighbour was murdered.'

Sam Heffernan watched his father squirm, trying to maintain a serious expression. 'Am I going to meet her?'

'She's gone over to the States for a month to see her sister. She's American but she's lived over here for years.' Gerry Heffernan felt like a naughty adolescent being interrogated for staying out late by a censorious parent.

Sam continued, enjoying the reversal of roles. 'What's she like?'

'She's a very nice lady. And we're just friends. She's a widow and . . .'

'You don't have to explain to me, Dad,' said Sam graciously. 'I just wanted to make sure her intentions were honourable.' His face broke into a wide grin. 'You can tell me all about it tonight.'

Gerry Heffernan thought it politic to make for the kitchen, where he made himself a swift cheese-and-pickle sandwich and pointedly washed the dishes. Then he left Sam searching through the job adverts in the local paper and returned to the police station.

When his father was safely out of the house, Sam put his feet up on the coffee table and ringed an advert, smiling to himself. He would phone later . . . discreetly. This was one job he didn't want his dad to know about.

Wesley Peterson sat at his desk, shuffling papers absent-mindedly as he waited for the phone call. The Copenhagen police had said they'd get back to him as soon as they'd managed to contact Sven Larsen, Ingeborg's next of kin. That had been three hours ago.

The telephone rang and Wesley grabbed at it eagerly. He heard Neil's voice, bubbling with enthusiasm.

50

'Sorry, Neil, I'm expecting an important call. Can you make it quick.' Wesley tried not to sound too dismissive.

'Yeah. Meet me at Stoke Beeching church tonight at five thirty. That quick enough for you?' The line went dead. Wesley, who had planned to get home early that evening – work permitting – was intrigued, if a little peeved by Neil's presumption. And he had forgotten to mention the hammer-shaped amulet Colin Bowman had found in the bones, which he now had safely in his pocket. But it could wait until they met at Stoke Beeching.

Gerry Heffernan appeared at the office door. 'Hi, Wes. Any word from Copenhagen?'

'Not yet. Still waiting. I presume Mr Larsen will speak English,' he said warily.

'I'd get your Danish phrase book out if I were you,' said Heffernan mischievously, before he disappeared into his office.

Rachel, who was staring at her computer screen, deep in thought, looked up. 'Wesley, does the name Laurence Proudy mean anything to you? It seems very familiar.'

Wesley shook his head. 'Sorry. Of course, his name might have cropped up before my time . . . I've not been here a year yet.'

'Seems longer,' muttered Steve resentfully as he sorted through house-to-house statements. Wesley ignored him . . . as usual.

The telephone rang on Wesley's desk. The Copenhagen police officer's command of English was truly breathtaking. Tradmouth CID would have been hard put to come up with two words of Danish between them. Sven Larsen, it appeared, was Ingeborg's brother. And as soon as he had heard the news of his sister's disappearance, he had packed his bags and made for the airport. He would be arriving in Tradmouth the following day. Stunned by this development, Wesley put the phone down and broke the news to the inspector.

'Let's just hope he doesn't get in our way. Anything else?'

'I suppose he'll be able to give us more information when he arrives. He might know what his sister got up to when she was over here last . . . who she knew, that sort of thing. The police there have told him to report to us.'

'I don't like this, Wes, I really don't. A woman goes missing . . . chloroformed . . . no ransom note or anything to suggest that it's a kidnapping. Hey, that's a thought. Are her family million-aires or anything?'

'I thought of that. When I asked the Danish police they said they were just an ordinary middle-class family . . . nothing too grand. Ingeborg's divorced and she's a college lecturer. I asked about the ex-husband too, of course, but he's in the clear. He was taking a party of students on a trip to some museum on the day Ingeborg disappeared and hasn't left the country for months. The Copenhagen police said he seemed quite concerned . . . asked them to keep him informed of developments.'

'So that's a couple of possibilities out of the window. How easy is it to get hold of chloroform?'

'It's also known as trichloromethane and it's pretty common. It's used as a cleaner . . . a solvent.'

Heffernan looked impressed. 'How did you know all that?'

Wesley shrugged modestly. 'Something I picked up in school chemistry lessons. Knew it'd come in handy some day.'

Heffernan sat and thought for a while. 'Know what, Wes? I think she saw something she shouldn't. Do you think her disappearance could be linked to the farm raids? If she saw them get away . . . or if she saw them watching a place and got their car number, or . . .'

Wesley had to acknowledge that it was certainly a possibility. 'But why burden themselves with a hostage? Why not just kill her if they wanted to shut her up?'

'They didn't kill Daniel Wexer . . . just shot to scare him probably. Perhaps they're just holding her till after they do an important job. Perhaps killing's not their style.'

'We can but hope,' said Wesley cynically. His years in the Met hadn't rendered him optimistic about the humanitarian urges of the average armed robber.

Gerry Heffernan announced that they should all get off at a reasonable time that evening because the following day would be a long one. And they couldn't really do any more until they had a full picture of Ingeborg's life . . . and perhaps even that wouldn't help them much.

Wesley looked at his watch, knowing he should head for home. But then Pam wouldn't be expecting him just yet, and Neil's brief conversation had sounded intriguing. He didn't hesitate long before getting into his car and pointing it towards Stoke Beeching.

Stoke Beeching was a pretty village half a mile from the sea. Its narrow streets were lined with pastel-washed cottages, some thatched, others with window boxes brimming with tumbling flowers. The pub next to the church was a low, white building boasting a fine floral display. The church itself looked ancient, its graveyard a haven of peace and twittering birds. The only sight that jarred was the cars belonging to the visitors eager to experience a real Devon village. The vehicles were parked all along the narrow streets, spoiling the very beauty that had brought them to the spot in the first place.

Neil was waiting in the churchyard, loitering around the newly mown graves, reading the headstones. An elderly man with a pair of shears trimmed the grass round the graves nearer the church and watched the long-haired scruffy young man and his smart black companion as if they were bound to be up to no good. When Wesley handed over the plastic bag containing the tiny hammer amulet, the man looked even more alarmed, suspecting that the drug-ridden horrors he witnessed nightly on his TV screen had at last reached Stoke Beeching churchyard.

Neil looked at the plastic-shrouded object with admiration. 'It's brilliant . . . and it confirms what we suspected. A Viking burial . . . quite amazing in this part of the country. Nice one, Wes.'

'Don't thank me; thank Colin Bowman. He found it stuck to one of the ribs.'

Neil took the plastic bag and put the prize in his pocket. Then he led the way to a small pink-washed house, just over the road from the church. 'I don't know this woman's name,' he said casually. 'She was just described to me as the old biddy who used to run the post office.'

'Great,' said Wesley. 'Are you sure she'll let us in?' He knew how security-conscious old people were in these lawless times.

'Just flash your warrant card. Tell her it's a raid or something.'

'I hardly think that'll put her in a co-operative frame of mind,' said Wesley, smiling at Neil's dim view of policing. 'Besides, I'm off duty.'

It was Neil who knocked on the pale yellow front door. With its pink stucco walls and yellow paintwork, the symmetrical house reminded Wesley of a giant Battenberg cake. A thin elderly woman with snow-white hair half opened the door and peered out suspiciously.

'I'm sorry to bother you but my name's Neil Watson and I work for the County Archaeological Unit. Some bones have been discovered at Longhouse Cottage . . . possibly very old. And Mrs Palister who lives there said you might know something about the history of the place, Mrs . . . er . . .'

'Crick. Who's that?' She looked at Wesley with open suspicion.

'This is Wesley Peterson. He was at university with me studying archaeology but now he's a policeman. Show Mrs Crick your warrant card, Wesley.'

Wesley obliged, acknowledging that Neil had been right. Mrs Crick opened the door wider and invited them into a front parlour crammed with family photographs and over-fussy china.

'You'll have a cup of tea,' the old lady ordered.

Not daring to refuse, they smiled and nodded while the best china was brought out and a plate of three-day-old scones was set before them. She had visitors . . . there were rituals to be observed.

'That Mrs Palister's a funny woman,' stated Mrs Crick as she handed out the teacups. 'I'm surprised she mentioned me. I've only talked to her a couple of times. They used to live up at Waters House but they sold it to some folk from London and moved down to Longhouse Cottage when her husband upped and left about three years back. Jock, her husband's name was – rough-looking character. He was never out of the Blacksmith's Arms, so I've heard.' She nodded knowingly. 'Her son Carl doesn't seem a bad lad, though . . . considering.'

'Mrs Palister said you told her about an old legend . . . some pebbles in the stream. A battle?'

'The Danes, it was.'

'Where did you hear that?' asked Wesley.

She looked at him curiously. 'It's just a story . . . something you hear. The pebbles are red because of the blood. I don't know how true it is. Mind you, there was that hoard found up there.'

Neil sat forward. 'What hoard?'

'There was a hoard of treasure found on that land. Don't know much, do you?' She frowned at the ignorance of this so-called archaeologist.

'When was this?'

'It was over a hundred years ago. The man who owned Waters House owned Longhouse Cottage too. He used to let it out to tenants but it was on his land. He was digging one day and found a load of treasure. I thought you'd know about it.'

'What happened to the treasure?'

'Oh, I think it went to London. It was very valuable . . . treasure trove and all that. But if you want to know more there's always the museum.'

'The County Museum?'

'No. His museum, in Tradmouth. I forget the name now . . . something to do with birds.' She screwed her face up, trying to retrieve the elusive snippet of information.

'Not the Peacock Museum. That little place near St Margaret's church?' Wesley had noticed the tiny whitewashed terraced house with an open door displaying the entrance fee. It had dusty windows and an uninvitingly shabby sign outside naming it as the Peacock Museum of Local History. The place had an unappealing, dry look which didn't promise much of interest within apart from a few birds' eggs, a menagerie of stuffed animals and rows of disintegrating ship models and farm implements.

'That's it. The Peacock Museum. His name was Peacock, you see, and he gave his collection to the town council. As well as Waters House he owned a house in Tradmouth, and he left that to the town as a museum to house his things . . . mostly junk if you ask me.'

'Is there any of this treasure in the museum?'

'I don't know. Not been since I was a girl. But they always take everything valuable to London, don't they,' she said resentfully. 'Leave us with the rubbish.'

Wesley smiled and nodded. He suspected that Mrs Crick had probably had revolutionary tendencies in her younger days.

She leaned forward and tapped Wesley on the knee. 'Those bones . . . I reckon I know whose they are. You're policeman, aren't you? Well, I suggest you ask that Palister woman up there what happened to her husband. He disappeared, you know . . . and he was a bad' un. She wouldn't be the first wife to do away with her husband, now, would she?'

Wesley refrained from saying that his boss was thinking along the same lines. 'Neil here thinks the bones are very old.'

'Well, I reckon he's wrong. He used to beat her up, you know . . . I've seen her with a black eye more than once. He got what he deserved, if you ask me.' The old lady sat back in her chintz-covered armchair, the fire of righteous indignation in her eyes belying her harmless appearance. Mrs Crick, Wesley thought, would probably have been more than capable of dealing with any recalcitrant husband in her younger days. He found himself wondering what had become of Mr Crick.

'You'll have another cup of tea,' she ordered. Neil and Wesley knew better than to refuse.

It was eight o'clock when Detective Constable Rachel Tracey finished loading the dirty dishes into the dishwasher in the cavernous kitchen of her family's farm. She turned round to find her mother looking at her appraisingly.

'I was wanting a little word, Rachel . . . now your dad's not here,' she said in wheedling tones. Her father and brothers were out of the way tending to the farm's evening chores. 'Are your lot any nearer catching the buggers who shot Dan Wexer?'

Rachel walked over the stone floor to the huge farmhouse table and sat herself down: she knew how long her mother's 'little words' took. 'Not really, Mum. We've had no leads, see. And they're professional . . . they cover their tracks.'

'That's four farms they've done now,' Stella Tracey said, the worry audible in her voice. 'I mean, we could be next. Have you thought of that?'

Rachel nodded. Being privy to the police's lack of progress, she'd thought of little else. 'We're doing our best, Mum, but they don't leave many clues. But we'll get 'em one of these days.' She tried to sound confident. 'Don't you worry about that.'

Stella Tracey looked at her daughter slyly. 'I was thinking, Rachel, what about asking Dave to come back. I mean, he's a big lad and very useful round the farm. And I'll bet he'd rather be here than stopping at that hotel in Morbay. They only give their staff the poky little rooms in the attic, you know. And you'd have him here again. That'd be nice, wouldn't it? I know he had the holiday flat last time, but if he wouldn't mind having the spare room . . .'

Rachel wasn't falling for the bait. 'I think we've got enough grown men around the place to put these robbers off, don't you?' Her father and three brothers, she thought, might be enough of a deterrent. She couldn't see how one extra, albeit a tall, good-looking Australian, would make much difference. She suspected her mother had other motives. Nature doesn't abhor a vacuum half so much as the conventional mother abhors her adult daughter's single state.

'So what do you say? Will you ask him next time you see him? The lads are busy with the farm and I need someone to help with the holiday flats now that you work such long hours.'

'I'll think about it, Mum. Don't push things, okay?'

Stella Tracey's round face was a picture of innocence. 'I'm sure I don't know what you mean, dear.' She began to arrange washing around the Aga, holding her fire for the time being. Then, as if to make her point, she turned round. 'Rachel, dear, could you do me a favour?' She pointed to an electric kettle standing on the windowsill. 'Could you take the kettle back to Flat Three in the old barn? Our Tom's put a new plug on it. The man there came over earlier to complain that it wasn't working.'

'Okay.' Rachel got up. 'Flat Three, is it?' The Traceys had five holiday flats on their farm, vital to make ends meet.

'That's right.' Rachel could tell by her mother's expression of disapproval that there was something about the occupant of Flat Three that she didn't like. 'It's a Mr Proudy . . . staying for three weeks, he is. He's there with his wife – if she is his wife,' she added disapprovingly. 'Funny pair, they are: all sorts of comings and goings at strange times. Some of the other guests have said they go out in the early hours, slamming doors and goodness knows what.'

'Laurence Proudy?' Rachel felt a thrill of excitement. The man who had quarrelled with Ingeborg Larsen was staying on her own doorstep.

Stella Tracey looked at her daughter as if she'd just performed a particularly amazing conjuring trick. 'That's right. How did you know?' Then her expression suddenly changed. 'He's not wanted by the police, is he?'

'Not that I know of, Mum,' Rachel said reassuringly, picking up the kettle. She stepped out of the kitchen door into the farmyard, which was flanked by huge corrugated-iron barns containing an impressive array of farm machinery. The old barn some way away was far more picturesque, and had been converted into three modern holiday flats. Two more flats were in a nearby outbuilding. The conversions had been expensive but had proved lucrative in an era of financial uncertainty for the farming community.

Rachel knew she'd have to tread carefully. She could hardly begin to question the man now. But she could see him, weigh him up. Knowing your enemy was the first rule of warfare, so she had heard.

She crossed over to the old barn, an ancient stone building gutted and modernised and boasting new, gleaming white windows and doors. Rachel knocked firmly on the door of Flat Three.

The door was opened by a tall woman, probably in her thirties, with a shining helmet of dark hair and wearing a short dress of fashionable simplicity. She chewed as she looked Rachel up and down. Rachel, having changed from her smart working suit into shorts and T-shirt, felt at a disadvantage – but then she realised that the best policy was staying undercover; playing the farmer's daughter rather than an off-duty policewoman.

'Your kettle's fixed,' she said, exaggerating her Devon accent. 'Everything else all right, is it?' She used all the skill learned during a brief sojourn in the divisional Amateur Dramatic Society to produce a friendly smile.

'Yes.' The woman's voice was unexpectedly deep, with just a hint of a foreign accent. 'Everything's fine.'

'You don't need more pillows? Only some people like more . . .'

'No. We're okay.'

A man appeared in the hallway. 'Who is it?'

'Just someone from the farm . . . about the kettle.'

'We've had it mended,' Rachel called through. 'It should be okay now.'

The man was probably in his late twenties, a little younger than his companion. He was smallish with a cropped hairstyle that didn't do much to improve his belligerent expression. He looked through Rachel as if she weren't there.

'Well, if everything's all right I'll leave you to it. If there's anything, anything at all, you know where we are, don't you?' She gave what she considered to be a sunny smile, which the woman attempted to return. The man, however, muttered something about being okay and shut the door in her face.

So that was Laurence Proudy, she thought, having taken an instant dislike to the man. She looked at the cars parked in front of the barn. A new silver BMW stood at one end with a noticeable dent in the nearside wing, presumably the result of his meeting with Ingeborg Larsen.

Rachel made a note of the registration number and walked back slowly to the farmhouse. Even if he'd quarrelled with Ingeborg, it was hardly a reason to do her harm. But then so-called road rage was becoming more common; there were new cases in the papers every day. It was with some satisfaction that Rachel contemplated Proudy being hauled off to Tradmouth police station the following day to answer some pertinent questions.

Stella Tracey noticed that her daughter was quiet as they spent the evening following the labyrinthine plot of one of Stella's favourite television detective programmes. Perhaps, she thought, it reminded Rachel too much of work. If Dave – such a nice boy and so good-looking – came back to the farm it would take Rachel's mind off things.

Waters House, perched on the hillside above Longhouse Cottage, was a imposing white stucco building of pleasingly Georgian proportions. Some said it had once been the vicarage for Stoke Beeching church, but Gwen Wentwood didn't believe that. It was too far away from the church for one thing – right out of the village – and she had heard that the place had another, more interesting history.

Gwen looked across at her husband, who had just closed the lid of his laptop computer. The machine emitted a satisfying final bleep and he sat back and closed his eyes. Gwen watched him lovingly: when they had first met she had thought him rather beautiful with his large brown eyes and long, poetic hair. Now the hair was shorter and, with his thirtieth birthday just passed, his waistline thicker. But the signs of strain on his face worried Gwen more than any signs of age. She reached across and touched his hand, a light, gossamer touch. He looked up at her and smiled weakly.

'Finished?' she asked gently.

'I've just got a bit more to do.'

'Is there anything you want? Something to eat? Shall I open a bottle of wine?'

A large antique clock ticked away on the mantelpiece but Christopher Wentwood looked at his watch out of habit. 'Nothing for me . . . not yet anyway.'

59

He carried his laptop over to the cluttered desk by the huge bay window. He really would have to tidy it . . . be more businesslike. He had left the security of a large firm in London three years ago to come back to Devon and set up on his own. If it hadn't been for Gwen's inheritance the whole thing wouldn't have been possible. He wanted to make a go of it for her sake . . . wanted to succeed. But there were times when he felt like giving up altogether.

He put the computer down carefully and touched the silver-framed photograph of his wife, smart in her uniform, which stood at the back of the desk. He looked up. Such a view: over the tumbling fields and down to the sea. But now the light had almost gone and the trees of the hilltop wood stood out black against the darkening sky. He could see the large coach house to the left. There was a light on in the window beside the great double doors: his sister, Ursula, was working in her studio, creating her bright, cheerful pottery.

Christopher reached for the curtains and drew them. Gwen had told him this ritual was unnecessary in such an isolated spot with no neighbours to pry, but he did it out of habit. He had lived in town too long to change his ways overnight.

As the thick velvet curtains swung closed, something caught his eye. He opened the curtains again and saw a figure flitting away soundlessly down the gravel drive.

He whirred round. 'Gwen . . . quick. He's there again.' Gwen rushed over to the window, but by the time she reached her husband the figure was just a shadow, fleeing down the drive towards Longhouse Cottage. 'We should tell the police.'

'It'll be poachers,' Gwen said hopefully, clutching at straws. 'There are always poachers about in the country.'

'We should tell the police,' Christopher repeated. 'If someone's watching the house . . . And what about Ursula on her own in that studio? We should do something.' Christopher Wentwood breathed deeply, as the books on stress had told him to do. If Waters House was being watched by a prowler, something would have to be done. He would contact the police in the morning.

Chapter Five

AD 997
Today the people from the country round about came to seek
shelter within the walls of the town and orders were given for
the town gates to be closed. It is said that the Danes were
sighted at the mouth of the river and that they killed the
brother who tends the shrine of Saint Peter and the holy well
there. Then they moved up to Tradmouth and laid waste the
village there and many perished.
From the chronicle of Brother Edwin, monk of Neston Minster

At eight o'clock in the morning Gerry Heffernan was just
contemplating rising from his bed. He generally walked to work;
it took five minutes at the most. If he got up now, made himself a
couple a rounds of toast and threw on some clothes, he could be at
work by half past.

The telephone rang and Gerry leaned across the bed to
answer it, hoping it wasn't bad news about Ingeborg
Larsen: the discovery of a body that would set CID into
overdrive.

But the ringing stopped. The phone had been picked up
downstairs. Surely Sam wouldn't be up at this unearthly hour.
Gerry listened for a few moments then, satisfied the call wasn't for
him, climbed slowly out of bed and made for the bathroom,
lumbering like a large, sleepy animal: he wasn't at his best first
thing in the morning.

As he emerged from the bathroom, rubbing his face with a
towel, he nearly collided with Sam, who was darting along the
small landing towards his room.

'Hi, Dad. I've just had a phone call about a job I applied for. I've got it . . . I start tonight.'

'Good. What is it?'

Sam looked sheepish and hesitated. 'Er . . . public relations. Quite well paid.'

'So what have you got to do? What does it involve?'

Gerry Heffernan, a detective of considerable experience, knew when a question was being evaded.

'Er . . . I don't really know yet. I'll find out when I get there.'

'Is it legal?' said the anxious father sharply.

'Oh, yes. You don't think I'd do anything iffy, do you?'

Gerry didn't answer, just gave his son a fatherly pat on the back. He looked at his watch. He was cutting it fine.

He left his son drinking coffee and rushed to the police station, where he found Rachel disgustingly awake. She made straight for his office like a speeding bullet, and announced her discovery with an enthusiasm that made him feel tired.

'So this Laurence Proudy's staying right under your nose, Rach. Let's have a word with him, eh? Brighten up his holiday.' Gerry Heffernan stifled a yawn and leaned back, causing his standard-issue inspector's executive swivel chair to creak dangerously. 'What's he like?'

'Small and aggressive I should say, sir . . . like one of those pit bull terriers.' Rachel smiled conspiratorially. 'Look, sir, I'd rather someone else interviewed him. He knows I'm from the farm and . . .'

'Of course, Rach. Enough said. I'll go with Wes. After all, it's the best lead we've got at the moment . . . as the actress said to the dog handler.'

Rachel rolled her eyes and marched back into the main office. She sat down at her desk and called over to Wesley. 'The boss wants you. Laurence Proudy's staying in one of the holiday flats on my parents' farm. He wants to go over and have a word with him. And that's not all: my mum seems to think that Proudy's been going out a lot in the early hours of the morning.' Wesley raised his eyebrows but passed no comment. 'I'll look him up on the computer,' Rachel continued. 'See if he's got any form.'

Wesley walked over to Rachel's desk and watched, leaning on the back of her chair, as she retrieved the information. Laurence Proudy was originally from York. He had three convictions for car theft in his youth. He had been on a training scheme for young offenders where he had learned car mechanics and he now owned a garage in London. In addition, last year he had done six months for a lucrative little racket in bent MOTs, and he had been convicted of actual bodily harm four years ago. Rachel shuddered. If her mother knew what kind of man was occupying her thoughtfully modernised apartment, she would be bound to panic.

She wished Wesley luck as he set off, knowing that she could rely on him not to alarm her mother . . . but she wasn't so sure about the inspector.

Little Barton Farm – home to the Tracey family for six generations – was just outside Tradmouth, down a network of dark narrow lanes. Rachel had given them directions, suggesting that they headed straight for the old barn: there was no need to disturb her mother.

Laurence Proudy – known to his associates as Lol – opened the door with an apparent lack of caution, wearing a navy blue towelling dressing gown, the material thick and luxuriant – not cheap. He looked alarmed to see the two strangers standing there, and even more alarmed when they produced their warrant cards.

'What do you want? I'm busy . . . just getting in the shower.'

'Laurence Proudy? We just want a quick word. Won't take long,' Wesley assured him as he stepped firmly inside the flat.

It was a comfortable apartment; plainly furnished and modern. Proudy sat on the edge of the dark green sofa as if prepared for flight, like an athlete on the starting blocks.

'We understand you had words with a Danish lady last weekend. She backed into your car. Her name was Ingeborg Larsen.' Wesley sat forward in the armchair expectantly as Heffernan watched Proudy's expression.

'I had words with her, yeah. The stupid cow wasn't looking where she was going.'

'How long are you staying in Devon, sir?' asked Wesley politely.

Proudy looked awkward. There was something in Wesley's last question that caused him to perform mental somersaults. 'Er . . . we've booked in here for three weeks. We've got a week to go.'

'We hear that you're out and about a lot . . . all times of the day and night.' Heffernan watched Proudy as a snake watches a rabbit.

Proudy looked astonished. 'Who told you that?'

'Let's just say it's been noticed,' Heffernan said quickly, not wishing to implicate the Traceys.

'I'm on holiday, aren't I,' said Proudy defensively. 'And I'm doing some business here and all. I've got a garage up in London and . . .'

'You see, we think this Ingeborg Larsen's been abducted. And whoever abducted her would have to take a bit of time out to feed her . . . if she's still alive.'

Proudy looked alarmed. 'Look, I don't know anything about this. She backed into my car, I gave her a mouthful. She got her side of the insurance sorted out . . . rang me on my mobile to tell me it was all going through. That's all, I swear it . . . I swear it on my mother's life.' Proudy stood up, agitated, grabbing his dressing gown to stop it falling open. 'I'm down here on holiday. Someone backed into the car and I made a fuss and the insurance got sorted out.'

'I thought you owned a garage, sir,' said Wesley, trying to sound naïve. 'The damage doesn't look very bad to me. Couldn't you have mended it yourself?'

'Er . . . well, bodywork's an expensive business and . . .'

'So you claim a fortune from the insurance company and you do the work yourself on the cheap. Bit naughty, isn't it?' Heffernan grinned widely. 'And illegal.'

Proudy began to panic. 'Look, I've not done nothing that . . .'

'What can you tell me about Ingeborg Larsen?'

'Nothing. I only saw her the once. Honest.' He sat looking from one policeman to the other. He didn't resemble a pit bull now so much as a kicked mongrel. Laurence Proudy knew defeat when it was staring him in the face.

'Well, sir,' said Wesley, 'If you'd make a statement about your dealings with Ms Larsen I'm sure we can leave you to get on with your holiday in peace.'

Proudy was only too happy to oblige. As he was signing the statement, a slim, dark woman emerged from the bedroom wearing only a thin T-shirt, her eyes heavy with sleep. She spotted Wesley and looked him up and down appreciatively.

'Morning, madam,' said Wesley. The light behind her shone through the thin material of her T-shirt, revealing the contours of her body underneath. He averted his eyes. 'Do you know an

Ingeborg Larsen? A Danish lady who backed into your . . . er, Mr Proudy's car?'

'I know some woman backed into Lol's car . . . but that's all. I wasn't there.' The woman lit a cigarette and waved the packet at Wesley. He shook his head, wondering how Mrs Tracey felt about her guests smoking in her apartments: if Rachel's attitude to smoking was anything to go by, she wouldn't be best pleased.

Wesley stood up. 'I think that's all for now. Thank you for your co-operation. If you remember anything else . . .'

Laurence Proudy and the woman stared as the policemen left; the woman coolly calculating, the man with relief.

'What did you make of all that?' asked Gerry Heffernan as they climbed into the car.

'He might be as crooked as a corkscrew, but I don't think abduction's his style. He was nervous about something, though. Don't you think?'

'Oh, definitely, Wes. I think we'll ask the traffic lads to keep a lookout for his car . . . just in case.'

Wesley smiled. 'I was thinking along the same lines myself. He's up to something . . . it's just up to us to find out what it is.'

'Lucky we've got our Rach on the premises, isn't it?'

'Very,' answered Wesley as he negotiated the narrow lane that led away from the farm. 'What time's Sven Larsen arriving?'

'About eleven. I can't wait to hear what he's got to say.'

'Neither can I.' Wesley drove on, his mind on an abandoned car and a small pad soaked in chloroform.

Constable Johnson knew that sunshine was good for his spots. He climbed out of the patrol car and stood, his face raised towards the sky, outside Waters House, breathing deeply and enjoying the warm, beneficial rays. Then he put on his hat, drew himself up to his full height, and prepared to meet his public.

The heavy wooden front door, in sore need of a coat of varnish, opened. 'Morning, madam. I'm PC Johnson from Tradmouth police station. Someone rang us from this address this morning to report a prowler?'

The statuesque woman who stood there, dressed in a sleeveless denim shirt and khaki shorts, smiled nervously and invited him in.

She led PC Johnson into the living room. 'It was my husband who rang you but he's out at the moment,' she said quickly. 'He only caught a glimpse of him, but he said he seemed to be watching the house. I said it was probably a poacher and that it wasn't worth calling you but . . .'

'Can you give me a description of this man, madam? It was a man, I take it?'

'I don't know. It was just a figure . . . a shadow really. I'm sure it was just a poacher.'

Johnson smiled to himself. The romantic solitary poacher after a couple of rabbits for his pot had been superseded years ago by gangs from the cities, slaughtering anything they could sell for a profit. This woman was from the town – a newcomer buying into the rural dream. That much was obvious.

'I think it's unlikely he's a poacher, madam. You've not got any game birds – deer, salmon, anything like that – have you?' Gwen Wentwood shook her head. 'There's been a spate of robberies recently,' Johnson continued. 'Mostly isolated farms. They've been after money and small valuables . . . and vehicles: four-wheel drives; quad bikes, that sort of thing. Where do you keep your car?'

Gwen Wentwood looked worried. 'In the coach house. You passed it on the way in. My husband's sister has her flat and studio there. She keeps the van she uses for her pottery business in there too. It's locked up at night.'

'I'm sure your vehicles are quite safe there, madam.' Johnson thought for a moment. 'Would you like to show me where you saw this prowler . . . where he was standing?'

Gwen Wentwood led the way out of the front door, across the wide gravel drive to a clump of bushes and small trees, once ornamental but now reverted to a semi-wild state. The garden, thought Johnson, needed a bit of attention.

'About here, I think. We only caught a glimpse each time so I can't be absolutely sure.'

Johnson looked round at the barrier of trees behind him. 'Do the woods belong to you?'

'Yes. But we don't venture in there very often,' she said quickly. 'Hardly at all. They came with the house and they're a bit of a liability.' She attempted a smile.

'How often have you seen this prowler?'

'My husband says he's been there a few nights. I thought it was his imagination at first, then I looked out last night and caught a glimpse of him. If he was a burglar he would have done something by now, wouldn't he?' There was a note of panic in Gwen Wentwood's voice. She was more worried than she was letting on.

Johnson began to search the ground. It certainly looked as if someone had stood here for a long time. The grass was flattened and scuffed in places, as if someone had waited there, shifting from foot to foot.

'And he's only been seen at night?'

'Yes.'

'And does he run away or . . .'

'It was dark, hard to see exactly where he went, but he seems to disappear down towards Longhouse Cottage . . . it's a small-holding just down the hill.'

Johnson bent down again to examine the ground. He had not been mistaken: there were definite signs that someone had been standing there. 'Have you any idea why anyone should be watching your house, Mrs Wentwood?'

'I've no idea,' she said, her mind racing. 'It's a complete mystery.'

Sven Larsen felt hot and sticky. He longed for a shower. He looked at his watch. Ten o'clock. He had set off early from Heathrow in the hire car and now he took the room key gratefully from the pretty girl on the reception desk at the Tower Hotel, too tired to exchange flirtatious pleasantries. He made for his room and locked the door carefully behind him.

As he stood beneath the refreshing waters of the shower he contemplated his next move. He was worried . . . very worried. It wasn't like Ingeborg to do something like this. She was such a capable woman – flirtatious and vivacious but always in control. Disappearing without a word in this theatrical manner wasn't Ingeborg's style at all. And the police had sounded concerned on the phone, which meant they feared the worst. He had an appointment with an Inspector Heffernan at eleven. And he dreaded what the inspector might say.

Sven dressed again and began opening the drawers and cupboards of the room, putting his neatly folded clothes away, filling in time until his appointment. He noticed the local telephone directory lying in a top drawer and pulled it out, idly flicking through the pages until he came to a name he recognised.

67

He stared at it for a couple of minutes: perhaps he should ring; it would do no harm surely. Ingeborg could be headstrong, impulsive. But surely she wouldn't have been so foolish as to contact him again after all these years. Sven had warned strongly against it. Some things were better left alone . . . best forgotten.

He picked up the telephone, and dialled the number. A couple of minutes later he replaced the receiver, feeling a little better after what he had heard. He wouldn't tell the police: he had been asked not to and it was best not to involve them. This was something he must deal with alone.

'Larsen's late.' Gerry Heffernan sat back in his seat and took a sip of the coffee so eagerly provided by WPC Walton. 'I thought he'd be here at eleven.'

'He has had a long way to come. If he's had to hire a car at the airport and . . .'

'Yeah, Wes, you're right. I don't suppose Tradmouth is the easiest place to get to, is it . . . not by land,' added the sailing enthusiast wistfully.

Wesley passed the inspector a sheet of official-looking paper covered in appalling handwriting. 'Have a look at this, sir. All the houses have been visited near to where Ingeborg Larsen's car turned up. Here's one of the house-to-house reports . . . the statement of a Mrs Jerworth of Honeysuckle House, about a mile down the road from where the car was found. Makes interesting reading.'

Gerry Heffernan screwed up his eyes in an effort to decipher the writing. After a few minutes he flung the report onto the desk and leaned forward. 'Well, well, well. This changes things a bit. We'd all assumed that our Ingeborg got lost trying to take a short cut down the lanes on her way back from Neston. But this . . .'

Wesley picked up the statement and read. ' "I was dusting in the front room at about three o'clock on Monday afternoon when I saw a white car draw up outside the front door. Nobody got out of the car for a while and I watched, standing back a bit so the occupant of the car couldn't see me. It was a woman, and she was sitting in a white car, watching the house. It must have been five minutes before she got out. She came to the front door, rang the bell, and I opened the door. She was a very attractive lady with fair hair, aged about thirty-five with a foreign accent, but she spoke perfect English. She looked nervous, then puzzled when she saw me. I asked her who she wanted and she seemed confused. She said she was very sorry but she must have come to the wrong house. She kept apologising and said she was sorry to have bothered me. Then she got into her car and drove off. I watched her go then I went back into the house. I got the impression that another car passed as I was closing the door but I can't be certain.' What do you make of it, sir?'

'I don't know. Her behaviour was a bit strange. If she'd gone to the wrong house you'd think she'd just ask for directions to the house she wanted . . . after all, her English is good. Has anyone talked to the other people who live on that road? There can't be many of them. It's only a country lane with the odd house or cottage dotted here and there . . . hardly a high-rise estate.'

'As soon as I saw Mrs Jerworth's statement I asked a couple of PCs to go back and double-check. There are several houses and cottages on that road but nobody else saw her that day. Nobody saw anything suspicious and nobody had ever heard of Ingeborg Larsen. Some of them noticed the white Opel parked in the lay-by but hadn't thought to investigate. But they all say she definitely didn't call on them on Monday afternoon. Mind you, most of them were at work.'

Gerry Heffernan sat for a minute, deep in thought. 'I don't like this, Wes. I don't like it at all. This Mrs Jerworth heard a car passing when she was closing the door. Do you reckon someone was following Ingeborg?'

'It's very possible. But if Ingeborg was frightened, why didn't she tell Mrs Jerworth? Why didn't she ask her to call the police?'

'She might not have known she was being followed. And she'd probably got the wrong road . . . taken a wrong turning. She'd just have felt embarrassed when she arrived at the wrong house.'

'So we widen the house-to-house enquiry . . . see if anybody around that area saw Ingeborg or was expecting her that day.'

Heffernan shrugged. 'Can't do any harm.' He sat back, contemplating the case. 'What have we got so far? A woman is probably abducted. She's been to this part of the world before but we've no idea when or if she still knows anybody here. She has a minor prang in her car with an unsavoury character staying at Rachel's farm, but he claims it was all sorted out . . . no hard feelings. On the day she disappears she goes into Neston and heads back to

Tradmouth along the network of lanes. It's a short cut if you're local but a stranger can get hopelessly lost. She stops at Honeysuckle House, watches the house for a bit, then she knocks on the door, says she's come to the wrong house and hurries off, possibly followed by another car . . . or not as the case may be. Is that all we've got so far?'

Wesley nodded. 'That's just about it. Not much, is it?'

'And what about the farm robberies? Any developments?'

'No . . . except that we've had a report from PC Johnson that a prowler's been watching a house near Stoke Beeching. It's that big place on the hill just above Longhouse Cottage.'

Heffernan sat up, suddenly interested. 'Waters House?'

Wesley nodded, thinking it strange that the name Waters House, once home to Jeremiah Peacock of museum fame, should crop up again that day.

'That's the place Jock Palister bought when he came into money. Then when he scarpered, Maggie sold it and most of the land and moved down the hill to Longhouse Cottage. It can't be a coincidence. First skeletons and now prowlers. It's all go, isn't it?'

A shy knock on the door heralded the arrival of Trish Walton. 'Excuse me, sir,' she began deferentially, 'Mr Larsen is down in reception. Shall I bring him up?'

'Yes, Trish,' said the inspector, licking his lips. 'You do that.' He turned to Wesley. 'Right then, Wes. How's your Danish?'

'My sister and her husband divorced six months ago. I let Bjorn know I was coming over here, of course. He is very concerned.' Sven Larsen took a sip of police station coffee and wrinkled his nose in barely disguised disgust. He was a tall man with neatly cut fair hair. Wesley recognised him from the photograph he'd found in Ingeborg's room. His clothes were elegantly casual – a pair of pristine jeans, an open-necked shirt and a tailored linen jacket. He made Gerry Heffernan feel positively scruffy; but then so did most people.

'So her ex-husband's at home in Copenhagen?' Wesley felt he had to make sure of this basic fact.

'Yes, Sergeant. That's right. I understand the police in Copenhagen confirmed that he could have had nothing to do with Ingeborg's disappearance. I know you always investigate the

70

spouse first in such cases, but I can assure you that Bjorn and my sister parted amicably. And besides, Bjorn has not left Denmark in the last year . . . except for a brief trip on my boat last September when we sailed up the coast of Sweden. Sailing is a great interest of mine, you understand.'

Gerry Heffernan looked up eagerly. 'Me too. I keep a twenty-seven-foot sloop here on the river. In a right state when I bought her . . . did her up myself. Having a spot of trouble with the engine at the moment. She's in the boat yard over at Queenswear . . . or I'd have taken you out on her.'

Sven Larsen smiled. He hadn't put this large, dishevelled inspector down as a sailing man. 'That is very kind of you, Inspector. I was thinking of hiring a boat while I was here. I think sailing is so good for the spirit. Good for the stresses of life.'

The two policemen nodded in agreement. All Gerry Heffernan's talk of phrase books had been unnecessary. Sven Larsen had a better command of the English language than many people Wesley had come across in the course of his police career.

'Did your sister say why she was coming to Devon?' said Wesley, steering the conversation away from nautical matters. 'I believe she'd been here before.'

'She said she needed a holiday . . . to get away from routine. It was a sudden decision to come to Devon . . . an impulse. I believe she did visit this part of the world before when she was very young – a teenager. I'm three years younger than Ingeborg, you understand. I didn't take much interest in my sister's life at that time. I think she stayed with a family here as an au pair to learn English . . . such arrangements are common, I believe.'

'Do you know the name of this family?'

'I must have heard it but I'm afraid I don't remember. She didn't keep in touch with them,' he added, a hint of anxiety in his voice.

'And did anything happen during her stay . . . anything, er, unusual?'

'I remember her telling our parents that the family were very dull and that she didn't like their children. But that is all. I remember nothing more,' Larsen said convincingly.

'And how old was she when she came to stay here?'

'Eighteen, I think. It was before she started at the university.'

71

'So as far as you knew she was just coming over here for a holiday?'

'That's right, Sergeant. She remembered that your scenery and towns are very . . . er, how do you say it, picturesque. Many people take holidays here. Yes?'

'Yes.' Gerry Heffernan raised his head. 'You're right there. So she brought her car over on the ferry, did she, and drove down?'

'Yes. I warned her that the roads were busier here than in Denmark, but she thought it best. Is her car damaged at all?'

Wesley glanced at his boss. It was now time for the painful truths the Copenhagen police had probably not revealed. 'A slight bump at the back but nothing serious. But I'm afraid there's every indication that chloroform was used to render your sister unconscious. We're treating it as a case of abduction.' He paused. 'I'm sorry if it comes as a shock but . . .'

Sven Larsen took a deep breath, avoiding Wesley's eyes. 'I know you're doing everything you can, Sergeant.' He looked up at Wesley. 'I have no idea who would want to do this to Ingeborg. We are not a wealthy family . . . there is no point in kidnapping somebody who has no money.'

'There have been a number of armed robberies in the area recently. It's just possible that somehow Ingeborg stumbled on the criminals and they abducted her to silence her. What kind of a woman was she? Would she have tackled anybody she thought was doing wrong?'

'It is possible, Sergeant. My sister was very . . . er, confident, outspoken sometimes. It is possible this led her into danger.'

'Can you think of anything that might help us . . . anything your sister talked about, anywhere she planned to go while she was over here, anyone she mentioned? Anything?' Wesley was beginning to feel helpless in the face of all the possibilities . . . and their lack of clear leads.

Sven Larsen shook his head. 'Nothing. I'm sorry. There is nothing,' he mumbled, avoiding Wesley's eyes. He looked at Gerry Heffernan, who was leaning back, playing with his ballpoint pen. 'Can you recommend somewhere where I may hire a boat? As you are also a sailor I . . .'

'Of course.' Heffernan reeled off an address and instructions to mention his name. Tradmouth's boating fraternity were a close-knit lot.

Sven stood up to go. 'If that is all I should like to make arrangements to hire a boat. If I can be of any more help . . .'

'We'll keep in touch . . . let you know of any developments. Tower Hotel all right, is it?'

'Very good, thank you, Inspector. Most satisfactory.'

'I hope we'll have better news soon,' said Wesley with some sincerity as Larsen left, Gerry Heffernan following behind to see his fellow sailor off the premises.

A few minutes later the inspector returned. 'Well?' said Wesley. 'What do you think?'

'Nice bloke. Got a thirty-footer moored in a little harbour just north of Copenhagen.'

'I mean apart from his boating activities. Don't you think it's odd that his sister disappears yet all he can think about is going off sailing?'

Heffernan looked at his sergeant as if he were two planks short of a deck. 'It's not odd at all. There's nothing like a run on the river for calming the nerves, taking your mind off things. It's a lot better than digging up old artefacts . . . you should try it some time.'

Wesley – sick on the cross-Channel ferry – smiled and shook his head. Whatever the inspector said, he still thought Sven Larsen was hiding something.

Pam Peterson had said nothing to Wesley about her plans for the day. She felt slightly furtive, almost guilty, as she drove to Neston. But, she told herself, it was time she did something to keep her mind active . . . and Michael had been happy to stay with Mrs Miller, his childminder-elect, for the morning.

She found the assembly hall easily enough and arrived five minutes early, which gave her the opportunity to study her fellow volunteers. For the life of her, Pam couldn't see most of the men in the assembled company as Viking warriors. The majority were middle-aged or elderly and possessed the warlike demeanour of the average retired bank manager. But the re-enactment group was there to put everyone through their paces. The whole procedure would be entertaining, if not historically accurate.

Pam sat near the front, determined not to miss the action. Groups of people chattered nervously around her, sharing her apprehension; the fear of the unknown. When a young man jumped up onto the platform at the front of the hall and announced in ringing tones that his name was Odin and he was the leader of the re-enactment group known as Thor's Hammers, the hall fell silent.

He was tall and well muscled, with long fair hair and finely chiselled features. Standing there, straight-backed and authoritative, he was the dashing Viking warrior to the life. He welcomed them all, his piercing blue eyes scanning the audience, assessing his raw material. Odin was dressed in the full regalia of his calling – a hand-woven blue tunic edged with rich red braid and a sword belt bearing a fierce-looking weapon. He would have looked more at home on the prow of some mighty longboat than there in that shabby modern school hall.

Pam noticed that his eyes were fixed on her as he spoke, and she wriggled a little on her uncomfortable plastic seat.

'None of you are expected to join in the actual fighting,' Odin continued. 'Thor's Hammers have trained hard in authentic Viking warfare, and it would be dangerous for anybody inexperienced to attempt it. Your role is to be bystanders in contemporary dress. Some of the men, perhaps, could indulge in a bit of mock fighting in the background with wooden weapons to swell our numbers, and the women will act as camp followers, administer first aid or, er . . . be carried off by our warriors.' He grinned meaningfully. 'Thor's Hammers have been in the area for two weeks now, performing re-enactments at various venues, including Nesroy Castle and the Dukesbridge Carnival. But the Neston Viking Festival will be the highlight of the tour for us. Then, next week, we will be giving a demonstration of Viking warfare at Tradmouth Naval College's annual charity fête.'

Somebody began to clap at the back of the hall, and soon the whole room joined in as Odin stood, triumphant, on his makeshift platform. He raised his sword in salute, and Pam looked up to find that his eyes were still on her. She looked away quickly and scrambled to her feet. Everyone was to assemble on the school playing field next door for a brief rehearsal, so she followed the crowd, teaming up with a formidable elderly lady, a retired headmistress who introduced herself as Dorothy Weston and confided that she was looking forward to being 'carried off', but feared that she would be landed with the first aid. Pam smiled sympathetically, adding that she'd be only too happy to be in charge of the bandages.

The rehearsal was a tame affair – nothing to frighten the warhorses – and Pam found herself 'tending to the wounded' for the duration of hostilities. But, Odin announced, things would hot up a bit on the actual day when they would all be in costumes kindly provided by the festival committee. When the thing was over, Pam set off for the carpark, bidding farewell to the feisty Dorothy, who headed off briskly in the opposite direction.

She felt a touch on her shoulder and swung round. Odin was there, looking her straight in the eye. 'I'll see you tomorrow for the next rehearsal, then, er . . .'

'Pam,' she said automatically, her heart beating against her chest. 'Is Odin your real name?'

He smiled. 'It is now,' he said mysteriously.

A couple of men – one tall, with tattoos decorating each bulging muscle and a sly weasel face, the other crop-haired and burly with a beard that hid a multitude of sins – had just appeared, hovering behind Odin, trying to attract his attention. Thor's Hammers, Pam thought, were a very mixed bunch; this pair resembled nightclub bouncers, but the rest, the vast majority, looked like off-duty computer professionals and civil servants. And Odin? What was his role in the humdrum present day? The question intrigued Pam as she tried to envisage him in a number of modern-day occupations . . . and failed.

'I'd better get back. I've got to pick my son up from the child-minder's,' she mumbled nervously, her heartbeat quickening.

She was not mistaken. There was a flash of disappointment in Odin's eyes; then another look, a hint of determination. She said goodbye as casually as she could manage and began to walk away but, when she'd gone a few yards, she turned round, just in time to see the two thickset men march away from Odin in her direction. Odin watched them go, his hand resting defensively on his sword, then he saw Pam and smiled, although his eyes remained cold.

The two men strode past her without a glance, but she caught a few snatches of their animated conversation. She heard the words 'wheels', 'tonight' and 'farm', but she couldn't make sense of the rest.

But the words somehow brought to mind the case Wesley was working on – the robberies at local farms. She could easily visualise these characters brandishing sawn-off shotguns. But then she stopped herself: she was being too imaginative. Whatever they were discussing didn't concern her . . . which, in view of Odin's obvious interest, came as a bit of a relief: she had enough on her mind. Since Michael had been born she had frequently felt exhausted and unattractive – however much Wesley tried gallantly to assure her otherwise. And, like most women, she was flattered by a little light-hearted male attention. But there had been something in Odin's eyes that suggested danger. Could it be that he was so immersed in the culture of the Vikings that he had absorbed some of their more undesirable attitudes? But, she told herself firmly, it was nothing she couldn't handle.

As Pam began walking again towards the carpark, Odin fingered his sword and watched her go, the smile still playing on his lips.

Wesley dreamed all day of arriving home, taking a long soak in the bath, then enjoying a mouth-watering supper. He told himself he must be getting old if he was beginning to relish such simple domestic pleasures. But, unrepentant, he rang Pam and asked her to order a Chinese takeaway. Pam, feeling mildly distracted by her experiences of the afternoon, and not being inclined to cook, readily agreed.

But Neil Watson had other plans. As Wesley was tidying the papers on his desk, ready to abandon the fight against crime for the evening, the telephone rang.

'Hi, Wes. I'll meet you at the Peacock Museum in fifteen minutes. Okay?' Before Wesley had time to answer the line went dead. He looked at his watch. It was five thirty already and the progress he and his colleagues had made that day in tracking down Ingeborg Larsen and the farm robbers was negligible. Things were moving at the pace of an elderly and arthritic snail, and Wesley felt frustrated.

He hurried from the office and down the stairs. When he reached reception he heard a booming voice behind him. 'Wesley, can I have a quick word?' He turned round to see Bob Naseby, the desk sergeant, giving him a huge lopsided grin. Wesley had once made the error of admitting that his great-uncle had played cricket for the West Indies, and Bob, obsessed with the game, had come to regard Wesley as a trophy to be won for the divisional team. Wesley hadn't the heart to tell him that his cricket-playing left much to be desired.

'Sorry, Bob. I've got a suspected abduction, a series of armed robberies and a wife who'll resort to murder if I don't spend my days off in the bosom of my family. I'm afraid my debut on the cricket field will have to wait a while.'

'Oh, it's nothing to do with cricket . . . not this time.' Bob looked from side to side, as if preparing to share a great secret, and beckoned Wesley to come closer. 'I'm worried about my daughter,' he said in a loud whisper. 'She's married to a farmer out near Stokeworthy . . . isolated place it is. The wife and I have been worried sick with these farm raids, especially after what they did to Dan Wexer. Someone could get killed next time. And it's haymaking. What if they take it into their heads to set fire to the barns? Are you any nearer catching the buggers?'

Not for the first time in his career, Wesley felt helpless. 'Sorry, Bob. We've not made much progress yet. Sorry,' he added feebly.

'You don't know where they're going to strike next,' Bob called out as an afterthought as Wesley disappeared through the swing-doors.

As Wesley walked past St Margaret's church, he said a silent prayer that the robbers would soon be caught and that the misery they were bringing to the already beleaguered farming community would cease. But something told him they hadn't finished their evil work just yet.

When he reached the Peacock Museum, Neil was waiting, leaning against the wall, looking more like a loitering mugger than an archaeologist. His face was a picture of impatience and disappointment. 'They're bloody closed,' he announced indignantly. 'Bloody tourist season and they're closed.'

Wesley looked at his watch. 'Well it is five forty-five.'

'Yes, but it says they're open till six. Look.' He pointed at a weathered board hanging on the wall outside the entrance which displayed a list of opening times and admission charges.

The Peacock Museum was unimpressive, to say the least. It was a small, whitewashed house with flaking black paintwork and a large front window. It had clearly once been a shop like its neighbours; a small establishment selling greetings cards stood on one side and an expensive-looking antique shop on the other. The museum window displayed a pair of intricately constructed model ships which flanked a huge dust-shrouded turtle shell. A notice above these artefacts announced that the museum housed the collection of Jeremiah Peacock Esquire, local antiquary and collector, of Waters House, Stoke Beeching, 1828–1903.

Neil pressed his face to the glass set into the sturdy oak door. There was no sign of movement; no sign of life. Wesley joined him, and they stood like a couple of small boys with their noses pressed to a toyshop window, trying to make out the shapes within. But it was useless. The interior was in darkness, and they could see nothing. They would have to return another day.

'Fancy a Chinese? Pam's ordered one.'

Neil grinned, licking his lips. 'Sure there'll be enough?'

'We always order too much. Come on.'

Wesley tried to banish all thought of Bob Naseby's frightened daughter and Sven Larsen's missing sister from his mind as he led the way up the narrow hilly streets that led towards home and chicken chow mein.

Sven Larsen jumped aboard the yacht he'd hired earlier that day and prepared to cast off. As a cautious man he checked his life-jacket and ensured that the small dinghy bobbing behind was securely fastened.

'I see you don't take any chances,' said his companion softly.

'I am what you might call a perfectionist,' replied Larsen. 'It is not in my nature to take chances.'

'And the police don't know you're meeting me?'

'I told them nothing. I think that matters should remain between ourselves. There are certain things about my sister I should not wish the world to know. Do you not agree?'

His companion smiled as they set off down the River Trad towards the open sea, the warm salty breeze in their faces.

The takeaway from the Golden Dragon had been up to its usual high standard, and Wesley sat back on the sofa, his appetite satisfied, while Neil delved into the oblong foil container, polishing off what remained of the beef and cashew nuts.

Pam sat watching them, wondering how to broach the subject. 'By the way, dear, I've just volunteered to be ravished by Vikings' sounded a little foolish.

But it was Neil who gave her her cue. 'You'll have to come and see the work we're doing in Neston parish church. We've uncovered a whole section of the Anglo-Saxon stone foundations . . . and they show signs that the building was destroyed by fire. I reckon the original minster wasn't as big as the present church, but it was quite substantial. But then it should have been, I suppose. Neston was an important place.'

'A burgh?' Pam grinned. She was only too familiar with Neil's single-minded enthusiasm for his work. She had gone out with him in their first year at university . . . until she had met Wesley.

Neil gestured with his fork. 'Yeah . . . right. I reckon it was destroyed in Viking raids. All the evidence points to it. They were very fond of that sort of thing, the Vikings. Raided and burned churches and monasteries and carried away their treasures; pillaged towns and villages – pinched everything they could lay their hands on, including people to sell in the slave markets of Bristol or Rouen. Slaughtered, raped . . . you name it, they did it. Good craftsmen, though. And their longboats were the stealth technology of their day.'

'Actually . . .' Pam looked at her husband, then at Neil. 'I've volunteered to take part in those Viking re-enactments . . . for the Neston festival. It sounded fun so I . . .'

Wesley leaned forward, surprised. 'You've not mentioned this before.'

'I saw the leaflet and I thought I'd go along and give it a try,' she continued. 'I thought it would do me good to get out of the house . . . and get Michael used to his childminder.'

Wesley, as an educated husband of the modern age, felt that he couldn't argue with this. 'Yes, I suppose it is a good idea. What do you have to do?'

'To be honest I don't know yet. At the rehearsal I was tending the wounded. The Vikings weren't renowned for their equal opportunities policies.' She smiled. 'But as long as I don't get ravished . . .'

'Or pillaged,' said Neil with a slight sneer. As a professional historian he was sceptical about the authenticity of such events. 'So what kind of people are taking part . . . and how do they ensure historical accuracy? Sometimes these re-enactment groups are excellent and put a lot of research in.'

'I can't say how accurate it's going to be. It's being organised by a group called Thor's Hammers.'

'Never heard of them,' said Neil dismissively. 'What are they like?'

Pam shrugged. 'They seem a very mixed bunch,' she said with a grin. 'They've been going round the area for a couple of weeks now, taking part in various events.' She looked at Wesley. She had just remembered the two thickset members of Thor's Hammers and their half-heard words. 'Actually . . .' She paused.

'What is it?'

Pam glanced at Neil, who was watching her intently, and suddenly felt foolish. 'Nothing. It's nothing,' she said, dismissing her nebulous feelings of unease. She was getting too imaginative in her old age.

The yacht drifted on the calm summer ebbtide out into the open sea of the English Channel. The flames were small at first, licking the cabin, then creeping slowly along the deck. But as the sun sank and the sky darkened, the fire took hold, growing in intensity until the whole craft was aflame.

It bobbed like a flaming torch on the water and drifted slowly out to sea . . . until it disappeared into the sunset like a stately, blazing funeral boat of old.

Chapter Six

AD 997

Today the Danes came to Neston. They ravaged and burned and took with them to their ships indescribable plunder. They killed many and had no mercy upon women and children and many they took as slaves aboard their boats. I witnessed such cruelty that I was certain the Devil guided the actions of the heathens. I saw babes slaughtered in their mothers' arms; I saw women horribly ravished and their violators cut their throats when they had done; I saw men and women and even children cut with axes and impaled on swords; many died screaming in the houses and churches that were burned; many of the nuns who took shelter with us were violated and murdered. The Danes rejoiced in this evil.

Our Minster is burned and its treasures and relics taken. But I, Edwin, by God's good grace, did escape the town by fleeing when the enemy breached the walls. I took with me for her protection Hilda, a young nun. We give thanks to God each hour that we escaped the horrors of the evil ones. I, Edwin, shall no longer keep the Minster chronicle as the Minster is no more: but I shall record my deeds and thoughts on the blank parchments I took from the scriptorium. I took also an ivory casket, a treasure of our house, that it would not fall into the hands of the heathens. It is our intent to travel to Stoke Beeching: to the house of my father and mother. I fear what we shall find there.
From the chronicle of Brother Edwin

Rachel Tracey arrived home to find her mother hurrying around the kitchen with a secretive smile on her face. She went upstairs to change out of her working clothes, and when she came down her mother was standing by the Aga, grinning with triumph. A tall, fair-haired young man sat at the kitchen table sipping a mug of tea.

'Hi, Rach.' The young man turned and smiled. He was good-looking by any woman's standards, even though he had lost the deep bronze tan he had brought with him from his native Australia a year before. He had met Rachel when she had arrested him and, once his innocence had been established, he had stayed around, abandoning his plans to backpack through Europe for the company of his arresting officer.

Rachel looked at him, tight-lipped. 'Well? Have I got the day wrong or what?'

'Your mum's asked me to stay for a while. With your dad and brothers doing the haymaking and these bastards breaking into farms . . .'

Rachel stood in the doorway. 'What about your job at the hotel?' she asked coolly.

'I've taken a few weeks off . . . told them I'm going away.' He shrugged and looked at her appealingly, puppy-like. 'Which was sort of true, I suppose. I thought you'd be pleased. Means we can see more of each other, eh?'

Rachel turned on her heels and marched off into the living room, where her youngest brother, Joe, was watching an Australian soap opera on television. He ignored her and stared at the screen. It wasn't long before her mother appeared in the doorway.

'I don't know what you're thinking of, Rachel, I really don't. Dave's a nice boy and you treat him like dirt.'

Rachel swung round. 'I wish you'd asked me first. I'd like to make my own decisions.'

Joe grabbed the remote control and turned the sound up on the television.

'I thought with these raids and . . .'

'Oh, come on, Mother, I didn't come down in the last shower. I know exactly why you invited Dave to stay. It's time you realised that I'm capable of running my own life.' She marched out of the room, leaving her mother speechless as the deafening strains of the soap opera signature tune oozed from the TV set.

She swept past Dave, who was hovering, uncertain, in the

hallway. He shrugged, abandoning all hope of understanding the opposite sex.

He decided to leave Rachel to it and strolled outside into the evening sunshine, towards the old barn and the open fields, hoping to receive a warmer welcome from Rachel's male relatives. Then he heard something that made him stop and dart behind a convenient tree.

Voices were raised, bitter, quarrelling. Yet another skirmish in the battle of the sexes. The woman stood, furious-faced, while her companion struggled to load a suitcase into a silver BMW with a dented nearside wing. One of the couples from the old barn were having a humdinger of a row.

After emitting a stream of expletives that almost made the young Australian blush, the woman stormed into the barn, the man making a one-fingered salute to her retreating back.

'If you open your big mouth you're dead meat,' came a threatening shout. 'Dead meat.'

Dave waited until the car had driven away before he made his way down to the fields.

Sam Heffernan stood in the dingy offices of Funograms Unlimited – situated above the butcher's shop in Tradmouth High Street – preparing for his first night in his new job . . . and feeling a fool.

'You look great,' said the curvaceous blonde on reception, perched on her desk, displaying a pair of alarmingly long legs. 'Very, er . . .'

'Daft?'

'I think you look very . . . manly.' She emitted a bubbly giggle, and Sam thrust out his chest and rewarded her with a wide grin.

'So you think it's okay?' he asked, waving his plastic sword about, thrusting and parrying the cigarette-smoke-filled air.

'You look great. Wouldn't mind being carried off myself.' She winked suggestively.

'It can be arranged . . . er . . .'

'Carly . . . Carly Pinkerton,' she giggled, then suddenly became more businesslike. 'Have you got your assignment card?'

'Yeah.' He delved into the pocket of his furry trousers and produced a pink card. 'A Gemma Munro at the Whale and Whelk in Morbay at ten o'clock. It's her twenty-first.'

'Right. I've given you directions. Don't be late, now, will you. Nervous?'

'Petrified.' He looked at his reflection in the long mirror on the wall. 'I just hope I don't get stopped by the police. I'd have a job explaining this lot away to my dad.'

With his heart thumping, Sam slunk outside to his battered car, fearing that he was about to experience the most terrifying night of his life.

Rachel turned over in her narrow single bed, glad she had told Dave that her parents wouldn't approve of them sleeping together under their roof. There were times when parents with traditional values could be a positive asset.

She looked at her alarm clock. Four o'clock. It wouldn't be long before dawn and the start of the day's work for her parents and her brothers. Police officers kept more civilised hours than farmers . . . if they were lucky. She closed her eyes and began to drift back to sleep. But something woke her. She jerked her eyes open and sat up, surveying the shadows of her room. There it was again. A car door slamming. She climbed out of bed and crept over to the window.

But before she could get there she heard a splintering crash. She froze and listened. There were noises downstairs, and she could hear mumbled, panicked voices; feet creeping on the landing. Her door opened.

'Rach. They're downstairs . . . the robbers.' Dave's voice was anxious. 'I told your dad I'm going down.'

'Don't be stupid, Dave. Don't take any risks.' She reached for the handbag beside her bed and took out her mobile phone. 'I'm ringing the station.'

'Okay. But we can't just wait for the cops to arrive.' He disappeared from the doorway.

She called after him. 'Dave, don't be stupid. Come back.' But he was gone. Her hands trembling, she reported the incident, trying to keep calm . . . professional. There were noises outside – shouting; barked instructions. She put on her long thick winter dressing gown. The robbers weren't going to have the satisfaction of seeing her half naked.

She crept to the top of the stairs and looked down at the scene below. Her parents were there, clinging to each other in their dressing gowns. Her brothers stood to the side of them, defiant. Dave stood in front of them all, squaring up to the man in the ski mask pointing the gun at him threateningly.

'Get the money. Move,' Ski Mask barked. 'And jewellery. Everything you've got.' He waved the gun in Stella Tracey's direction. 'Come on. Don't waste my time.'

Rachel listened carefully from her post, hidden at the top of the stairs. The accent was local, definitely local. She would recognise it again . . . anywhere. There were another two figures behind the man, both with guns. One kept the family covered while the other searched the room for valuables, placing anything that took his fancy into a large red hold-all.

'Where are the quad bikes? We know you've got quad bikes. Where are they?'

'None of your business,' shouted Tom, Rachel's eldest brother. She saw him ease back the trigger 'Tell me . . . now.'

'Just tell him, Tom. It's not worth it,' sobbed Stella.

Rachel stood there, fists clenched with frustrated anger as her brother told Ski Mask that the farm's four quad bikes were kept in the new barn. She wanted to go down there and rip the masks off their evil faces, ram their guns down their throats. She had investigated many crimes, but she had never before experienced the helpless fury of the victim.

It happened so quickly . . . yet so slowly. Unreal: like something watched on film. Dave leaned forward with a sudden jerk and grabbed Ski Mask's gun. As they wrestled over the thing, pulling it one way then another, Rachel held her breath, expecting the night-shattering explosion then the awful silence as one of them lay bleeding on the ground. But she heard only her mother's screams and her father's anxious instructions to leave it, it wasn't worth it.

Rachel heard herself shout but her voice was disembodied . . . like a voice on a tape recorder. She heard the words but she wasn't aware of speaking them. 'I've called the police on my mobile,' she shouted from the top of the stairs, stepping out into the vision of the two armed men, who seemed to be watching, stupefied, as Dave fought their colleague. 'The police are on their way.'

The officer in the approaching patrol car timed it just right. As soon as Rachel had finished speaking, her words were reinforced by the sound of a distant siren. Dave managed to wrest the gun from his adversary's hands as Ski Mask gave him a mighty push, sending him cannoning backwards into an oak dresser. The gun flew upwards and dislodged Mrs Tracey's best china, which crashed down on Dave's head as he lay there, unmoving.

Then, without a word, following each other by instinct like migrating birds, the robbers fled; one of them running backwards, pointing the gun, sweeping it over the assembled company, emphasising a point. A car door slammed and they were off. Tom ran to the window and watched as they drove away, lights out, tyres screeching. A large dark van, probably intended to accommodate the quad bikes, followed behind.

The rest of the family had gathered around Dave, who lay motionless on the floor. Stella Tracey knelt and checked his pulse, tears streaming down her face. 'Ring for an ambulance, somebody.' She looked round desperately. Her husband lifted the receiver on the telephone but soon replaced it in disgust. The wires had been cut.

Rachel still stood at the top of the stairs, frozen, numb. 'Is he all right?' she called down. But nobody answered.

She forced herself to turn away from the horrible fascination of the scene and walked slowly back to her bedroom, taking deep breaths. She took her mobile and dialled 999 automatically as she heard the police cars squeal to a halt outside her window.

When Wesley reached the CID office the next morning he found Steve Carstairs alone.

'Is the boss in yet?'

Steve looked up resentfully. 'Not seen him.'

The awkward silence that followed was broken when PC Johnson rushed into the office waving a typed report. To Steve's disgust he made straight for Wesley.

'Sarge . . . have you heard? He's still unconscious, and Rachel's suffering from shock, her mum said . . . mind you, her mum sounded a bit shaken and all.'

'Hang on, Paul, what are you talking about? What's happened?'

'Has Steve not told you?' he said incredulously.

Both men looked at Steve for some explanation. 'I never had a chance,' he muttered.

PC Paul Johnson drew himself up to his full and considerable height and prepared to relay the latest news. 'There was a robbery at Rachel's farm last night. Rachel managed to call the police on her mobile so the gang were disturbed. They didn't get away with much.'

'So who was hurt?' Wesley asked impatiently.

'Rachel's boyfriend, Dave. Concussion. He's not regained consciousness yet. It seems he had a go at disarming one of them ... got pushed backwards and hit his head. The whole family are pretty shaken. And Rachel's not coming in today.'

Wesley picked up his jacket. 'I'll go up to the farm and see her. Do you know where the inspector is?'

Johnson's look of concern was replaced by a grin. 'I reckon it's his old trouble.'

Wesley nodded knowingly. The inspector was renowned for his frequent inability to wake up in the morning.

'I'm going up to Little Barton Farm anyway to take statements after SOCO are finished,' said Johnson. 'I'll give you a lift over if you like.'

Gerry Heffernan chose that moment to lumber into the office like an outraged gorilla. 'I know I'm late. That son of mine got in at two in the morning from goodness knows where and woke me up. I overslept. What's this about our Rach? I've heard her place was done last night. Who's over there?'

'I'm on my way to take statements now, sir. Sergeant Peterson's coming with me ... and SOCO are there,' Johnson said, standing to attention, his spots standing out as he blushed.

'I think Rachel's all right, sir,' said Wesley quickly. 'But her boyfriend, Dave, was knocked unconscious. I don't know the full details yet.'

Gerry Heffernan was a churchgoing man, not usually one to swear, but he emitted a colourful string of expletives, learned in his navy days, to make his opinion of the men who had raided the Traceys' farm clear to all who cared to listen. 'So the bastards got away, did they?'

'Seems like it, sir. Are you coming with us to Little Barton Farm?'

'You try and stop me, Wes, you just try and stop me.'

'We're off out, Steve,' said the inspector as he passed DC Carstairs' desk. 'If anyone wants us you know where we are. Okay?'

'Yes, sir.' Steve sat back in his chair, glad to be alone in the office with nobody watching him. He had an interesting-looking magazine in his desk drawer which his mate at the snooker club had lent him. He anticipated with considerable glee a couple of hours in the company of Big-Bosomed Sadie and her well-endowed playmates. Then he suddenly remembered the message for the inspector that he should have passed on.

He called out. 'Have you got the message from the coastguard, sir? I put it on your desk.' But he was too late. Gerry Heffernan was already halfway down the stairs. Steve shrugged and opened his desk drawer. The message from the coastguard probably wasn't urgent. It would just have to wait.

Stella Tracey felt she had to keep busy. If she stopped she would begin to think about last night . . . what happened, what could have happened. The men were working in the fields. There was hay to be made at this time of year before the main harvest, cows to be milked, sheep to be seen to. Robbers or no robbers, the work of the farm never stopped.

The kitchen had been cleaned to within an inch of its life. The policemen in white overalls – the scenes of crime officers or SOCOs, as Rachel insisted on calling them – were in the living room searching for fingerprints and goodness knows what else. It had been Stella's first instinct to give the place a good clean . . . to try to eliminate all trace of those evil men from her house. But Rachel had given strict orders that things were to be left as they were: even a quick going over with the Hoover would destroy vital evidence.

Stella looked around, anxious for something else to do. Rachel was still in bed. And the SOCOs were awash with tea: she had made them three pots already. Then she thought of the guests in the holiday apartments. She presumed they were all right: she certainly hadn't heard otherwise. The old barn being well out of earshot of the farm itself, none of them had been up to enquire about the strange goings-on in the night. But it would do no harm to check . . . to make sure everyone was okay and to have a good chat to Mr and Mrs Smithers – regular visitors to the farm who, Stella considered, were a nice, sensible couple.

She took off her rubber gloves and walked purposefully over to the old barn, noting that most of the cars were still parked outside. Except Mr Proudy's.

She knocked at all the doors in turn, just to make sure everything – and everyone – was all right. She recounted the events of
the previous night to a captive and sympathetic audience. Mr and
Mrs Smithers – a recently retired couple whose new-found
freedom seemed to have endowed them with boundless energy –
invited her in for a medicinal brandy – to steady her nerves. Stella
was feeling better already, and if it hadn't been for Dave she
might even have begun to enjoy the excitement.

'Did you hear anything last night?' she asked Mrs Smithers.

'I heard the police car sirens, of course, but I didn't realise they
were so near.'

'I hope they didn't wake you up.'

'Oh, no. As a matter of fact we were woken up before then . . .
by that man in number three. He was slamming his car door and
revving his engine long before the police cars arrived. Then
eventually he drove off.'

'Mr Proudy?' Stella wasn't surprised. If one of her guests was
going to go slamming car doors at unsocial hours she would have
laid money on it being Mr Proudy.

'Yes. That's right. He went out in the small hours . . . and I
don't think he's back yet.' Mrs Smithers leaned forward. She was
a woman who liked a gossip. 'I wonder where he's gone,' she said
with relish.

'Yes,' said Stella thoughtfully. 'I wonder.' She pondered this
question all the way back to the farmhouse, wondering whether to
mention it to Rachel.

Stella opened the back door and was surprised to find her
kitchen full of police officers. A good-looking young black man
sat at the huge pine table next to a tall, spotty uniformed constable
and a large untidy man with a barely ironed shirt and a couple of
disreputable-looking tattoos on his chubby forearms. She had
heard all about Rachel's colleagues, but this was her first
encounter with them in the flesh. Wesley Peterson – whom Rachel
seemed rather taken with – lived up to her expectations, but
Inspector Heffernan was certainly no advert for the police force.
He needed to smarten himself up a bit. But then Stella
remembered that he had lost his wife and her censure turned to
instinctive sympathy.

Rachel herself had dressed and was seated at the head of
the table. She smiled weakly at her mother and made the

introductions. 'We need statements from everyone, Mum,' she said. 'And I've just phoned the hospital. There's no change.'

Stella sank into a vacant chair and shook her head. 'If I hadn't asked him to come back here . . . it's my fault . . .'

'Of course it's not your fault, Mrs Tracey. You couldn't have known. You mustn't blame yourself.' Wesley spoke quietly, his voice full of sympathy. Stella could see why Rachel liked him . . . why she talked about him such a lot.

They were interrupted by one of the SOCOs, who poked his head round the door and asked if he could have a word. Wesley and Heffernan followed him to the living room, one corner of which was covered in broken china.

The white-overalled officer produced a large plastic bag. Inside was a sawn-off shotgun – a weapon favoured by many of the constabulary's not-so-valued customers. 'One of them dropped this in the struggle,' he said. 'It's strange . . .'

'What is?' said Heffernan.

The officer looked nonplussed and carried on. 'Well, I was very surprised to find that it's not loaded.'

'Not loaded?' said Heffernan incredulously. 'But they shot Dan Wexer.'

'Perhaps after that they lost their nerve,' said Wesley.

'And began to help old ladies across the road? Oh, come on, Wes, that type don't lose their nerve . . . they just get more desperate, more vicious,' answered Heffernan, sceptical.

Rachel stepped into the room and looked around. 'I thought I'd better tell you, sir. My mum's just told me that she's been over to the old barn this morning . . . to the holiday apartments. She says Laurence Proudy drove off in the small hours and hasn't come back. Do you think it's important?'

Heffernan and Wesley looked at each other.

'Could be,' said the inspector with barely concealed excitement.

No sooner had PC Johnson dropped DI Heffernan and DS Peterson back at Tradmouth police station than a message came through on his radio. The prowler had been up at Waters House again last night. Mr Wentwood thought he'd better let the police know. Johnson wondered why he had waited so long; why hadn't he reported it while the prowler was actually there rather than the morning after when he was long gone? But his not to reason why . . . his just to deal with the paperwork.

It was Christopher Wentwood he spoke to this time, his wife standing behind his chair protectively like a mother watching over her young. Beside Gwen he looked young, immature, with his wavy brown hair and anxious eyes. Wentwood clearly didn't follow Johnson's reasoning. He had seen the man run away. It would have been no good contacting the police last night. He had gone.

Gwen Wentwood seemed tense. She appeared a capable woman, but perhaps the thought that her house was being watched was getting to her too.

Johnson took out his notebook, longing for a cup of tea, but he wasn't offered one. 'So what did the prowler do? Did you get a better look at him this time?' he asked hopefully.

Christopher shook his head. 'It was the same as before. I saw this figure in the bushes. Then he ran away. It was too dark to get a proper look at him.'

'You're sure it was a man?' Christopher nodded. 'And what direction did he run off in?'

'Towards Longhouse Cottage . . . just like before.' Gwen Wentwood put a protecting hand on her husband's shoulder and shot Johnson a mildly resentful look.

Johnson thought for a moment. Longhouse Cottage – a body had been found there. He recalled that Sergeant Peterson had had some interest in the place. He made the appropriate reassuring noises and made his exit.

As Johnson walked down the drive towards his patrol car, he pushed the button on his radio and spoke. 'Can someone get a message to DS Peterson? Can you ask him to meet me on the main road outside Longhouse Cottage, Stoke Beeching, in half an hour?'

Wesley Peterson drove out to meet PC Johnson feeling optimistic for the first time that day. He had just taken a call from Neston police station. Daniel Wexer's Land Rover had been found parked on a street near the middle of the town, its presence reported by an irate householder, complaining that its owner's thoughtlessness was denying her husband a precious parking space. The Land Rover was being brought to Tradmouth for forensic examination. The villains must have left some trace: fingerprints or hairs . . .

maybe even traceable possessions. After a depressing start at Little Barton Farm, this was the best news he'd had all day. Just before he'd left the station he'd rung the hospital to ask how Dave was. There was no change. It was just a matter of waiting.

Johnson met him, as arranged, at the side of the main road out of Stoke Beeching. He was leaning on his patrol car, and he raised a hand in greeting as Wesley drew up beside him.

'I just thought I'd let you know, Sarge. The prowler reported at Waters House always runs off in the direction of Longhouse Cottage. I know you had some dealings with the people there . . . wasn't there a body found?'

'That's right. A skeleton. According to Doc Bowman it's almost certainly centuries old, so officially it's not our problem. Tell me about this prowler.'

'Mr and Mrs Wentwood who live up at Waters House say there's a man standing in the bushes watching the house. It's happened a few nights now and Mr. Wentwood's getting a bit worried. He seems the nervous type . . . jumpy. Do you think it could be these robbers? One of them might be casing the joint,' he suggested with relish.

'Anything's possible.' Wesley looked around. 'I think we should pay a call on Maggie Palister to ask if she's seen anything. Have you heard of the Palisters?'

Johnson shook his head. Jock Palister's notoriety had been before his time.

'According to Inspector Heffernan Jock Palister was a local villain who came into money. He bought Waters House and owned all this land, then he disappeared suddenly and left his wife, Maggie, and her son in the lurch. They sold Waters House and most of their land and moved into Longhouse Cottage – which had been farm workers' accommodation – and now they just run a smallholding there. The inspector has a theory that the skeleton belongs to Jock Palister, but I'm afraid he's going to be proved wrong. Anyway, it's always possible Maggie might have seen this prowler, so it's worth a call.'

Wesley led the way up the farm track and spotted a half-naked Carl Palister, his torso glistening with sweat, digging in the field near the house . . . probably still labouring away at the drainage. Wesley called to him and Carl looked up, shielding his eyes from the sun.

'Found any more skeletons, Carl?'

'No . . . nothing. I filled in that hole. Your mate said it was okay and I was scared of losing a sheep down there. They're not too bright, sheep. Get into all sorts of trouble if you don't watch 'em.' He leaned on his spade and wiped the beads of sweat off his brow, watching Wesley and Johnson warily. 'Is that all you've come for? To see if any more bones have turned up?' There was a hint of anxiety in his voice, and Wesley wondered if Carl Palister was hiding something.

'I wanted to know if you and your mother have noticed anyone suspicious hanging around. There's been a prowler reported up at Waters House . . . seems to run off in this direction when he's spotted. Well?'

Carl Palister studied his spade for a few seconds. 'The drive to Waters House runs just the other side of the stream. Anyone can go that way. Doesn't mean they have to come on our land.'

'Have you seen anything?'

Carl shook his head.

'Is you mother in?'

Carl looked up. For a split second Wesley saw panic on his face; then the mask of boredom was swiftly replaced. 'She's somewhere about. I'll fetch her.'

He began to walk towards the house and the two policemen followed. Carl turned round. 'There's no need for you to come. I'll bring her out. Okay?'

'That told us, Sarge,' whispered Johnson as Carl disappeared towards the dilapidated house. They stood watching as Maggie Palister walked towards them, arms folded defensively, to the unmusical accompaniment of distant hens, clucking angrily. Their feeding time had been disturbed. Carl followed her, looking from left to right as if he suspected there were snipers in the bushes that lined the field.

She looked Wesley up and down and squared up to him, arms akimbo. 'Our Carl says there's prowler up at Waters House. What's that got to do with us?'

Wesley mustered all his charm. 'We just wondered if you'd seen anyone suspicious, Mrs Palister. The prowler was seen to run off in this direction.'

Maggie seemed to consider the question carefully. Then she nodded. 'Come to think of it there's been a car parked just next to

93

the entrance to their drive. Just on the main road. Carl's noticed it a few times when he's been out to the village in the evening, haven't you, Carl?'

Carl nodded, still wary. 'Big black car it was.'

'Make?'

'Didn't notice. It was just a big black car.'

'Saloon? Hatchback? New? Old?'

'Saloon. Didn't look old. Not anything flashy like a Roller or a Jag. Just something ordinary . . . Japanese maybe or a Ford. I didn't take much notice.'

'And when did you see it?'

'It's been parked there a few nights now.'

'If you see it again will you ring us . . . or at least write down the registration number for us: it'd be a great help.' Wesley handed him his card. Carl studied it for a moment then stuck it in the back pocket of his cut-off jeans that served as shorts.

'I don't see why he has to do your dirty work for you,' said Maggie, hostile.

'Call it self-protection, Mrs Palister. Who knows, this man might come prowling round your house next if he's not caught.' Wesley gave a quick businesslike smile and nodded to Johnson. It was time to leave. But he had one last parting shot. 'By the way, have you heard about the treasure that was found on this land in the last century?'

This got a reaction. Maggie Palister's eyes lit up greedily, and Carl thrust his spade into the ground and stood up straight. 'What treasure?' asked Maggie.

'Neil Watson and I had a word with Mrs Crick who used to have the post office in the village. She said a hoard of treasure was found by the man who owned Waters House in the nineteenth century . . . a man called Peacock. It was buried somewhere near here.'

'I've not heard nothing about that,' said Carl, surprised. This was certainly news to the Palisters.

'You never know, Carl, there might be some more about. Let us know if you find anything, won't you. Neil'd be interested.'

Carl didn't reply. He nodded to Wesley and started to dig again with renewed enthusiasm, wondering whether it would be worth borrowing a metal detector from a man he knew in the village pub.

Maggie Palister made no comment. She turned on her heels and

94

walked quickly back to the house, looking back once to make sure the two representatives of the local police force were safely off her premises.

The mobile phone is a wonderful invention . . . at times. From Stoke Beeching, Wesley was able to speak to Neil at Neston parish church and arrange to meet him in Tradmouth that lunchtime.

After a quick sandwich in the Tradmouth Arms and a résumé of Rachel's misfortunes, they walked the short distance to the Peacock Museum.

'So you think Carl Palister's going to go on a treasure hunt of his own?' said Neil with quiet amusement as they passed the ancient bulk of St Margaret's church.

'You should have seen the way his eyes lit up when I mentioned the treasure. He almost grabbed his spade and started digging there and then. Any more thoughts on the skeleton?'

'I reckon that amulet Colin found clinches it: he's Viking. I suppose he could have been killed in the so-called battle that was supposed to have taken place there and been buried by his shipmates. Perhaps he was their leader so they gave him a good send-off. He had his boat to sail to Valhalla in, didn't he . . . the hall of the slain,' he added with relish.

Wesley changed the subject. 'What do you make of the Palisters?'

'Carl's okay but the mother's a bit odd. I asked if I could have a look at the house to see if there were any clues about how old it was and she looked at me as if I'd made an indecent suggestion.'

Wesley smiled. There had been times when Neil's enthusiasm for his work had been misinterpreted. 'According to Gerry Heffernan, Maggie Palister hasn't had an easy life.'

'Not surprised,' Neil mumbled uncharitably. They approached the museum and Neil's eyes lit up with excitement. 'It's open.'

Indeed, the door to the Peacock Museum stood open, but it hardly invited the casual visitor. The two men stepped inside the narrow hallway and the bare, splintery floorboards creaked to announce their arrival.

The man who appeared at the door of the front room was in his sixties with a shock of grey hair and a pair of reading glasses perched on the end of his beak-like nose. He wore a sports jacket with leather patches on the elbows in defiance of the summer heat, and his shirt was slightly frayed at the collar. The effect was completed with a red spotted bow tie. The man looked rather like a museum exhibit himself: undoubtedly an endangered species.

He looked the newcomers up and down with alarm. 'Can I help you?' His voice was as dry as his appearance. 'It's two pound each, you know,' he added, as if the exorbitance of the entrance charge might put them off.

It was Neil who decided to do the talking. 'My name's Neil Watson from the County Archaeological Unit, and this is Detective Sergeant Peterson from the local CID. He studied archaeology with me at university. Actually we're here professionally.'

The suspicion lifted from the man's face. He held out his hand. 'Geoffrey Bate-Brownlowe. Curator. So pleased to meet you.' He shook each hand in turn heartily. 'And what have we here in our little museum that would interest a pair of archaeologists, eh? Let me guess . . . our little collection of flint arrows and axe-heads. Jeremiah Peacock was a remarkable collector and a well-travelled man. Come along.' He began to lead the way down the corridor before Neil could get a word in. 'I'm sure the detective sergeant will be interested in our small collection of African artefacts . . .'

Wesley and Neil exchanged looks. 'I'm sure they're very interesting, sir, but we're here about the treasure hoard that was found on Mr Peacock's land in the last century.' Wesley thought the direct approach would be best.

Bate-Brownlowe stopped and turned round. 'Why didn't you say?'

He squeezed past them and led the way back to the museum's small front room. Once a shop, it at least had the advantage of a large window. The sunlight streamed in and caught the dust particles which danced and swirled, suspended in the air. The room was crammed with silent creatures, stuffed and sad in their dirty glass coffins; faded cases of birds' eggs; regiments of seashells with faded brown writing beneath; dusty turtle shells propped against the wall.

Bate-Brownlowe took something that looked like an old-fashioned ledger from a large black cupboard in the corner. 'It's all in here,' he said, tapping the book. 'The whole collection. What kind of treasure did you say it was?'

'We know that Peacock found something valuable on his land, most of which was sent to London,' said Neil. 'That's all we have to go on at the moment.'

'So you've called in the CID, have you?' Bate-Brownlowe looked over his glasses at Wesley, a smile playing on his lips. 'Do you mind me asking why you're so interested in Jeremiah Peacock's discoveries?'

'A skeleton has been found on what used to be Peacock's land,' said Wesley. 'It could have connections with Viking raids on this part of the country in the late tenth or early eleventh century. If we knew what Peacock had found there already it might help us piece together a few clues.'

'I see.' Bate-Brownlowe fingered through the great book, its pages foxed with age. Eventually he looked up, an expression of triumph on his face. 'Is this what you're looking for, do you think?' He pushed the glasses up his nose and read. 'One Anglo-Saxon silver pin; two Anglo-Saxon strap-ends; one Anglo-Saxon disc brooch; fifteen silver pennies of Ethelred the Unready; all discovered buried in the field known as Blood Field near to Longhouse Cottage and found to be treasure trove. The bulk of the Longhouse hoard as it is called was presented by Her Majesty Queen Victoria to the British Museum. That's all there is, I'm afraid. Would you like to see them?'

Neil nodded eagerly. The curator led the way up the uncarpeted staircase to the dimly lit upper floor. They watched as he searched in musty cupboards, taking out boxes and looking inside. Wesley didn't need telepathic powers to know what Neil was thinking. This was hardly a professional way to run a museum.

'I'm afraid my speciality is natural history,' Bate-Brownlowe said by way of explanation, brushing the dust from his jacket. 'I haven't taken much interest in the later archaeological exhibits. I've only been here six months and I haven't really found my way around yet.' He drew out a large flat wooden box and opened it carefully. 'Here we are, gentlemen. The Longhouse hoard.'

He opened the heavy oak box, which was lined with rich blue velvet. The silver stood out, shining, moon-like, against the dark cloth. There wasn't really much there, but what there was was impressive.

'Bet the British Museum got the best bits,' said Neil bitterly.

'Very likely, Mr Watson. I've never been quite clear on the laws of treasure trove. Er . . .'

'It's easy,' said Wesley casually. 'If it was hidden deliberately it's treasure trove and belongs to the Crown; if it was lost by accident the landowner can keep it. The coroner must have decided that what was found on Longhouse Cottage was hidden deliberately. Was anything else found on Peacock's land?'

Bate-Brownlowe thought for a few moments. 'Now I'm sure I've seen a label . . . do bear with me . . .' He knelt down again and began rooting in the cupboard, leaving Neil holding the Saxon treasure. It occurred to Wesley that if they'd been impostors they could have walked away with Tradmouth's share of the Longhouse hoard with no problem. But perhaps his time in the police force had rendered him over-suspicious.

The curator took another box from the cupboard, a long, grubby cardboard specimen this time. 'Here it is. I noticed the label on the side. "Sword and shield boss found with skeleton in the bottom field near to Longhouse Cottage. Skeleton reburied undisturbed. Possible Anglo-Saxon." Is this any help to you at all?'

Wesley took the box and opened it carefully, feeling as excited as a child opening a particularly intriguing Christmas parcel. The sword lay there, a corroded length of rust, giving few clues as to its original fearsome splendour. Beside it lay a round, rusted shield boss, about the size of a dinner plate; the wooden shield surrounding it had long since rotted away.

Neil looked up at the curator, grinning. 'This is just what we were looking for,' he said, his eyes glowing with anticipation.

Gerry Heffernan sat at his desk contemplating lunch. He had bought a ham roll and a banana – a combination that seemed to him sadly inadequate for a grown man. Normally he would have patronised the station canteen, but with Wesley out on unspecified business and Stan Jenkins in hospital he would probably end up eating his sausage and chips in solitary splendour with nobody to talk to.

Besides, he was busy . . . which was more than could be said for his son, who was no doubt spending the day in bed after his mysterious excursions of the night before. When the fond father had enquired how the job had gone, Sam had blushed and answered with a mumbled 'okay'. But Heffernan had been young once himself and knew that Sam was hiding something. He just hoped that it was nothing immoral, illegal or unhealthy.

The telephone on Heffernan's desk rang just as he was about to bite into his ham roll. He picked up the receiver and grunted. It was the coastguard, who told him reproachfully that they had rung first thing that morning and left a message. They thought he'd like to know that a hired yacht had been found drifting and ablaze off the coast near Stoke Beeching. Heffernan's name had been mentioned at the time it was hired. The fire had been extinguished and the boat searched but there was no sign of anybody on board . . . alive or dead. The police launch had towed it back into Tradmouth.

'Hang on a minute. Where do I come in? Who hired this yacht?'

'It was a Danish gentleman,' said the coastguard on the other end of the line. 'A Sven Larsen. Just thought we'd let you know personally, seeing as your name came up. I'll leave it with you, then.'

The phone went dead and Heffernan bit into his roll, longing for a plate of sausage and chips to sustain him. It was going to be a long day.

Chapter Seven

AD 997

*We followed the river to Stokeworthy where we found much
destruction. But one old man and a young child were left
living in that place. They had been collecting firewood in the
trees when the evil ones arrived and so hid and were spared.
The man whose name was Ethelheard told of such cruelty and
said the child's mother had been taken as a slave and its
father slain. The village was burned . . . laid waste.*

*Hilda wept much at the sight and clung to me. I have vowed
to protect her. She looks upon me with great affection and she
has great beauty but I should not think of her as men
commonly think of lovely women . . . I should not.*

From the chronicle of Brother Edwin

Rachel Tracey sat by the hospital bed, watching Dave intently.
She turned to her mother, who was standing behind her.

'I saw his eyelids move, Mum. I'm sure I did.'

Stella took hold of her hand and squeezed it. 'I don't know, my
luvver. I never saw. The nurse said we should talk to him. She said
that helps . . . sometimes.'

Rachel looked back at the young man in the bed. 'What should
I talk about?'

'Anything, I suppose. I don't know. You know him better than I do.'

The tears began to flow down Rachel's cheeks and Dave's
eyelids flickered open.

Gerry Heffernan's first reaction to the news from the coastguard
was to look for Wesley. But then he remembered he'd gone out to
Stoke Beeching and then to lunch. He could be some time.

His second thought was to ring Sven Larsen's hotel. The receptionist said that he wasn't there . . . hadn't been back all night. Somehow Heffernan wasn't surprised.

He looked through the glass partition and saw that Steve was back at his desk, apparently engaged in some tedious administrative task. Heffernan stood up and opened his door. 'Steve,' he shouted. DC Carstairs looked up with a start. 'Any sightings of that silver BMW yet . . . Laurence Proudy's?'

'No, sir, nothing yet,' came the half-hearted answer. 'Bet he's halfway up the M4 by now.'

'Don't be so defeatist. Let me know if you hear anything, eh? And when Sergeant Peterson comes back tell him I've gone to see a man about a boat.'

Steve nodded and returned to his paperwork.

Gerry Heffernan strolled out of the police station into the summer sunshine and weaved his way through the meandering tourists who thronged the quayside, enjoying the spectacular view across the river. Some hung around brightly coloured ticket booths, deciding whether or not to brave a trip aboard one of the many pleasure craft that plied up and down the river to the accompaniment of a lively commentary by the skipper on local places of interest or notoriety.

But these delights held no interest for the inspector. Avoiding the ubiquitous children with their crabbing lines, he descended a series of stone steps that led onto a wooden jetty and made for a notice that said 'River Trad Boat Hire'.

'Hi, Jim. I had a call from the coastguard. What's been going on?'

The man he addressed was tall and lean with the weather-beaten look acquired only through a lifetime spent out of doors. He was standing on the deck of a small cabin cruiser, a coil of rope in his hand. He put the rope on the deck and looked up at Heffernan solemnly. 'That bloke you sent . . . the foreigner. Yacht I hired him was found drifting half a mile off Little Tradmouth Head . . . been set alight, it had. Next time you send someone to hire a boat off me just make sure he's not going to torch it, eh?'

Gerry Heffernan couldn't tell whether or not Jim was truly annoyed with him, but he didn't want to take any risks. He felt an apology was in order. 'Sorry, Jim. The bloke was an experienced sailor. I never thought . . .'

Jim smiled ruefully. 'Not your fault, Gerry. Good job I'm insured.

You'll find her over there at the end of the next jetty . . . just by the police launch. Your lot have been giving her a going-over.'

Heffernan looked across and saw the craft tied up next to the gleaming blue-and-white launch. It sat low in the water and the cabin had been reduced to a shell – definitely an insurance job. 'So how did Sven Larsen seem when he came to pick her up?'

Jim shrugged. 'Fine. He appeared to know what he was doing. He just said he was going for a trip round the head and up the coast a bit. He said he'd be back by ten yesterday evening . . . never turned up. The coastguard had a report of a boat on fire about eleven last night. When the fire was put out they searched and found nobody on board. They've had the helicopter out, and the lifeboat . . . but no sign of Mr Larsen.' He sighed. 'How do you know him, anyway? One of your criminals, is he?'

'Not that I know of, Jim. But you can never be sure in this game.'

He was about to take his leave when Jim called him back. 'The dinghy's missing, you know. She was towing an inflatable dinghy with an outboard motor . . . he said he wanted it in case he decided to go ashore anywhere. It's gone.'

'Thanks, Jim.' Heffernan strolled down the jetty, hands in pockets. Maybe things weren't looking too bad for Sven Larsen after all.

Wesley noticed that his boss had a bit of colour in his chubby cheeks when he returned to the office. And he looked more cheerful. A walk in the sunshine had done him good.

'Good lunch, Wes?'

'Yes, thanks, sir. I met Neil and we found a sword and shield boss that had been buried with that skeleton at Longhouse Cottage.'

'What would Jock Palister want with a sword and shield boss? Now if it was a pickaxe handle and a baseball bat . . .'

'It's not Jock, sir. Dr Bowman assured me that the man was over six foot and the bones were very old,' Wesley said patiently. 'And we've found a reference to a skeleton being found near Longhouse Cottage in the last century. The sword and shield were taken from the grave, then the body was covered up again. It would explain a lot.'

Gerry Heffernan looked disappointed. His theories were fast disintegrating. He liked Wesley, but there were times when he was too clever by half. He really would have to have another word with the Super about his promotion. He decided to change tack. 'Have you heard about the yacht?'

'What yacht?'

'Sven Larsen hired a yacht. It was found adrift and on fire with nobody aboard. The inflatable dinghy it was towing is missing and Larsen didn't go back to his hotel last night.'

Wesley gave a low whistle. 'Oh dear. To lose one Dane may be regarded as a misfortune but to lose two looks like carelessness,' he misquoted with a grin.

'You what?' Gerry Heffernan looked at him blankly.

'Never mind, sir. Any news of Ingeborg yet?'

'In a word, Wesley, no.' Heffernan scratched his head. 'The whole thing's a complete mystery. Are you going to tell the Copenhagen police that we've mislaid another of their citizens or shall I?'

'If he managed to get away in the dinghy he might turn up at any time. Let's wait a bit, shall we? He could be wandering round dazed somewhere.'

'Mmm. We'll give it another twenty-four hours or so, eh?'

The phone rang on Heffernan's desk. Wesley watched as the inspector's expression during the brief conversation changed from one of funereal solemnity to one of positive glee. When he put the phone down he rubbed his hands together with relish.

'Dave's come round, Wes. Looks like he's going to be okay.'

When they reached Tradmouth Hospital, Gerry Heffernan went up to C Ward to break the news to Dan Wexer that his new Land Rover had been found, apparently undamaged. Dan was making an excellent recovery and would be discharged the next day. If the shot had hit him a couple of feet higher, things might have ended quite differently. Heffernan remembered that and shuddered inwardly. Life is a precarious business.

Wesley had volunteered to visit Dave. Rachel met him at the entrance to the ward, pacing up and down, chewing her finger-nails. She looked pale and strained – not her usual chirpy, efficient self. Without a word she walked into the deserted day room with its ripped wallpaper and suffocating haze of cigarette smoke.

'How are things?' was all Wesley could think of saying. 'I hear Dave's going to be all right. That's great.'

Rachel said nothing. But her eyes brimmed with tears. Wesley had never smoked in earnest, but there were times when he could see the attraction of it: the calming of the nerves; the casual offer of the packet . . . of shared comfort. That day room must have witnessed countless scenes of anxiety . . . of terror. No wonder it stank of burnt tobacco. He touched Rachel's hand, a gesture of sympathy . . . of solidarity.

She drew closer, burying her face in his shoulder. He put a tentative arm around her and Rachel clung to him as if reluctant to let him go. Then, after a few long minutes, she took a deep, shuddering breath and stepped back. 'Sorry,' she whispered, straightening her back.

'Don't worry about it. You've been through a lot.' He took hold of her hand again and gave it an encouraging squeeze. 'So how is he? Have they said how long they're keeping him in?'

'They say he'll be fine. But they're keeping him in a few days for observation. You know how cautious they are.' She attempted a smile.

'Is it all right if I talk to him now . . . take a statement?'

'I suppose so. Wesley . . .'

'What?'

'I feel so guilty.'

'What about?'

She took another deep breath. 'I was thinking of telling Dave it was all over before this happened.'

He sensed Rachel wanted to talk . . . to confess some imagined wrong. He looked at his watch, careful not to let her see him doing so. If it would make her feel better he would listen and make sympathetic noises. A row of grey-upholstered institutional chairs stood against the wall beneath a cheap Constable print. Wesley sat down and Rachel sat beside him.

'I don't see why you should feel guilty,' he said, trying to sound reassuring. He could think of little else to say. Playing agony aunt was hardly his thing.

She shook her head, near to tears again. Then she reached up and touched his shoulder, looking into his eyes. He looked away quickly. Perhaps he was misreading things. He hoped he was.

'Look, Rach. You're upset now . . . you're bound to be. But what's happened to Dave isn't your fault. I'd like to see him now and take a statement, if he's up to it.' He stood up; crisis averted.

Rachel looked mildly embarrassed. As someone who liked to

be in control, she sensed that she had almost made a fool of herself. She led the way to the ward, walking briskly, as efficient as any blue-uniformed sister.

Dave greeted Wesley with a weak smile of recognition. 'Hello, mate. How's it going?' he muttered breathlessly, lying back on the plump hospital pillows, his fair hair spread out like a halo. His face looked thinner, drawn.

'Are you feeling up to making a statement yet, Dave? If you're not I can come back . . .'

'No . . . I want you to get those bastards. Things are still a bit hazy, but I'll tell you what I remember.' Dave replied with feeble determination.

Wesley prepared to write. 'Let's start at the beginning, shall we? Before the robbery, did you notice anything suspicious? Anyone hanging around or . . .'

'No, nothing like that, mate. The only unusual thing was early on that evening . . . before the robbery. I was walking down to the bottom fields to give Rachel's dad a hand when I saw two of the people staying at the old barn – that Proudy character and his missus. They were really having a go at each other, so I stopped behind a tree where they couldn't see me. He was loading a big suitcase into his car . . . big flash BMW. They were really going at it hammer and tongs. Then he drove off.'

'What time was this?'

'About six, quarter past . . . something like that.'

'Is there any chance Proudy could have been the man you heard talking later . . . the man you fought with?'

Dave shook his head. 'No, different accent. The man with the gun was local. Proudy was from up North somewhere, I guess. But he could have been one of the others: I never heard them speak.'

Wesley patted the patient comfortingly on the shoulder, trying not to show his disappointment. Dave hadn't told him anything he didn't know already: that Laurence Proudy was aggressive; a nasty bit of work. But Wesley's instincts told him that Proudy was somehow involved in the farm robberies, and he wondered whether he had returned to Little Barton Farm yet.

He met Gerry Heffernan in the hospital's main reception and shared his suspicions.

'We'd better get someone round to Little Barton Farm to see if this Proudy's turned up . . . or failing that, see if his lady friend –

wife, partner, whatever – is still there,' said Heffernan wearily. 'Let's face it, he's the best suspect we've got at the moment. It's just a matter of finding some proof.'

'How's Dan Wexer? Pleased about his Land Rover?'

'Oh, aye. And so was that wife of his. Although she was more concerned about the jewellery she had nicked . . . asked about that antique locket. She's a bit of all right, she is. Apparently he traded his old one in for a new model. Don't know how these blokes manage it . . . I always reckoned that Kathy was the only one who'd put up with me.'

Wesley, who could hardly envisage Gerry Heffernan with a glamorous young blonde on his arm, smiled in agreement. 'So what do we do now, sir?'

'You go back to the station and see what you can find out about Proudy and I'll pop up to E Ward and pay Stan Jenkins a visit.'

'What exactly is the matter with him, sir? Nobody'll say.'

Heffernan winked solemnly. 'Don't ask, Wes. Just don't ask.'

With that the inspector turned and disappeared down the long, bright hospital corridor.

Wesley walked back to the police station slowly, enjoying the sunshine and the holiday bustle of the quayside. Flowers tumbled from lamp-posts and municipal tubs – the happy result of the town's efforts to win some coveted horticultural prize – and their sweet scent mingled with the aroma of seaweed, fish and chips and boat fuel, borne in on the breeze. He stopped to buy a pasty then hurried back, thinking of the paperwork piling up on his desk . . . and trying not to think about Rachel.

He walked through the Memorial Park where a brass band were puffing bravely at their instruments on the bandstand. They had gathered quite a crowd – men in shorts displaying pale, hirsute legs; women with bright dresses and equally bright bare shoulders; and children whinging with the heat or appeased with large, half-melted ice creams. A raucous seagull yelling overhead made Wesley look up. Then he saw something that brought him to a sudden halt.

At night, in the height of the season, the park attracted gangs of local youths, bent on troublemaking. The camera fixed to the top of a tall thin pole was a recent innovation: video surveillance, the town council's latest foray into the brave new world of high technology. Wesley's mind raced as he considered the possibilities. Did Neston have similar arrangements? Even if the streets weren't covered, the shops probably would be. Had Ingeborg Larsen's movements on the day she disappeared been caught on camera? Had she been with anyone . . . or had she been followed?

Back at the office Trish Walton greeted him with an anxious enquiry about Rachel while Steve spoke softly, almost furtively, into his phone, making no acknowledgement of Wesley's arrival.

There was a smug smile on Steve's face as he put the receiver down. 'I've got a lead,' he said with almost childlike pride. 'I was just on the blower to my snout and the word is the farm gang are using a wheel man from up North who owns a garage in the smoke. They've got a lock-up in Morbay and this geezer resprays the motors and gives 'em new plates and chassis numbers, then they ship 'em up to the smoke with bent documents and sell 'em as kosher. Quad bikes and all . . . big demand for quad bikes.' Steve sat back, looking very pleased with himself.

Wesley tried hard to suppress a smile. Steve assumed that the patois of the Met would give him a certain cachet in Tradmouth CID, even though he'd never lived further east than Morbay. 'Good work, Steve.' He felt a little encouragement might be in order. 'Have you got a name for this, er . . . geezer?'

'His name's Lol. That's all I've got so far, but I've asked my snout to keep his ear to the ground.' Wesley could have sworn he detected a note of cockney in Steve's voice.

'Good. Get on to Morbay, will you, and tell them to keep an eye on any premises the gang might use. And let the boss know when he gets back. He's just gone to visit Inspector Jenkins. He shouldn't be long.'

'What exactly's wrong with Inspector Jenkins, Sarge?' asked Trish shyly.

Wesley smiled at her. 'I've no idea. I was told not to ask. Look, Trish, I've had an idea. Ingeborg Larsen went to Neston on Monday. If we can check the video surveillance tapes from any shops she might have visited that day . . .' Trish nodded, quick on the uptake. Steve looked blank. 'If you and Steve could go over to Neston and ask around . . . And if she went to Neston first thing in the morning and wasn't seen at Honeysuckle House till three, that means she must have had lunch somewhere. Take her picture and ask around the cafés too.'

Trish nodded enthusiastically. 'I think we should have another look through her things too.'

'Yes. Rachel's back tomorrow. I'll ask her to deal with that.'

'What about tracking down this Lol?' asked Steve indignantly.

'That's all in hand.'

'So you knew about him already?' Steve sounded resentful.

'It was just a suspicion but you've confirmed it. Any news on Sven Larsen?'

Steve turned away.

'No, Sarge. Nothing,' said Trish apologetically. 'Do you want us to go over to Neston right away?'

'What's this, Wes? Why are you sending this pair on the hippie trail to Neston?' Gerry Heffernan thundered as he strode into the office. 'Is anything happening that I don't know about?'

Steve got in first, proudly telling the tale of Lol the wheel man. Then Wesley explained about the proposed Neston trip. Heffernan's eyes lit up with the excitement of the chase. 'We'll need to get a patrol car over to Little Barton Farm. If Laurence Proudy's made a reappearance we'll need to ask him some questions . . . or his lady friend'll do. I reckon he's our Lol: garage owner; now lives in London but originally from the North. I want his holiday flat given a good going-over and all once he's been brought in. Tell 'em to leave it spick and span . . . don't want to create work for Mrs Tracey. Come on, Wes. We're off to the Tower Hotel first. I want to have a quick look through Sven Larsen's things.'

Wesley nodded. If Larsen had disappeared, it had to be done. There was always a possibility, however slight, that there would be a clue of some kind among his belongings. He thought of the yacht Larsen had hired, adrift on the sea, sailing off aflame into the sunset. It was strange that Gerry Heffernan had described just such a scene when they had found the skeleton at Longhouse Cottage: the common, though inaccurate, view, gleaned from Hollywood movies, of the traditional Viking funeral. Only there had been no dead body on Larsen's boat to be consumed by the flames.

He knew it was going to be another long day. He picked up the phone and dialled his home number to warn Pam that he would be late. But the phone rang and rang. There was no answer. Then Wesley finally remembered where his wife was that Friday afternoon.

Michael was growing more used to Mrs Miller: Pam could tell. His little face lit up with a wide toothless grin every time he saw her. Although this brought considerable relief, it also brought a small nagging ripple of pain – a dread that by the time September came and she was back teaching her class full time, her baby son would be so enamoured of his new childminder that he might not miss his mother at all.

As she parked her VW Golf in the carpark of Neston High School, she noticed a strangely dressed figure standing outside the school entrance beside three large hold-alls, two black, the other bright red. Odin was in full regalia as before. Pam walked self-consciously across the carpark towards him in her short lime-green dress, aware of his eyes upon her.

Somehow Odin didn't look odd in his rough-woven blue tunic, leaning against the wall of the box-like 1960s building, his sun-bronzed arms folded. It was she who felt out of place. He smiled, his bright blue eyes fixed on hers as she approached.

He said something softly in what she guessed was Danish . . . or an old version of that language, used by the Vikings. Then he translated. 'Greetings, Pam. Welcome. I've been waiting for you.'

She blushed, her heart pounding. 'Er . . . are we in the hall again?' she asked, matter-of-factly. 'Sorry I'm late. I had to drop my son at the childminder's. Sorry.' She didn't know why she was apologising: it must have been nerves. She cursed herself for not putting into practice what she'd learned in that assertiveness class she'd attended when she'd lived in London. But she'd not had much need or opportunity to assert herself recently: she'd got out of the habit and had sunk back into the quicksand of coy British politeness.

'You're not very late,' he said, looking her up and down appreciatively. 'Don't worry about it.'

At that moment, with a mixture of relief and regret, she spotted Dorothy, the feisty ex-headmistress. And she raised her hand to greet her.

'See you later, then,' Odin whispered in her ear before disappearing through the double glass doors.

'Is he bothering you, dear?' asked Dorothy, whose dealings with sly and frequently dishonest youth had taught her to read body language from a great distance.

'He's not bothering me,' said Pam, feeling more confident now. 'Everything's fine.'

Sven Larsen's room at the Tower Hotel had yielded nothing of interest. All Wesley and Gerry Heffernan had learned about the man from his possessions was that he had travelled light. A few changes of underwear, a spare set of clothes, a razor and a toothbrush. His room was as neat as his sister's.

'Tidy lot, these Larsens,' commented Heffernan. 'Bet their mum didn't have to nag them to clean their rooms. My kids' bedrooms always made the municipal rubbish tip look like a luxury penthouse.' He winked at Wesley. 'You've got all that to come,' he added smugly.

'How's your Sam doing? Got a job yet?'

'So he says, but he hasn't told me what it is. He said it was public relations, but I reckon he's working behind a bar . . . he didn't get in till the early hours last night. He probably doesn't want his old father turning up expecting free drinks and embarrassing him . . . that'll be why he hasn't confessed.'

'More than likely. Where to now?'

The two policemen left the hotel under the hostile gaze of a young blonde receptionist, who clearly thought that a police presence was lowering the tone of the place, and drove out to Little Barton Farm.

It was a slow journey, as they were forced to crawl along behind a caravan for the first two miles on the main road out of Tradmouth: one of the increasingly familiar perils of the holiday season. Wesley turned onto the narrow, hedge-lined lane leading to the farm and drove carefully, slowing down for blind bends. He still hadn't gained the confidence of local drivers like Rachel, who knew what lay beyond each turn in the road. Gerry Heffernan sat slouched in the passenger seat, a small smile of anticipation on his face.

The police cars had gone. With all the evidence gathered, Stella Tracey would be clearing up her living room. There was no need to disturb her, so they made straight for the old barn and parked outside.

It was a long time before Proudy's door was opened: it was the woman who stood there, uncertain, a hint of apprehension in her eyes.

'Mrs Proudy?'

'Ms Jones, Astrid Jones.' Wesley detected a faint, but barely audible, hint of a European accent.

'We're looking for Laurence Proudy. Is he in?'

'No. He's gone.'

'When will he be back, love?' Heffernan asked.

'He was called back to London on urgent business. Why?'

'Can we come in, love? We're catching our deaths out here,' said Heffernan cheekily.

Astrid looked confused. The temperature was in the seventies. But the tactic worked. She stood aside meekly, and Gerry Heffernan made straight for the living room, looking in each room, making certain that Proudy wasn't lurking behind a closed door. When he looked in the second bedroom something he saw there surprised him.

'Hey, what are you doing?' asked Astrid, indignant.

'It's okay, love. Mr and Mrs Tracey own the place and they don't mind.'

'But I do,' she said. 'You have no right.'

'Three armed men broke into the farmhouse here last night and threatened the family. A lad got hurt. Did you know about it?'

'I saw a lot of police about. I didn't know what had happened.'

Wesley could tell the woman was lying.

'These robberies started just over a fortnight ago . . . just when you and Proudy arrived in the area for a so-called holiday. What made him decide on a holiday down here? I didn't think rural Devon would be his scene.'

'Lol had some business down here . . . some cars he wanted to look at.'

'So you're combining business with a little holiday. That's nice.'

'It was till you started harassing us. I'm going to complain about our treatment,' she said half-heartedly, as if she thought a token protest was expected of her.

'I'm sorry to hear that, Ms Jones. Me and the sergeant here like to promote peace and harmony when we interview suspects, don't we, Sergeant? Make it more like a friendly chat. And we serve a lovely cup of tea down at the station . . . and biscuits. So if you'd like to come with us and make a statement . . .' Gerry Heffernan gave her his most beatific smile, bearing a strong resemblance to a degenerate cherub. 'You see, we've had information that your Lol's involved with these robberies and we'd like to have a little word about what he's been up to down here.'

Astrid Jones began to look uncertain of her ground. 'I told you

111

I don't know anything and Lol went back to London early this morning. Business.'

'And will he be back?'

'I don't know.' She folded her arms, defiant.

'I believe you had an argument with Mr Proudy yesterday. What was it about?' asked Wesley softly.

Astrid's expression changed. She looked from one policeman to the other nervously. 'Nothing much. I thought it was a bit off him going back to London and leaving me here on my own in the middle of nowhere. That's all.'

'How long have you known Proudy, Ms Jones?'

'Only for a few weeks.'

'I see you're not sharing a bedroom,' said Heffernan softly.

'That's none of your business,' retorted Astrid, outraged. She hesitated. 'He snores, if you must know . . . and I like to get a good night's sleep.'

'How did you meet him?'

'I went to get my car fixed at his garage,' she said quickly. 'All this is nothing to do with me . . . really.'

'I think it would be best if you came down to the station to make a statement.'

Astrid fell quiet as Heffernan led the way to the car. When she was safely installed in the back seat, he shut the back door and turned to Wesley. 'Think she'll tell us much?'

'I don't think there was a great deal of loyalty there, sir. And if she's feeling badly done by, we can only hope she might want to get her own back.'

'Hello sir, hi Wes. I thought I saw your car.'

Wesley swung round. Rachel was standing there, her fair hair loose around her shoulders. She wore shorts and a T-shirt. Wesley, used to seeing her dressed smartly for work, hardly recognised her.

'Arresting our guests, are you?'

'We're sure Laurence Proudy's our man. An informant told Steve that a man from London called Lol is involved in the robberies, specialising in disposing of the stolen vehicles. Proudy owns a garage in London, and we suspect he's gone back there.'

Rachel shrugged. 'Can't say it surprises me. Good job he paid for the apartment in advance, isn't it?' She gave Wesley a shy smile.

112

'Is your mum okay?'

'Yes . . . now that Dave's on the mend. See you tomorrow, then.'

'See you tomorrow.' Wesley stood by the car, watching her walk away.

Pam was relieved to find that the long Anglo-Saxon dress she was given fitted nicely over her thin summer clothes. Somehow, the prospect of stripping down to her bra and pants in the cluttered classroom off the hall, imagining lustful watching eyes peering through the small window in the door, didn't appeal to her.

Besides, it looked as though Thor's Hammers used the room too: their costumes and weaponry were heaped up over by the teacher's desk. It was probably the only room that the school – security-conscious as schools were forced to be in this lawless age – was willing to leave unlocked. There was no way she was going to take off a stitch when there was the possibility of Odin bursting in.

She found Odin's obvious interest flattering . . . if slightly disturbing. It was a long time since a man had looked at her like that: she and Wesley, like most couples with a young baby, had settled for the deep peace of domesticity. And she felt a guilty discomfort that the lustful eyes of a fake Viking warrior should conjure such forbidden excitement. It was silly . . . stupid. But it made her feel alive; attractive again after the months of lumpen pregnancy and new motherhood. As long as it stayed light-hearted, it was nothing she couldn't handle.

She forced herself to think of practical matters and picked up the length of fine white cloth which, she had been assured by the artistic-looking lady in charge of the costumes, would serve as her head-dress. She strolled over to the tarnished mirror propped against the wall, draping it over her hair and pulling a thin circlet of braid down to secure it. But the braid kept springing up. Something was needed to keep it in place.

Being a teacher herself, Pam knew the tricks of the trade – where things attractive to young fingers were likely to be hidden. The drawers of a teacher's desk were always crammed with everything from dull drawing pins and sticky tape to thrilling objects of desire confiscated from hapless pupils. All Pam wanted was a hairgrip or a safety pin. She made for the desk, picking her way over helmets, shields and other unrecognisable items of Viking equipment.

She was about to open the top drawer when her foot kicked something large and soft. She looked down. A bright red sports hold-all lay on the ground, the one she had seen Odin guarding earlier. It must have been left partly unzipped, because when her foot had come into contact with it, it had sprung open and the contents now peeped out tantalisingly.

Pam looked around, making sure she was alone, then she bent down and (as she had instructed many a child on school trips) looked with her eyes but not with her fingers. She could see something shiny and wooden. After a few seconds she touched it tentatively, then, her curiosity fully aroused, she pulled the zip back a little. She had not seen a firearm before at such close quarters, and she stared at it in fascination. She pulled the zip back quickly when she heard the door opening, her fingers fumbling, and kicked the hold-all farther under the desk. Then she sprang to her feet and opened the top drawer.

'Just looking for some safety pins,' she called out breathlessly, trying to sound innocently cheerful.

Odin closed the door quietly behind him and walked towards her slowly. She pretended to delve in the drawer, trying not to show her discomfort . . . her fear. She had seen him with the red hold-all. Did the gun belong to him?

She could hear her heart thumping as he drew closer to her. She could smell his aftershave – musky, sensual. Then he touched her cheek gently, his hand moving downwards slowly, brushing her breast. Pam knew that a well-aimed kick to the groin and a calm, efficient exit would be the sensible option. But she froze, wondering how she could regain control of the situation . . . of herself.

His arm crept round her waist like a hungry boa constrictor, tightening, pulling her towards him. 'What are you up to in here, eh?' His voice was heavy with suggestion. He looked down at the hold-all, then his eyes met hers, questioning. Suddenly afraid, she began to pull away, preparing her knee for a sudden upward movement. Then the door opened with a crash.

Chapter Eight

AD 997

*We feared what we would find at the shrine of St Peter at
Tradmouth Head. And we were right to fear. The evil ones had
slaughtered the brother who tends the shrine there and had
used his body so ill and wrought such mutilations upon him
that I shielded Hilda from the sight and I cannot write of the
dreadful things that were done to him in this journal. I dug a
grave and gave our poor innocent brother a Christian burial.
A man from the village of Tradmouth who had come to give
the brother food and sustenance found the body and, when we
came upon him, his wits had departed with the horrors he had
witnessed.*

*I could wring no sense from him but that he had hidden
himself as the evil ones went about their bloody business and
they did not discover him. I asked if he had word of my mother
and father in Stoke Beeching. But he spoke and gibbered like
a madman and would say no more. I fear the worst and take
my comfort from the Lord . . . and Hilda's sweet presence. She
looks upon me with great affection.*

From the chronicle of Brother Edwin

Astrid Jones was a model witness – innocently caught up in the situation and only too willing to help the police. She had met Proudy
when she had taken her car to be mended. He had told her he was
renting an apartment in the Devon countryside and had invited her
down. Then what had begun as a light-hearted affair with a holiday thrown in had developed into something more threatening. He
had acted strangely, secretively. He had left her alone for long peri-

ods at all hours of the day and night. When she had asked he had been evasive at first, then threatening. She knew nothing.

When the interview was over, Astrid expressed a wish to return to London . . . and never to see Lol Proudy again. She wanted to get home . . . forget it ever happened.

They left her with a WPC in the interview room, sipping a cup of unspeakable station coffee, while Gerry Heffernan made a phone call.

After a few minutes the inspector put the receiver down, a smug expression on his face. 'I've spoken to Proudy's local nick in London and they said they'd be delighted to pick him up for us if he turns up back home . . . suspicion of armed robbery.' He thought for a moment. 'Where are Steve and Trish?'

'Don't you remember? I've sent them out to Neston . . . trying to trace Ingeborg Larsen's last movements.'

'So if she was seen on one of these video cameras being bashed over the head by a one-legged, red-haired man with an eye patch and a purple dog we'll know who we're looking for.'

'Something like that,' said Wesley with a sigh. 'Let's hope they come up with something. It's not going to be an easy job trawling through those surveillance videos. Neston's packed with visitors at the moment. Even Pam's gone there this afternoon.'

'What for?'

'It's the final rehearsal for the Viking Festival. She's volunteered to tend the wounded.'

'With any luck she might get rid of some. You know what we could do with round here, Wes?'

'What?'

'A few less Vikings,' the inspector said as he charged the swing-doors in desperate search of a decent cup of tea.

Dorothy Weston, retired headmistress of St Werburgh's High School, looked at the young woman beside her.

'Are you sure you're all right, Pam, dear? Would you rather go home?'

Pam smiled at her. 'Thanks, but I'm absolutely fine. It was nothing I couldn't handle,' she said confidently, jutting out her chin. 'Probably all part of the Viking experience.'

'As long as he doesn't try anything like that with me,' said Dorothy Weston with determination. She began to chuckle. 'But at my age, chance'd be a fine thing. Mind you, he's a handsome

116

devil, isn't he . . . and he did look disappointed when I burst in. If you weren't a married woman, eh?'

Pam smiled weakly, feeling a little foolish. Then she caught Dorothy's eye and the two women, seated on the wooden school bench in their long Anglo-Saxon garb, began to rock with laughter. Odin walked past, his hand resting on his sword, and glanced over at them. Pam's face reddened and she avoided his eyes, praying that he hadn't seen her looking in the hold-all . . . but she couldn't be sure. And even though Odin had appeared to be looking after it, she couldn't be absolutely certain that it was his . . . but she didn't feel inclined to take any chances.

She took a deep breath and made a decision. A man who went around carrying a firearm in a hold-all was potentially dangerous. She should get a message to Wesley. If she could get to a phone now, he might be able to send someone over before the rehearsal finished. 'Do you know if there's a phone round here?' she asked Dorothy.

'There's a pay-phone in the corridor outside. But I noticed it's out of order.'

'Shit,' said Pam under her breath. Dorothy gave her a disapproving look.

'It's like looking for a needle in a bloody haystack.' Steve Carstairs swaggered out of the shoe shop first, leaving Trish Walton to carry the increasingly heavy carrier bag filled with videotapes from the security cameras of the shops lining Neston's busy High Street.

They had omitted the numerous New Age shops – those whose windows were crammed with healing crystals and wholefoods – and concentrated on the more mainstream establishments selling clothes and souvenirs. But the task was still a daunting one. Trish hoped that somewhere, on one of the tapes she carried, Ingeborg Larsen would appear . . . followed or accompanied by her unknown abductor.

Steve led the way into an expensive clothes shop and Trish lingered behind, looking in the window at a particularly mouth-watering dress which would have cost her a week's wages.

'Come on, Trish. Get a bloody move on,' said Steve, bad-tempered. 'I don't know why we're wasting our time on this. It's like looking for a needle in a bloody haystack,' he muttered again, making his point.

*

Pam wasn't the only one who was trying to contact Wesley Peterson. Neil Watson put his mobile back in the pocket of his jeans. Detective Sergeant Peterson was unavailable, the voice on the other end of the line had said. Could someone else help? Neil hadn't answered and had hung up in disgust. If Wesley couldn't come with him to Longhouse Cottage, he would go alone.

He looked at his watch. Time to pack up for the day. He glanced across at Matt squatting at the far end of the extended trench, scraping at a section of blackened stone wall with his trowel. Jane stood at the edge of the trench with a clipboard, drawing earnestly. The trench had been enlarged that morning, and the layout of the Saxon foundations could now be seen more clearly.

'I'm going over to that place where we found the skeleton,' said Neil. Matt looked up and nodded. 'I've had a call from the lad who lives there. He says he's found something else. If Wesley rings, tell him where I've gone, will you?'

A lady of the parish who was arranging flowers near the church porch looked across disapprovingly. It was enough that the life of the church had to be disrupted by the excavation of the floor, without the soil-stained young diggers shouting to each other across the echoing building.

'Okay, Neil. Will do.' Matt held up a large piece of pottery for Jane's inspection. She took it from him and put it in a plastic finds tray, her hand touching his for slightly longer than was necessary.

Neil gave the flower lady a brisk smile that was not returned as he left the church.

Carl Palister had rung him an hour before to say he'd found something else in the lower field, and Neil found it hard to contain his curiosity. He drove his Mini towards Tradmouth, cursing the dawdling holiday traffic, and turned right onto the road to Stoke Beeching.

Maggie Palister heard Neil's struggling engine approaching. She stood by the window, chewing her nails. 'What the hell's he doing here?'

Carl looked up from his copy of the *Sun*. 'Who?'

'That bloody archaeologist . . . he's coming up the drive.'

'Good. I asked him to come over.'

Maggie rounded on him, her eyes blazing. 'You stupid little bugger. You're as daft as one of your bloody sheep. Get rid of him.'

'I wanted to show him these coins I've found,' said Carl, pleading, indignant.

'Get rid of him. Just show him the coins and get rid of him. And don't bring him in here. Right?' Carl sat staring at his mother, defiant. 'Well, go on . . . get out there before he knocks on the bloody door. Keep him away from the house. Go on.'

Reluctantly Carl pushed his newspaper aside and stood up. He collected the plastic box containing the shards of pottery he'd dug up and the coins he'd found with the help of the metal detector borrowed from a mate in the pub, and hurried outside.

Maggie Palister wiped her hands on her skirt. They felt sweaty, tingling: perhaps it was her nerves. She listened. She could hear Carl talking outside, his voice excited, showing off his finds. She listened again. There was no sound from upstairs. It was safe.

She lifted the edge of the threadbare rug near the great inglenook fireplace and felt for the tiny hole in the floorboard. It was her secret . . . only she knew about the secret place; the stone-lined space beneath the floor, a hiding place built into the ancient foundations. The board came up smoothly and she took the tin box out and opened it. The money was still there.

She heard a small furtive sound behind her and held her breath, hurriedly replacing the tin and flicking the rug back. She knelt there, pretending to search for some small thing lost on the faded, patterned pile. Her heart beat faster as hostile eyes watched her, and she hoped desperately that her act was being convincing.

Then she heard the door close. She was alone again. Maggie sat back and took a deep breath. She couldn't keep this up for much longer.

A few minutes later Carl burst in with the bubbling enthusiasm of one half his age. 'He said they were worth a bit, Mum. He said the coins were the same age as that other one. And the pottery's Anglo-Saxon, he said. And he said that long thing I found was a stylus, a sort of pen . . . and he said they were usually only found in monasteries. He told me to keep 'em safe.'

'He's not coming back, is he?'

'He said he would.'

Maggie Palister turned on her son, exasperated. 'You're a bloody idiot, Carl. His mate's a bloody detective sergeant . . .'

'I never brought him in the house. I wasn't that daft.'

Maggie shook her head, despairing of Carl's naïve confidence. 'Just keep him out of here, that's all.'

'So I shouldn't call the police, then?'

'What?' She looked up at him, wide-eyed with disbelief.

119

'That car they were interested in . . . the black one. The one that might belong to that prowler up at Waters House. It's there again with someone sitting in it and Neil's mate said to ring if I saw it . . .' He drew the card Wesley had given him out of the pocket of his shorts.

Maggie grabbed the card and tore it in half. 'Leave it, Carl. Just leave it.'

'But he said it might be that prowler . . .'

'It's none of our business, Carl. Just leave it.' Her voice was hoarse with emotion.

'Okay, Mum,' said Carl, touching her thin shoulder gently.

Wesley had tried his home number several times, but there was no answer. He wondered fleetingly what went on at these Viking re-enactments.

The telephone on his desk emitted a series of electronic squeals and he picked it up with a sigh of resignation. More crime. More work. Somewhere at the other end of the office he could hear Gerry Heffernan singing softly but melodiously as he sorted through a pile of forensic reports that had just come in: 'A policeman's lot is not a happy one,' he crooned appropriately.

'Wes? Is that you?' Pam's voice on the other end of the line sounded breathless and urgent. 'I've only just got home. I tried to get to a phone before but I couldn't.'

'What is it?' Something was wrong. He could tell.

'I went to the rehearsal today and I accidentally opened this hold-all . . . and there was something that looked like a gun inside but I didn't get a proper look. It was just in the room where we changed, pushed under a desk.'

'Who did it belong to? Do you know?'

'I can't be sure.' She wondered whether she should mention Odin. She had assumed that the hold-all was his . . . but she had no real proof. Besides, she felt foolish when she thought of him. There were some things it was best not to tell your husband.

But, she told herself, if Odin did own the hold-all, why should she shield him? She owed him no loyalty; she owed him nothing. 'The leader of the Viking group came in and I just had the impression . . . But it could have belonged to anybody.' She tried to imagine Odin threatening someone with a sawn-off shotgun – those cold blue eyes in that handsome face watching a terrified victim – and, reluctantly, she succeeded.

'What's this man's name?'

'He calls himself Odin but I assume that's not his real name. I tried to ring you from the school but the phone was out of order. He went off in his car at the end of the session . . . a big four-wheel-drive.'

'Did you get the number?'

Pam hesitated. 'Er, yes.' She had written the number down in the back of her diary, taking care that nobody saw her do it. Suddenly she felt a pang of awkward guilt.

'Well done. What is it?' Pam recited the number; it was too late to back out now. Wesley tapped the registration number into the computer on his desk. 'Did he take the hold-all with him?' he asked, hoping the answer was no.

'Well, it was gone when I looked.'

'Does this Odin have a local accent, by any chance?'

'No. Slight London if anything.'

Wesley thought for a while. Rachel had said the man who spoke was local. Proudy was Yorkshire; this one from London. How many of them were there? Perhaps armed robbery was becoming a summer pastime like barbecues or cricket.

He glanced over at Gerry Heffernan, who had just answered the telephone on Rachel's desk. He watched as his boss's face lit up with excitement. 'Wes,' Heffernan called across cheerfully. 'Come over here. Quick.'

Wesley said goodbye to his wife, impressed by her contribution to the fight against crime. There were times, he thought guiltily, when he underestimated Pam . . . when he took her for granted.

He joined Gerry Heffernan, who was grinning widely as he always did when a breakthrough was imminent.

'They've got Proudy,' he announced, excitedly. 'Couple of our lads out on patrol spotted his car and pulled him up in Morbay. He hadn't gone back up to London after all. He probably told his lady friend that to get her off his back. Anyway, the Morbay lads have found the lock-up. And two stolen Range Rovers and six quad bikes. He was giving the Range Rovers new number plates and logbooks and selling them on to a London dealer he knows. He's passed a couple on already.'

'What about the rest of the gang?'

'He's not telling. He said he just did the driving and disposed of the stolen vehicles. He doesn't know anything about the guns or the other stuff they nicked. That's his story and he's sticking to it.'

121

Wesley told his boss about Pam's phone call and Heffernan rubbed his hands together with glee. 'We've got 'em, Wes. Shall we pull this Odin in and ask him a few questions?'

'According to the computer his car's registered in the name of Cecil Mitchelson. No wonder he calls himself Odin. His address is in London and he's got no criminal record. Trouble is we don't know where he's staying round here.' Wesley smiled. 'But if we turn up at the Viking Festival tomorrow he'll be there . . . leading his merry band of Vikings.'

'Nice one, Wesley.' Heffernan gave his sergeant a hearty slap on the back. 'Here.' He thrust a sheet of paper into Wesley's hand. 'This forensic report's just come in. Have a look at that, will you. Unidentified fingerprints on Dan Wexer's Land Rover . . . won't be unidentified for long, eh?' He chuckled. 'And two of Proudy's prints on the barrel of the gun they abandoned at Little Barton Farm. No other prints, though. It's my guess that the others wore gloves but Proudy handled the gun at some time and forgot to wipe his prints off. Silly mistake . . . but where would we be if the criminals all used their brains, eh?'

The office doors swung open and Trish Walton staggered in carrying a couple of heavy carrier bags, looking as though she'd just spent a fortune in the local supermarket. Steve followed sulkily behind, like a man forced to accompany his wife on a shopping trip.

Trish deposited the bags on her desk and flexed her arms. 'We visited all the likely shops and we've got most of the surveillance videos for Monday. There were a few who'd already recorded over them but . . .'

'Well done,' said Wesley. 'Did you speak to anyone who remembered Ingeborg?'

'No. They said Monday was a busy day . . . lots of holidaymakers about. Nobody remembered seeing her. Sorry,' she added, as if Neston's collective failure of memory had been her fault.

'Well, tomorrow you can start looking through them. If she was shopping in Neston it's my bet she'll appear on them somewhere.'

Gerry Heffernan noticed Steve glowering in the background. 'And you can give her a hand and all, Detective Constable Carstairs. They may not be pornographic videos, but concentrate on them as though they are, will you?' Steve shuffled his feet moodily as Trish stifled a smirk.

The inspector looked at his watch. It was five o'clock. 'I'm going over to Morbay to have a word with Proudy before choir practice.'

Wesley remembered it was Friday night: the night when Gerry Heffernan exercised his voice in preparation for Sunday morning's service at St Margaret's. 'Do you want me to come with you?'

'No, Wes. You go and interrogate your wife . . . there might be something else she remembers. And tell her I'm looking forward to seeing her doing a spot of pillaging tomorrow.'

'I'll tell her,' said Wesley as he prepared to head for home.

Laurence Proudy was co-operation itself. He knew when he was beaten. But for all his anxiety to confess his part in the farm robberies, he still refused to name his accomplices. He was no grass, he kept assuring the officers present, before he entered his cell in the bowels of Morbay police station with the same reluctant resignation as a schoolboy enters a classroom for a maths lesson. And he hadn't seen Ingeborg Larsen since she had bumped into his car. He swore that on his mother's life, his grandmother's life, and anybody else's life he could think of. There was no way he had anything to do with her disappearance.

Gerry Heffernan heard all this but said nothing. He would see what progress they made with the elusive Odin before he questioned Proudy further . . . if, indeed, Odin was the owner of the red hold-all: there was always the chance that it belonged to someone else entirely.

He arrived back at his whitewashed cottage at the end of Baynard's Quay at seven o'clock, his stomach rumbling with hunger, longing for the fish and chips that lay wrapped in newspaper in his hands, the tempting aroma wafting up to his nostrils.

Sam answered the door with a sheepish expression on his face, and hungrily accepted his father's offer of a chip, explaining that he'd already heated a pizza from the freezer but, in the way of the young, was still starving.

Even after almost four years, certain things – like a lonely father and son sharing takeaway food – brought memories back, raw and painful. And for a few seconds, Gerry Heffernan felt the acute pain of his wife Kathy's death. There were times when he was glad that he led a busy life, when he was almost grateful for a little criminal activity to take his mind off his loss.

'I'm off out to choir practice,' he said to Sam, who was sitting with his feet up watching *Coronation Street* intently. 'Will you be in when I get back?'

'No, Dad, I'm . . . er, out later. Work,' Sam replied evasively, before returning his attention to the latest goings on at the Rover's Return.

Heffernan didn't enquire further. No doubt Sam would feel the urge to enlighten him about this mysterious new job in due course.

He closed the front door behind him and walked out onto the busy, cobbled quayside, still teeming with holidaymakers and their offspring. And he paused for a moment, looking out at the river, watching the boats scuttling to and fro on the glittering water.

One particular boat caught his eye. It stood out clearly, painted in immaculate blue and white. The police launch chugged purposefully along, towing something behind. Heffernan shielded his eyes from the lowering sun and stared. But it was too far away to see clearly.

He began to run, weaving in and out of the strolling tourists. And by the time he reached the passenger ferry he was breathless, pausing, bent double, on the pavement as passers-by stared. When he had recovered a little he trotted at a more sedate pace down the stone steps and onto the long wooden jetty towards the police launch's habitual mooring.

The officer on the deck looked up. 'Hello, sir. Wasn't expecting to see CID here for a while.' He glanced at the thing bobbing behind the launch. 'As you can see, we've found the dinghy. The coastguard reported it floating out to sea about a mile off Bloxham . . . must have drifted. Jim's confirmed it's the one that went missing from that burned-out yacht. I suppose you'll want Forensic to give it a going-over.'

'Do you think they'll find anything?' Gerry Heffernan stared at the grey inflatable dinghy, willing it to give up its secrets.

'I reckon there's a smear of blood just next to the outboard motor. But only time will tell,' said the officer philosophically. 'And there's no sign of a body. Nothing's been washed up anywhere that we know of.'

Gerry Heffernan was late for choir practice that evening; and when he finally arrived in the ancient oak choir stalls of St Margaret's church, he found himself concentrating on a small grey inflatable dinghy adrift in the English Channel rather than the music in front of him. The resulting harmonies were worthy of some discordant avant-garde composer . . . hardly a fitting requiem for Sven Larsen.

Chapter Nine

AD 997

From the cliff top we could see the boats of the evil ones sailing out to sea. They were most fearsome and their carved prows reared from the water like monsters of the deep. They went away round the coast to bring more destruction on our land. Hilda and I watched them. We lay down so that we were not seen. She was so near and I could feel the warmth of her body. I know that many of my brothers at Neston married discreetly and their wives bore children. But I never knew a woman.

As I lay beside Hilda I touched her. Then she raised her face to mine and looked at me with such love. She said she adored me . . . that she would be mine always. I kissed her. I never knew such sweetness before. We are but a short way from Stoke Beeching. How I fear what we shall find at the house of my mother and father. Hilda's company gives me comfort . . . yet I fight my desire for her.

> *From the chronicle of Brother Edwin*

Of all the things Gerry Heffernan found deeply offensive, alarm clocks were at the top of his list. He hated the things, shouting their rude interruptions to well-earned rest. He reached across his bedside table and knocked the clock onto the floor. It gave a disgruntled squeak but carried on ringing. It wasn't going to give in that easily.

The house was silent as he staggered down the stairs. When Sam had returned home late the previous night he had made straight for his room. Presumably he was still asleep after the night's exertions. Heffernan stumbled his way into the living room and picked up Sam's coat, which lay discarded on the floor. As he lifted it, a clump of brightly coloured streamers fluttered to the ground. Wherever Sam had been last night, someone had had a good time.

He left the house quietly, shutting the front door carefully behind him. No doubt Sam would tell him in his own good time what he got up to at nights . . . but he wasn't holding his breath.

When he arrived at the police station he found that Wesley was already at his desk, tackling his paperwork. Rachel sat near by, quiet and self-contained, tapping at her computer keyboard.

'They've found the dinghy belonging to Sven Larsen's boat. It was drifting out to sea,' Heffernan announced loudly as he entered the office. He glanced across at the photograph of Ingeborg Larsen that was pinned to the wall, fearing that her brother's would soon join it, then he turned to Rachel. 'How's your Dave, then?'

'Much better, thanks. They're not going to keep him in much longer,' she said quietly.

'Going to have him back at your farm, then? Give him a bit of tender loving care?'

To Heffernan's astonishment, Rachel stood up and swept out of the room. He turned to Wesley. 'What have I said?'

'I think she's going through a bit of a crisis,' Wesley answered, his voice lowered.

'That's not like our Rach.' Heffernan shrugged. 'Where are Steve and Trish?'

'Watching videos,' said Wesley. 'Let's hope that Steve hasn't substituted something more spicy for the surveillance videos.'

'I wouldn't put it past him. All ready for this afternoon? The Viking raid on Neston?'

'I wouldn't miss it for the world. Pam's ready to point this Odin out. I asked her last night if she knew anything more about this group, Thor's Hammers, and she said they did some re-enactments in Sussex around Easter time. I rang the Sussex police first thing and they told me there were some similar raids on farms at the time Thor's Hammers were there. Nobody hurt but a lot of valuables and vehicles taken.'

'Well, I think that confirms our little theory. Well done, Wes. Looks like we've found a link. And I've sweet-talked the Super into giving us extra back-up for the festival.'

Wesley smiled. 'How did you do that?'

The inspector tapped the side of his nose. 'I used my charms.' He winked. 'Then when these robbers are enjoying the custody sergeant's lavish hospitality, we can concentrate on finding Ingeborg Larsen . . . wherever she is.' His face clouded. 'Do you think her brother's disappearance has anything to do with hers? Or do you think he's just had some sort of accident? Any ideas?' he asked anxiously. Wesley suspected the question had been preying on Heffernan's mind.

'We won't know until Sven Larsen's found, will we? You seem to think he's dead.'

'I thought he'd got away from the boat in the dinghy but it was found drifting out to sea. And there's a bloodstain near the outboard motor. It doesn't look good, Wes.' Heffernan shook his head, clearly worried.

Rachel walked slowly in through the office door. There were dark rings beneath her eyes: she hadn't slept. She approached Wesley's desk, giving him a weak smile. 'I believe Trish suggested we have another look through Ingeborg Larsen's things. Do you fancy coming up to Newpen Road?'

Wesley nodded. 'Good idea. We've some time to kill before the Neston Festival. Come on.' He stood up and grabbed the jacket from the back of his chair.

Rachel was quiet as they walked through the streets of Tradmouth. The seagulls wheeled overhead, emitting raucous cries as they climbed the steep street up to Newpen Road, with a precipitous drop down to the river on one side and a row of genteel whitewashed houses, the kind once owned by respectable sea captains, on the other. Wesley paused, enjoying the view. The boats scurried below them like pond-skating insects, and the buildings of the hill-hung town of Queenswear on the opposite bank of the river gleamed in the sunshine.

'Nice view,' said Rachel quietly.

'Is something the matter, Rach?' He decided on the direct approach.

She leaned on the low wall and stared out across the river. It was a while before she spoke. 'It's Dave. I feel pressured, Wesley. I'm not ready for anything serious.'

'Is there any reason why you should be?'

She shook her head. 'It's my mother. She's dropping hints ... pushing us together all the time, piling on the pressure.'

'That's mothers for you. I had the same problem once. My mother decided that a girl who went to our church was the one for me. She was training to be a solicitor and her parents came from Trinidad like my parents, so they kept pushing us together. She was a nice girl and I did like her ... but I can't say it was true love. Then I met Pam at university and ...'

'But they didn't move the girl into your house, did they? At least you got away to university. I feel the whole thing's out of my control ... I feel that any moment my mother will be buying me a wedding dress and marching me up the aisle with a shotgun at my head.'

Wesley smiled to himself. It wasn't like Rachel to be so melodramatic.

'Why don't you just tell her?'

'Did you tell your mother?' she asked challengingly.

'No. Sheer cowardice on my part, I'm afraid. Look, Rachel, don't let it get to you. If you're not ready for commitment, you say so.' It amused Wesley to think of the cool, self-sufficient Rachel feeling like a frustrated teenager locked in a battle of wills with her mother. But, he thought philosophically, to one's mother one is always ten years old and in need of advice and control. But at least, unlike others, mothers mean well.

'Yeah, you're right. I'm making too much of it ... letting it get to me. It's all the strain of the robbery and ...' She leaned across and gave him a quick kiss on the cheek. 'Thanks, Wes.'

He looked at her, certain he could detect tears in her eyes. 'Come on. Let's go and have a word with Mrs Questid.'

When Barbara Questid answered her front door, she looked a little flustered. 'I'm afraid I've had to let Ms Larsen's room,' she babbled apologetically. 'I really didn't have any option. It's the height of the season and I couldn't afford to turn people away with one of my best rooms standing empty.' She stood there, her arms folded as if to make her point.

'That's all right, Mrs Questid,' said Wesley comfortingly. 'What have you done with Mrs Larsen's things?'

'They're quite safe. I packed everything away in her suitcases and put them in the cupboard under the stairs. I don't suppose there's any word . . .'

'I'm afraid not. Sorry. Has her brother been in touch with you at all?'

'Her brother? No. Should he have been?' She looked worried, fearing some dreadful omission had been made on her part.

'No, not necessarily. If we could just have another look through her things . . .'

Barbara Questid led them to the stairs and opened the cupboard door. A couple of expensive-looking suitcases stood there inside the immaculately clean cubby-hole, side by side.

Wesley took the larger case out and opened it carefully. Barbara Questid had packed it well, folding each garment with professional neatness. He sighed and looked at Rachel. There was probably nothing here that could tell them anything they didn't know already.

'What exactly are we looking for, Wesley?'

He shrugged. 'I don't know. Something . . . anything we missed the first time we looked.'

He began to unpack the case, placing the clothes in a neat pile on the floor. He came to a snowy-white jacket, swathed in thin clingy polythene, and picked it up carefully by its wire hanger. 'Look at this.' He located the pink ticket and examined it. 'Pilington's Cleaners. That's in Market Street, isn't it?'

Rachel nodded. 'If she wore white jackets that need dry cleaning, what could she expect? Must have cost her a fortune,' she said censoriously. Wesley suspected that Rachel would never be caught doing anything so extravagantly impractical.

'I think we should pay a visit to Pilington's to see if anyone remembers her. She might have been with someone . . . or mentioned something to the staff. It's unlikely, I know, but . . .'

Rachel shrugged, unconvinced by the idea. She looked at her watch. 'Have we got time?'

'We'll have to get over to Neston soon, so I suppose it can wait.' Wesley placed the dry-cleaning ticket in a plastic bag and put it in his pocket. It was a long shot but, he thought, it was worth a try. He checked his watch again. 'We'd better think about grabbing something to eat. Pam's making her debut at one-thirty . . . can't miss that, can I?'

Rachel smiled weakly as she helped Wesley to pack Ingeborg

Larsen's worldly possessions back into the suitcases, wishing that there was some way she could avoid visiting the Neston Viking Festival that afternoon.

Neil Watson was looking forward to the Neston Festival ... looking forward to noting Thor's Hammers' appalling historical inaccuracies. He toyed with the idea of ringing Wesley to see if he was free that lunch-time. But, he reckoned, the chances of his friend being able to get away were slim, given the crime wave that seemed to have engulfed the district in recent weeks.

After buying himself a humble cheese sandwich from the busy supermarket in the middle of Tradmouth, he decided that he had just enough time for a swift visit to the Peacock Museum. Perhaps Bate-Brownlowe had managed to dig out some more information on the finds at Longhouse Cottage.

He found the curator sitting outside the museum on a rickety wooden chair, enjoying the sunshine, a flask of coffee at his feet. He stood up when he saw Neil approaching.

'Lovely day. You've not brought your friend with you this time?' He looked anxious, as though Neil were some sort of inspector come to report on the museum's shortcomings.

'He's busy. Crime wave,' Neil said simply. 'I don't suppose you've found out anything else about the finds from Longhouse Cottage?'

'I'm sorry. I've been busy cataloguing the natural history collection. But you're welcome to take a look at Jeremiah Peacock's old catalogue, if you like. There might be something else in there,' the curator said, anxious to please. He led Neil inside and pulled the massive volume from the cupboard before excusing himself. He had a collection of birds' eggs to remount.

Neil flicked through the book, glad that Jeremiah Peacock's copperplate handwriting was legible. Peacock had been an avid and eclectic collector. Natural history had been his main passion, with a smattering of foreign and local history around the edges, as it were. He had obviously predicted the imminent obsolescence of much of the equipment used on the district's farms in the last century, and had collected seed drills, butter churns and horse-drawn ploughs as if they were going out of fashion. Neil turned the pages, scanning them for anything archaeological or anything remotely connected with Longhouse Cottage.

But, he had to admit, the entries in old Jeremiah's catalogue were remarkably dull. There were some Roman coins and a few shards of medieval pottery, but nothing that Neil would describe as exciting.

Until he came to the next-to-last page.

Wesley dropped Rachel outside the police station and rushed into the nearest sandwich shop in search of lunch before his trip to Neston. Coming out with his prize, chicken tikka on rye bread, he put his change into his pocket and his hand came into contact with a plastic bag. He pulled it out, and the pink dry-cleaning ticket sat there between his fingers, challenging.

As he had half an hour spare, he would get the visit to Pilington's over with . . . not that he really expected it to be productive.

He made for Market Street, no great distance away, where he found the dry cleaner's empty of customers, and the woman behind the counter staring at him with undisguised curiosity. Wesley guessed she was about fifty, but she might have been younger . . . or older. She was a big, strong-looking woman with dull brown hair, peppered with grey, which framed a plain, doughy face with a tiny button of a nose. She had the careworn look of one who had worked hard most of her life for little reward.

'Can I help you?' she asked, pulling down the sleeves of her thin blue nylon overall defensively.

Wesley produced his warrant card and the woman fidgeted, avoiding his eyes. Then he placed the bag containing the pink ticket on the counter in front of her.

'A lady called Ingeborg Larsen brought a white jacket in here for cleaning.' He produced the photograph of Ingeborg he had carried around in his inside pocket since the investigation began and laid it beside the ticket. 'Do you recognise her?'

The woman glanced at the photograph for a second then shook her head. 'So many people come in here. I can't remember them all, can I? And if she wasn't a regular . . .'

'So you don't remember her?'

The woman obviously found it hard to utter a blatant lie. 'Well, I remember her vaguely . . . but she just came in and went out, I never talked to her. Why?'

'She's gone missing and we're looking for her.' Wesley gave a

131

quick, businesslike smile. 'Sorry to have bothered you, er . . . Mrs . . .'

'Tensby. Sorry I couldn't be more help . . . but as I said, we get a lot of people in here.' Wesley could detect relief in her voice.

When he was halfway down the road, taking a bite from his sandwich, Mrs Tensby went into the back of the shop and picked up the telephone.

Neston was filling up nicely. The steep narrow High Street, now closed to cars, thronged with colourfully dressed citizens and summer visitors. Children, tetchy in the summer heat, were appeased with ice creams and brightly coloured helium balloons which bobbed above their heads. Barriers had been erected at the sides of the High Street, and there was a carnival atmosphere as people stood around expectantly, chattering loudly and cheering everything that moved down the centre of the road. Wesley Peterson and his boss stood on the expanse of grass in front of the ancient parish church, which stood back from the rest of the street. Wesley watched the church porch in the hope of spotting Neil and his colleagues, but there wasn't an archaeologist in sight.

'Where do we start?' asked Gerry Heffernan, as he narrowly avoided an assault with a loaded ice cream held by a small boy standing to his right.

'The parade starts by the river then comes up the High Street, past the castle, and ends up on the school playing fields for the battle re-enactment.' Wesley looked at the printed programme in his hand. 'It all seems well organised.'

Heffernan looked round at the large police presence, officers in uniform standing chatting awkwardly in the heat, not quite knowing what to do. 'So where do you suggest we put this lot, Wes?'

'I'd keep a few uniforms here and get the rest up to the school playing fields.'

The inspector nodded and pushed his way through the crowd towards the uniformed sergeant who would relay his orders. To Wesley's surprise he returned with two large ice creams. 'Well, we're undercover, aren't we?' he said by way of an excuse as he took his first lick.

Then Wesley heard the strains of the approaching band. First a deep rhythmical drumbeat, then distant brass turning out a barely audible tune. The parade was on its way. The crowd quietened, straining to hear; screaming children were shushed by their mothers. All eyes turned downhill towards the river.

The first thing to appear was the band, puffing solemnly on their instruments, marching in their ill-fitting uniforms and setting feet tapping on the dusty pavements. Then came the boat. A longboat replica on wheels, towed by a local agricultural feed merchant's newly polished lorry. The vessel trundled along proudly, its great square sail raised, the tall carving of the fearsome dragon on the prow glowering threateningly down on the crowd.

The Vikings stood on the boat in their gleaming helmets, waving their swords and shields at the bystanders in an inappropriately friendly manner, raising a hearty cheer. Their predecessors, a thousand years before, would not have been granted such a welcome, Wesley thought as he scanned the smiling faces on the boat, wondering which one was Odin. To Wesley, they all looked pretty harmless . . . but then appearances often deceived.

More Vikings marched behind, waving cheerfully. Then came a large and motley group of townspeople in Viking and Anglo-Saxon dress. He spotted Pam among them, marching next to a formidable-looking elderly lady, and nudged Gerry Heffernan.

'There she is,' the inspector cried, waving what was left of his ice cream. 'Oi, Pam. See you later,' he shouted, causing people to turn and stare. Pam, looking demure in her pale blue homespun gown and white veil, waved at them with a smile of relief.

The spectators fell in behind the parade. It seemed as if the entire population of Neston was marching on past the castle towards the school playing fields. Wesley and Heffernan allowed themselves to be swept along with the crowd.

Wesley wondered if the burghers of Neston had noticed the increased police presence on the playing fields. Normally the event would have been policed by a handful of smiling community constables, but today it looked as if they were expecting a heated demonstration at least, possibly a minor riot. Tents and marquees had been erected on the far side of the field for the use of those taking part, and strangely dressed figures scurried in and out, preparing for their big entrance. But Pam was nowhere to be seen.

The announcement over the public address system was loud but indecipherable. As the distorted words boomed out across the parched field, the Vikings emerged from the smaller marquee, brandishing their swords murderously. The other participants, Pam included, emerged from the tents and stood about the edge of the field, watching.

Wesley had to admit that the battle itself was impressive. He looked around as the swords and axes crashed on the shields, searching the crowd for Neil. Surely he wouldn't be missing this, if only to scoff. Neil was nowhere in sight, but Wesley spotted Rachel pushing her way towards them through the crowd, her face serious and determined. When she finally reached them she stood silently by Heffernan's side.

The fighting was reaching its climax. Bodies lay about the field, gory with scarlet stage blood, as Pam and her colleagues ran on to tend to the wounded. Pam looked as though she was enjoying herself . . . and not taking the proceedings too seriously.

'Which one's this Odin, then?' asked Heffernan.

'Pam said she'd point him out.'

As if on cue, Pam scanned the sea of faces and caught her husband's eye. The fighting was down to two men, the rest having been dispatched or retired wounded. The combat now seemed somewhat more professional as the last two warriors engaged in a fake duel to the death.

Wounded Vikings propped themselves up on their elbows to watch as sword thudded against shield.

'How come they don't cut each other to pieces?' asked Gerry Heffernan rhetorically as he watched the battle, his attention, like everyone else's, focused on the two combatants.

But Wesley was looking at Pam. The two battling Vikings parted for a moment, preparing for a second deadly meeting. Pam pointed at the nearest and mouthed 'Odin'. Wesley nudged his boss. 'That's Odin . . . the fair-haired one fighting. That's him.'

But Gerry Heffernan wasn't listening. Something else had caught his eye. Near the two fighters some wounded Vikings had stood up and moved back, so as not to get in the way of the main attraction. One man who stood there, stocky with a beard, looked unsettlingly familiar, and Heffernan stared, growing more and more certain that he wasn't mistaken.

'Wesley,' he whispered urgently in his sergeant's ear. 'I think I've just seen a ghost.'

*

It was over. Odin was the victor, receiving the crowd's applause and standing triumphant, his great sword raised. The other Vikings, now miraculously revived, milled around, not to be left out. Aggression had given way to cheerful banter as the costumed participants began to mingle with the crowd. The band struck up again, and the many stalls dotted around the edge of the field opened for business as the public began to wander onto the battlefield.

Pam strolled around looking for Wesley but, in the press of people, he was nowhere to be seen. No doubt he was discreetly arresting Odin, she thought with mixed emotions. It would probably be best if she wasn't there when it happened.

She decided to look for Dorothy. With Wesley busy, they could go round the stalls together. She searched in the crowded marquees first, with no luck. Then she came to the smaller tent where the clothes and equipment were stored. Dorothy had mentioned that she might get changed before enjoying the dubious pleasures of the Neston Festival. Pam raised the flap of thick cream canvas and stepped inside, calling Dorothy's name softly. But the tent was empty. Clothes and bags were strewn every-where. Pam looked at the pile of hold-alls belonging to Thor's Hammers that lay on the floor: the red one that had contained the gun was there, near the top. Pam would have recognised it anywhere.

The flap of the tent opened and she gasped involuntarily. Odin stepped into the tent, his eyes on hers. He was dishevelled after his long fight, his clothes soiled and his skin glistening with sweat. She stood quite still as he walked towards her slowly, an accusing half-smile on his lips.

'I've been looking for you,' he said softly as Pam took a step back.

Chapter Ten

AD 997

*I write now for my eyes alone. In the days when I wrote the
Minster chronicle I wrote for all in our house, but now I set
out thoughts that I should not wish others to know.
Concerning Hilda, last night, in a barn preserved by some
great miracle from the fire of the Danes, we spent the night
and I had knowledge of her. To lie beside her and then enter
her warm body was the sweetest moment in my life. Hilda is a
creature of such beauty and of such devoted nature and I
thank the Lord that he has left me by His grace something
good and lovely after all the evil we have witnessed. And she
clung to me, saying that she loved me with the love we must
reserve for our Maker. I told her she should not say such
things; that I am merely a man like any other. But it may be
that I should not scold her: it may be I am truly blessed by her
great love.*

*If the church at Stoke Beeching has been spared we will ask
the priest to marry us there. But I have heard word of much
destruction from those we have met on the road and I pray
that the church has been left standing. We will come to Stoke
Beeching tomorrow. We pray earnestly that all will be well
when we arrive. I have had no word of my mother and father.*

From the chronicle of Brother Edwin

'Where are you going, sir? Shouldn't we be looking for Odin?'

'All in good time, Wes. I'm sure he went this way,' Gerry
Heffernan muttered as he pushed through the crowd.

Wesley looked round, wondering if Rachel had followed them.

But she wasn't there. 'I wish you'd tell me what's going on,' he said, exasperated. 'I think we should have a word with Pam before we . . .'

'Hang on, Wes. There he is. He's with another bloke . . . big chap, see?' Heffernan spotted his quarry and watched him like a deerstalker, weaving in and out of the throng, never taking his eyes off his prey. 'Get on your radio, will you,' he whispered. 'Say we need some back-up here.'

Wesley took his radio from his pocket. As he did so, the bearded man turned round and his eyes met Heffernan's with horrified recognition. Then he began to run. His companion saw what was happening and did likewise. Soon they were lost in the press of people.

Heffernan emitted a string of colourful expletives which made some around him tut in disgust. 'I'm getting on to the Super . . . get a search warrant organised. At least I can guess where he'll be heading,' he said to Wesley with a sly grin.

'Where?' Wesley, who had expecting to be questioning Odin, still felt somewhat confused.

'Longhouse Cottage. Maggie Palister's been acting a bit strange every time a policeman hoves into view. Now I know why. Can you organise someone to bring in this Odin character?'

'So who is it we're after exactly? Who's that man with the beard?'

'Jock Palister, of course. You were right about that skeleton all along,' said Heffernan with a regretful grin.

Odin stepped towards Pam, slowly, his eyes on hers. She pulled herself up to her full height.

'What do you want?' she asked, casually. To her surprise she felt calm, completely in control. Any attraction she had felt for this man had now disappeared. The moment of flattery, of madness, had long passed. But then she asked herself why she felt so calm. In all probability this man was an armed robber, and it was likely that he had expectations of their tenuous relationship which she had no intention of fulfilling. She suddenly felt an over-whelming wave of cowardice, but tried hard to fight it.

'I just wanted to talk.'

'What about?'

He took another step forward. 'I just wanted to . . .'

'Look,' she said, taking a deep breath, 'I've arranged to meet . . .'

At that point a bearded man in full Viking regalia exploded into the tent. He saw Pam and hesitated. Then he grabbed the red hold-all that had contained the gun. He heaved it off the pile, causing the other bags to tumble onto the ground in an untidy heap, and pushed past, bashing Pam's legs with his heavy burden. He ran from the tent, breathless; a man in a hurry.

'Steady on,' Odin shouted after him. 'You've knocked all these bags down. Hey, Jock, come back . . .' Odin stood there helpless, his authority as the Viking leader diminishing by the second.

'That red hold-all,' said Pam tentatively. 'Was it yours?'

Odin looked at Pam, deflated; the sexual desire that had beamed so clearly from his blue eyes before replaced by uncertainty.

Pam sensed the change. 'Well?' she prompted in the voice she used to interrogate naughty pupils. 'Was it yours?'

'No. It's his . . . Jock's. Why?' Odin sounded genuinely puzzled. Either he was an extremely good actor or he was telling the truth.

'No reason.' Pam had the uncomfortable feeling that she'd made an embarrassing mistake. 'Now what did you want to talk to me about?'

'Oh, it's, er . . . I just wanted to apologise for the other day in the changing room. I was out of order. And if you've forgiven me I wondered if you'd fancy coming out for a drink,' he added sheepishly.

The tent flap opened again and the police piled in. Gerry Heffernan led the way, followed by Rachel and PC Johnson. Wesley brought up the rear.

'We saw him come in here. Where is he?' Gerry Heffernan addressed Odin in a voice that indicated he'd stand no nonsense. He looked surprised when he spotted Pam. 'Pam,' he said urgently. 'Did a man come in here . . . beard, shifty face?'

Rachel stared at Pam – the woman she'd heard so much about but had never before met – making a swift appraisal. Pam was attractive, she thought, and the long blue Saxon dress enhanced her looks. She glanced over at Wesley, who had just exchanged a smile with his wife, and took a deep breath, torn between jealousy and embarrassment at harbouring such unspoken and barely acknowledged thoughts about a colleague. She avoided looking at

138

Wesley, cursing herself for the foolish, unadmitted fantasies that had crept into her idle hours.

'He grabbed the red hold-all and ran off.' Pam glanced at Odin nervously. 'Apparently it belonged to him. His name's Jock.'

'Thanks, love. We think we know where he'll go to ground.'

'I wondered why Maggie Palister was so anxious to keep Neil and me away from the house,' said Wesley. 'Do you think he's been hiding out there?'

'If it's Jock you're talking about,' began Odin apprehensively, 'he said he was staying with friends about ten miles from here.'

'And you are?'

'Er . . . Odin,' he said, having put aside completely the swagger of a Viking warrior. Even his voice now seemed meek, anxious to please. 'Alias Cec Mitchelson,' he added with a feeble smile. 'I'm the, er, leader of Thor's Hammers. Look, I don't know what this is about, but . . .'

'It's about armed robbery . . . possible abduction of a witness . . . possible murder,' said Gerry Heffernan, pulling no punches. 'Pam here said that she found a hold-all containing a firearm we believe to have been used in a series of armed robberies. What do you know about it?'

Odin fingered his sheathed sword nervously. 'Nothing,' he said in seemingly honest panic. 'I don't know anything about it.' He looked at Pam in horror. 'Jock joined us recently. I really don't know anything about him,' he added, convincingly. He looked again at Pam, warily. 'So you went to the police?'

'I didn't have to,' she said. 'I happen to be married to Detective Sergeant Peterson over there. Call it pillow talk,' she added mischievously.

Odin looked across at Wesley and blushed, his hopes concerning Pam finally and brutally dashed.

'So what can you tell me about Jock Palister?' asked Heffernan.

Odin straightened his back and became more businesslike. 'Jock joined us just before our Easter trip to Sussex. Most of us are based in London, and we all have other jobs. We only do this for a few weeks a year. For some of us, me included, it's a way of life . . . more than just a hobby. But there are others who just come along for a bit of fun . . . a bit of company, bit of acting. I'd say Jock falls into the last category. And his friend Darren, of course. That's the big bloke he hangs around with. They both joined at the same time. As I said, I don't know much about them. They tended to keep themselves to themselves . . . never joined in with any of our social activities.'

'Would you be willing to make a statement?'

Odin nodded. 'Yes, of course. This won't stop us going on to our next booking, will it? We're doing a display up near Plymouth, then another at the Naval College fête in Tradmouth.'

'You might be a couple of Vikings short of a longboat, but I think once everyone's made statements you'll be free to go. By the way Mr, er . . . Mitchelson, when you're not plundering and pillaging, what is it you do for a living?' Gerry Heffernan asked, more by way of curiosity than pursuing a police enquiry.

'I'm a tax inspector. Why?'

'Bit of a busman's holiday for you, all this, then.'

Pam struggled to contain her laughter while Wesley and PC Johnson dutifully smirked at the inspector's wit. Rachel, her mind on other things, hovered at the tent entrance, anxious to be away.

'Come on, then,' said Heffernan jovially. 'I feel a raid coming on.'

Neil Watson pushed his way through the crowd, his stress levels reaching new and unfamiliar heights. He had circled Neston at least four times looking for a parking space, only to discover that, with the festival on, half the roads had been closed and all the spaces taken. He had had to park his yellow Mini on the industrial estate a mile out of town and walk. As he neared the playing fields he realised that although the festival was still in full swing, he had missed Thor's Hammers' performance.

He reached the crowded field, looking out for Wesley. But the police force was represented only by a couple of cheery-faced constables in their shirtsleeves who were mingling affably with the crowd. The CID was nowhere to be seen.

He felt a tap on his shoulder and swung round. Pam was standing there grinning at him, fetching in her Saxon gown and demure white veil.

'You on your own?' she asked. 'You've missed all the excitement. A couple of Thor's Hammers were using the group as a cover for armed robberies . . . or at least that's what I think was going on. Wes and Gerry have gone off after them.'

'Pity,' said Neil regretfully. Armed robbery didn't interest him much. 'I wanted to see Wes. I've something to tell him. Something he'll be interested in. Do you know when he'll be back?'

'Your guess is as good as mine. What is it?'

'Tell him I found another reference to Longhouse Cottage in Peacock's catalogue, will you. Tell him I found a casket that was supposed to have had some parchments inside. Looks Anglo-Saxon. It was hidden in the attic of that apology for a museum . . . bloody amateurs. No sign of the parchments, of course. They'd have disintegrated years ago. But Peacock was thoughtful enough to make a copy of them which I found stuffed in the back of the catalogue. I've told the curator I want to call in someone from the county museum to have a look . . . get the stuff that's left conserved properly. Will you pass the message on to Wes?'

Pam sighed. She knew Neil and his single-minded enthusiasms of old, and she knew how Wesley tended to be swept along with them. But at least, she told herself, it was better than Wesley having another woman. 'I'll tell him,' she said, resigned. 'Actually I think he's heading for Longhouse Cottage now . . . something about a Jock Palister.'

Neil smiled like a cat that had just caught a particularly plump bird. 'Me and Wes told Gerry Heffernan it wasn't Jock in that grave. We told him it was a Viking. But would he listen? Fancy an ice cream?'

Pam could think of nothing she would like better . . . apart from her husband's company.

The one thing Gerry Heffernan hadn't expected at Longhouse Cottage was the wholehearted co-operation of their quarry's son. Carl Palister came running out, making straight for Wesley. They had parked away from the house, having summoned the firearms unit. Jock Palister was inside; possibly with his companion, Darren, and possibly holding Maggie as hostage . . . and Ingeborg? Was Ingeborg in there too? One thing was certain – Jock was armed. They were taking no chances.

'There's no need for all this,' were Carl's first words when he arrived beside Wesley, breathless. 'He's a right bastard. There have been times over the past couple of weeks when I could have happily killed the old bugger, the way he knocks Mum about. But you can go in and get him now . . . easy.'

'He's armed, Carl. He's got a sawn-off shotgun with him. We're not taking any chances.'

'Who told you that?' asked Carl in disbelief. 'He's got a shooter all right, but it's not loaded. He's got no ammo. I know. I looked. He might give you a nasty knock on the head, but he's not going to shoot anyone. Same goes for his mate, Darren. He's been hiding out with Dad for the past couple of weeks. He's not armed neither. Go on. Go in and get 'em. I'll be bloody glad to see the back of him.'

'Your dad – or one of his mates – shot a farmer a few nights ago . . .'

'That couldn't have been him. Aren't you listening? He's got no ammo. He just uses the shooters to frighten people . . . he said.'

'You seem very keen to see your dad behind bars,' said Gerry Heffernan.

'Too right. He waltzes in here after three years, threatens Mum and acts like he bloody owns the place. I told him to get out . . . that we didn't want to know him. But then he worked on Mum. When you were here I nearly gave him away. I should have done but I was afraid of what he'd do to Mum.'

'Where's your mum now?'

'Out. In Tradmouth. Go on. Get him while you've got the chance . . . before she comes back.'

'Is anyone else up at the house . . . apart from your dad and Darren?'

Carl shook his head. 'If Mum had been in I wouldn't have come out. I'd be scared what he'd do to her, but . . .'

'And you're sure they're not armed?'

'Positive.'

Gerry Heffernan gave Carl a quick pat on the shoulder. He believed him. But what if he was mistaken? The firearms unit would have to be involved, just to be on the safe side. Steve Carstairs would be livid at missing it all: to Steve this was what policing was all about. The inspector looked at his watch, wondering just how long this armed stake-out would take.

But Steve would have been bitterly disappointed. After a few minutes of tension while Gerry Heffernan spelled out the situation to the others in no uncertain terms, Jock Palister and the well-built Darren emerged from the front door of Longhouse Cottage, still dressed in Viking garb, their hands high in the air and an expression of surly defeat on their faces. They knew when they were beaten. They meekly submitted to the flak-jacketed officers, who frisked them for weapons as they lay prone on the rough ground of the yard, and they were led away to the waiting police cars.

'Well, Wes, that's a good day's work. Three of the farm raiders in custody. Wonder if there's any more of 'em.'

'If Proudy drove the getaway car and three did the actual robberies then there must be one more,' said Wesley, putting a slight dampener on the proceedings. 'Mind if I have a look inside the farmhouse?'

Heffernan looked towards the house, where swarms of officers were preparing to search the premises. 'It looks a bit crowded over there . . . like the January sales, all sawn-off shotguns half price.'

Wesley strolled over to the house, thinking that Maggie was going to get a shock when she returned from her shopping trip to find hordes of unwelcome uniformed guests going through her belongings. But it wasn't just crime that was on his mind at that moment. He wanted a look at the house itself . . . wanted to see if there were any clues to its age and origins.

He wandered through the shabby rooms, greeting his colleagues, sharing quips and words of encouragement. But all the time he was looking at floors, stonework, fireplaces, blocked-in windows and doors: the lack of any attempt at modernisation made the task easier. The place was very old, the core of the house medieval at least; but exactly how old he couldn't tell without expert advice. And even then a medieval longhouse could have been built on the site of an earlier structure. Recycling was nothing new.

After a while he wandered out into the sunlight, where Gerry Heffernan was still talking to Carl Palister. The inspector spotted him and walked quickly over, taking his arm confidentially. 'You go back to the station, Wes. I'm going to stay here and have a word with Maggie when she gets back . . . make sure she's okay.'

Wesley climbed into his car and started the engine, navigating slowly down the uneven drive of Longhouse Cottage, terrain that would bring delight to the heart of any exhaust replacement company. When he reached the gate and the main road he depressed the brake pedal, looking left and right.

It took a split second for his brain to make the connection, filled as it was with armed robberies and medieval domestic architecture. He watched as a large black saloon car pulled over onto the grass verge near the gate. It waited there for a few seconds then drove off. Then Wesley remembered: this was the car that appeared every time the prowler was spotted at Waters House. He grabbed his notebook and wrote down the registration number as the car disappeared in the direction of Tradmouth. He pulled out. With any luck he might be able to follow it . . . see where it went.

But this being the holiday season there was too much traffic around to make pursuit easy. The car disappeared from view, having overtaken a new, shiny camper van just before a bend in the road. But he had the number. He would check it on the computer when he got back to the station. He drove through the narrow, crowded streets of Tradmouth, trying his best to avoid the slowly strolling pedestrians, feeling a warm glow of professional exhilaration. They had three of the farm raiders, he had the number of the prowler's car. All they needed now was to find Ingeborg and Sven Larsen safe and they were well on the way to driving crime from the district . . . for a day or so.

Shopping was one of WPC Trish Walton's favourite activities. The exploration of clothes shops – in Neston, Morbay, or even Plymouth if she was feeling extravagant – with her sister or her friends was one of the cherries on life's cake. Or so she'd always thought. Until now.

If she had to see the interior of one more shop on the flickering television screen, she might be put off shopping altogether. Steve Carstairs had left her to it half an hour ago. He had claimed he had to make an important phone call to an informant he'd met at a snooker club in Morbay. Trish strongly suspected this was a ploy. She had noticed more than once that when the going got tedious, Steve got going.

She sat in front of the screen, watching shoppers come and go; some purposeful, some merely browsing. She pressed the fast-forward button, staring at the speeded-up figures rushing jerkily in and out of the shop. If Ingeborg did appear on one of the tapes, she asked herself, would she actually recognise her? Perhaps another coffee would pep up her fuzzy brain and make her more alert.

She paused the tape and went to fetch the coffee from the

machine. When she sat down again, she sipped the hot muddy liquid, staring at the frozen picture on the screen.

Then a slow smile came to her lips. There she was . . . in the corner of the tape, browsing through the racks of sunglasses. Ingeborg Larsen.

She wound the tape forward a little. Ingeborg soon disappeared from the camera's view. But a few seconds later a familiar figure appeared, walking through the shop's open glass doors. Trish's heart beat fast as she wound the tape back to make sure she wasn't mistaken.

She let it play. There they were. They had met by the display of sun cream near the counter, Ingeborg and the man. They were walking out of the shop together.

Trish treated herself to another sip of coffee. The inspector would be impressed when she showed him the evidence in black and white – Ingeborg Larsen talking to Laurence Proudy on the day she disappeared.

Gerry Heffernan had spent some time with Maggie Palister before returning to the station. It was hard to tell whether she was relieved or upset by her husband's arrest. But he guessed she had mixed emotions. There were some dregs of attachment there, but also considerable relief that he was gone; that she'd no longer have to endure his abuse and cover up for him. When the patrol car had driven away, Heffernan had looked back at Maggie and her son standing there in the yard, Carl's arm firmly around his mother's shoulders. Hopefully now Maggie could get on with what passed for her life. Jock would be going away for a long time.

Jock and Darren proved only too willing to talk, especially when they heard about Lol Proudy's arrest. They both confirmed that Lol was the wheel man, driving them to their destination, then waiting outside in the car in case a quick getaway was needed. They had taken turns to drive the stolen vehicles and the lorry for the quad bikes. This, of course, begged a question. If Lol had been outside in the car and there were three raiders who went into the houses, who was the other man? Jock and Darren, like Proudy, stayed silent on the subject. Heffernan would work on it.

They made a full statement to Heffernan and Wesley. Rachel had wanted to sit in on the interview but Heffernan had not considered it wise, given her involvement. She did, however, identify Jock Palister's voice. He had been the man who had pushed Dave against the dresser. They confessed to four robberies. One near Stoke Beeching; one just outside Bereton; one near Dukesbridge; and Little Barton Farm.

'What about Wexer's Farm? You shot the farmer . . . put him in hospital.'

Jock and Darren, interviewed separately, had both shaken their heads. 'That's not down to us,' they each announced with apparent sincerity. 'We didn't do that one. We only carried shooters to frighten people . . . never had them loaded. Looks like someone's trying to imitate us.'

It was unanimous. Proudy, Jock and Darren all denied it vehemently. They didn't raid Wexer's Farm and they certainly didn't shoot Dan Wexer.

Heffernan's heart sank. This could only mean one thing. There were two lots of villains going around the district raiding farms. 'Oh, Wes,' he said with desperation as the two men left the interview room, 'what are we going to tell the Super?'

Lee Territ and Natalie Barker, on holiday together for the first time, away from parents' prying questions and restrictions, emerged from their tiny tent without many clothes on and ran down the steep fields towards the shore. Natalie giggled as Lee caught her naked waist.

They walked together, their arms entwined, only separating when the time came for them to negotiate their way in single file down the steep narrow track leading to the beach. The track, pitted with tree roots and sandy rabbit-holes, made them stumble, laughing, clinging to one another for support. They looked down at the beach. Because of its inaccessibility to young families, it was deserted . . . just as they liked it.

It was Natalie who hit the beach first, running, turning to challenge Lee to follow her, to catch her, to kiss her. They had the sands to themselves; the sun was shining in a cloudless sky; they were together, away from the daily routine of the Redditch and District Building Society. Life was good.

Lee threw himself, exhausted, onto the warm, gritty sand, but Natalie continued running, down to the sea, where the waves were teasing the seaweed-strewn shore. She took off her shoes and dipped her toes in the foaming water; in spite of the day's heat, the water was ice cold.

She strolled along the shoreline, glancing back at Lee. He was stretched out now, waiting for her. But she wasn't ready to join him just yet. The seaweed lay around like litter on the pristine beach. She walked on towards a huge clump of the stuff, strewn thickly over some sort of rock or driftwood.

Lee sat up with a start when he heard her scream. Disorientated, his heart thumping, he shielded his eyes from the sun and looked to see where she was. She was screaming . . . as loud and insistent as a burglar alarm. He ran towards her, scooping her up in his arms when he reached her. The screaming stopped.

There on the damp sand lay what seemed to be a clump of seaweed. But a hand, ash white and water-wrinkled, protruded from it. On closer inspection Lee saw water-matted hair, the colour of wet rope; a dark cavity where an eye should have been. He held Natalie closer, rocking her to and fro, comforting her as he would a child.

'Let's get out of here and call the police, eh?'

As they scrambled slowly back up the rough path, neither of them uttered a word.

Chapter Eleven

AD 997
*I was afeared when we came to Stoke Beeching. We came first
to the village and found it destroyed. What the evil ones could
not steal, they burned. The church, our fine wooden church,
was but ashes piled upon the earth, the treasures it contained
plundered. I sat in the ruins and wept. Hilda comforted me;
held me and said little. There are no words that describe the
wickedness of the pagans.*

*But some people of my village had escaped; had taken their
families and hidden in the woods. Now they creep back to the
village and begin to rebuild their homes. I met with some who
told me the priest had been burned alive in his church. They
had buried him and others slaughtered in the churchyard. I
saw the fresh graves and wept once more, for I knew many of
the dead.*

*I asked for news of my parents. They would say nothing,
only that my father was dead, buried with the others. I fear
there is news too horrible for telling, but I must go there and
see for myself.*

From the chronicle of Brother Edwin

'Lovely day for the beach, Wes,' said Gerry Heffernan cheerily.
'Brought your bucket and spade?'

They stood watching as Colin Bowman disentangled the
corpse's limbs from their seaweed bonds. The face was now
visible, and Wesley looked away. Sea creatures had devoured the
eyes. It was not a sight for weak stomachs.

'Shall I have a word with the people who found him, sir?'

148

Wesley wanted to absent himself before things became too gruesome.

'Yeah. They're over there. Young couple on a camping holiday. They're in a bit of a state – especially her – so be gentle with 'em.'

'Aren't I always?' said Wesley before striding over to where Lee and Natalie were standing, pale and shocked, clinging to each other for support.

'Well, Gerry,' said Colin Bowman. 'Our friend here has been in the water a couple of days by my reckoning. It's amazing how quickly a few hungry crabs can do that sort of damage. Any idea who he is? Anyone reported missing?'

'I know who he is all right, Colin. I've met him. His name's Sven Larsen; brother of that woman who's gone missing. He came over from Denmark a few days ago. He hired a boat and it was found ablaze floating out to sea. There was a dinghy and all but that was found drifting . . . had a smear of blood near the outboard motor. Any idea of the cause of death?'

'I won't be able to tell for certain until I do the post-mortem but at a quick glance I'd say it's possible that he was knocked unconscious and fell in the water. Look at that wound at the back of the head. It could have been done if the body was dashed against rocks after death, I suppose, or he could have been knocked out by the sail and fallen overboard, but . . .'

'But you think it could be suspicious?'

Colin Bowman paused, looking intently at the well-defined wound, half hidden by the matted hair. 'Yes, Gerry. I think it could be. But as I said, we'll have to wait . . .'

'For the post-mortem. I know, Colin. I'll just have to learn patience. Me mam always used to say it was a virtue.'

Rachel sat back in her office chair, hot, exhausted, feeling a fool. She had liked Wesley from the time they had first met. He possessed a sensitivity, a quiet, unassuming intelligence, that she hadn't come across in many men she'd known. At first she had been glad when they had teamed up together on enquiries; then she had begun to engineer it. Then she had begun to compare Dave, her straightforward, rather macho Australian boyfriend, with Wesley . . . and had found him wanting. The liking had

149

developed into affection which in turn had become . . . she hardly liked to think about it.

She had known that he was married, had a young baby. And she had also known that he and Pam had had their problems, especially before Michael was born. But seeing Pam face to face had shaken her . . . had made the whole thing real. It wasn't a game . . . a fantasy to while away the idle hours. There were people who could get hurt.

She knew that when she saw Wesley again she would experience a bewildering cocktail of attraction, guilt and acute embarrassment. He had given her no sign that he saw her as anything but a colleague and friend; and the way he had looked at Pam today had told her all she needed to know. Rachel Tracey had the horrible, sinking feeling that she could have made a fool of herself. But she was lucky. Things hadn't gone too far . . . hadn't even started. And she felt curiously relieved.

She heard a polite cough behind her and swung her chair round. Trish Walton was standing there. She looked pleased with herself, as smug as a precocious child who'd just won a talent competition. She proudly placed a videotape on the desk in front of Rachel and took a step back.

'Do you know when the inspector will be back?'

'He's gone over to Widerspool Sands. A body's been washed up there. Why?'

'Has Sergeant Peterson gone with him?'

Rachel blushed. 'Yes. Why?'

'I found Ingeborg Larsen on a few tapes . . . just looking in the shops. But on this one she's met someone. Laurence Proudy. She was talking to him on the day she disappeared. It's all on the tape.'

Rachel picked the tape up and turned it over absent-mindedly. 'Are you sure?'

'Positive.'

The office door burst open, making Rachel jump. Gerry Heffernan's voice boomed out. 'If any of you lot were hoping to have a day off tomorrow, think again. We've just found Sven Larsen's body . . . possible case of murder.' Wesley lurked behind him, his expression serious.

Rachel nudged Trish and handed her the videotape. She'd let the new recruit have her moment of glory.

Heffernan reacted to Trish's discovery with a satisfied smirk.

'We'll bring Proudy over from Morbay tomorrow morning . . . get him to tell us the truth for once. I don't believe in coincidences . . . Sven Larsen's death has something to do with his sister's disappearance.' He looked over at the notice-board, where an enlarged photograph of Ingeborg Larsen smiled out at them. 'And I've got a horrible feeling that now we've found Sven dead, we're not going to find his sister alive.'

The inspector turned and walked into his office. Wesley knew he was worried.

The Golden Dragon was doing good business from the Peterson household. As Wesley didn't arrive home till after seven, and Pam was exhausted from the rigours of Viking life, they put Michael in his cot and ordered a takeaway. When they had finished they sat ignoring the empty foil dishes on the coffee table, Wesley's arm round Pam's shoulders, and prepared to watch a popular archaeology programme they had recorded some nights ago. Pam closed her eyes, prepared to doze through the discoveries. But her rest was disturbed by an urgent ring at the doorbell. It was Wesley who summoned the strength to answer the door.

He was surprised to see Neil standing there, grinning. 'Hold the door open, Wes, I'm bringing the stuff inside.' Neil made for his Mini, parked up on the kerb outside.

'Hang on, Neil. What are you bringing in?' Neil didn't answer, and Wesley stood there, feeling somewhat helpless in the face of his friend's determination.

Neil returned from the car with two large cardboard boxes, each containing something mysteriously bulky. 'I'm getting these over to Professor Harvey at the museum on Monday. Just thought you'd like to see them . . . and they need to be kept somewhere dry and safe till then.'

'What are they?'

'Didn't Pam give you the message?'

'She said something about a casket and some papers but, to tell you the truth, today's been a bit hectic. We've arrested a gang of armed robbers and we've got another murder on our hands. I haven't really had time to think about . . .'

'Well, make time,' said Neil, pushing past with his heavy burden.

At this point Pam joined them in the hall, rubbing her eyes. 'Hi, Neil. Should have known it was you.'

Without a word Neil went into the living room and cleared the remnants of the takeaway off the table, making sure that no stray traces of chicken chow mein remained.

'What are you doing, Neil?' asked Pam, more in amusement than in anger.

He didn't answer but placed the boxes on the table. The rusted remains of the sword lay there against the crisp white acid-free paper, next to the round shield boss. Then Neil carefully added the *pièce de résistance* to the display: the second box contained an ancient carved casket, crafted from ivory or bone. It wasn't large – about eighteen inches wide and a foot high – but it teemed with busy carved figures and was topped by a powerful crucifixion scene in the centre of the lid.

'Wow,' said Wesley. 'Where did you get it?'

'At the Peacock Museum. It was just stuck up in a dusty attic with a water leak in the corner . . . not even on display. I couldn't leave it there, could I? It needs to be kept in proper conditions. And it needs proper conservation . . . so do the sword and shield boss. I'd like them X-rayed and all. I told that useless Bate-Brownlowe character that they weren't being treated properly and I said I thought they should go to the County Museum for conservation and proper display. I gave him a receipt, tried to do everything properly, but he wasn't pleased.'

'You mean you took them without permission?'

'Well, er . . . sort of, technically, I suppose.'

'Neil, I'm a police officer. I can't handle stolen goods.'

'Well, I'd prefer it if you didn't handle them, actually . . . the fewer people the better. You can watch while I open the casket. Okay? Does that salve your delicate conscience?'

Wesley turned round and saw that Pam was grinning. Neil had always been single-minded. If he considered that a valuable piece of archaeological history was being abused, he would consider it his bounden duty to confiscate it from its abuser, regardless of the legal niceties.

'I hope you realise the importance of this, Wes. It's Anglo bloody Saxon . . . a thousand years old. Unique.'

'Worth a fortune?' asked Pam, eagerly.

'You can't think in terms of money,' said Neil, reverently lifting the lid of the casket. 'This is a major find. Look.'

They craned to see inside the box, Wesley's interest defeating his brief bout of conscience. Then Neil closed the lid carefully and produced a cardboard file containing a sheaf of brown-tinged papers covered in neat, even copperplate writing.

'These are the papers I found at the back of Peacock's ledger. They're obviously copies of something much earlier. It's my guess he had some ancient documents copied, then lost the originals ... or just neglected them so that they fell to bits. Scandalous,' he added with quiet indignation.

'What do they say?' asked Pam.

'How's your Old English? Mine's not too hot ... I couldn't really understand them.'

Pam's eyes lit up. She knew her three years at university studying English hadn't been completely wasted. 'A bit rusty but not too bad. I must admit that when everyone else on my course was moaning about having to study *Beowulf*, I actually liked it. I even enjoyed reading it in the original Old English.'

'Swat,' muttered Neil with a grin. 'So you can translate this lot?'

Pam shrugged modestly. 'I'll have a go. How long have I got?'

'Well, I'm taking everything over to the County Museum on Monday, so you've got a day or so. You don't mind if I kidnap your husband and take him for a drink, do you?'

Pam gave her consent, for once without resentment. She looked at the papers with eager anticipation. At the top they bore the words 'exact copies of parchments found in carved ivory box discovered in floor cavity during structural renovation of Longhouse Cottage, Stoke Beeching, the originals being in very poor condition'. After long months of sleepless nights and nappy-changing, Pam was eager to exercise her brain again. She took a notebook from the sideboard drawer and settled down to work.

Now he was feeling better, Dave was enjoying the attention he was receiving in hospital; enjoying his banter with the prettier nurses, too ... although he would never have admitted this to Rachel.

Rachel sat by the bed, picking at a bunch of grapes absent-mindedly, as if her thoughts were somewhere else.

'Penny for 'em, Rach.'

She looked up guiltily. 'What? Oh, sorry, Dave. I was miles away. It's been quite a day.'

'Yeah. Right. Great you've got that load of bastards behind bars. Awful to think that Proudy must have been keeping an eye on your place all the time he was staying in the old barn. Still, it's all over now, eh?' He touched her hand.

She gave him a slight, sad smile. 'We reckon one of them's still on the loose . . . but they might have headed back to London by now. Apparently the whole thing was arranged in London using the Viking re-enactment group as a cover, with Jock Palister providing the local knowledge for this series of raids. Proudy had had some dealings with Palister in London, so they brought him in on it because of his garage expertise. That woman hasn't left yet – Proudy's girlfriend . . . Astrid or whatever her name is. I suppose someone'll have to tell her what's going on. So much for a free holiday with a bloke you've just picked up, eh?'

'Now she's a nasty bit of work,' said Dave unexpectedly. 'What is it they say? The female of the species is deadlier than the male?'

'What do you mean?' Rachel was helping herself to another grape, only half listening.

'When she threatened him. It was all a bit hazy after I was knocked out, but now it's coming back. I heard them arguing, her and Proudy, on the evening before the robbery. She told him he was dead meat if he said anything . . . she sure sounded vicious.'

Rachel stood up, placing the bag of grapes firmly in Dave's hand. 'I've got to make a phone call,' she said before rushing out of the ward, hoping Dave's revelation hadn't come too late.

At half past nine that Saturday night Astrid Jones was packing her suitcases into her car. The police had swallowed her story whole, and she hadn't told anyone she was going. It was better that way – to leave quietly, to get out of the area and back to London before any of her associates took it into their heads to betray her.

When two police cars arrived to arrest her she ran off towards the fields, her last desperate attempt at escape guided by the instinct of self-preservation rather than reason.

It wasn't long before she was caught and led away to the waiting cars, swearing colourfully and cursing the fickle cowardice of men.

*

Gerry Heffernan lay awake, the anthem he was to sing with the choir in church the next morning echoing in his head. He wished he could forget it. He wished he could get some sleep. There would be no day of rest for him this coming Sunday.

He had received the call about the arrest of Astrid Jones earlier that evening, and he made a mental note to congratulate Rachel on a good piece of deduction. Astrid had fooled them into thinking she was an innocent bystander, accidentally involved by the foolish acceptance of the offer of a free holiday. How wrong could they have been?

She was known to the police under the name Astrid Johnstone, a German national who had married – and later divorced – a British serviceman. She had lived in Yorkshire – at Catterick – when she arrived in Britain. There she had first met Lol Proudy, and she had met up with him again when she moved to London. She had been suspected of conspiracy to rob a series of post offices a year ago but had been released owing to lack of evidence. Using Thor's Hammers as a cover had been her idea, and Jock Palister had given her the idea of robbing isolated farms. She was a good organiser, a clever woman. And she had taken Gerry Heffernan in completely. Perhaps, he thought in the self-doubt of the small hours, he was losing his touch.

He was just drifting off to sleep again when he heard a sound outside his bedroom door. Surely Sam couldn't be back so late. He got out of bed, pulling up his pyjama trousers to ensure decency, and crept out to the landing, where a series of floorboards creaked musically beneath his feet. He was just in time to see a strange sight – a tall figure dressed in shaggy skins with a pair of alarming horns protruding from its head. The figure disappeared rapidly and soundlessly into Sam's room.

Heffernan quickly shot back into his bedroom, leaning on the door that he had closed firmly behind him and telling himself that he must be dreaming . . . or the beer in the Tradmouth Arms wasn't agreeing with him.

When he finally drifted off to sleep, Gerry Heffernan dreamed of strange horned creatures, seven feet tall, driving stolen quad bikes on the choppy river . . . and they all had Sven Larsen's dead, disfigured face.

*

'Where's the boss gone?' Rachel Tracey asked the next morning. Her manner was guarded, quiet. Wesley could tell her mind was on things other than police work . . . but in view of the recent events at Little Barton Farm, this was hardly surprising.

'He's nipped off to church . . . the choir can't function without him, apparently. He should be back soon.'

'How did the post-mortem go?'

'Larsen was knocked unconscious then somehow he found his way into the water and drowned. Colin Bowman reckoned he was knocked out with something like a fire extinguisher. He found tiny traces of red paint in the wound. That means someone was out there on the boat with him.'

Wesley and Heffernan had gone to the mortuary early that morning to watch Colin Bowman examine the mortal remains of Sven Larsen. His conclusion was that Sven had been murdered. He had been hit over the head with a blunt instrument, then he had fallen overboard, perhaps in an attempt to escape. The sea had done the rest, and the actual cause of death was drowning. The forensic tests on the yacht concluded that an accelerant of some kind had been used to set it alight – probably the spare fuel stored aboard for the petrol engine. It was no accident. It was murder. And the murderer – on the yacht with Larsen – had used the dinghy to escape after setting fire to the vessel.

The fire suggested that the murderer had thought Larsen dead or deeply unconscious and that his body would be consumed in the flames, along with any other forensic evidence. But somehow Larsen had met his death in the cold waters of the English Channel. There was one question that would have to be answered. Just who had shared Larsen's last voyage?

Wesley's thoughts were interrupted by the distant strains of 'For Those in Peril on the Sea' being sung enthusiastically by a tuneful baritone voice.

'He's back,' said Trish Walton as the singing grew louder.

The inspector burst in, beaming around at his assembled team. He carried on singing as he made his way to his office. Wesley followed him.

'Very appropriate hymn,' he said as his boss sat down with a heavy creak. 'For Sven Larsen, I mean.'

'You're right there, Wes. When we sang it this morning I kept thinking about him lying there on Colin's slab. He was in peril on the sea all right . . . or rather from whoever was out there with him. I talked to Jim from the boat hire company again. He was in church and I caught him after the service. He said Larsen was definitely on his own when he set off.'

'He must have picked someone up on the way.'

'Someone he knew . . . someone he didn't mind going sailing with. Who?'

'His sister?'

'Oh, come on, Wes. She's been kidnapped . . . the chloroform.'

'It was just a thought. After all, it's his first visit here. He didn't know anyone in the area. What about fingerprints on the dinghy?'

'There are loads of them. But nothing that helps us.' Heffernan sighed. 'Anyway, with the farm robbers safely banged up we can concentrate on this case. Do you believe that they didn't do Wexer's farm?'

'I don't know what to believe. They're certainly unanimous that they had nothing to do with that one.'

'Well, let's hope they're lying, eh? Armed robbers aren't exactly renowned for their open honesty, are they? They've just brought Lol Proudy over from Morbay. Shall we have a word about that video of him talking to Ingeborg?' Heffernan rubbed his hands together with gleeful anticipation. 'Come on, Wes. Let's see what Proudy's got to say for himself.'

Laurence Proudy had had a busy morning. He had been transferred to a cell in Tradmouth police station, where his fellow robbers were being held, and now he was being shown a video by that big Scouse inspector and his posh black sidekick. He couldn't complain that the police weren't keeping him entertained.

He had admitted everything about the robberies. And now Astrid, the brains behind the whole operation, had been caught, he had confirmed her part in it all as well. There was too much evidence against them to get away with it. And confession, apparent repentance, was good for the soul, so he'd heard . . . and always impressed juries. But this . . . Somehow he had to convince these men that he had had nothing to do with the disappearance of that Danish woman.

He looked at the stilled image on the television screen. Him and Ingeborg. 'Yeah, okay. I met her. I just bumped into her in Boots. I told her the insurance was being sorted out . . . that everything was going through. That's all. Honest. She just asked me when I was getting my car fixed . . . all polite, like. There wasn't no aggro. We only talked for a minute. I didn't mention it before, cause I didn't want no trouble. I only saw her for a minute. It wasn't important.' He looked from Heffernan to Wesley, his piggy eyes pleading for them to believe him.

'What happened after you left the shop?' asked Wesley quietly.

'We just said goodbye. She went off up the hill towards the castle and I went the other way. I'd just gone into Neston to pick up some shopping.'

'Why not Tradmouth? That's nearer to Little Barton Farm, surely.'

Proudy looked awkard. 'Er . . . I was going to meet up with Jock and Darren in the pub. Astrid was meeting us there and all. Jock and Darren had a Hammers rehearsal that afternoon so it had to be Neston. You can ask them, they'll tell you,' he said with confidence.

'Was anyone else around when you met her?' asked Wesley. 'Anyone who might have been following her?'

Proudy thought for a moment. 'That video . . . wind it on a bit, will you.'

Wesley obliged. Proudy stared at the moving figures on the screen, people coming and going. 'I'm sure a woman came out of the shop at the same time as us. I can't see her here . . . no, there she is, just a glimpse, see.'

Wesley froze the video. A woman in a straw sunhat and large dark glasses flashed into the picture and then disappeared.

'She was sort of hanging about, near where, er . . . Ingeborg was. Then she left at the same time . . . nearly bumped into me, that's why I remember. I told her to look where she was going. Then she hurried off after Ingeborg towards the castle.'

'Could she have been following Ingeborg?' asked Wesley, winding the tape back to see if the woman made any other appearances.

'No idea. That's your job, isn't it,' Proudy said, defiant. He had had enough.

Wesley and Heffernan watched the tape again, but the straw-hatted woman only made fleeting appearances. Her protection from the summer sun made her unrecognisable anyway. But

Wesley stored it in his mind for future reference and continued with the questioning.

'Did you ever meet Ingeborg Larsen's brother, Sven?' he asked, searching Proudy's face for a reaction.

Proudy looked puzzled. 'Nah . . . didn't even know she had a brother. Why?'

'Because he's just been found murdered.'

Proudy looked horrified. 'Well, that's not down to me. How could it be when I didn't even know he existed?' Proudy was starting to sound worried. 'Look, just because I put my hand up to robbery doesn't mean I'm a murderer. We never even used loaded shooters. We said before we started out. No unnecessary violence.'

'That's very public-spirited of you,' said Heffernan sarcastically. 'Maybe you'll be in line for next year's Nobel Peace Prize. But there's the small question of Daniel Wexer . . . the farmer who was shot. Why did you abandon his car in Neston?'

'I didn't abandon no car. What kind was it?'

'You know that, surely. It's a Land Rover. Brand new.'

'Well, if I'd nicked it it'd be driving round the M25 with new number plates on by now. That proves it wasn't us,' he said with finality.

Heffernan stood up. 'Right, Mr Proudy. I think that's all for now.'

Wesley switched off the tape machine and followed his boss from the interview room.

'Believe him?' asked the inspector as soon as they were safely out in the corridor.

'Yes, I think I do,' replied Wesley, deep in thought. 'I don't think he knows anything about Ingeborg Larsen's disappearance.'

'And Dan Wexer?'

'All my instincts tell me that Proudy's telling the truth but . . . I really don't know.' Wesley sighed and looked at his watch.

Gerry Heffernan slouched in front of him as he walked back to the office, silent in thought. Wesley watched as the inspector slumped down in his chair, head in hands. After a few seconds he raised his head and looked his sergeant in the eyes.

'I can't put it off any longer, Wes. I'll have to ring Copenhagen again . . . tell the police there about Sven. And I think it might be an idea if we spoke to Ingeborg's ex-husband some time in the next few days . . . he's obviously in the clear, but he might be able to tell us something. If the same person abducted Ingeborg and killed Sven, that means there could be somebody around here who has it in for the Larsen family. But why?'

Wesley shook his head. He had some ideas, unformed and nebulous, but they were hardly ready to put into words, let alone test and prove.

'I'll make the phone call, Wes. You get off home and think about it, eh?'

'Thanks. But I don't know whether Pam'll be pleased to see me. Neil's landed her with a job . . . translating some Old English documents.'

Heffernan raised his eyebrows. 'Don't you think the poor woman went through enough yesterday with them Vikings? Give her my regards, eh?'

As Wesley left the office he looked back and saw Gerry Heffernan pick up the telephone.

Pam Peterson had had a frustrating day. It was as if Michael resented something else claiming his mother's attention. And he was teething, which only made matters worse. At last, by three o'clock, she had managed to get him down for a sleep and was able to continue the translation.

She wrote in a spiral-bound notebook, in pencil. The words had come slowly at first, but then she became attuned to the unfamiliar early version of the English language and her pencil moved rapidly across the paper.

By the time Wesley came in she was totally absorbed. Dinner would have to wait. The events unrolling in Jeremiah Peacock's carefully copied manuscripts were becoming very exciting indeed.

The man left his large black car parked on the main road and walked slowly up the drive to Waters House. He glanced to his left at Longhouse Cottage, squatting in its scrubby fields, a rusting collection of disintegrating vehicles lying in what passed for a yard. Whoever lived there couldn't be the most desirable of neighbours.

He could see the front door of Waters House. The driveway had once been satisfyingly crunchy with white gravel; now the gravel only remained in trodden-in patches. The rest was bare earth, pitted with holes that swelled into puddles when the rain came. He hesitated. Should he watch again tonight? Or should he knock at the door? Confront them?

He had spent so much time watching. Sometimes he would almost summon the courage to approach the house. Then his nerve would fail and he would stand there, camouflaged by the laurel bushes, staring into the bright rooms where they moved about like figures in a peep-show. It had been so long . . . so many years. But the doctors had told him that he was dying. What had he got to lose?

The man walked slowly, stiffly, up to the house. When he reached the front door, he raised his hand to the great wrought-iron knocker and brought it down with a thunderous crash, loud enough to wake the dead.

Chapter Twelve

AD 997

It was just before noon when Hilda and I arrived at my parents' farm, and, with much relief and rejoicing, I saw the house was still standing and had not been burned like those in the village. I took Hilda's hand as we approached, half fearful of what we would find within.

Then we came upon my mother. She sat before the house weaving on her loom. She was most joyous to see me and greeted Hilda as befits my future bride with a warm embrace. But there lay sorrow beneath her joy. My father, she told me, had been killed by the Danes on the sands as he brought a catch of fish ashore. They struck him down with their axes. He was buried near to the church with the others who perished.

I embraced my mother to comfort her . . . but she shed no tears. She told me then that she had buried all of value, her jewellery and coins, in the earth nearby for safekeeping. I rejoiced in her good wisdom.

Then I heard a noise from within the house.

From the chronicle of Brother Edwin

It was almost eight o'clock when Gerry Heffernan received the phone call from Wilkins the Jewellers in Neston High Street. Mr Wilkins, having been issued by his local constable with a full description of the items stolen from Wexer's Farm, had displayed admirable vigilance. A locket had been brought in by a young man who offered it for sale; an unusual Victorian locket, the one described in the constable's list. He had taken the young man's name and address and had kept the locket for valuation. He thought the inspector would like to know.

Mr Wilkins assured Gerry Heffernan most earnestly that he considered it every citizen's duty to help the police in every way they could . . . particularly in such lawless times. Five minutes later he eventually came up with the name and address of the young man with the stolen locket.

When he put the phone down, Heffernan sat back in his executive swivel chair, deep in thought. The name Mr Wilkins had given him was the last one he had expected to hear.

After a few minutes' thought he dialled Wesley's number.

The pubs were normally quiet on Sunday nights . . . which meant that as soon as Sam Heffernan set foot inside the Ship and Compass on the seafront at Morbay, he would be the centre of attention.

He was convinced that his father didn't know his secret. He had almost caught him last night, and Sam had waited with bated breath for the knock on his bedroom door. But it hadn't come: he was safe for now. He looked at himself in the mirror that hung, slightly askew, on Funograms' office wall.

'You're doing really well,' giggled Carly Pinkerton as she flicked the grey caterpillar of ash from the end of her cigarette. 'People are asking for you, you know. Word gets round. And you do suit that costume,' she added with a suggestive wink. She paused, a smile hovering on her lips. 'Have you, er . . . got a girlfriend up in, er . . . where is it you're at university again?'

'Liverpool. There's nobody special at the moment. Why?'

'Oh, no reason,' said Carly innocently. 'I don't suppose you've got your own place down here,' she added, maintaining eye contact and hitching her skirt up a couple of inches.

'No . . . 'fraid not. I'm staying with my dad. He's on his own since Mum died.'

'Does he work, this dad of yours? Is he out in the day?'

The implication of the question was as obvious as a blazing beacon on a hilltop. Sam adjusted his headgear nervously. Carly was keen. The trouble was that he didn't know whether he was. Perhaps she was a little obvious for his taste.

'Yeah . . . he's, er . . . police, a detective inspector.'

Carly raised her beautifully plucked eyebrows. 'Well, we'll just have to be careful we don't break the law, then,' she said, the words pregnant with innuendo.

Sam looked at his watch. 'I'd better be going. It's a Sharon Daley at the Ship and Compass, isn't it?'

'That's right. It's her hen party. Give her a good send-off.' Carly walked over to him and fingered the neckline of his fake fur tunic. 'But not too good, eh, Sam?' She stood on tiptoe and pressed her mouth to his. At first the smell of cigarette smoke caught in his throat as they kissed. Then, as he grew accustomed to it, he began to relax, and explored Carly's lithe body with his hands as her lips clung to his like a hungry limpet.

Suddenly she jumped back. 'Bloody hell! What's that?' she shrieked.

Sam looked down in horror. 'Oh, sorry, it's my sword. It seems to have a life of its own. Er, look, Carly, I'd better be off. I mustn't be late. Wish me luck.'

Carly Pinkerton rose on tiptoe again and planted a final, firm kiss on his lips. 'Business before pleasure. Off you go.'

Wesley sat back in the armchair, enjoying the peace of a domestic night in. He closed his eyes. The only sound was the ticking of the clock on the mantelpiece and the scratching of Pam's pencil on the paper of her notebook.

'Want some wine?' he asked.

She didn't look up. 'Better not. I'd be terrified of spilling it on these papers.'

'How are you getting on?'

'Fine. Peacock's transcription is very clear. Brother Edwin must have had excellent handwriting.'

'Brother Edwin?'

'A monk . . . talks about Neston Minster.'

'If it's about the minster, Neil'll be over the moon. That's what he's digging up at the moment . . . on the site of Neston parish church.'

'Oh, it's not just about some stuffy old monastery. It's much more exciting than that. You wouldn't think the modern Danes were the descendants of the Vikings, would you? They seem such nice, civilised people . . . all educational toys and tasteful interior design.'

'Remember what I used to say when I kept getting stopped by

the police in London, 'cause I was black . . . beware of racial stereotyping,' said Wesley with a wry grin.

'I know, I know,' she said. 'And I know that most Scandinavians in those days were just farmers and traders. But these Vikings were such a vicious lot . . . all that butchery and destruction. You should read what Brother Edwin has to say about them.'

Wesley's eyes lit up, and he made a grab for her notebook. She held on to it, teasing. 'Not yet. I haven't finished.' She leaned across and kissed him. 'And I'm just getting to the juicy bit.'

Wesley was about to make further enquiries when the telephone began to ring.

When Wesley announced that Gerry Heffernan needed him over at Neston to bring in a suspect for the Wexer's Farm robbery, Pam sighed and returned to her work. She had married a policeman: she had known what to expect, but that didn't make it any easier.

The tiny box-like modern semi, exiled in a new housing estate on the outskirts of Neston, loomed before Wesley and Heffernan in the evening light. It had been designed by some unimaginative architect on an off-day and jammed up against its neighbours for maximum profit.

'This is the address, sir,' said Wesley. 'Bit of a contrast to Wexer's Farm.'

The two policemen climbed out of the car and walked up the concrete front path, past the parched square of scrubby grass that passed for a front garden.

The woman who opened the door was probably in her forties, and not unattractive. Her figure, although inclined to plumpness, was shapely, her dark brown hair well cut in a shoulder-length bob.

It was Gerry Heffernan who did the talking. Claire Wexer looked alarmed when he asked if they could talk to her son, Pete. He had a job in a pub in Morbay, she said. He was working.

'What's it about? He's not in trouble is he?' asked the anxious mother. 'Since his dad and I split up, he's not been the easiest of teenagers . . . but he's never been in trouble with the police,' she assured them.

'It's in connection with the robbery at your ex-husband's farm,

Mrs Wexer. A lad giving your son's name tried to sell a locket stolen in the robbery to a jeweller in Neston. We'd just like a word with your Pete. And I'm afraid we might have to send someone to search his room,' he said, with genuine regret.

Penny, Wexer's daughter, came up behind her mother in the hallway and put a thin protective hand on her shoulder. Wesley recognised her from the hospital. 'What is it, Mum?'

'The police think Pete's taken something from the farm. It can't be true. He wouldn't have gone there. He won't even talk to his father. There must be some mistake.'

She looked at Heffernan, her eyes pleading with him to believe her. Gerry Heffernan felt sorry for her . . . as he felt sorry for every innocent mother who found out her child was in deep trouble. But he couldn't leave it there. 'Where was your son last Tuesday night?'

Claire clutched her daughter's hand, confused. 'I don't know. I can't remember.'

'He was in Morbay. He works in a pub there,' said Penny, confidently. 'I don't know what that Jen bitch has accused him of but . . .'

Heffernan had no wish to become embroiled in family arguments. He asked for the name of Pete Wexer's place of work and left the two women clinging to each other in the doorway.

'I don't half feel sorry for those two,' he said as Wesley pointed the car towards Morbay.

Sharon Daley and her flock of human hens weren't difficult to find; their high-pitched hilarity could be heard throughout the large, modern barn of a pub. As soon as they saw him they cheered. Sam stopped in his tracks, trying to ignore their suggestive, drunken invitations, preparing himself for his performance. He straightened his shiny plastic-horned helmet, drew a sheet of typewritten paper from the pocket in his furry tunic, and began.

'My name's Eric the Viking and my longboat's parked outside.
My mates are a-raping and pillaging until the turn of the tide.
But I've come to wish you, Sharon, the very best of luck
And I'm bringing you this message today in the hope that
    you'll give me . . . a great big kiss. Come on, Sharon.'

Amid hooting laughter, Sharon was pushed forward by her mates, her plump, pretty face flushed. Sam always felt some affinity with his victims: they were usually as embarrassed about it all as he was. He lifted Sharon up in his arms and carried her round the pub, followed by comments ranging from the witty to the obscene. Then he kissed her with mock passion, raising bawdy cheers from her fellows. He sensed an encore was needed (his public expected their money's worth) so he swept her up in his arms again and carried her off out of the pub, kicking the door open dramatically. He planned to chat with her outside for a few minutes, asking her about her wedding and wishing her luck, before making his last dramatic entrance.

As soon as they were outside he put her down beside a large four-wheel-drive vehicle. 'Sorry about all this,' he said with sincerity.

But the wine had got to Sharon before he had. She giggled. 'I've never been carried off by a Viking before,' she gasped, breathlessly. 'I'm not getting married till Saturday, so if you're not doing anything tomorrow night I've got my own place and . . .' Like Carly earlier that evening, Sharon pressed her lips and her body to his. Sam decided not to battle with fate and twisted his sword belt round so that it wouldn't impede his activities.

After a few minutes Sam slowly detached himself from Sharon's lips. 'We ought to get back inside. Your friends'll be getting the wrong idea.'

'Let 'em.' Sharon attached herself again but Sam broke free, taking her hands firmly. 'Are we still on for tomorrow night, then?'

'I thought you were getting married next weekend. What will your fiancé say?'

'What the eye doesn't see . . .' she replied meaningfully.

'Big bloke, is he?' asked Sam nervously, taking her hand and guiding her back towards the pub.

Things had degenerated in the Ship and Compass while Sam had been outside. He sat down, perched on the edge of his seat, avoiding groping hands, while around him the hen party got even more out of hand.

The human hens had downed enough alcohol to floor several elephants, their conversation growing coarser with each empty glass. It was when they began to throw their knickers across the pub floor in a newly invented game, seemingly based on crown green bowls, that Sam decided he'd had enough. He disentangled himself from Sharon and made for the gents', thinking that a strategic withdrawal would be wise.

'Hell,' he muttered to himself as the pub doors swung open. Standing there facing him, mouth gaping, was his father, accompanied by a smartly dressed young black man.

Wesley Peterson stood by his boss, trying in vain to suppress a grin. 'What is it you were saying about too many Vikings around here?' he whispered in his boss's ear.

But Heffernan didn't answer. He continued to stare at the apparition in the horned helmet. Until the apparition spoke.

'Hello, Dad.'

Heffernan scratched his head. 'So that's what you mean by public relations, is it? What are you doing, son? Working for the Scandinavian Tourist Board?'

'Er . . . actually, Dad, I'm a kissogram – Eric the Viking,' explained Sam. 'Goes down very well with hen parties,' he added by way of justification.

'I'm sure it does.' Heffernan turned to his sergeant. 'Wesley, you've not met my son, Sam.'

Wesley and Sam shook hands. 'I've heard a lot about you. You read archaeology at Exeter, didn't you?'

'Come on,' said Heffernan impatiently. 'This isn't *University Challenge*. We're here to have a word with one of the barmen. Young, mousey hair, goes by the name of Pete. Ring any bells?'

Sam shook his head, and Wesley prepared himself for discreet enquiries at the bar.

Pete Wexer wasn't hard to find. And when they asked him, in time-honoured fashion, to accompany them to the station, he said nothing but climbed into the back seat of their car, his face bearing an expression of cool resentment.

Sam followed them outside and stood, holding his horned helmet and looking coyly at his dad.

'Have you got that rust bucket with you or do you want a lift back to Tradmouth?' shouted Heffernan from the passenger seat.

'I came in the car. Honest Dad, can you imagine me getting the bus dressed like this? Anyway' – he winked – 'I've got some unfinished business back in the pub.'

Sam disappeared back inside and his father watched him go, shaking his head. 'By heck, Wes, you do some daft things when you're young, don't you.' He turned and looked at Pete Wexer, who was sitting in the back seat, looking decidedly nervous.

Monday morning dawned, promising another day of semi-tropical heat. As he crunched on his cornflakes, Wesley listened to the local morning news on the radio, with its grim predictions of drought and water rationing. But the words didn't register. His mind was on other things.

Pete Wexer was Daniel Wexer's son: he had admitted that much when they had interviewed him the previous night. But he had refused to explain why a sawn-off shotgun and ammunition had been found hidden at the back of his wardrobe during the search of Claire Wexer's house that Heffernan had organised soon after the arrest. Pete Wexer – a young man with no previous criminal record – had spent a night in the cells. Gerry Heffernan reckoned that this introduction to the world of crime and punishment would concentrate his mind wonderfully.

Pam was still in bed, asleep and exhausted after a night tending to a teething baby. Wesley looked at the cupboard where she had stowed away the Peacock papers and her notebook, wrestling with his curiosity. But a glance at his watch told him he had no time for history, however intriguing. Brother Edwin would have to wait.

When he finally arrived at the police station, Gerry Heffernan was nowhere to be seen.

'I've a message for you from the boss,' Steve Carstairs announced as Wesley walked into the office. Steve was sitting in front of a flickering computer screen, leering unpleasantly. 'Hey, Sarge, I heard about him finding his lad last night dressed up as a Viking. He'd got a job as a stripagram or something. His dad found him with a load of naked girls . . . orgy it was.' The story had obviously been embellished by the ever-efficient station grapevine as the night had progressed. Steve emitted a lecherous laugh. 'They were a randy lot them Vikings, eh?'

Wesley smiled and nodded but thought it best to make no comment. Why spoil a good story? And besides, this was the friendliest Steve had ever been. He would make the most of it before the old, unreconstructed Steve returned . . . as he inevitably would. 'Is the inspector in already, then?'

'Yeah . . . not like him at all, is it? He was here at eight. Rachel got in early and all and they're interviewing Pete Wexer now. He left you a message . . . said he'd deal with Wexer if you carried on with the Larsen case.' Steve, chirpy for once, returned to his computer screen and carried on typing.

'Thanks,' said Wesley as he sat down at his desk. He looked over at the notice-board, at the photographs of Ingeborg Larsen and her dead brother, and wondered where to start.

He opened his notebook, organising his ideas, scribbling likely avenues of investigation on a spare piece of paper. He would arrange for everyone with a boat moored anywhere on Sven Larsen's probable route to be interviewed in case they had seen anyone boarding his yacht. He would have to contact Ingeborg's ex-husband. And then there was the mystery woman in the sunhat and dark glasses who appeared on the videotape. There was something about her that wasn't quite right. He was about to have another look at the tape when something in the notebook caught his eye: the registration number of the black car he had spotted near Longhouse Cottage. He typed the number into the computer and the owner's details flashed up on the screen.

It was fortuitous that PC Paul Johnson chose that moment to walk into the CID office. Wesley called him over.

'Paul, there's something here that might interest you.'

Johnson leaned over to see the computer screen.

'It's the owner of that black car . . . the one that Carl Palister thinks might belong to the Waters House prowler. Look at the name.'

'Address in London. Perhaps he's a visiting relative.'

'Then why not drive up to the house like everyone else? It must be the prowler. Carl's sightings fit the times the prowler was reported. I think we should go and have a word with Mr and Mrs Wentwood when we've got time . . . ask them who exactly this Harry Wentwood is.'

PC Johnson nodded earnestly. He had to admit that he wanted to know the answer to that question himself.

Gerry Heffernan stared at the young man who sat opposite him in the grey, institutional interview room. He was an unprepossessing lad. Neither tall nor small, with mousey hair, grey eyes that were placed too close together above a bulbous nose, and not even enough spots to make him stand out in a crowd. But he had a presence, an aura – hatred, like electricity, positively crackled around him.

Heffernan stared at the tape machine whirring at the edge of the table and paused before he asked the next question. 'So let me get this straight, Pete. You hate your dad and you persuaded this mate you won't name to drive you to your dad's farm to stage a robbery at gunpoint just to frighten him?'

Pete Wexer nodded. 'When I heard about these farm robberies I thought it'd be a good idea. I wanted to make him pay for what he'd done to my mum. She was so cut up when he said he wanted her out . . . when he brought that . . . that bitch into our house. Mum had given him everything . . . she'd never messed about with anyone else. She'd just helped him run the farm and brought us kids up. Then that . . . that . . . she came along to do the farm accounts and they ended up in bed. Mum's been on tablets ever since . . . been backwards and forwards to the doctor with her nerves. And that evil slag . . .' Pete didn't finish the sentence. There were tears in his eyes. 'I wanted to kill him,' he said quietly.

Rachel handed Pete a tissue. He took it from her and blew his nose loudly. 'I love my mum,' he said, sobbing. 'That's why I did it. I saw what he did to her.'

'Does your mum know what you did?' asked Rachel gently. Pete Wexer shook his head. Rachel already knew the answer: Claire Wexer had been shocked at the discovery of the shotgun in her son's room.

'Or your sister?' asked the inspector. 'I met her at the hospital. She didn't seem too fond of your stepmother either.'

'No. Penny's not involved. It was my idea, right? Nobody else's. I shot him and if I go to court I'll tell them all why. I'll tell them how that bastard deserved everything he got and more. He's always been a randy old goat. My uncle told me he got some foreign girl into trouble just before he got married . . . some girl who came to stay on the farm to help my gran. He never could keep his trousers up. I bet that old devil has caused more misery . . . and as for that bitch Jen . . .' He spat the name. 'She didn't give a shit about what she did to my mum. All she wanted was to

171

get her hands on the farm and . . .' The words stopped, their flow plugged by bitterness.

Heffernan could feel the waves of anger and hatred, almost palpable. He hoped his own children would never have cause to speak of him like this. This was not just a thankless child – it was a bitter, wounded one.

Gerry Heffernan and Rachel Tracey took his written statement, then left the room in silence. Neither felt like talking.

After assigning what detective constables were available to waterfront enquiries to discover whether Sven Larsen had been seen with anyone on the evening he died, Wesley Peterson wandered down the corridor in search of PC Johnson. The identity of Harry Wentwood was preying on his mind. The sooner he called at Waters House and asked a few pertinent questions the better.

But Gerry Heffernan, charging down the corridor towards him like an irritated bear, had different ideas. Waters House would have to wait.

'We're off to see Dan Wexer,' Heffernan announced cheerfully. 'His lad told me something interesting. Apparently Dan's been a bit of a lad in his time. According to Pete Wexer, he got a foreign girl into trouble many years ago when he was young . . . a girl who came to help at the farm. Are you thinking what I'm thinking?'

'That it was Ingeborg. She came to stay with a family over here when she was about eighteen. Does the timescale fit?'

'My maths has never been that good, Wes . . . but I think so. We might have found a connection at last.'

'Of course, foreign could mean anything,' said Wesley, pouring cold water on Heffernan's enthusiasm. 'You've got the whole world to choose from.'

'Well, there's only one way to find out. We'll go and ask Wexer.'

'Sven never mentioned that Ingeborg had had a child.'

'She might have had an abortion, or had it adopted . . . anything. Come on, Wes. Let's get over there.'

The inspector sat in the front seat of Wesley's Ford in expectant silence, his eagerness bubbling below the surface. When they drew up at Wexer's Farm, Jen came out to meet them. Heffernan greeted her curtly; Pete's version of her arrival at the farm made

172

him look at the woman in a different, more critical way. She was pretty, certainly, but there was also a hardness in the eyes. Heffernan could well believe that Pete's account was true.

She led them into the house, where Dan Wexer was sitting at a bureau in the corner of the room, filling in official forms, his leg still bandaged and a pair of steel crutches propped up against the wall within easy reach. He turned as the policemen walked in and greeted them with a friendly 'Hello'.

But the smile faded from his face when Gerry Heffernan revealed the identity of his attacker. He seemed shocked – but somehow not surprised – that his own son should attack him, that his own flesh and blood should harbour such hatred. But then, Wesley told himself, it was hardly unusual for people's nearest and dearest to be the focus of such emotions: most murders were family affairs.

He listened while Heffernan asked the questions. Jen, he noticed, was standing near the door, arms folded defensively. She said nothing and her expression gave nothing away. If she felt bad about the misery she had caused in the Wexer household, she certainly didn't show it.

It wasn't long before Heffernan's questioning changed tack dramatically. 'Tell me about this foreign girl you got into trouble before you were first married.'

Wexer's rugged face froze into an expression of shock. He stared at the inspector, his mouth open. Jen stepped forward and sat down on the sofa, interested, curious, rather than disturbed.

'It were only a fling. It were nothing. I can't even remember her name. What's it got to do with our Pete anyway?'

'Tell me about the girl,' Heffernan persisted.

'She were just a girl. Pretty. I were a young lad. Nature took its course. I don't know what it's got to do with . . .'

'And where was she from?'

'I don't know. She was foreign . . . can't remember.'

'What kind of foreign? Italian, Spanish, French, Australian?'

'None of them . . . Swedish or something. I really can't remember.'

'And her name?'

'I can't remember.'

'You slept with a girl who was living here, on your family's farm, and you can't remember her name?' said Wesley with incredulity. 'Charming. Could it have been Ingeborg?'

Wexer wrinkled his brow in an effort of concentration. 'I told you, I don't remember. She was blonde . . . I remember that. And pretty. And it was haymaking; lots of opportunity for . . .' Wexer's wide mouth formed into a sly, lecherous grin.

'I think we get the picture,' said Wesley quietly. 'Did she tell you about herself, where she came from? What did you talk about?'

'Didn't do much talking.' Wexer's grin widened.

Jen Wexer stood up. This had gone far enough. 'I don't know what all this is about but my husband's just come out of hospital and . . .'

'Don't worry, madam, we won't take up any more of your time. Just one more thing, Mr Wexer. Did you ever meet the girl's brother?'

Wexer looked puzzled. 'Brother? I didn't even know she had a brother.'

'But surely if she was pregnant her family . . .'

'Who said she was pregnant? First I've heard about it. About twenty years back I had a fling in a haystack or two with a pretty au pair. That's all. End of story. I've not seen or heard of her since and I certainly don't know if she had a brother. Okay?'

Wesley and Heffernan exchanged looks. There was a finality about Wexer's last words which told them they weren't going to get any more that day. Jen was standing, pointedly waiting to see them off the premises.

'What do you think?' asked Wesley as they climbed into the car.

'I think he's our man. I think he's done away with Ingeborg because of something she threatened to drag up from the past and I think Sven found out about him somehow and got bumped off for his trouble.'

'But what could she drag up? Not their affair, surely . . . that wouldn't bother anyone, least of all Wexer. And Wexer's leg's injured. He could hardly have killed Sven.'

'What about Lady Macbeth in there? I reckon she's capable of most things. She's brought a hell of a lot of misery to that family.'

'Jen Wexer? She might be a ruthless bitch but I don't see her as a murderer. You sound like Pete Wexer.'

174

'Maybe, Wes. What is it they say nowadays? Don't be judgemental?'

'Something like that.'

'But I still reckon it's him . . . or him and Jen. Maybe Ingeborg knew something about Wexer . . . something really bad. Let's find out if anything suspicious happened on Wexer's Farm around the time all this romping in haystacks was going on.'

Wesley nodded. He'd been thinking along the same lines himself. 'Rachel's mother might be able to help. If there was anything untoward going on in the farming community around here, word would surely have got around.'

'Aye. Stella Tracey strikes me as being the kind of woman who has her ear to the ground . . . like daughter like mother, as they say. We'll have a word with Rach then we'll pop along for a gossip this afternoon, shall we?'

Gerry Heffernan sat back in the passenger seat looking pleased with himself while Wesley concentrated on driving down the narrow country lanes.

'You realise where we are, don't you, Wes?'

'Where?' Wesley had been concentrating too much on his driving to notice his surroundings.

'We've just passed the place where Ingeborg's car was found. We'll reach that house she knocked at in a minute – what was it called?'

'Honeysuckle House.' Wesley spotted it. 'There it is on the right.'

They slowed down as they passed the house. Gerry Heffernan leaned across and stared out of the window. 'Nice place, isn't it? Big. You and Pam could do with something like that.'

'Chance'd be a fine thing on a sergeant's salary,' said Wesley without bitterness.

Heffernan's lips twitched upwards in a secretive smile. 'Did I mention I'd had a word with the Super . . . recommended you for promotion?'

'Thanks,' said Wesley simply, feeling the gratifying glow that comes with the knowledge that one's efforts are appreciated . . . at least by someone. 'I was thinking, sir,' he said, changing the subject. 'I'd like to have another look through Sven Larsen's things. There could be something we've missed . . . some mention of someone in this country . . .'

175

'Wexer?'

'Perhaps.'

'Okay, Wes. You get over to the hotel . . . see if anything useful turns up.'

As Wesley turned the car into the police station yard, he had a nagging feeling that there was something he had seen in the past half-hour that held the key to the mystery of Ingeborg's disappearance and Sven's murder. But he couldn't, for the life of him, think what it was.

'There you are, Sergeant,' said the young, smart-suited receptionist as she handed Wesley the key to Sven Larsen's room. She smiled, the distantly friendly smile she had been taught to use during her initial training. Wesley half expected her to add 'Have a nice day', but she controlled herself. Nice days weren't often the lot of police officers.

'Thank you. I'll bring the key back when we've finished,' said Wesley, returning the smile.

'What exactly are we looking for?' asked Rachel as they mounted the thickly carpeted stairs.

'I don't know. Anything.' Wesley marched, determined, towards Larsen's room. 'Did the boss tell you he wants to talk to your mum . . . about Dan Wexer?'

'He did mumble something.'

'He wants to know if anything untoward happened on Wexer's Farm about twenty years ago . . . when Ingeborg was supposed to have been over here. And we need to find out whether this foreign au pair Wexer romped in the hay with was actually Ingeborg.'

'Why don't you ask him?'

'We have. He said he couldn't remember her name.'

'Charming,' said Rachel as Wesley pushed the door to Sven Larsen's room open.

'It shouldn't be this difficult to find out where Ingeborg stayed when she was over here, surely. Her parents are dead and her brother claimed he didn't know. But there must be some way of finding out.'

'Do you think Sven was telling the truth? Do you think he knew who she stayed with?' asked Rachel.

Wesley shrugged. 'There's no way of finding out now, is there?'

They stood together in that neat, tasteful hotel room. Rachel looked at Wesley. He was stroking his chin, deep in thought. She had recovered from her feelings of foolishness. Wesley hadn't realised how she felt . . . neither had anyone else. The situation was retrievable. They were colleagues, friends; nothing more.

'I haven't asked you how Dave is,' said Wesley unexpectedly.

'He's coming out of hospital later today. They wanted to keep an eye on him but he's fine.'

'And what about your little problem?'

She looked at him in alarm. Perhaps he had guessed after all. 'What little problem?'

'Your mother . . . have you put her straight?'

Rachel smiled with relief. 'Yes. I told her and she seemed to understand. If I catch her looking at wedding hats I'll know she hasn't got the message.'

'And Dave?'

Their eyes met and she smiled. 'The jury's still out on that one,' she said simply. 'Where shall we start?' She looked around the room, wondering exactly what it was that Wesley was after. Surely nothing had been missed in the first search.

She rummaged through the wardrobe while Wesley stood by the bed, looking for inspiration. But none came. The room was as bare of clues as when he had last seen it. He sat down on the bed and idly opened the bedside drawer. Inside was a small Gideon Bible, an assortment of leaflets describing local tourist attractions, and a local telephone directory. He pulled them from the drawer and arranged them on the bed. There must be something in this room he had missed the first time around.

He flicked through the Bible, pausing briefly when he encountered familiar verses, learned on the rainy London Sundays of his childhood. He placed it back in the drawer and picked up the telephone directory, searching for anything hidden within its pages.

He hadn't seen it at first, but after he had flicked through the directory a couple of times he noticed a small piece of tissue paper wedged between two pages, as if to mark the place. 'Rach,' he said. 'Look at this. Do you think it could have found its way in there by accident?'

Rachel examined the improvised bookmark. Then she opened

the suitcase at the end of the bed and took out a half-full box of tissues. 'No. I don't think so. It's a piece of one of these tissues from Larsen's case. See? They've got the same imprinted pattern. Larsen must have put it there.'

Now they were getting somewhere. Wesley opened the directory at the marked page. *Wem* to *Wex*. 'Look at this.' He read, 'D. Wexer, Wexer's Farm, Little Shute Lane, Brofton, near Stokeworthy.'

He looked up at Rachel, eager to share his triumph.

'No,' the young woman on reception said in patient, well-trained tones. The phone system used in the hotel recorded only the cost of the call, not the number dialled, unless it was long-distance. There was no quick way of discovering whether Sven Larsen had rung Daniel and Jen Wexer. She was sorry she couldn't help, she said with apparent sincerity.

That was it . . . a tantalising clue but nothing that could be proved. The receptionist hurried to the other end of the marble counter to answer the telephone and Wesley picked up the hotel register, idly flicking through the pages, looking for Sven Larsen's entry. But it was another name that caught his eye. A name with a familiar car number written beside it.

He turned to Rachel. 'Look. There's a Harry Wentwood staying here. Do you remember the Waters House prowler . . . the one we thought might be connected with the farm robberies?'

Rachel nodded, wondering where this was leading.

'A black car was seen parked near Waters House at the times the prowler was reported. I checked the number on the computer and found that it belonged to a Harry Wentwood. Now we haven't had a chance to speak to the people in Waters House yet, but their name's Wentwood, so it could be a relative of theirs. It's probably quite innocent but . . .'

'But you want to see this Harry Wentwood to get his side of the story?' Rachel could see the sense in this.

'Might as well talk to him while we're here . . . if he's in. Excuse me,' he called to the receptionist, who had just finished her phone call, 'is Mr Wentwood in?'

She checked, a model of efficiency. 'Yes. Shall I ring his room for you?'

'Er, no . . . we'll go up and have a quick word.'

The young woman's helpful expression changed to one of officious challenged authority. 'I don't know whether . . .'

'What number is it?' asked Wesley, ignoring the woman's misgivings.

'Thirty-two, but . . .'

Wesley marched up the stairs towards Room 32. Rachel, following, glanced back and saw that the receptionist had lifted the phone, no doubt warning Wesley's quarry of their imminent arrival.

Room 32 wasn't locked. Wesley discovered this after he had stood knocking politely on the door for a full minute without receiving an answer. He turned the door handle and the door swung open smoothly.

On the bed lay an elderly man, his eyes shut, as in sleep. He had the distinguished appearance of one used to authority and he had, in his younger days, been good-looking: that much was obvious to Rachel even from the brief glimpse she had of his face. He lay on his side, his six-foot frame curled in foetal comfort. The shirt he wore tucked into a pair of grey cavalry twill trousers was good quality but frayed at the collar and cuffs. And a pair of expensive but well-worn brown brogues lay with military neatness at the side of the bed.

'He's asleep,' mouthed Rachel. 'Let's leave him, eh?'

But Wesley stepped towards the bed and touched the man's face gently. Then he touched the neck and kept his fingers pressed there till he was sure.

'He's not asleep,' he said gently, almost in a whisper. 'He's dead.'

Chapter Thirteen

AD 997

I asked my mother what was the sound I heard from within. She seemed greatly afeared and said it was her Christian duty to care for the sick and wounded. I agreed that this was so but I knew that she was keeping something from me that I, as her son, should know.

So I left her with Hilda and went into the house. There, through the gloom and the smoke of the fire, I saw a man. He was tall of stature, the tallest man I have seen. His hair was light and he stared at me with eyes blue as summer sky. I saw that his body was wounded and bound with cloth about the shoulder. He showed no fear of me. I asked him who he was but he spoke in some foreign tongue, words I could not comprehend.

Then he reached for a great sword that lay beneath the window and held it at me and I was greatly feared. My mother entered and shouted to him that I was her son and not to hurt me. I shielded her with my body, to protect her, but she went to him, taking the sword from his hand which he allowed most meekly. 'My son,' she said. 'This man is wounded and in my care. I pray you, do him no harm.'

'What manner of man is he?' I asked, fearful of our safety.

'His name is Olaf,' my mother said, standing by his side. 'And he is a Dane.'

From the chronicle of Brother Edwin

'What are you doing, Wes? Killing 'em yourself? We're not on piece-work, you know. Don't you think we've got enough on our plates at the moment without you going round finding more dead bodies? When you or that Neil aren't digging 'em up, you go searching for 'em in hotel rooms.'

Gerry Heffernan paced up and down his office floor, wondering how much worse things could get.

'I wouldn't worry about this one, sir. Colin Bowman says it looks like natural causes, probably a heart attack. And he found some heart pills in the dead man's bedside drawer. He's doing a post-mortem some time tomorrow but . . .'

But Gerry Heffernan wasn't listening. 'And the Super's going berserk about the budget,' he said, still pacing, scratching at his bare, tattooed forearms.

Wesley had worked with Heffernan long enough to know his moods and ignore them. 'I'm going over to Waters House to see if they know anything about the dead man, Harry Wentwood. I've told you that his car's been seen up there when they've reported that prowler, haven't I?'

Heffernan took a deep breath and stopped pacing. 'Yeah, you do that, Wes. And call in to see how Maggie Palister's getting on while you're up there, will you?'

'If I've got time. I think I'll take Paul Johnson with me. He's been up to Waters House before. They know him.'

'Right you are. And I'll pay Mrs Tracey a little visit . . . see what gossip I can pick up about Dan Wexer's amorous exploits. Have you had any feedback on those enquiries of yours yet? Found anyone who saw Sven Larsen on the day he died?'

'A local fisherman said he thought he saw him on the deck of his yacht with an elderly man but he couldn't give a description. And a woman on a visiting yacht said she might have seen someone possibly fitting Sven's description with a woman in dark glasses . . . but again she couldn't be sure. The trouble is that in the holiday season there are so many strangers around that people don't take much notice.'

Wesley left his boss contemplating modern man's ever-weakening powers of observation. Ten minutes later he was sitting beside PC Johnson, heading out to Stoke Beeching, enjoying the view as Johnson steered the patrol car along the winding coast road. As the car swung into the long drive of Waters House, Wesley looked to his left. Over a tumbling stone wall, he could see Longhouse Cottage, where half a dozen skinny sheep grazed unperturbed by the events of the past week.

Johnson parked neatly in front of Waters House next to a tiny blue, rust-encrusted Fiat. Over by the garage stood a blue Volvo estate. Wesley hoped the Wentwoods didn't have visitors.

They were unfastening their seat belts when the front door opened and a woman rushed out. She was plain, middle-aged; hardly one to turn heads or stand out in any sort of crowd, however small. Wesley stared as she climbed into the Fiat and drove quickly away down the drive. He had seen her before but he couldn't remember where. His mother had always said that if you stopped thinking so hard it would come to you eventually. So he tried to put the woman's face from his thoughts as he knocked on the once-imposing front door of Waters House.

It was Gwen Wentwood who answered. She looked anxious, and there were deep, dark rings beneath her eyes.

'We're sorry to bother you, Mrs Wentwood,' Wesley began, trying to put the woman at her ease. 'But I think we might have some news about your prowler.'

A fleeting expression of alarm passed over Gwen's face as she stood in the doorway defensively.

'May we come in?' asked Wesley, as an invitation didn't seem to be forthcoming.

Without a word Gwen Wentwood led them through to the back of the house. Wesley noted the shabby, half-finished look of the decor. Wallpaper was stripped off in places but there seemed to have been no serious attempt at redecoration; fireplaces were ripped out, awaiting replacement by something more fashionable. He had the strong impression of grand ideas thwarted when the money – or the inclination – ran out. The Wentwoods had, perhaps, overreached themselves.

'I'm sorry to bring bad news, Mrs Wentwood,' said Wesley gently as he sat down in a large, lumpy armchair which had seen better days. 'But a Mr Harry Wentwood has been found dead in a hotel in Tradmouth. Suspected heart attack. We wondered if he was a relation of yours.'

He waited expectantly. Johnson took his notebook from his uniform pocket and sat on the edge of his seat, preparing to write.

'What makes you think he was a relative?' said Gwen without emotion.

'His car was seen by your neighbours at Longhouse Cottage. The number gave us his name and address. The car was seen around the times your husband reported your prowler.'

There was a long silence while Gwen considered her reply. 'Harry Wentwood was my husband's father. They didn't get on . . . never spoke. Of course, when he reported the prowler he'd no idea it was his father. It wasn't until he called here last night that we knew. There was a knock on the front door at about nine o'clock and there he was . . . just standing there.' She shook her head. 'I can't believe he's dead. He seemed so . . .'

'It seems he had a heart attack.'

'He did say he was very ill. But I don't think Christopher believed him . . . I mean, people say that, don't they . . . when they want sympathy.'

'Can you tell us what happened last night?' Wesley glanced across at Johnson, who was rearranging his long legs in preparation for a writing session.

'He came here and my husband said he didn't want to see him. I know they've not talked for years . . . in fact, I'd never met Harry before. Then my husband's sister, Ursula, came over from the studio and found him here. She went mad. Told him to get out. Said she never wanted to see him again. She can be very determined . . . far more so than Christopher,' she added fondly. 'Then Harry left and he gave me his phone number at the hotel in case Christopher changed his mind. That's it really.'

'Do you know what they'd fallen out about?'

'Christopher and Ursula just said it was a family matter. Families are sometimes like that, aren't they, Sergeant?' she said with an awkward smile. 'They fall out over a will or some trivial matter and the thing festers for years.'

'What about Christopher's mother?' asked Johnson, beating Wesley to the question.

'She died when the children were young. Then they went to live in London with their father. It must have been after that they fell out.'

'Where were they living when their mother died . . . before they moved to London?' asked Wesley.

'It was somewhere round here but I'm not sure where. Christopher wanted to get away from London, from the rat race . . . start his own small business in the country.'

183

'It seems to be a common dream these days,' said Wesley sympathetically. 'I came here from London myself . . . used to be in the Met.'

Gwen Wentwood looked up, suddenly interested. 'I should really be used to moving about: I was in the army before I married. But it's not easy, is it . . . moving somewhere where you don't know anyone? And Christopher's working so hard . . . and he's not been well.' She looked around. 'We had all these plans to do up this place. I thought it would be good for Christopher to have an interest but . . .' She didn't finish the sentence.

Wesley nodded sympathetically. 'Does your husband's sister live with you?'

'In the studio at the side of the garage.'

'Perhaps we should have a word with her. Is she in?'

'No. She's out selling her pottery.' Gwen picked up a brightly coloured dish, decorated with leaping dolphins, from the rickety coffee table. 'It's good, isn't it? She makes it here and sells it through craft shops . . . and there are enough of those in Tradmouth and Neston,' she added with a bitter smile. 'Not much else really. I miss the shops in London, don't you?'

Shops had never come high on Wesley's list of priorities. 'I expect my wife does,' he said for the sake of politeness. 'When will your husband and your sister-in-law be back? We should really have a word with them about their father.'

'Your guess is as good as mine.'

'Will you ask them to get in touch with me?' He handed her his card. 'I'm sorry about your father-in-law,' he added formally as Gwen saw them off the premises. 'By the way, a woman left as we arrived . . . middle-aged, drove a blue Fiat. I'm sure I've seen her somewhere before.'

'Her name's Millie. She used to work for my husband's family when he was young . . . some sort of cleaner or housekeeper.' Gwen Wentwood changed the subject. 'What was going on at Longhouse Cottage the other day? There seemed to be police cars everywhere . . .'

'We, er . . . had to make an arrest in connection with a series of armed robberies. But it's all cleared up now . . . nothing to worry about.'

As Wesley climbed into the police car beside PC Johnson he looked back at Gwen Wentwood standing in the doorway of

Waters House and noted that his last words to her didn't seem to have reassured her in the least. She looked worried. Very worried indeed.

Rachel wondered how Gerry Heffernan and Steve were getting on with her mother. No doubt they were being stuffed full of home-made scones and regaled with Mrs Tracey's brilliant deductions. Rachel knew that her mother had never taken to Dan Wexer; but she had liked his former wife, Claire. She had made no secret of her disapproval when Dan had replaced Claire with some flashy young thing who worked for a firm of accountants – a calculating young woman in more ways than one.

She feared that before the afternoon was out her mother would have Daniel Wexer tried and sentenced for Ingeborg Larsen's abduction, Sven Larsen's murder and any other unsolved crimes in the area that happened to spring to mind.

But Rachel had other things on her mind: there was something she wanted to check. She strolled casually over to Trish's desk. Trish looked up, suspicious, and Rachel flashed her a conspiratorial smile.

'Trish, have you got time to give me a hand with something? It's just an idea, but you know those videos you looked through?'

'Yes,' said Trish, wary. 'What about them?'

'Do you remember Proudy said that there was a woman hanging around when he saw Ingeborg?'

Trish nodded. She knew what was coming.

'Can you go through all the tapes where Ingeborg appears and see if this woman's there too?'

Trish looked out of the office window at the sun-drenched scene outside – the boats bobbing on the sparkling river, the brightly clad holidaymakers meandering slowly along the water-front – and nodded, resigned to spending the next few hours cooped in a small stuffy room.

But Trish's sentence was shorter than she had feared. The tapes on which Ingeborg made a fleeting appearance had been separated from the rest and the task was fairly easy. After half an hour she emerged, triumphant. 'She's there,' she announced proudly to Rachel. 'I've found her.'

'Well, I wouldn't leave that Dan Wexer alone with any daughter of mine,' Stella Tracey said righteously. 'Not that my daughter

185

can't take care of herself,' she added swiftly, not wishing to criticise Rachel in front of her boss and her bored-looking colleague, who was sitting with his feet up on a neighbouring chair.

'In fact,' she continued, 'I reckon that Jen's young enough to be his daughter. And his ex-wife Claire's a lovely woman. He's just a randy old sod, that's what he is, chucking his wife off the farm and installing some . . . dolly bird.' Steve smirked at this archaic expression, earning himself a look of disapproval from Stella.

'And I'm not surprised about young Pete attacking his dad. Those kids were so angry at what happened. He told them they could stay on the farm but there's no way they wanted to. They went with their mum. Poor Claire,' she muttered, shaking her head at the injustice of it all. Then she looked up with a sudden, gloating smile. 'Mind you, I've heard that Claire's gone and got herself a new bloke . . . a widower who works at Neston Pottery. Good luck to her, that's what I say.'

Steve looked impatiently at Gerry Heffernan, who was nodding in agreement.

Stella regarded Steve with renewed distaste. 'I thought you'd bring that Wesley with you. He seems such a nice young man.'

'He's over at Stoke Beeching,' said Heffernan cheerfully. 'I thought our Steve here could do with some fresh air.'

'He could do with a few lessons in manners,' she said pointedly. Steve, getting the message, took his feet off the chair, reddened and sat up straight.

Gerry Heffernan gave Steve a withering look and took a sip of tea from the colourful mug, decorated with leaping sheep, on the table. 'Nice mug . . . very appropriate for a farm,' he said, feeling he had to make up for Steve's shortcomings.

'Yes, they're lovely, aren't they. Rachel bought them for me for Christmas. They're made by a woman out at Stoke Beeching . . . Ursula Wentwood. She's getting to be quite well known round here.'

Wentwood? Heffernan wondered if she was any relation to the late Harry, whose untimely death had caused such a ripple in the Tower Hotel's normally calm surface. He leaned forward. 'I wonder if you remember a foreign girl staying on Wexer's Farm . . . before Dan Wexer was first married. It must have been about twenty years ago, give or take a couple of years.'

Stella sat down at the kitchen table and thought hard. 'Yes,' she announced, looking up. 'I remember hearing something about it through the grapevine. I never actually saw the girl, of course.'

'What did you hear?'

'Just that young Dan had been having a bit of how's your father with this girl who'd come as an au pair to help his mother in the house.'

'You don't remember the girl's name, I suppose? Or her nationality?'

'Sorry,' Stella said, shaking her head. 'I never even saw the girl.'

'And can you remember anything unusual happening at Wexer's Farm around that time? An accident, a death ... anything?'

Stella thought for a few seconds. 'That was about the time Jos Wexer, Dan's father, was killed . . . an accident. Tragic, it was. He fell into a baling machine. I mean, farms can be dangerous places if you're not careful . . . these things happen.'

Gerry Heffernan was sitting up and taking a great deal of notice. 'Was there ever any suggestion that it might not have been an accident?'

'Not that I know of. No.'

'Where was Dan at the time?'

'Oh, I think he was there . . . helping with the harvesting.'

'Is Dan's mother still alive?'

Stella shook her head. 'No, she passed away about five years back.'

'And this accident happened at the same time as this au pair was on the scene?'

'Yes. I think it was around that time. I heard she went home after the accident. I suppose it was upsetting for her.'

'I bet it was,' said Gerry Heffernan, picking up his mug and taking a long hot drink of tea. 'I bet it was.'

'Why are we here exactly, Sarge?' PC Paul Johnson parked the patrol car in front of Longhouse Cottage, took off his hat and scratched his head, puzzled.

'The inspector wanted me to check whether Maggie Palister's all right. What did you think of Mrs Wentwood?'

'They seem to be struggling a bit up there in that big house, don't they? Overreached themselves financially, I reckon. That bit about him not being well was just an excuse.'

'You could be right. She certainly looked worried about something.'

As Wesley began to climb out of the car, he heard someone calling his name. He looked round and noticed Neil's disreputable Mini parked among the rotting vehicles at the other end of the yard. Neil himself was marching towards him across the field where the skeleton had been found. Carl Palister was following behind, hanging back a little at the sight of the police car.

'Wes. What are you doing here?'

'I might ask you the same question.'

'Loom weights.'

'I beg your pardon?'

'Loom weights. Carl's found a load of them over by the door. He thought they were just stones, then he saw they had holes in so he called me up to have a look. They're late Saxon, I reckon, which fits in with the other finds round here. Carl's found a load of late Saxon pottery and all.' Neil grinned widely, getting into his stride. 'I think we're building up a picture of this place, Wes. I reckon the present building's medieval – classic Devon long-house – but I think there was an earlier, Saxon house on the site.' He looked around hungrily. 'I'd love to do a proper dig here . . . get everything excavated and recorded.' He paused, examining the loom weight in his hand. 'I think that when the Danes were rampaging around this area, one of them was killed and buried in the field down there, along with his sword and shield and a boat for him to sail to Valhalla in . . . the hall of the slain. And I reckon he either died in some sort of battle – in which case you'd expect to find more bodies – or he was murdered,' he concluded with satisfaction. 'So it's over to you, Detective Sergeant.'

'I don't know what you expect me to do about it after a thousand years. I've got enough on my plate with modern-day crime . . . more than enough. Is Mrs Palister in?'

'Mum's in,' muttered Carl. 'But I don't know if she wants to see any filth at the moment.'

'Inspector Heffernan asked me to see whether she's okay.'

Carl thought about this for a moment, then nodded.

Wesley signalled to Johnson to stay where he was and knocked softly on the front door. Maggie Palister answered and stood aside resentfully to let him in.

'I'm sorry to bother you, Mrs Palister, but Inspector Heffernan asked me to look in and check you're all right.'

Unexpectedly Maggie gave a bitter smile. 'I wouldn't say I was all right but I'll survive.' She lit a cigarette and flashed the packet at Wesley. He shook his head. 'I started on these things again when Jock turned up out of the blue. I never thought I'd see him again. It was a bloody shock, I can tell you. I thought it was all over . . . the bullying, the black eyes. But when he turned up again – and with that Darren, a mate to show off to – it all started again.' She slid the shoulder of her shabby dress down to reveal a thin shoulder, bruised blue. 'I wasn't sorry to see the police here that day,' she said quietly. 'I've struggled to keep this place going . . . for Carl and me. Then he just turns up and acts like it's all his . . . like I'm all his and all. He comes in here after three years thinking he can just take up where he left off. Carl doesn't know the half of it.'

Wesley watched her as she sucked desperately at the cigarette. 'It's all over now, Mrs Palister. He's going to be in prison for a long time.'

'But what about when he gets out? He'll be back.'

'Let's hope not.'

'I told the policeman who arrested him that if any money's found on him it's mine. I had a bit put by . . . hid it in a little hole near the fireplace, under the floor. But he bloody found it, pinched it . . . a hundred and twenty quid.'

'I'll ask for you. There's a chance you'll get it back if he had it on him.' Wesley smiled sympathetically. 'How much did you know about the farm robberies?'

'I knew he was up to something but I didn't know what. Then Carl went and found that bloody skeleton and called the police. When Jock saw you lot crawling over the place he went berserk. It wasn't long after that that Carl found out what he was really like. Then we had to be careful. Jock could be violent, you see. Oh, I don't mean in robberies or anything like that, only to his family . . . and like all bullies he liked to throw his weight around.'

'It's over, Mrs Palister. You can get on with building this place up now. Carl seems a bright lad.'

'Thank God he doesn't seem to have taken after his father,

that's all I can say.' She gave one last desperate suck on what was left of her cigarette and stubbed it out in a dirty saucer. 'And I'm going to try to give these up and all,' she added as she gave the cigarette a last, violent stab, crushing out the memory of Jock Palister.

Wesley decided it was time he changed the subject. 'Do you see much of your neighbours up in Waters House?'

'No. They keep themselves to themselves.'

'Do you know anything about them?'

'I know it's a couple called Wentwood . . . and there's another woman who's turned the old coach house into a pottery. Why?'

'You don't know if they used to live round here years ago?'

'I think they did years ago; then they moved to London after one of their parents died. That's all I know . . . and that's just what they told me when they bought the place. But I wasn't taking much notice at the time. I had enough problems of my own without taking notice of other people's.'

'That black car which you and Carl saw parked on the main road . . . it belonged to an elderly man. Did you ever see him going up there?'

Maggie shook her head.

Wesley walked slowly towards the open front door. 'Inspector Heffernan says that if ever you need anything you can get in touch with him. You've got his number, haven't you?'

Maggie Palister nodded and watched as Wesley walked away across the uneven stony yard and down towards where Neil and Carl were deep in conversation. PC Johnson, he noticed, had returned to his patrol car and was sitting with the door wide open, enjoying the sun.

'Wesley,' called Neil. 'How's Pam getting on with that translation?'

'I think she's just about finished. I haven't read any of it yet but . . .'

'I'll call round for it later, then I can get all the stuff over to the County Museum. Do you want to see what we've found here? The broken loom weights were all together as if the loom was knocked over violently.'

Neil held out a plastic box containing shards of pottery which Wesley recognised as late Saxon. Beside them lay half a dozen broken pieces of clay, about the size of a fist with holes in the centre. A thousand years ago they had hung from a loom to weigh down the threads. Wesley picked one up and examined it, deep in thought.

He had the uneasy feeling that somewhere in the Palisters' struggling smallholding, in the strange, obsolete object he held, lay a clue to Ingeborg Larsen's fate.

'I've found her on five tapes, sir. She never gets too close to Ingeborg but it looks like she might have been following her.'

Gerry Heffernan, newly returned from Little Barton Farm and sated with Stella Tracey's freshly baked scones topped with home-made jam and thick clotted cream, slumped into the chair beside Trish. 'Let's have a shufti, then.'

'The woman keeps her identity well hidden. She's wearing dark glasses and her hair's hidden by a straw sunhat. I couldn't even tell whether she was blonde or dark-haired. Sorry, sir.'

'Not your fault, Trish. That was probably the intention.'

Trish put the first tape in the video machine and they watched as Ingeborg Larsen, in grainy black and white, searched through racks of summer dresses. Near by, seemingly engrossed in a selection of T-shirts, was another woman, her hair concealed by a hat and her face by a pair of large dark glasses. In any other weather she would have looked conspicuous, but not in a heat wave. Heffernan studied her carefully.

Trish put on another tape; then another. There was no sign that the woman was following Ingeborg, or that Ingeborg was aware of her presence, as the woman always took care to keep her distance. But it was too much of a coincidence that she should choose the same time to browse in the same shops. And Gerry Heffernan wasn't a great believer in coincidence.

'Rach!' he called through to the outer office. Rachel came hurrying in, and he rewound the tape and played it again for her benefit. 'What do you reckon, Rach? Do you think that woman there in the dark glasses looks like Jen Wexer?'

Rachel peered more closely at the screen.

As Wesley Peterson looked out of the window of the patrol car, he didn't notice the fields of ripening crops and fattening livestock that flashed by outside. His mind was working, making connections, piecing together elusive fragments. There was an answer to the mystery of Ingeborg Larsen's disappearance and her brother's murder. It was just that, so far, he hadn't been asking the right questions.

'Paul,' he said quietly, 'can we drive along the B road from Neston to Stokeworthy – the one where Ingeborg Larsen's car was found?'

'Sure thing, Sarge,' said Johnson enthusiastically as he flicked the indicator to turn left onto the road out of Tradmouth.

They drove for a while in amicable silence, and Johnson slowed down as they came to the spot where the car had stood.

He was surprised when Wesley asked him to drive on farther towards Neston and stop outside a large, creeper-clad pink-washed house. Wesley sat and stared at the house.

Johnson watched him with patient curiosity. 'Well?' he said after a few minutes.

Wesley looked at him. 'I'm just going to see if anyone's in. It's just an idea . . . if it doesn't come to anything there's no need to tell the boss, eh?'

Johnson grinned and nodded as Wesley got out of the car. He watched the sergeant stroll up to the highly polished front door of the house and knock. Then, when the door was opened and Wesley stepped inside, Paul Johnson took a Spanish phrase book from the glove box and settled down for a little light self-education.

Honeysuckle House was every bit as desirable inside as it was out. Pam, Wesley thought, would have loved it. The hallway was spacious and airy, painted in delicate Wedgwood blue and lined with highly polished antique furniture. Mrs Jerworth, a slight woman in late middle age with steel-grey bobbed hair and a floaty summer dress that made her look younger than her years, invited Wesley into the elegant sitting room and offered him tea with scrupulous politeness. He thought of Johnson waiting outside, felt a small pang of conscience, and declined the offer.

'I'm afraid I've not remembered any more about that poor woman, Sergeant. I've really told the police all I know,' Mrs Jerworth said apologetically, sitting on the edge of a brocade-covered armchair.

'I appreciate that, Mrs Jerworth. We're trying to discover as much as we can about the missing woman's background, and it's possible that you might be able to help us.'

'If I can,' said Mrs Jerworth with the co-operative enthusiasm of the law-abiding citizen.

'I've been wondering why Ms Larsen chose to call at this house. Could you tell me how long you've lived here?'

'Twenty years, Sergeant. My late husband had just retired from the Royal Navy – he'd been posted at the Naval College in Tradmouth – and we were looking for somewhere local. We saw this place and we fell in love with it. There were those who said we shouldn't buy it, of course. There are always superstitious people around but I took no notice.'

'Superstitious? What about?'

'About the suicide. A woman who lived here committed suicide shortly before we moved in. I never asked any details, of course . . . I didn't want to know. And it has always been a happy house for us. My husband passed away last year, of course, but that was his heart . . . nothing to do with the house.' She smiled sadly. 'We've been very happy here, Sergeant.'

Wesley sat forward. There was one question he was burning to ask. 'Could you tell me the name of the people who lived here before you? The people involved in this alleged suicide.'

'Of course.'

As Mrs Jerworth told him the name, Wesley Peterson began to feel more confused than ever.

Chapter Fourteen

AD 997

*I wandered back to the village, my mind distracted. Hilda
followed me, fearing for my safety. I had to know the truth of
how that creature, Olaf, came to be in my mother's house and
in her care. It was Ordgar who was once my playfellow who
told me. He had escaped the evil ones but had heard the tale
from others. He told of how my father was on the shore and
was killed by the heathen as they came off their ships. He told
how my mother had found one of the Danes sorely wounded –
Ordgar said it was the man who slew my father. Ordgar said
also that my mother had given herself to the creature. I struck
Ordgar and would have killed him but Hilda knelt, comforting
me, begging me to come away . . . not to add to all the killing
and wickedness our people have endured.*

From the chronicle of Brother Edwin

Wesley rushed into the foyer of Tradmouth police station, his eyes
fixed on Bob Naseby. If he could get Bob's mind off the cricket
pitch for a few minutes, he might be just the man to help.

But Bob was otherwise engaged. A woman and a tearful child
were reporting a missing dog. Wesley waited, trying not to show
his impatience, until Rex's details had been meticulously recorded
and Bob's professional sympathy dispensed.

As the bereft dog-owners left the station, Bob gave Wesley a
knowing wink and leaned his bowling arm on the desk. 'What can
I do for you then, Wesley?' His face lit up. 'You've not changed
your mind about playing on Sunday, have you? There's always
room on the team for a good all-rounder, you know.' He beamed

at Wesley hopefully, so eager that Wesley felt churlish for not volunteering immediately.

'It's nothing to do with cricket, I'm afraid. Who can I ask about a case of suicide twenty years ago? It was at a place called Honeysuckle House on the road from Stokeworthy to Neston.'

Bob Naseby scratched his chin, deep in thought. 'You'll want Billy Cawthorne over at Morbay. He was attached to Neston for years until he was transferred. There's not much that went on that he didn't know about.' Bob shook his head. 'Old Billy, eh . . . must be nearing retirement.'

'Is it Sergeant Cawthorne . . . Inspector?' asked Wesley tentatively, not wishing to offend.

'Oh, no . . . just Constable. Billy never had much ambition. One of the old school is Billy . . . more at home on the beat than filling in forms. I'll ring him for you, if you like.'

'Thanks. That'd be a great help.'

Wesley wandered back to the CID office, turning over the possibilities in his mind. He pushed open the office door and found Gerry Heffernan holding court, the assembled officers hanging on his every word. And he was looking remarkably pleased with himself.

When the speech was finished and the troops rallied, Heffernan took Wesley to one side. 'We're bringing Wexer in . . . and that wife of his,' he announced in a stage whisper. 'I think we've cracked it, Wes. Stella Tracey told me that Wexer's father was killed at the farm about the time this foreign au pair was staying there. I suspect old man Wexer's death wasn't an accident . . . in fact there was a bit of a question mark over it at the time, so I've sent for all the files. I think Dan bumped his dad off and this au pair – possibly Ingeborg – was a vital witness. I think she came back and threatened to let a very fat cat out of the bag. Then she got murdered for her trouble and so did her brother, who was on her trail. It all fits, Wes.' He rubbed his chubby hands together in excitement. 'And you've not heard the best bit.'

'What's that?' Wesley felt faintly disappointed. It did all fit, as the inspector said. But Wesley's thoughts had been progressing along very different lines.

'Trish had another look through those videos, the ones where Ingeborg appeared. On a few of them there's this other woman . . .

not with Ingeborg, just near by. I think she was following her, and you know who the woman looks like?'

'Who?'

'Jen Wexer. She's got dark glasses on and her hair's all covered by a big hat but I'm sure it's her.'

'Good. Now it's a matter of proving it.'

'Oh, we'll do that, Wes. Don't you worry. The sun's shining and I'm feeling lucky.'

Wesley decided to take a break; to go home, remind his wife of his existence and grab a swift meal before returning to the fray. If Dan and Jen Wexer were being brought in, it was likely to be a very long day indeed.

There was something different about Pam, a sparkle in her eyes. She sat by the kitchen table shovelling baby rice into Michael's open mouth, with a secretive smile on her lips. Wesley bent down and kissed her cheek. He thought he'd better get her in a good mood before telling her that he'd have to spend the evening at work.

Pam took the announcement philosophically. Then she looked up at him, a satisfied grin on her face. 'Neil called half an hour ago for those things he's taking to the County Museum. And you've got a treat in store,' she added intriguingly.

'What's that?'

'A murder. And one that's not your problem because it's a thousand years old.'

Wesley sat down beside her. 'Go on.'

'No. You'll have to read it for yourself. I managed to finish translating all that Old English and it turned out to be quite a story. A Brother Edwin fled from the minster at Neston when the town was raided by the Vikings. He took some parchments with him and wrote the whole story down . . . apparently he was the monk whose job it was to keep the minster chronicle. Anyway, he met up with this nun called Hilda who was crazy about him and they became lovers. They made their way to Stoke Beeching where his family lived and found that the Vikings had destroyed all the villages on the way. So when they got to Stoke Beeching they found . . .' She stopped, her eyes twinkling mischievously. 'No. You'll just have to wait till you read it.' She grinned at him, teasing, lifted the baby from his highchair and placed him carefully in his carrycot, stroking his tiny, golden-brown cheek and being rewarded with a wide, toothless smile.

Wesley grabbed her waist and started to kiss her. 'You can't leave the story there.'

'Can't I?' She kissed him back, gently at first, then more eagerly, more passionately, pressing her body on his. 'Haven't you got to go back to work?'

Wesley glanced at the clock on the mantelpiece. 'I reckon I've got an hour before Gerry gets back,' he said, taking her hand and leading her up the stairs. 'And I enjoy a good story,' he said softly, Brother Edwin's exploits being the last thing on his mind.

The first thing Wesley Peterson did when he returned to Tradmouth police station after his brief spell of connubial bliss was to open the drawer of the large filing cabinet that stood in the corner of the office. It was high time he talked to Ingeborg's ex-husband. He pulled out the plastic exhibit bag containing Sven Larsen's address book, placed it on the desk and flicked through the pages. Now all he had to find was a Bjorn.

To his dismay there were three Bjorns listed. The first was a casual acquaintance who seemed to show no curiosity as to why the English police were ringing him out of the blue; the second didn't answer his phone; the third was the Bjorn he had been looking for – Ingeborg's ex-husband.

Luckily for Wesley, Bjorn Sorensen spoke excellent English. Although Wesley couldn't see his face, he was confident that the shock and grief Bjorn expressed at the news of Sven's death were genuine. Sven had been a friend as well as a former brother-in-law. And when Bjorn asked about the progress they had made in the search for Ingeborg, it was clear that he still had some feelings for his ex-wife; he assured Wesley that he would do anything he could to help find her. He asked whether Wesley thought there was any chance she was still alive. Wesley had to be honest. He said he didn't know; all they had was hope.

Much as he longed to leave this unfortunate, unseen man across the sea alone with his grief, there was a question Wesley had to ask.

'Mr Sorensen, Ingeborg came to England – to Devon – when she was about eighteen to work as an au pair. I don't suppose you

197

know the name of the family she stayed with. I'm sorry to have to ask you at a time like this but it could be important.'

There was a silence on the other end of the line while Bjorn Sorensen gathered his thoughts. 'I don't know, Sergeant. It was long before we met. I'm sorry. But . . .' He hesitated. 'Ingeborg has a lot of old documents and letters still at my house. She left them here when she moved out. They go back to when she was a child.'

Wesley took a deep breath, trying to control his excitement. 'I don't suppose you could . . .'

'They are all in a big case – what do you call it? – a trunk up in the roof . . . the attic. I will look and ring you back if I find anything. Yes?'

'Please . . . if you could . . .'

'And there is something else I must tell you, Sergeant. Before he left for England, Sven said that Ingeborg told him she planned to visit someone in Devon. He had seemed worried about this. He said she was being foolish. I told him he must tell the police everything when he arrived in England but he said that he did not wish to involve the authorities. He said he would deal with the matter himself. I asked him what it was all about but he said it was better that I did not know. That is all the information I have. I am sorry.'

'Thank you, Mr Sorensen. You've been a great help.'

At that point Wesley heard a loud and gleeful Liverpudlian voice bellowing in the distance. 'Wes, where are you? I've got a surprise for you in the interview room.'

Wesley put the phone down and went out of the office to investigate.

'We'll have a drink tonight, eh, Wes? Celebrate. We've got him.'

'Who, sir?'

'Dan Wexer. He says he wants to make a full confession. Rach and Trish are interviewing Jen and all. We'll crack it by tonight.'

'And Ingeborg?'

'What about her?'

'Is she still alive?'

Gerry Heffernan looked at his sergeant as though he were mad. 'I doubt it. But he'll tell us what he's done with the body.'

'And what about Honeysuckle House?'

'What about it?'

'What I've just told you. What Mrs Jerworth said about . . .'

'Oh, that's got nothing to do with it, Wes. Just a coincidence . . . she called there for directions or something. There's no evidence to connect . . .'

'No, sir. I suppose you're right.'

They opened the door to the interview room. Seated at the table was Daniel Wexer, his crutches in the care of the young constable stationed by the door. He looked up, an expression of resignation in his eyes.

'I've come to get it off my chest,' he said with a sigh.

Gerry Heffernan switched on the tape recorder and gabbled the legally required words. 'Now, Mr Wexer. What would you like to tell us?'

Wexer hesitated, watching the whirring tape. Then he spoke in a loud, clear voice. 'I want to confess to murder.'

Chapter Fifteen

AD 997

*Then we returned to the house. I had feared what I should
discover there but I had not prepared myself for the sight. My
mother and Olaf, like beasts of the field, taking their pleasure
in the bed she had shared with my father. I watched as they
sweated and groaned in their shame. At that moment my
mother was dead to me. Hilda begged me to leave them to
God. But I pushed her away. I knew what must be done.*

From the chronicle of Brother Edwin

'It was twenty years back ... more maybe. Late summer –
harvest. The baler was going and my dad was standing up top.
We'd been having trouble with it and he was checking it didn't get
clogged up, like. We'd had a row, me and Dad. He treated me like
dirt sometimes and I knew I could run the place better than him. I
had all these new ideas and ... Anyway, he called me up and told
me to keep an eye on the machine while he went off. He said
something – I can't remember what exactly – something like he'd
better not be long because he couldn't trust me to do anything
right. He starts to come towards me and I tell him to get lost ...
that I'm sick of being treated like a child, that he was past it and
he had no idea how to run a modern farm and he was holding us
back. Then he starts to shout ... says I should be taught a lesson.
He takes a swing at me and I grab hold of him and he loses his
balance and falls into the baler. I could hear his screams ... it
were awful. People came running and I pretended I'd just arrived.
But I'd killed him, murdered him ... my own father.'

Dan Wexer put his face in his hands and sobbed. Wesley and

Heffernan looked at each other. After a while Wexer drew a clean handkerchief from his trouser pocket and blew his nose loudly.

'So you're saying you made your father lose his temper, then he lost his balance . . . but you didn't mean to kill him?' Heffernan thought he'd better get things straight.

'I never meant to kill him. The coroner at the inquest said it was an accident and in a way it was. I never meant to kill him . . . never.'

'What about the au pair? Where was she when all this was happening?'

Wexer looked puzzled. 'No idea. Why?'

'Have you remembered her name yet?'

Wexer shook his head. 'No. I've tried but I don't remember. But I think she was Swedish or something. I remember my father thought she was German when she first arrived . . . said he'd had enough of fighting Germans in the war without bringing them into his house – typical of that old bigot. But my mother told him she wasn't German and to leave her alone. The poor girl must have had a miserable time – I was the only one to pay her any attention. But even so, I hardly remember her. I don't know why you keep asking about her. She's got nothing to do with all this.'

'And you haven't seen her since?'

'Of course not. What are you getting at?'

Heffernan produced a photograph of Ingeborg and placed it on the table in front of Wexer. 'Is this her? Is this the au pair who stayed on your farm twenty years ago?'

Wexer shrugged. 'No idea. They all look alike to me, these Scandinavian girls.' He leered.

Wesley looked away in disgust. He could quite imagine Dan Wexer thinking he was the Lord's gift to the opposite sex and claiming the young au pair's body as his by right. In his arrogance he had goaded his father. But as for it being murder, he wasn't so sure.

'Aren't you going to charge me with murder, then?'

'In a word, Mr. Wexer, no. At least not based on what you've told me. You're free to go now, but we might have to ask you some more questions.'

Wexer looked at Gerry Heffernan, surprised. 'But I came here to confess to killing my father . . .'

Heffernan stood up and strode from the room with Wesley in his wake, Wexer's protestations of guilt ringing in their ears.

201

'What do you think, sir?' asked Wesley when they were back in the office.

'I think he's playing games . . . trying to distract us from the real murder he's committed. I mean, why bring his father's death up now? I don't believe all this about his conscience, do you? From what he's said it sounds like an accident. I think it's all a smokescreen.'

'But if he's confessed, then that takes away the motive for silencing Ingeborg, surely?'

'A double bluff?' Heffernan sounded unsure of his ground.

Rachel and Trish returned to the office, crestfallen. They'd got nothing out of Jen Wexer. She vehemently denied being the mystery woman on the videos, claiming that she wouldn't be seen dead in a hat like that. She denied all knowledge of Ingeborg Larsen and said that her husband's guilt about his father's death had been preying on his mind since Pete's attack on him – he saw family history repeating itself. He wanted to get his own gnawing feelings of guilt off his chest.

'We know where they are, Wes,' said Heffernan, trying to be cheerful. 'We can pull 'em in any time. Let's get home, eh?' He grinned mischievously. 'I'm off out tonight with my lad, Sam. I'm going to watch him at work. Wish me luck.'

'They'll have him up there dancing in a horned helmet,' said Rachel when the inspector had disappeared from view. She looked at Wesley shyly. 'You don't feel like coming with me to have a look . . . purely in the line of duty, of course.'

'Sorry, Rach. Pam's expecting me home.'

Rachel watched sadly as Wesley left the office.

The morning streets were filled with the scent of the flowers tumbling from tubs and window boxes as Wesley walked to work the next day. It was too early for the tourists to be out and about, so he strolled down the steep, narrow thoroughfares towards the heart of the town and hardly saw a soul. He enjoyed this walk in the fine weather – the exercise; the opportunity to think. And he had a lot to think about.

The previous night he had begun to read Pam's translation of the Anglo-Saxon documents . . . her tale of murder dating back a thousand years. He had read about Brother Edwin and the terrible events that had plagued the district in 997. He had read of Edwin's discovery that his father was dead and that the man who had allegedly killed him had been taken in by his mother, injured, and had become her lover. Then that morning, over his cornflakes, he had read of the incensed Edwin about to kill the interloper to avenge his dead father. But then Wesley had looked at the kitchen clock and realised that if he read on he would be late for work. But he could guess what the end of the story would be: the brutal blow, then the burial with full Viking rites at the bottom of the field. As he had left the house he had stuffed the notebook pages into his jacket pocket. If he had a spare moment during the day, he would finish the story: it would give him a welcome break from modern police work.

Thoughts of Longhouse Cottage spread and connected with other thoughts. The house above the smallholding, Waters House: once home to Jock and Maggie Palister in more prosperous days and, long before that, home to Jeremiah Peacock – collector, antiquary and local busybody. Peacock had robbed Olaf's grave of the sword and shield that were to see him safe to Valhalla; had dug up Edwin's mother's hidden hoard of silver and had somehow filched the precious casket containing Edwin's writings and had consigned them to the neglected attic of his pet museum. Somehow Wesley felt he wouldn't have liked Jeremiah Peacock very much.

Then the sight of a rusty blue Fiat chugging past him down Market Street prodded his memory. An image flashed through his mind – a white jacket with a pink ticket attached. Wesley quickened his steps. It was starting to fit together.

Bjorn Sorensen rang at half past nine, at the exact moment Gerry Heffernan chose to roll into the office and regale his team with loud tales of his adventures of the previous night. His Sam's Viking exploits during an unsuspecting woman's fortieth birthday celebrations caused hoots of hilarity throughout the CID office.

Wesley picked the phone up, covering the mouthpiece and pleading for silence. His colleagues obliged, even Steve, and went about their work. Gerry Heffernan came over and sat on the edge of Wesley's desk expectantly.

'I spent last night going through Ingeborg's papers,' Bjorn began. 'I found two letters concerning her stay in Devon. The first from an au pair agency in Exeter saying they were arranging things, and the second from the mother of the family she stayed with saying that she was looking forward to seeing her.'

Wesley did his best not to sound impatient. 'What was the family's name?' he asked.

As Bjorn Sorensen answered his question, Wesley allowed himself a smile of satisfaction.

Trish Walton rushed up to his desk just as he was replacing the receiver. 'There's a Constable Cawthorne just arrived to see you, Sarge. Sergeant Naseby's sending him up.'

No sooner were the words out of Trish's mouth than Constable Cawthorne appeared in the doorway. 'I'm after a DS Peterson. Is he about?'

Constable Cawthorne was a big man in his late fifties, slow in his movements with silver-grey hair. A pair of spectacles sat perilously on the end of his nose, and he possessed the world-weary look of one who had lived through halcyon days – when the local constable could dispense wisdom and a night in the cells to members of a community whose worst misdemeanour was a spot of light poaching – but who was now witnessing a downward spiral into crime, misery and wickedness for which he was quite unprepared. Constable Cawthorne was looking retirement in the face with eager anticipation.

Wesley stood up and introduced himself and Cawthorne looked at him with barely disguised curiosity. 'I've heard all about you,' he announced. 'Liking it down here, then, are you?'

Wesley nodded, wishing Cawthorne would come to the point.

'I found that file . . . Honeysuckle House. I had a young constable with me at the time – probationer, wet behind the ears. It was his first suicide, poor lad, and I don't think he forgot about it in a hurry.' He handed Wesley a musty-smelling file. 'Before the days of the great god computer, it was . . . I don't reckon these floppy disk things'll last like good old paper.'

'I think Inspector Heffernan would agree with you there,' said Wesley as he opened the file and flicked through the reports. 'So what happened up at Honeysuckle House? Did you ever find out why the woman killed herself?'

'Oh, yes. The housekeeper there was only too ready to tell us. It seems this poor lady's husband was having it off – if you'll pardon the expression – with this young girl. He said he was leaving his family for her . . . crazy about her, he was. Anyway, the wife went into this outhouse on the edge of their land where they kept a tractor and a couple of old rowing boats, parked her car inside, took a few sleeping pills and left the car engine running. When they found her she was dead, poor woman . . . and her with a couple of kiddies and all. Tragic.'

'Do you know what happened to the husband? Did he go off with the girl?'

'I don't know. If he had any decency about him he'd have left well alone. But then people don't have much decency about them, do they? If they did we'd all be made redundant,' Cawthorne pronounced philosophically.

'This young girl . . . was she foreign?'

Cawthorne thought for a moment. 'Can't really say. I never saw her.'

'And you don't know her name?'

'I think the husband wanted her kept out of it. Her name was never mentioned. Why? What's the case being reopened for after all these years? Cut and dried it was. Suicide.'

'It's a long story,' said Wesley. 'It's in connection with a recent murder and a woman's disappearance.' He thought Cawthorne deserved some sort of explanation for his efforts.

He opened the file and saw the name of the principal witness – the housekeeper, whose words showed that she was consumed by a wave of vengeful fury against the young girl who had so cheerfully broken up a happy family and caused the suicide of a woman she described as being a lovely lady, a perfect wife and mother.

And Wesley knew where that housekeeper was now. Her name, according to the files, was Mrs Mildred Tensby. Last time Wesley had seen her she had been coming out of Waters House; but the time before that, she had been working behind the counter of Pilington's Dry Cleaners.

Wesley thanked Constable Cawthorne, who reluctantly returned to keeping law and order in the large seaside town of Morbay. Just as the picture was starting to emerge from the fogs of time and deception, it looked as if fate had dealt them another suspect.

'I haven't got your good manners, Wes,' observed Gerry Heffernan as he opened the glass door of Pilington's Dry Cleaners. 'I don't believe in going round the houses.' He went up to the counter and stood there until the woman behind it had served her last customer.

'Right, love. Mrs Tensby, is it?' Heffernan produced his warrant card and the woman nodded, terror on her plain, doughy face. 'We're making enquiries into the disappearance of a Danish woman . . . Ingeborg Larsen. I believe you told my colleague here that she came in to have a jacket cleaned.'

The woman looked at Wesley and swallowed nervously. 'That's right.'

'When was this?'

'Friday night . . . latish. She picked it up on Saturday.'

'We have reason to believe you knew Ms Larsen when she lived nearby about twenty years ago. You were housekeeper to a family who lived in Honeysuckle House near Neston. Am I right?'

There was no use denying it. Mildred Tensby nodded, wary.

'Did Ingeborg Larsen live with the family as an au pair?' asked Wesley confidently. He already knew the answer. Bjorn Sorensen had told him earlier that morning. Ingeborg had stayed at Honeysuckle House with a couple called Wentwood and their two children.

'Yes.' Mildred Tensby pressed her lips together in disapproval. 'Why?'

'Ms Larsen's brother, Sven, was found murdered recently,' Wesley began formally. 'And we have reason to believe that Ms Larsen herself has been the victim of an abduction. Do you know anything about it?'

At that moment the bell on the shop door jangled and an elderly lady entered, bearing a winter coat crammed into a large carrier bag. Gerry Heffernan turned. 'Sorry, love, shop's shut. Come back later, eh?' The woman, confused, obeyed without a word, and the inspector refocused his gaze on Mildred Tensby. 'Well?'

'I did it. I killed Ingeborg Larsen. And her brother . . . I killed him too.' She looked at the officers defiantly, challenging them to disbelieve her.

'First Christopher Wentwood's father turns up dead in a hotel room and now all this. They say the past catches up with you eventually, don't they,' said Wesley philosophically as they pulled up outside Waters House.

They hadn't got much out of Mildred Tensby. She had given

them a statement of the bald facts and refused to elaborate further. She had been deeply attached to the Wentwood family and had witnessed the carefree young au pair, Ingeborg, tearing the happy family apart with no hint of regret. Things had started well: the girl was happy, willing . . . and beautiful. But then Harry Wentwood had become infatuated with her . . . obsessed. She had gone along with it, enjoying Harry's attentions as if the whole thing were a joke. Then Harry announced he was leaving the family . . . moving in with Ingeborg. The pair disappeared to some unspecified love-nest leaving Mary Wentwood distraught and in financial difficulties.

Mildred Tensby, the faithful housekeeper, had comforted Mary; had listened to her woes and witnessed her slide into the despair of depression. Then Mary had ended her life. At this point in her statement, Mildred had broken down in tears.

Harry Wentwood returned when he heard of his wife's death, sold Honeysuckle House and took the children to begin a new life in London. Ingeborg was no longer on the scene, having returned home to Denmark, the adventure over. The grand passion hadn't lasted long after all. The children, Christopher and Ursula, never forgave their father, and left home at the earliest opportunity, cutting off all communication with Harry. It was when Harry knew that he was dying that he made one last, desperate attempt to be reconciled with his children. He hadn't succeeded. Christopher and Ursula had wanted nothing to do with him and he had returned to the Tower Hotel to die alone.

Mildred claimed she had discovered where Ingeborg was staying when she had left her white jacket, soiled during the long journey from Denmark, to be cleaned. Ingeborg hadn't recognised the former housekeeper of Honeysuckle House, but Mildred had recognised her all right – she would hardly have forgotten her, even after all these years. Monday had been Mildred's day off work. She had followed Ingeborg Larsen on the day she disappeared, had tricked her into opening her car door and had managed to abduct her and murder her. She had thrown the body into the River Trad at high tide. When Sven had arrived he phoned her, as Ingeborg had mentioned her name. She arranged to meet him on the yacht he had hired, where she killed him before setting the vessel alight. She had smiled in satisfaction at this point. Mary Wentwood and her children had been avenged, she said. She didn't mind how long she spent in prison. It had been worth it.

Gerry Heffernan left the interview room quite crestfallen. He had been so sure that Daniel Wexer had been involved, but he had been wrong. But at least they had unravelled the case. What with the farm robberies and Dan Wexer's shooting being cleared up, not to mention the truth behind Jos Wexer's accident twenty years back, it looked as if, for once, they were on a winning streak. Gerry resolved to stand his team a drink tonight to celebrate – he might even get his Sam to do his Viking act by way of entertainment.

Heffernan hung back, smiling to himself in anticipation, as Wesley hammered on the front door of Waters House. Although there were two vehicles parked outside – a small red van and a shiny blue Volvo – there was no answer.

'Wentwood's daughter, Ursula, has a studio in the coach house,' said Wesley. 'We'll try there.'

They walked the short distance to the two-storey coach house. Next to the huge double doors was a smaller door, leading to what had been, in more prosperous days, the coachman's residence. Wesley rang the tarnished brass doorbell.

He didn't recognise the woman who opened the door. She was tall with long dark hair and pale green eyes. Her hands, he noticed, were grey with dried clay. She looked at Wesley warily, as if he were about to begin a sales pitch for double glazing. When he produced his warrant card, her face became a mask of indifference, only the eyes betraying concern.

She introduced herself as Ursula Wentwood and led them through a tastefully minimalist living room – a contrast to the shabbiness of the main house – into a huge, bright pottery, created by knocking down the walls of a series of large workshops behind the coach house. The walls were sparse white-painted brick, and the place was filled with racks of grey, half-finished pots. A large, modern kiln stood in the far corner, and the wall near the door was filled with shelf upon shelf of vivid pottery. On a shelf above a clay-shrouded sink on the far wall stood a collection of battered bottles and cans of fierce-looking cleaners and chemicals.

Gerry Heffernan studied his surroundings, spotting the brightly coloured finished products. 'Nice stuff,' he commented casually. 'Colourful.'

Ursula, having other things on her mind, made no answer.

Gwen Wentwood was perched on a stool near the sink. She stood up and walked over to Wesley, looking at Heffernan with curiosity.

'Sergeant, I believe my husband went down this morning to identify his father's body. Has he been in touch with you?' Gwen Wentwood sounded anxious.

'I think it would be the coroner's people who would deal with all that, Mrs Wentwood. We're here about something else entirely. I believe you know a Mrs Mildred Tensby.' He turned to Ursula. 'She used to be a housekeeper for your family when you lived at Honeysuckle House.'

'Yes,' said Ursula, tentative. 'We've known Millie for years. Why? What's happened to her?'

'She's confessed to the murder of a Ms Ingeborg Larsen.'

Ursula gasped and put her hand to her mouth.

'You remember Ingeborg Larsen?'

'Yes,' Ursula said quietly. 'She was responsible for my mother's death.'

Gwen turned to her sister-in-law, a look of horror on her face.

'Can you tell us the whole story, Miss Wentwood? From the beginning,' Wesley suggested quietly.

Ursula sighed. 'We had an au pair by the name of Ingeborg.' She said the name bitterly, almost spat it. 'She had an affair with our father and he consequently left our mother. Our mother killed herself. End of story. I don't know who was more cut up about it all, us or Millie. She certainly took it hard . . . she'd known Mum for years, was devoted to her.'

'Did you know Ingeborg was in Tradmouth?' asked Wesley.

Ursula thought for a moment. 'Millie works in the dry cleaner's. Ingeborg brought something in for cleaning and Millie came up here and told us. She said she'd deal with her. I thought – so did Christopher – that she was just going to give her a piece of her mind . . . tell her what trouble she'd caused. I never thought she'd . . .'

'Yes. It all makes sense now,' said Gwen eagerly. 'Millie said justice would be done . . .'

Heffernan leapt on this. 'So you knew what she planned to do?'

'Oh, no . . . of course we didn't. How could we?'

'Were those her exact words . . . justice would be done?' asked Wesley, deep in thought.

209

'I can't remember. Does it matter?'

'When was this? When did she say it?'

'I can't remember.' Gwen was beginning to panic.

'Can I see Millie?' asked Ursula, unexpectedly.

'I don't see why not,' said Heffernan. 'Want a lift down now?'

'No thank you, Inspector. My van's outside. I'll drive myself.'

Ursula Wentwood gave her sister-in-law a withering look as she brushed past.

Jock Palister was starting to treat the cells at Tradmouth police station as home. The food wasn't as good as Maggie's, admittedly, and the custody sergeant's tea was a little on the weak side, but they were keeping him entertained. They had even laid on a couple of officers who had come all the way from Sussex Constabulary that afternoon to ask him a few pertinent questions about raids on farms in their area earlier in the year.

It was the young, flash DC with the big mouth who led him to the interview room – Carstairs, Steve Carstairs. Jock had the impression he enjoyed his work, enjoyed mouthing off at villains . . . probably putting the boot in too if he thought he could get away with it. Typical copper. Not like that posh young black one and Gerry Heffernan, the scruffy Scouser: Jock couldn't make those two out. At least he knew where he was with the likes of Steve Carstairs: the kind of copper he knew and despised.

Steve led Jock on down the corridor, standing to one side to let an attractive dark-haired woman past, glancing down apprecia-tively at her legs. She was being taken to one of the other interview rooms by Trish Walton. She disappeared inside and closed the door.

Jock gave Steve a nudge. 'I'm not the only one who lives up that way you should be pulling in, you know. Her that's just passed . . . the one with dark hair. Lives up at Waters House. Ask her about the goings-on there. I got fed up staying cooped up at Maggie's place so I took it into my head one night to go for a walk. I hopped over the wall to my old place – Waters House – to the woods. I reckoned nobody'd be out there at that time so I went to look at the old folly . . . the place where I used to keep all my booze and that. When I got there it was locked . . . bloody great padlock on the door. Then I heard sounds, like moans coming from inside. I don't know what was going on in there but I

210

scarpered bloody quick, if you know what I mean. You ask her about the folly. Okay?'

Steve rolled his eyes and pushed Jock into the interview room where the officers from Sussex were waiting. Then he hung around for a few minutes, waiting for Trish Walton to emerge. He didn't have to wait long. As she closed the interview room door behind her, Steve grabbed her arm and took her to one side, putting his face close to hers.

'That woman, the one you've just taken into Interview Room Two . . . what's her name?'

'It's Ursula Wentwood. She lives up at Waters House. Why?'

'Where's the boss? I've got something important to tell him.'

The two sober-suited officers from Sussex watched with considerable interest as Gerry Heffernan asked Jock Palister to repeat what he'd just told DC Carstairs.

Jock was only too pleased to provide it all. Strange moans . . . orgies, most like. Then he decided to embellish the story: screams, terrifying, bloodcurdling screams – a feature of Jock's narrative certainly added for dramatic effect. He went through it all with relish; after all, it was nothing they could fit him up for. As far as any untoward events at Waters House were concerned, his conscience was as clear as the stream than ran past Longhouse Cottage.

Gerry Heffernan said nothing as he and Wesley marched back to the CID office. It was Wesley who broke the silence.

'Do you believe Jock, sir?'

'Knowing Jock, he's probably making it up, having a laugh at our expense . . . or they might hold wild orgies up at Waters House. You never know these days.'

'Do you know what I think, sir?'

'What do you think, Wes? I'm past thinking. I just want to get Millie Tensby charged and then go home.'

'I think Ingeborg Larsen's still alive.'

Gerry Heffernan stopped and stared at his sergeant. 'You what?'

'She's still alive. But I don't know how long she'll stay that way.'

211

Chapter Sixteen

AD 997
My mother had fallen against her loom and now it fell, broken
to the ground, the weights shattered. Olaf went to her . . . I
think he went to help her. Then I saw the axe . . . Olaf's axe.
One of his weapons of war that he used to kill my people.

   How could I have let him live, the man who caused my
gentle father's death and made a whore of my mother? I was
a man of God, never a man of violence and death, but I could
not leave this unavenged.

                       From the chronicle of Brother Edwin

'What do you mean . . . alive? She's dead. Mildred Tensby
said she killed her.' Gerry Heffernan looked at his sergeant,
exasperated. Why did Wesley have to complicate things?

'Do you believe her?'

Heffernan thought for a moment. 'Aye. I do. She hated
Ingeborg for what she did all those years ago . . . and Ingeborg had
treated it all as a great joke. She'd show no remorse for all the
grief she'd caused. When Millie had the chance to teach her a
lesson she took it . . . and things probably escalated when Sven
arrived.'

'Do you think she's physically strong enough?'

'Don't let Rach hear you say that. She reckons women can do
anything men can. And in this case she's probably right. Tensby's
a big woman . . . and anger makes some people capable of
anything. And she's confessed. I wouldn't take what Jock says too
seriously, Wes. He's just trying to stir it. There's nothing Jock
Palister would like better than to think of the local constabulary

running round like a bunch of headless chickens because of some fairytale he'd made up.'

'But I'm sure Millie Tensby's not the woman on the videos. Our mystery woman seems slimmer . . . younger.'

'You can never tell with those surveillance videos – the quality's awful. I've looked at them again and it could be Millie . . . or someone totally unconnected with the case,' Heffernan added mischievously. 'I'm going out for me lunch. Coming, Wes? Fancy a pint at the Fisherman's Arms and one of Maisie's hotpots?'

'Er . . . no, sir. I've got a pile of paperwork to catch up on. I'd better just grab a sandwich.'

Heffernan looked disappointed, like a little boy whose friend had just refused to come out to play. 'Suit yourself. Don't say you weren't asked.' The inspector almost collided with Steve Carstairs as he lumbered out of the office in search of refreshment.

Steve spotted Wesley and made straight for his desk. 'Can I have a word, Sarge?'

Wesley looked up. 'Sure. What is it?'

'It's Jock Palister again. When I was taking him back to the cell after the blokes from Sussex had finished with him, he kept rabbiting on about Waters House. He kept asking if we'd looked in the folly yet.'

'Is that it?'

'That's it. And he kept laughing. What is a folly anyway?'

'It can be anything . . . a small castle, a Greek temple, a mock ruin. The Victorians used to build them to liven up their gardens.'

Steve shook his head in disbelief.

Wesley looked around the office. Rachel was sitting at her desk typing a report, and other members of the team were drifting off in a quest for midday sustenance. He looked at the large notice-board that covered half of the far wall. Ingeborg's enlarged image hung there, smiling, beautiful, full of life. Surely, Wesley thought, her body wasn't caught in weeds, nibbled by fish and decomposing at the bottom of the river.

'I'm going down to have another word with Jock,' he said to Steve before marching resolutely through the swing-doors and down the stairs to the cells.

Steve watched him with a sly grin. It would give him great satisfaction to see Wesley Peterson slip up badly.

*

Gerry Heffernan had still not returned from his long celebratory lunch in the Fisherman's Arms when Wesley set off for Waters House. Rachel Tracey sat in the passenger seat beside him, her short linen skirt riding up and revealing a portion of suntanned leg. Wesley concentrated on his driving.

'Are you sure about this, Wesley?'

'No. But I'm not willing to take the risk. If this woman's still alive then I doubt she will be for much longer.'

Rachel sat back and watched the beauties of the South Devon scenery flash past the window. The words wild, goose and chase sprang to mind . . . but, all things considered, she thought Wesley had a point. If Jock was telling the truth and Wesley was right, then they had a chance of saving a woman's life. If he was just giving them the runaround, then there was no harm done.

Wesley brought the car to a halt at the end of the drive leading to Waters House, near the spot where Harry Wentwood had parked when he had kept watch on his estranged family. Rachel followed Wesley up the uneven drive, wishing she'd worn sensible shoes. As they neared the house they kept to the trees. Wesley didn't want to be seen.

Jock Palister had given detailed directions to the folly. When he and Maggie had lived at Waters House in happier days, he had used it to store bottles of booze gleaned from trips to the Continent – gallons of the stuff, he had said with pride. The folly was situated well away from Waters House in the overgrown woods, and Jock was adamant that when he'd wandered there that night he'd heard moans coming from inside the locked building. Wesley left the drive and followed Jock's instructions, walking down the overgrown pathway, wide enough to allow a car to pass, past rambling bushes and trees that provided welcome cover. The sprouting vegetation on the path was flattened here and there as though a vehicle had used it recently.

The folly wasn't obvious if you weren't looking for it – a tiny stone castle, about the size of a large garden shed, well camouflaged by trees. Exactly as Jock had described it. Wesley walked slowly towards the battered wooden door, feeling a sudden stab of fear.

He looked at Rachel, and she gave him a quick smile. 'Well? The door's ajar. Do we go in?'

Wesley nodded. Without a word he approached the door and

214

pushed it open, noting the strong, new-looking padlock that dangled from its fastening. The first thing that hit them was the smell. Excrement. Jock would hardly contemplate storing his precious booze supplies here now. They covered their noses as they stepped inside.

Wesley had come equipped. He pulled a torch from his pocket and shone the beam around the walls. In one corner stood a plastic bucket which, on closer inspection, they saw had been used as a lavatory but had not been emptied – this was the source of the foul smell. In another corner was a mattress covered by a couple of filthy blankets. There was debris on the floor: another pad of chloroform-soaked gauze, like the one found in Ingeborg's white Opel; strong strips of sticking plaster; short lengths of washing line, enough to bind hands and feet; an empty pill bottle which, on examination, they could see had contained strong sleeping tablets. Wesley and Rachel looked at each other.

'Someone's been kept here,' said Wesley quietly.

'Ingeborg?'

Wesley nodded. 'You can still smell the chloroform ... amongst other things. She must have been here when we came about the prowler. And I don't think she's been gone long either.'

'What do we do now?' asked Rachel, making nervously for the door. This place, apart from the stench, gave her the creeps.

'We call for back-up ... and get SOCOs to go over this place. Then we go up to Waters House and ask some questions.'

'So Mildred Tensby kept her here?'

Wesley didn't answer. He made the necessary calls as soon as they were outside, his mind racing. He began to think of two stories he'd come across during the past few days. There was Pete Wexer's revenge on his father ... and then there was the ancient story Pam had translated. The vengeful child rights the wrong, kills the lover who had caused all the grief. It was probably a story old as time itself ... a story that had repeated itself here in Stoke Beeching when Ingeborg Larsen had turned up out of the blue and awakened the suppressed desire to avenge Mary Wentwood's suicide. But whose desire? Who had abducted Ingeborg and kept her prisoner in the folly? And where was Ingeborg now?

'I don't think Mildred Tensby could have known about that place,' said Wesley as they walked towards Waters House. 'It was one of Mary Wentwood's children – Christopher or Ursula ... or

215

both. I'm certain Mildred's covering up for them. She let them know Ingeborg was in Tradmouth but I think that was the extent of her involvement.'

Rachel looked sceptical. 'How can you be sure?'

'I can't. But everything Mildred's told us so far is long on generalities and short on detail . . . she could have got the lot from newspaper reports. And Pam's been translating this story,' he added with a smile. 'It just reminded me of this case. If one of Mary Wentwood's children wanted to kill Ingeborg to avenge their mother, then it all makes sense.'

At the mention of Pam's name, Rachel fell silent and looked at Wesley regretfully.

The police cars were rolling up the drive as they stepped into the large, gloomy hallway of Waters House. Gwen Wentwood looked uneasy, as though she sensed than this was no routine visit. She led Wesley and Rachel into the living room. Christopher Wentwood's laptop computer lay neatly in the centre of the desk in the corner. The desk was tidy, files piled up to one side.

'Where's your husband, Mrs Wentwood?'

Gwen looked fearful. 'He's gone out . . . with Ursula.'

'Where?'

'The fête at the Naval College in Tradmouth. Ursula has a stall there . . . selling her pottery. Is this about Millie?'

Wesley leaned forward, watching Gwen's face. 'We've just had a look inside your folly.'

Gwen took a tissue from her pocket and twisted it in her hands. 'I don't know what you mean. The previous owners told us the folly was dangerous. Nobody's been in the place since we moved in. We've kept well away.'

'It looked fine to us,' said Rachel.

'We've never even looked at it. We've had enough to do in this place without bothering about . . . What is all this?'

The telephone on the desk rang and Gwen grabbed at it. A brief conversation followed. 'I can't. I've made other arrangements,' she mumbled guardedly into the mouthpiece. There was a brief pause, then she grudgingly gave in. 'All right, then. I'll bring it down as soon as I can.'

She replaced the receiver, obviously annoyed, resentful. 'My

216

sister-in-law's forgotten the cash float for her stall at the fête. She wants me to take it over now. I really can't be long.'

Rachel looked at Wesley, who appeared to be deep in thought. She decided to continue. 'We won't keep you much longer, Mrs Wentwood. But we have reason to believe that Ingeborg Larsen was kept in that folly against her will . . . imprisoned. And we want to talk to your husband . . . and your sister-in-law . . .'

'No,' said Gwen firmly. 'There's no way Christopher would be involved in anything like that. You're mistaken.' She looked at Rachel, woman to woman, pleading for her to understand. 'Now Ursula, she's a very' – she searched for the word – 'determined person. I sometimes think that she was given all the strength in that family.' She put her hand to her mouth as if she'd realised she'd said too much. 'Of course, I'm not saying she'd do anything . . . But perhaps with Millie. I don't know. All I know is that Christopher isn't involved. He can't be. Please believe me.'

Gwen Wentwood looked from Wesley to Rachel, desperate, willing them to believe her.

'We'll have to talk to your husband . . . and your sister-in-law. You do realise that, Mrs Wentwood?' said Wesley softly. Gwen nodded and put her face in her hands.

Wesley stood up. 'They're at the fête, you say?' Gwen nodded, resigned. 'You said you had to take something over to them. Do you want a lift there?'

'No . . . I'll drive myself. Er . . . thank you,' she said, her mind elsewhere. They said a quiet goodbye and left her, gnawing at her fingernails in that room without sunlight.

Rachel drove them into Tradmouth, making, like everyone else, for the grounds of the Naval College, which stood on the hill above the town. Wesley rang Gerry Heffernan on his mobile and asked him to meet them there. Then he sat, quiet, thinking.

After a while Rachel broke the silence. 'You think they did it? Both of them? Christopher and Ursula?'

'I think Millie's covering up for someone and that that someone is one or both of her beloved Mary's children. Don't you agree?'

'Oh, yes. This is revenge. You can positively smell it.'

Wesley sat back. He felt in his pocket absent-mindedly and pulled out the pages of Pam's notebook.

'What have you got there? Been making notes?'

'No. This is that thing Pam translated. I was going to finish reading it this morning but I ran out of time . . . Not that I can't guess what's coming next.'

'You've got ten minutes till we get there. Enjoy yourself,' Rachel replied sarcastically. She could never see the appeal of the ancient.

Wesley began to read.

I took up the axe but I could not strike. I could not kill him. I sank to my knees, weeping like a child. I looked at Hilda and saw such love, such pity on her face, for I know she loved me with the love we should reserve for our Maker. I was all to her and she saw my grief. Gently she took the axe from my hand then, with a great cry, she did strike Olaf who stood before me, thinking himself safe. There was amazement on his countenance as he fell. The axe fell from Hilda's hands and she ran from the house.

'What's the matter, Wesley?' Rachel could see the shock on his face.

'It's, er . . .' He paused. 'Who reported the prowler?'

'Er . . . Christopher Wentwood, I think.'

'Would you invite the police up to your house if you were holding someone captive in the grounds?'

'I wouldn't,' Rachel said with a smile. 'But then I don't go in for kidnapping. What are you getting at?'

'I think we might be after the wrong person, Rach.'

'Well, do we go to the fête or not?'

'Oh, yes. We go to the fête.'

Rachel drove on through the ornate gates of the Naval College, slowing to walking pace to avoid the strolling, brightly clad crowds who invaded the august establishment for one day each year to enjoy the fête held in its grounds to aid local charities. She parked the police car in a spot marked 'No Parking', using the power of the law, and Wesley followed her to the hub of activity, the massive playing field edged with stalls. It didn't take them long to spot the Wentwoods. Wesley recognised the brightly coloured pottery – it was hard to miss it. If the Wentwoods hadn't been suspects in a murder enquiry, he might have bought some . . . it was just the kind of thing Pam liked.

'The Wentwoods are both there on the stall,' he managed to say before the cheerful music blaring over the Tannoy was interrupted by an announcement. Thor's Hammers were about to give a demonstration of authentic Viking battle techniques. 'Not that lot again,' said Wesley. 'All through this case we've been dogged by Vikings.' He smiled.

'Too right,' said Rachel bitterly as Wesley began to walk purposefully towards the stall. 'Shall we wait for back-up?'

'I don't think there's anything to be gained by waiting . . . not if there's a chance she's still alive.'

Ursula had spotted them. She nudged her brother and whispered something in his ear. Customers were drifting away to watch Thor's Hammers' demonstration. When Rachel and Wesley reached the stall they had Ursula and Christopher Wentwood to themselves.

'Good afternoon,' Wesley began formally. 'Lovely day for the fête.'

The Wentwoods glanced at each other, then nodded warily. Wesley had seen Gerry Heffernan taking suspects off their guard: it was a technique that usually worked. 'We've just been to your place . . . we had a look in the folly.' He waited for a reaction. But Christopher and Ursula Wentwood displayed no panic . . . not even a flicker of concern.

'Really?' said Christopher, touching his ear nervously. 'I don't know why you'd want to do that. I haven't been down there for months. I was planning to store some tools and things in there but it was much too damp. Bit of a white elephant really. I've even thought of knocking it down.'

'It has a new padlock.'

'Yes. I bought one when I planned to keep the tools in there. I just left it on with the key in. Why? What is all this? Surely the police can't be interested in a glorified garden hut.' He looked at his sister and she nodded eagerly in agreement.

'I don't understand, Sergeant. What's all this about?' Ursula asked with what sounded like genuine concern.

Wesley glanced at Rachel. 'We've found evidence that the missing woman, Ingeborg Larsen, has been held there. The woman who had an affair with your father and caused your mother's suicide.' Rachel looked from one to the other, waiting for some indication of guilt. But the brother and sister looked horrified, then puzzled. Christopher began to chew his knuckles, tense.

'You mean Millie kept her in there . . . that's awful,' said Ursula, seemingly sincere. 'We never knew . . . honestly. It's so far from the house and . . . unless . . .'

'Unless what?' asked Wesley, eager for any suggestion.

A few yards away Thor's Hammers had emerged from their marquee and were indulging in some preliminary skirmishes. It was to be a purely professional demonstration this time – no amateurs involved. Wesley noticed Odin swaggering at the forefront of the group. Odin looked around the watching punters, caught Wesley's eye and looked away quickly before raising his great sword in salute to the crowd.

'Unless what?' he repeated, returning his attention to police matters.

'Our father must have been hanging around for days before he called at the house. We thought he was a prowler, if you remember. He could have met up with Ingeborg and . . . After all, I suppose she blighted his life as well as everyone else's,' Ursula said convincingly.

'But he wasn't to know that the place wasn't used, was he?' said Wesley gently. 'You're out a lot on business, I believe, Mr Wentwood?'

Christopher Wentwood nodded anxiously. 'Yes,' he whispered, barely audible.

'And Miss Wentwood, you're usually working in your studio or out selling your pottery.'

'Yes. That's right. Why?'

Wesley didn't answer. As he turned to watch Thor's Hammers, who were getting into their stride with clashing steel and blood-curdling screams, he saw a familiar figure walking across the parched grass towards the pottery stall. Very familiar . . . a woman whose identity was concealed beneath a straw sunhat and dark glasses.

Rachel touched Wesley's arm. 'It's her, in the videos . . . it's her.'

The woman saw Wesley and Rachel staring at her and halted, removing her dark glasses. Then she began to back away, wary.

'Isn't that your wife, Mr Wentwood?' said Wesley as casually as he could. 'I think we'd better have a word with her.'

At that moment Wesley spotted Gerry Heffernan lumbering towards them past the empty stalls. Gwen Wentwood turned and nipped into the crowd, weaving her way through until she was out of sight.

'Let's get after her,' said Wesley quietly. He took Rachel's arm and steered her towards the crowd. 'Didn't she say that nobody had been in the folly since they moved in? But her husband just said he planned to keep tools in there . . . even fitted a padlock. Which way did she go? Can you see her?'

'I think she made for the arena . . . over there.'

Wesley took off in pursuit, followed by Rachel. He heard a shout of 'Hey, Wes, where are you off to?', and glanced round to see Gerry Heffernan and Steve Carstairs puffing after them. Of the two Gerry appeared the fitter.

A shout went up from the cordoned-off battlefield. 'Hey, get out of here . . . you could get hurt. Get back.'

The crowd parted to reveal Gwen Wentwood running between two ranks of hefty Vikings, their swords raised in mid-air, blank expressions of amazement on their faces.

'Stop her . . . police,' shouted Wesley.

It was Odin who took the initiative. He placed himself in Gwen's path, shield raised. 'Well, come on, lads, you heard . . . stop her,' he yelled to his bewildered Vikings.

But Odin's crew had lost its fighting edge when it had lost the services of Jock Palister and Darren. The chartered accountants, civil servants and computer professionals who were left lacked the ruthlessness necessary for victory against a desperate opponent. Gwen was too quick for Thor's Hammers. She weaved her way past them and doubled back. Some of the watching crowd thought it part of the performance and the laughter and applause began. Odin threw down his shield and snatched at Gwen's arm, catching her off balance. But Gwen had been trained for just such a situation; she brought Odin down swiftly and efficiently, leaving him sprawled on the parched grass of the arena. Then she ran on, disappearing through the puzzled crowd, which parted to let her through. Odin staggered to his feet, red-faced, and brushed grass from his tunic.

Wesley stopped. They had lost her. He looked at Rachel, breathless by his side, as Gerry Heffernan and Steve drew level with them.

'Where did she go, Wes? The way she brought that Odin down . . . like something from a self-defence course. She's good, I'll give her that.'

'I remember her saying she'd been in the army . . . obviously not forgotten what she'd been taught,' said Wesley, looking around, trying to locate the sunhat among the sea of heads. 'Radio whoever's on duty at the entrance,' he said to Steve. 'Tell them to stop a woman driving a blue Volvo.'

But it was too late. Steve reported back that a woman had indeed passed through the entrance driving a blue Volvo. She had driven through at speed, demolished the crash barrier and was last seen heading out of Tradmouth on the Neston road.

'I think I can guess where she's going,' said Wesley quietly as Gerry Heffernan scratched his head in stunned silence.

Gwen Wentwood's hands shook as she grasped the steering wheel. Not much farther now. In a few minutes it would be over. She stared ahead, her eyes seeing the narrow lane, darkened by the high hedgerows, but her mind on Christopher . . . and the happiness, the life, that one woman had denied them.

When Christopher had come to the army camp that day to install some new software on the computers, she, Sergeant Price, had fallen in love with him almost at first sight. He had been so good-looking, so gentle. She had been the one to make the first move, of course. She had asked him out for a drink in a pub near the barracks, her heart beating, fearful of rejection. But he had accepted, and over the following months the relationship had bloomed and strengthened. He was sensitive, considerate; not like the men she had known before. Then she had again taken the lead, suggested marriage, and he had seemed as keen on the idea as she was . . . had even introduced her to his sister, Ursula. But there had been something there, beneath the surface . . . something that, in her happiness, she had chosen to ignore.

The fact that Christopher didn't want to sleep with her had amused her at first. She had thought it rather sweet, rather old-fashioned . . . a refreshing change from the other men she had known, whose aim had been to inveigle or bully their way into her bed at the first opportunity. When Christopher had said he wanted to wait until they were married she had merely thought he had rare moral values. It was on their wedding night that she had learned the truth.

But she loved him . . . loved him with an almost maternal devotion. She soothed him when he awoke, screaming at night, sweating with fear and sobbing with despair. Christopher Wentwood had become her life, and when she left the army he became the focus of all her hopes, ambitions and emotions. She was in her thirties and longed so much for children, Christopher's children; children an impotent husband couldn't give her. Slowly, over the first months of their marriage, she had learned the whole story. Christopher Wentwood was a damaged man. The impotence was only one symptom. Then came the periods in the psychiatric unit, the hours with psychiatrists and counsellors, the inability to cope with the job in a multinational company. Gwen had thought it best if they spent the money she had inherited from her grandmother on moving to a less stressful environment – to Devon, where Ursula was building up a successful pottery business, where Christopher had been brought up. She had found Waters House. It needed renovation, but a bit of do-it-yourself would be good therapy for Christopher. And the consultancy was doing all right. Problems aside, he was good at his job.

Then one night, a year ago, sitting by the fire drinking wine with Ursula when Christopher was out with a client, Gwen had discovered the ultimate truth behind her husband's problems. As a child of ten he had discovered his mother dead in a fume-filled car.

Ursula had been thirteen at the time. She had known the reason for his mother's desperate action: a carefree, laughing young woman called Ingeborg Larsen, just five years older than herself. Christopher's grim discovery had scarred him, and throughout his youth he had been strange, withdrawn. Gwen was the first girl in his life. Ursula said he should never have married – it wasn't fair on Gwen. But Gwen disagreed. Her love for him would conquer all . . . eventually. He was everything to her – husband; child. Since she had found out the truth, she had come, over those months, to hate the woman who had brought Christopher to this . . . who had absconded with his father as some sort of adventure and caused his mother such despair that she chose to end her life.

There is no justice, she thought. The girl caused untold damage to two generations, denied Gwen the children she craved. And she had laughed. Ursula had told her that Ingeborg had laughed when she announced she was going off with their father. It was that laugh, that mockery of her beloved Christopher's feelings, that had sealed Ingeborg Larsen's fate.

When Millie had called that day to say that Ingeborg was back in Tradmouth, Gwen had sought her out. She had the address and description from Millie, so she wasn't difficult to find. Gwen hadn't confronted her: she had other plans. She followed her, and when the time was right, when they were on a quiet road with nobody else about, she rammed Ingeborg's car to make her stop. Gwen had not planned to kill her right away. She would make her suffer . . . make her repent. She had found the chloroform in Ursula's pottery, a solvent standing innocently on a shelf. She had used it on Ingeborg and bundled her into the boot of the Volvo, taking her to the disused folly. She fed her, never speaking, and used Christopher's sleeping tablets to keep her unconscious. Then, early that morning, the unconscious Ingeborg had made another journey – her last. And all the time, Gwen never told her why she was being kept prisoner. But she would tell her soon. When Ingeborg Larsen had come round, when she was about to die, Gwen would tell her why.

It was lucky she had taken the phone call from Sven. He had known what had happened all those years ago. And he feared that Ingeborg would make contact with Harry Wentwood, her old lover – since her divorce, according to Sven, she had mentioned him several times. But Sven hadn't wished to share his sister's secrets – secrets than hardly reflected well on her character – with the police. He had looked the name Wentwood up in the hotel phone book and telephoned the house, hoping to deal with things alone.

It was Gwen who had arranged to meet him, pretending she was Ursula. She had told Sven that she knew where Ingeborg was and she had met him in Tradmouth. She had hopped aboard his boat, having no firm plans, knowing only that this man knew of the link between her husband's family and Ingeborg and could lead the police to her. When she saw the dinghy bobbing behind the boat she knew it would be easy. She had knocked him out with a fire extinguisher, had spread fuel over the boat and set it alight. Then she had leapt onto the dinghy and had steered towards the shore; the blood on her hands was soon washed off in the sea. She had landed in a cove near Stoke Beeching, set the dinghy adrift and made her way home as though nothing had happened.

Millie had been wonderful – she had tried to take the blame, thinking it was one of the children, Christopher or Ursula, who had finally avenged their mother. And Gwen was happy to let her take the blame. As long as Christopher was free from suspicion, as long as he was there with her, in her arms . . . safe.

Gwen drove along the lane automatically, noting Honeysuckle House on her right. She wondered why Ingeborg had called there – the scene of her misdeeds – that day. Had she hoped to see Harry Wentwood, to take up again where she had left off? Had she intended to make some sort of apology? Or had she just felt curious?

Gwen looked in the mirror. There was a police car in the distance, gaining speed, following her. She put her foot to the floor. They wouldn't catch her. She would go away, go away with Christopher and look after him . . . but not before she had dealt with Ingeborg Larsen.

The car gained speed, lurching around blind corners, the police car no longer in sight. Faster . . . faster . . . her hands tightened on the steering wheel, her right foot pressing harder on the pedal.

There was a thundering crash as she met the tractor. Then all was silence except for the bees buzzing in the high, imposing hedgerows.

Rachel Tracey leaned on the steering wheel and stared at the scene of devastation before her. 'Oh my God,' she muttered. 'Oh my God.'

Wesley put a comforting hand on her shoulder. 'You call the ambulance.'

He left Rachel in the driving seat, glancing back with concern, and ran to the blue car. Gwen Wentwood, blood obscuring her features, lay like a rag doll halfway through the windscreen. She hadn't been wearing a seat belt.

'She was tearing down the lane, there was no way she could have stopped . . . she swerved then she hit me,' came a shaky voice from the cab of the tractor. 'There was nothing I could do.' Josiah Beaumont clutched the tractor's wheel as if for comfort.

'Are you okay?' asked Wesley gently. 'My colleague has called an ambulance. Just take it easy. Can you get down?'

Wesley helped Josiah down from his tractor, which hadn't been too badly damaged, considering. Gwen's car had swerved, giving the tractor a glancing blow, but the hedgerow had taken the main impact.

'Is she dead, then?' asked Josiah, his voice trembling with shock.

'I'm afraid so. Come on. Let's get you back to the car.'

Josiah seemed to be in a trance as Wesley led him to the police car. He climbed into the back seat, and Rachel turned and smiled with professional sympathy, having conquered her initial distress.

Wesley knew the farm worker was in shock, but he had an important question to ask – a question than couldn't wait. If Josiah Beaumont had been living and working in these parts for many years, he might just be able to help. 'Do you remember a woman called Mary Wentwood, who committed suicide about twenty years ago?'

Josiah looked up, surprised. 'Aye, I do. Why?'

'Do you know exactly where she killed herself? I know it was some sort of outbuilding on land belonging to Honeysuckle House, but where exactly? Do you know?' asked Wesley anxiously.

'Aye. It don't belong to Honeysuckle House now . . . the new folk there sold that bit of land but the place isn't used no more. Why?'

'Can you direct us to it?'

Before Josiah could answer the sound of urgent sirens heralded the arrival of the ambulance. As Josiah was swathed in a blanket and led away firmly but gently by a pretty ambulancewoman, he turned to Wesley. 'Straight on for quarter of a mile . . . you'll see a track on your right. It's at the bottom . . . can't miss it.'

Wesley signalled Rachel out of the driving seat of the police car. 'I'll drive. You look all in, Rach.'

'Where are we going exactly?' she asked as he negotiated his way past Josiah's abandoned tractor.

'Hopefully to find Ingeborg Larsen. Radio the boss, will you . . . tell him what's happened. I just hope we're not too late.'

They ran towards the wooden building, which stood silent and brooding. There was no sign of life.

'We're too late,' said Rachel quietly.

But Wesley pushed at the double doors. They had been shut firmly but not locked. They opened slowly, scraping on the

226

ground, dislodging the strips of sheeting that had been piled up against them in preparation. Wesley stood for a moment as his eyes grew accustomed to the gloom. Although a space had been cleared in the middle of the floor, the edges of the garage were stacked with ladders, sacks and boxes, filthy and dust-covered. Only the sheeting looked clean, freshly imported onto the scene.

Wesley could just about make out a shape at the far end of the garage. A small wooden rowing boat, old and probably unseaworthy, lay pushed up against the wall. He rushed forward, his eyes fixed on the prone, bound figure inside the boat. He bent down.

'Rachel,' he said softly. She ran over the rough earth floor to join him and stared at the still, silent woman.

Ingeborg Larsen lay unconscious, curled up on the floor of the boat, bound and gagged. The outbuilding had been cleared to make room for a car but the boat, awkward to move, had been pushed to the end to provide an improvised deathbed. The old sheets had been intended to seal the place so that the lethal fumes did not escape. Ingeborg had been sentenced to die in the same manner as Mary Wentwood. Gwen Wentwood had been on her way to carry out the execution.

Rachel leaned across, putting her fingers gently on Ingeborg's neck to feel for a pulse.

'She's alive,' she whispered, relieved.

The sound of police car sirens and vehicles screeching to a halt outside would have been enough to waken the deepest sleeper. Gerry Heffernan was the first to burst in on the scene. 'What's up, Wes? Have you found her?' He stopped and stared at the woman lying in the boat. 'Pretty, isn't she?' he commented, in Rachel's opinion unnecessarily. 'She's dead, I take it?'

'No, sir,' said Rachel. 'She's breathing and there's a strong pulse. The ambulance is on its way.'

'I heard about the Wentwood woman. Terrible business. Died instantly, the paramedics said. I got the shock of my life when I saw her in that hat and those dark glasses, just like on the videos, Wes. I'd never have thought it was her. I had the brother and sister down for it if Millie turned out to be telling porkies. So she bumped Sven Larsen off and all, did she?'

'That's right. She mentioned when I first saw her that she'd been in the army. She obviously put all her training to good – or should I say bad – use.'

'I never thought to find Ingeborg alive . . . not in a million years. Well done, Wes. But why did Christopher Wentwood's missus do all this?' Heffernan asked, puzzled.

'Love,' said Wesley, simply. 'Her husband found his mother's body here. That must have left him badly traumatised, and Gwen watched him suffer for years as a result. When Ingeborg arrived on the scene she took his revenge for him. But that's only a guess. I don't suppose we'll ever know the whole truth.'

Gerry Heffernan fell uncharacteristically silent as the paramedics arrived and lifted Ingeborg Larsen gently out of the boat. He questioned them quietly about her condition and watched as she was taken to the waiting ambulance. After a while he spoke to Wesley almost in a whisper. 'Come on, let's get out of here.'

Heffernan walked out through the splintery wooden doors and down the track to the waiting patrol car. Wesley walked beside him, subdued, with Rachel following closely behind. Heffernan turned to her. 'Rach . . . will you go and break the news to Gwen Wentwood's husband? I know you're good at that sort of thing.'

Rachel nodded, tight-lipped. She might be good at breaking bad news but she still hated the very thought of it. As she headed towards her car, Heffernan put a hand on his sergeant's shoulder. 'Wes, the paramedics said she's been drugged but she's already showing signs of coming round. We'll get her interviewed as soon as she's conscious then we'll head for the Tradmouth Arms.'

Wesley nodded. A quiet pint in the Tradmouth Arms was just what he needed.

Ingeborg Larsen was fit enough to talk after a couple of hours. Wesley listened as she gave the account of her terrifying ordeal to Rachel.

He could tell Rachel was still upset by the news she had had to take to the Wentwoods. Outside, in the grey hospital corridor, she had told Wesley how Christopher Wentwood had broken down in tears, how he had curled up into the foetal position while his sister held him, rocking him, whispering words of comfort. Rachel had left them with a young and sympathetic WPC. It was one of the worst jobs she'd ever had to do, she added bitterly.

When she was told of her brother's death, Ingeborg wept, and Wesley watched her beautiful face, the fair skin pale and drawn and wet with tears, the area around her delicate nose red and blistered from the chloroform pad. When she lay back, exhausted, on the hospital pillows, her statement made, Wesley decided he had had enough of death and pain. He needed the normality of the Tradmouth Arms . . . and then he needed Pam, and his son. He needed to return to the sunshine.

Gerry Heffernan was waiting for him in the pub, a full pint sitting on the table, bought in anticipation of his arrival.

'Come on, Wes. Sit down. I think we should be celebrating . . . the farm robberies are all cleared up, and the Larsen case. I rang the Copenhagen police when I got back to the station.' He smiled modestly. 'I think they were impressed by our efficiency.' He winked conspiratorially. 'And the Super's very impressed by your contribution.' He paused to take a long, thirsty drink. 'I went to see Stan Jenkins at home last night . . . they've let him out of hospital for good behaviour. It's my guess he'll decide to retire at long last, Wes. I think his little trouble might be the last straw.'

'What exactly was his little trouble?' asked Wesley.

'He was a martyr to his piles was Stan,' said Heffernan, shaking his head. 'And there's a lot of sitting down in the police these days . . . all this paperwork they make us do.' He gave a wicked smile and Wesley looked at his boss with curiosity. 'I don't want to say too much yet but the Super's been hinting at a few changes in CID if Stan leaves. Could be good news for both of us.' He paused, a sly grin on his face. 'But don't say anything. I don't want the Super to think I can't keep my mouth shut.'

Wesley opened his mouth to speak but no sound came out.

'Hello, you two . . . thought I might find the forces of oppression in here.' Neil Watson loomed over them, grinning. 'How's it going?' He sat down heavily on the stool, nearly spilling his pint.

'All the villains are locked up and crime has been forever driven from the land,' announced Gerry Heffernan, as convincing as a politician making promises.

'Good. You're out of a job, then, Wes. You can come and give us a hand. We've just been given permission for a dig at Longhouse Cottage. Not much funding as usual, but the powers that be think it could be an important site . . . and Carl Palister's keen on the idea – in fact it was him who suggested it. Maggie's tolerating the prospect; she said it was all right as long as we didn't make too much mess. I told her she wouldn't even know we were there.' He smiled angelically.

'Been to the museum?'

'Yeah. They were ecstatic about the casket . . . and the sword and shield. They've been X-rayed. You should see the workmanship that went into . . .'

'What did they say about the documents?' asked Wesley before Neil got carried away.

'They said it was a pity the originals couldn't be found. I said they'd probably rotted in that attic years ago . . . or Jeremiah Peacock used them to light his fire or something. Just the sort of thing he would do.' He snorted derisively. 'But they were thrilled with the copies. Said they were a very important find.'

'You've not read Pam's translations yet, have you?'

'Didn't have chance. I only saw the first bit about the raid on Neston.'

Wesley pulled the notebook from his pocket and began to read.

My mother cried as I carried him from the house. I dug his grave in the bottom field, away from the house, and threw the axe that had killed him into the pit. But my mother rushed from the house in great distress and said he must be buried as one of his kind. His gods were not our God and in Valhalla, the hall of the slain, he would have need of certain things. Olaf was buried within an old fishing boat that was my father's with his sword and shield by him. My mother wept most bitterly over his grave. I would she had wept thus over my father's.

He looked up at Neil. 'Ring any bells?'

Neil nodded. 'That's it. It's all there. The burial at Longhouse Cottage.' He grinned like a satisfied cat. 'And now we've got a name for our skeleton . . . Olaf.' He slapped Wesley on the back and stood up. 'I'd better be off. Things to do, site reports to write up . . . busy, busy, busy. Might see you in here later, eh?' He disappeared through the pub door like a man in a hurry.

Gerry Heffernan drained his glass. 'Well, as we've got everything cleared up bar the paperwork I'm off on my own little Viking raid.' He grinned at Wesley, expecting some display of curiosity. 'Do you remember Thor's Hammers? Chap called Odin?'

'Odin the tax inspector? Yes.'

Heffernan pulled a green ticket from his inside pocket. 'When PC Wallace was taking his statement about what happened at the Tradmouth fête, he gave him tickets for a do Thor's Hammers are organising tonight . . . sort of Viking social called an 'Evening in Valhalla'. Look, it says here: 'all the fun of a Viking feast in the hall of heroes'. I managed to get hold of some tickets. Rachel's going with her Dave.'

Wesley raised his eyebrows at this piece of information, relieved that things between Rachel and her handsome Australian were settling down. There had been times in recent weeks when he had felt uncomfortable. He was a modest man – no Steve Carstairs, who thought every woman longed to get him beneath her duvet – but he had noticed Rachel looking at him in a certain way . . . and he hoped he had been mistaken. Such things could lead to bad feeling at best, disaster at worst. He had seen a lot of it in the Met.

'I got two extra tickets for you and Pam and all,' Gerry Heffernan continued, as Wesley pushed these inappropriate thoughts from his mind. He leaned forward, looking around as if he were afraid someone might be listening and taking notes, and handed the tickets over to Wesley furtively. 'Can you get a baby-sitter? If you can't make it I can give them to my Sam . . . if he's not out somewhere pillaging.'

Wesley frowned. 'It's a bit difficult to get someone at such short notice. And Valhalla means the hall of the slain so, er . . . I think we'll stay in with a bottle of wine and a video.'

When he had drained his glass, Wesley Peterson left his boss contemplating an evening of Viking revels and walked back home up the steep streets, trying to absorb the sunny, holiday atmosphere of the flower-laden town . . . and trying to forget about Gwen Wentwood's limp, torn body and the lovely tear-stained face of Ingeborg Larsen.

Epilogue

AD 997
My mother told me of her love for Olaf . . . that he was not the
man who killed my father. But it may be that she deceives
herself . . . as we all do. Hilda is gone, I know not where, but
Ordgar saw her near to the shore in great distress. I fear that
she has come to harm. I searched for her two days and nights
but could not find her. My mother says I should let her go . . .
that her love for me was intemperate . . . that it consumed her
like a fire. But I had great affection for her . . . and desire. I
pray for her safety and her soul. Yet if she is gone it may be
for the best, and I shall henceforth dedicate my life to the
Lord. I leave tomorrow for the abbey at Tavistock. I will be of
use there. There is much rebuilding to be done, and a brother
who forms his letters well is always of use.

So ends this chronicle. I shall leave it with my mother for
safekeeping along with the casket which might be of some
value to her. I would not want the brothers of Tavistock to
know of these things. I shall have a new beginning.
                                    From the chronicle of Brother Edwin

Ten days later
'He's all yours,' said Colin Bowman cheerfully as he handed Neil
the large cardboard box. 'I'll be fascinated to hear what your bone
specialist makes of him. It's amazing what these experts can find
out from a few teeth and bones.'

'No doubt they'll come up with his full life story . . . minus the
saucy bits, of course.'

'What saucy bits?'

Neil swung round, nearly dropping his box in the process. Gerry Heffernan was standing in the doorway of the mortuary, grinning at him. Wesley stood behind him, serious.

'We've come to pick up the report on Gwen Wentwood . . . tie up the case,' said Wesley quietly. 'Who have you got in the box, Neil?'

'Olaf. He's destined for stardom down at the university.'

'Aren't you going to bury the poor bugger?' asked Heffernan bluntly.

'Eventually. Don't worry, he'll get a decent burial. Though I can't promise him the full Viking works this time.' Neil looked at his watch. 'Got time for a quick drink, Wes . . . you too, Gerry? I'll tell you all about the casket and the things from Olaf's grave going to Tradmouth Museum. Apparently the Peacock Museum has admitted that it hasn't the facilities to look after anything of real historical importance and . . .'

'I'm sorry, Neil, it'll have to wait till another time. We're meeting someone.'

Wesley wasn't in the mood for amiable chat. He thanked Colin for the report and the two policemen left. Neil watched them go, slightly puzzled. There was something on Wesley's mind . . . something that was bothering him.

The day was cooler. The height of the heat wave had passed, leaving the weather cloudy and unpredictable. The tourists glanced nervously at the sky as they toted their cagoul-stuffed bags around the town. Wesley and Heffernan walked in silence around to the hospital's main entrance.

Ingeborg Larsen was waiting for them on the steps, her beauty restored, her blonde hair like a smooth, shiny helmet, her body lithe and slender. She smiled as they approached, a smile that dazzled – confident, self-assured. There was no sign of the ordeal she had suffered . . . not outwardly, at least. Inward scars, the invisible ones, heal slowly. A man emerged through the swing-doors behind her. He was tall, athletic-looking, with a small fair beard and a calm, patient manner.

'Inspector Heffernan, Sergeant Peterson, I should like you to meet my husband . . . Bjorn. We are – what is the word? – reconciled. We will try again.' Her slight accent seemed to render her even more attractive. Wesley noticed Gerry Heffernan staring at her like an adoring puppy.

'That's good,' said Wesley gently. 'I wish you both luck. I hope you'll be able to put everything that's happened over here behind you.'

'I will try, Sergeant.' she smiled at Wesley, a sparkling smile with a hint of a giggle, displaying a set of perfect white teeth.

'That's that,' said Gerry Heffernan as Ingeborg Larsen climbed elegantly into Bjorn's car and they drove off into the narrow, traffic-filled streets.

'Ingeborg is the loveliest of the girls,' Wesley muttered, staring after the car.

'Pity,' said Gerry Heffernan with a philosophical grin. 'If she'd been ugly as sin it might have saved us a lot of work.'

They watched the car disappear around the corner; Ingeborg Larsen had left Tradmouth for the last time. There would be a new beginning.

Author's Note

The Viking raid on 'Neston' described in this book is, of course, purely fictional. However, Devon did suffer greatly from Viking attacks for many years. The Anglo-Saxon Chronicle tells us that in 997 'the Danes went around Devonshire . . . killing and burning each thing they met . . . and brought with them to their ships indescribable plunder'. It was monastic chroniclers who recorded these dramatic events, and the Church at that time added the words 'From the fury of the northmen, oh Lord, deliver us' to its litany.

The inhabitants of the threatened areas must have watched in terror as the fast, manoeuvrable longboats with their fearsomely carved prows (the most advanced seafaring technology of the day) moved relentlessly along the coasts and up the rivers. Some, fearing the raids, buried their precious possessions, and treasure hoards from the period have been unearthed.

The Viking graffito mentioned in this book claiming that 'Ingeborg is the loveliest of the girls' actually exists. It was written by Vikings who plundered the prehistoric tomb at Maes Howe in the Orkneys in AD 1150 . . . showing that even Viking raiders had romance in their lives!

Boat burials were a common Viking custom. Pagan Vikings were buried with cherished possessions for use in the afterlife: sword, shield and axe would be considered essential equipment for a warrior.

The vast majority of Vikings, however, weren't piratical raiders but ordinary people: farmers, craftsmen and traders who settled peacefully in many parts of Britain and mainland Europe. But the Vikings were also great explorers who made their indelible mark on history. The Normans who conquered England in 1066 were their descendants. And there is even evidence that it was a Viking, Leif Eiriksson, who discovered North America . . . five hundred years before Christopher Columbus.